NAVIGATORS YOU CAN TRUST

NAVIGATORS
YOU CAN TRUST

PATRICK FITZGERALD

Podium

To my father and mother

For instilling in me immortality and honor

Cover design by Paul Lycett

ISBN: 979-8-3470-0773-8

Published in 2026 by Podium Publishing
www.podiumentertainment.com

NAVIGATORS YOU CAN TRUST

PRELUDE

They said that dragons had roamed these parts, hurled their flames down from the sky and broke open the world. But all such beasts had died long ago, and really, it was just us Navigators.

No. Not those that direct routes and assist others in traversing passageways.

At least, not anymore.

In the here and now, steel crab cruisers sailed through the orange-colored skies, eclipsing the twin suns in frantic black blurs. The daggerlike obsidian dirt they stirred up in their wake sandblasted my long white-and-gold coat, and I threw an arm in front of my face to prevent being blinded. The scream of the engines and the explosions of multicolored energy deafened me briefly, and hot wind knifed at me, yanking on the dozens of hilts strapped to my belt, legs, and chest.

All these senses I'd felt a thousand times before, had them buried somewhere deep within my blood. Yet now, all I could think was, *Why did I ever come back?*

The wind died, enabling me to drop my arm and look out across the beach. Where trees had swayed in the breeze, where waves had splashed up against the glittering black sand, now ruin ruled. The beach had been carved away by cannonballs, stripped by the thick tracks of huge tanks, and tattered by the rainbow energy slashing and sparking every which way at once.

A great black fortress on a crooked hill jutted up into the orange sky through the chaos and the hazy mist that the conjured energy created above the battlefield. Beneath it, tanks moved en masse, purple flags bearing the silver stars of the Noda waving from their hulls. Though more than once, I spotted a second flag blowing among them: a glowering jackal head wearing a gold collar with orange eyes. Billowing atop the fortress's ramparts, those same eyes watched.

Not today.

Instead of falling to my knees, instead of indulging in the pain and the sorrow as I'd done in the past, I tracked the storm of metallic fury fired from a tank and did the only thing I could do. The only thing I should do.

I tapped into Ignis.

The world flashed bright white all around me. Grasping one of the hilts along my belt, a single white flame exploded from my heart out of my chest, until I was surrounded in a silhouette of churning pearlescent fire. The flames both cleansed and empowered me, stilling my nerves while heightening my eyesight, hearing, and strength. I felt more balanced, more comfortable. I felt the one thing I so desperately needed to feel since all this began: alive.

As I did every time I summoned Ignis up from within me, I wondered what it had been like to be a Dragon Lord, to have instant and eternal access to the well of power that was Ignis, unlike the temporary hold gifted to us humans. I wondered what the Great Dragon War had been like and how measly this so-called "Perpetual War" looked in comparison. The dragons hadn't had great war machines. All they'd had was their Ignis and themselves.

And now, there are none. Removing the knife from my belt, the silver blade became an ethereal white flame. Eyes wreathed in the same fire, I glanced over my shoulder at my companions. *Just us Navigators.*

"Thirty Nodan tanks and the Lords know how many more in waiting." Watching the crab cruisers sail overhead then land every other mile down the beach, Janne grinned. "I hope we aren't late."

"Focus," I said. I appreciated the younger Navigator's enthusiasm. But this wasn't another quest, another rainbow's end discovered. *It should be. But this is so much more than that.* "Take your squad and move north. You'll meet up with the others." I watched the shuttle doors to the distant crab cruisers slide open, unloading several groups of colorful individuals such as the ones I stood among. "Strength in numbers and that sort o' thing."

Janne was at least a foot taller but looked at me with stubborn respect. He was one of hundreds of my pupils: younger Navigators that a High Navigator was responsible for mentoring. Whose life I carried in my scarred hands.

"Strength in numbers," he repeated. "Aye. But what will you be doing off on your lonesome?"

The fortress squatted like a horned toad. The front gates had opened, vomiting forth a dozen more tanks and metal war machines. Weapons that allowed Ignis-less men to do the work of twenty Navigators. I had seen tanks like those run through a *thousand* Navigators.

"Doing what's to be done," I said, ignoring the way my shoulders had started to lightly shake with anger. "The Government will want me to make the charge."

I ignored the shaking so in turn, I could ignore the flag blowing some fifty yards behind me. A flag displaying a white G on a blue background. Another fifty yards behind that, the soldiers of the Archengardian Government sat quietly in a sea of iron vehicles like those that had spilled from the fortress walls.

Unbelievable. The Government's sworn enemies, the Noda, defended a fortress just a couple miles from them, yet they sat and did nothing. As immovable as the toad fortress itself.

Because that's what we're *here for.*

"It's our job anyway," I added emotionlessly.

Janne spat in the direction of the Government forces. He was a good spitter. War did that to young Navs, forced them to find new hobbies. "Our job is to mediate." The initial energy that had filled his voice drifted into desperation. "Not fight."

My fists tightened until I could feel my bones popping. "That's my job."

That seemingly wasn't enough for Janne. "I enjoy a bout as much as the next Nav. This ain't stopping anytime soon, that's for sure. But it's not your burden—"

"Bugger off." I scuffed a boot into the black sand. "Please."

Janne swayed briefly, eyes wide and worried, then shadow took his face and he slipped away. "Let's go!" I heard him holler over my shoulder, then the pounding of feet on sand as he and his squad of Navigators raced down the hill to join up with their brethren escaping the crab cruisers.

For a while, I just stood there, blade burning in my hand, watching both sky and sand as they were cast into inferno. Watching Ignis thrown from both us and our enemy, torching the air with serpentine tongues. A gift from the Dragon Lords, they called Ignis. Yet the Dragon Lords had torn themselves to powder in conflict over what to do with this race—this fragile, forsaken human race—and then that powder had settled over the atmosphere of Archengard.

Only the wisest knew that Ignis was not a gift, but a curse.

I reached my free hand across my waist and seized a second knife, then drew it from its worn sheath. Sucking in deep, tired breaths, I crossed the flaming knives over my chest, closing my eyes.

But I will use this curse for good.

Ignis formed around my legs, slinking down my body and filtering into my feet. Translucent white energy curdled around the dirtied, bloodied leather boots I'd worn since my swashbuckling days, and white fire trailed in my wake as I raced over the hills of sand into the heart of the raging battlefield.

I eliminated the roar of machinery, the shriek of other Ignis abilities sailing around me. In my ears was the gentle swaying of the Grand Sea as it lapped up onto the shore, nothing more. As my white-fire knives cut tanks open like fruit, spilling open their iron hulls, I recalled beaches so much farther from here, far from all the blood and the black diamond sand. As I spun across the battlefield, deflecting raging fireballs of Ignis with the flaming white blades of two simple knives, I swept aside the whirlwinds of purple-and-black flame beginning to spring up and recalled a warm sunset on a rocky cliff. Four young men watching the twin suns eclipse one another before sinking low in the sky, giving way to millions of stars.

Back when all we really were was just Navigators. Pathfinders. Adventurers.

A stray cannonball knocked a knife from my hand. I cast my flaming eyes in the direction of the approaching tank that had fired it, then fished for my belt and a replacement. Spinning the knife thrice, I worked up enough speed so that when I flung it forward, the Ignis knife became a javelin of white light that pierced the tank at ten times the speed of the cannonball. It sent the tank sailing backward where it collapsed in a smoking heap.

And now we're warriors. The memory of the four boys entrenched in my mind, I closed my eyes. *Killers. Something we never should've been.*

My hands moved on their own, seizing another knife from my belt, then I was whirling through the ranks of black-coated, helmeted soldiers, recalling foot- and bladework that could never leave me, no matter how hard I tried to forget. Ignis poured out of me in tidal waves, my weapons slashing through the hefty guns and crude metallic devices the soldiers carried with them, devices they had used to mow down ranks of Navigators.

But none of them touched me. None of the soldiers saw anything other than a brilliant flash of white as my knives ended each of their lives. The playing field was leveled, so to speak, for I never saw anything either. My eyes remained sealed shut the entire time.

There had been four boys once. Yes. But now, there was just one. And his head hurt, his joints ached, and his spirit was crushed. He no longer raced around the Light Isles with a bottle of rum in hand, the wind nipping at his hair. Now, he walked through walls of tanks, and indestructible iron exploded around him. *When all he wants is peace.*

The tides of the battle were turning. My arrival had already given the Navigators enough confidence to begin surging toward the fortress. The crab cruisers we'd thrown at the barriers hadn't yet had any success breaking through, but the Ignis that the Navigators within them had thrown down were definitely doing their job to the surrounding landscape. The barrage would continue for another hour before any massive success could be had.

Mayhaps we shorten that to forty-five minutes? I flung myself into a pack of soldiers that had begun to condense around the Navigational squad I'd arrived with, then watched them all crumble beneath my Ignis.

I attended to the squad. Janne had sustained a deep cut in his arm, but Sasha was a skilled healer and used her dark orange Ignis to seal the wound. I nodded in approval.

"Aye. Bloody good work." My voice sounded so much more gruff now. I couldn't recall the last time it'd sounded cheerful. "Now get back to the northside. The other squads will rendezvous there."

"We want to stay with you," Sasha said, ever the Charger—leader—of the squad.

"Well, you don't get to." When she stood her ground, I glared. "That's an order, young'uns."

"With all due respect, sir," Janne said. "I think we're gonna be defying that order. If the Government isn't going to watch your back, then we will." He lifted his chin, placing a closed fist across his heart. "And I swear on the Code that this day, I shall stand beside you."

I watched all five of them do the same, each swearing on the Code as they formed their hands into triangles, placing them to their hearts—

A portal of darkness opened between us. Tendrils of magenta-colored Ignis, spiked and crystalline, exploded outward, with black energy turning through them like thorns.

I was thrown back some thirty feet, wincing as my left shoulder struck the stone-like sand, then dug a knife into the ground to slow my tumble. Blood bubbled up from my throat, forcing out a ragged cough. Wiping the tiny black diamonds from my face, I squinted into the dark dust storm, searching for the other Navigators.

The tendrils of Ignis thrashed from their portal, the black spikes slowly edging outward until the churning energy around them began to darken, revealing that they weren't Ignis-created constructs at all, but humongous spiked tentacles covered in sickly pink skin, summoned from . . .

I reached a knee slowly, eyes wide.

A tall black-coated figure stepped out of the triangular portal, the tentacles briefly parting to allow them to step through. A pointed hood was drawn down over their face, rendering their features completely hidden, but not the glowing pink crystal around their neck.

My knives slipped from my grip. The white flames coating their blades sputtered out of existence when they plunged into the dark sand, their light extinguished.

Among the mass of tentacles writhing around the figure, the dust began to clear, revealing the mounds strewn about the field. Crumpled Navigator bodies, torn open and tattered. Youthful features turned cold and dead.

But the figure just stepped over the macabre corpses and walked toward me, dark mist swirling out of the pink crystal.

My fingers twitched, searching for the blades they'd once held but unable to retrieve more from my belt. The blood running down my face felt ice cold, the sand particles still coating me like tiny daggers. All of me was frozen, legs rooted to the ground.

And my eyes. They could not unsee what they'd seen. Couldn't undo what had been done. And never again could I close them without seeing the carnage and the loss.

I didn't scream. Just pried my jaw open in a wordless, thoughtless bellow. Emptied myself of the past three decades, of the conflicts and wars and ways that could've so easily been prevented, could've just faded away had we all kept to the words and oaths we'd all once sworn to each other.

I gazed deep into the cloaked figure's hood, searching while I roared. The darkness didn't respond, nor reveal its depths. I thought about throwing my remaining daggers of Ignis at it in hopes of being the Light in the Darkness I'd once been called, but my limbs were slack with fear. Too scared to fight, too pathetic to face someone I knew had stacked every odd against me.

ONE DAY.

So I did the only thing a Navigator never did: I turned and ran.

Explosions obliterated the sand around me. Pillars of black sand and brown smoke erupted every which way, forming a war-torn corridor. I sprinted through it, barely seeing a thing, barely feeling the sharp pain flaring through my face or the way my knees screamed with pain and discomfort. Blood poured into my eyes, blinding me. I tripped over a tattered shard of tank armor only to discover a fallen Navigator. The boy was missing half of his body.

One day.

I kept running, willing my aching body to move as fast as it once had. I felt myself run through the many legendary eras of the Brotherhood, turning back the clock and reducing all the vows and codes we'd kept to void. I abandoned honor, I abandoned connection, and as I emerged into the jagged brown hills that coated the outskirts of the beach like ridged gravestones, I threw myself up onto one of the spiked cliffs and fell to my knees.

One . . . day . . .

From my place atop the crag, I could see all of the beach, smoking and shattered. Through the black smoke, the fortress still stood, and tanks and crab cruisers rumbled across the sand and through the sky. One crab cruiser exploded, plunging into the Grand Sea off the coast of the fortress. A spurt of magenta fire lit up the dark sky, and the shadow of a massive tentacle swayed across the entire battlefield. And behind them all, the Government forces sat silent and unmoving.

I tangled my dirty fingers through my hair, trying to rip out whole locks.

You did this. I cast my bleeding, blurring eyes to the dark clouds, trying to tear beyond them to reach the Dragon Lords. *You gave us this, yet you do nothing.* But when that grew too pathetic, I jerked my head back down to my lap, watching the way my entire body shook ferociously. *You give us the power to burn, but we're too busy burning up—*

Movement forced my eyes to the right, to another crag, where a tall man clothed in white and brown bandages stood. Though the wind blew about him, tearing at my own coat, somehow his makeshift robes never swayed. And the only part of him visible beneath all the bandages were two smoldering blue eyes. Trickles of smoke poured from the corners of them.

"Have you come to watch it end?" I asked. "That's what you Shrouded Men do, isn't it?" I wiped a shaking hand across my mouth. It came back smeared in blood. "Watch the world and document its destruction?"

The Shrouded Man said nothing for a while. Until: *"I think you will find, Kaleo Ashai, that this is merely the resurrection."* He had a voice like mist. A voice that might've soothed anyone to sleep but today just made me want to rip his eyes out.

"Navigators lay *dead,*" I bellowed back at him. "There is no resurrection today. Nor was there one yesterday. Or the day before that. Or the years and years that this bloody stupid war has gone on for."

I remained on my knees, finally allowing the tears to pour free. The Shrouded Man watched me weep, saying nothing.

"This is it," I finally stated. "I swear this is it. The end of the Navigational Brotherhood." I tried wiping my eyes but found my hands too bloody to do so. All of me was bloodstained. All of me screaming. "All we were supposed to be were protectors. Protectors and guides of the world. Not killers." I ground my fist into my pants, staining them. "But since the Government and the Noda will not cease fighting, we will cease fighting for them. The Perpetual War will rage on, and from this moment moving forward, Navigators will not fight.

"Archengard can bleed out for all I care."

"*Then let it bleed,*" the Shrouded Man said. *"But the blood will remain on your hands. No matter how fiercely you seek to remove it."*

"Did the Jackals send you?" I spat. "I thought the Shrouded don't take sides, yet you're here berating me for actions I'd undo a million times over if I could."

"What is done is done." Then he paused. *"Yet* one day, *it might be undone."*

I looked up.

Though the Shrouded Man faced me, his eyes seemed to drift away, up toward the sky and possibly through the dark clouds I'd so desperately wanted to peel back. The power swimming through him was Ignis, yet the Shrouded were not known for looking to the Dragon Lords, as most Ignis users did. In fact, they saw the Lords as limiting. They looked beyond and read what they saw. Some said they knew the stars by name. Some said the prophecies they spoke were written in the souls of those stars.

"Long ago, I spoke to you." The Shrouded let himself take a slow step forward, to the very edge of the crag. *"And I told you that the age you found yourself prospering in would not last. I told you to beware of the black dog with the orange eyes, and that with it would come the dark. And with the dark, the War."*

Then he cast his head to the sky.

"But look." He pointed. *"There on the horizon."*

I followed his bandaged finger, searching, hoping.

"This Shrouded does think that through the black, he sees a star." He tilted his head, as though amused. *"A star of gold and green."* He nodded. *"Then we shall see."*

Though the cold winds continued to bite at me, the crags shaking as smoke and ash and Ignis-created fires continued to buffet them, a warm shiver slid down my spine, prickling the scorched hair on the back of my neck. And when I glanced back at the crag where the Shrouded Man had stood, he was gone.

Legs popping painfully, I rose to my feet, nearly tumbling down the side of the spire. The blood had dried on my face, sealing my left eye shut, yet the right eye saw clear as day. I placed a worn hand to the jagged tip of the crag—what I'd used for support to get to my feet.

Maybe I can make this right.

Grimacing, I wrenched my arms out of the ruined white-and-gold coat, then impaled the collar on the crag. The wind instantly caught it, turning it into a tattered flag.

Maybe I can. Not today.

I left the coat twisting in the wind.

But maybe one day.

CHAPTER 1

Murta

TEN YEARS LATER

I twisted to the side and caught the insect.

A moment after it happened, I had to blink and remind myself that I'd actually moved that fast. That I could catch insects mid-flight even without Ignis.

Tapping into the energy, I felt it pour out of my soul, flowing out into my hands and replacing them with claws covered in obsidian scales. I felt Ignis seep up into my eyes, turning my vision umber gold. I felt, above everything, alive.

Listening to the horrified squeaking from between my claws, I raised them to eye level. The orange-and-midnight-striped back was unmistakable: Jaguar hornets could carve through ranks of men. Whereas bees lived to pollinate, jaguar hornets lived to kill.

Just like me, I mused, then pressed my claws together.

Amber flames sprang to life between them, incinerating the hornet with a satisfying *snap-hiss*. I let go of Ignis, letting my scales fold back to human skin, and after rinsing off the hornet's remains, cast them to the cold wind rushing out of the temple.

Walking several feet in front of me, Nico spun when he saw the flash of gold. His eyes went wide with panic. "Murta, was that—?!"

"Not anymore," I said. *"De nada."*

He inhaled cautiously. The Shadarian language had had that effect for as long as I could remember. People liked to pretend we were a clan of demons, but we were just as human as everyone else. Sometimes.

Nico continued his spin in search of a nest. "What about the rest?"

"Who knows." I was losing patience. "Focus on the job."

Up ahead, the temple looked more stable than some of the older monasteries I'd sifted through in the past, but the darkness seeping out of the entrance was ancient. To counter it, I summoned Ignis once more, letting it convert my irises into brazen rings. In response, the dark parts of the temple lit up in every shade of gold.

I took the marble steps at a jog, Ret following closely. Bringing up the rear were Lee and Camble, two younger mercs whose lives I'd saved during my last mission.

I shook my head when I heard them scamper in my wake, trading childish insults. I'd just turned twenty sun cycles; Lee and Camble were still nineteen. We weren't a professional mercenary band. *Definitely* not something akin to a Navigational squadron. I agreed that Ignis users needed to stick together in these dark times, but that was hardly a reason for us to harken back to the ways of the Navigational Brotherhood.

Those ways are dead. The world took them out back and slit their throats.

So I ignored the other mercs and commanded Ignis to flow back down into my hand. Once more, its ethereal energy turned my human skin into draconic claws, and a curdling ball of gold fire ignited in the center of my palm. I inspected the high ceiling. Ret broke the line that he and the other mercs stood in by joining me at my side. He followed my gaze upward. The inner sanctum was entirely made of old iron, rusted and crude.

"This is the place?" he asked. "The one that the Jackals are looking for?"

I didn't respond.

The descent took five minutes. Camble and Nico were constantly tripping over chinks in the stone, flames flickering in their hands as they concentrated more on their footing than controlling Ignis. Camble's flame sputtered out completely, and I offered a spark of my own to reignite his. He nodded, and I watched his Ignis ability return: a triangular column of violet light spinning in his hand. Like all Ignis when first summoned, it started within his chest as a spiral of colored flame, then expanded to take over his entire outline. Even wielded by fools like Camble, it was a brilliant aura of color, a fragment of draconic power.

I watched it spin out of Camble slowly, almost methodically. I watched as he leaned in close, and before he could sear my face off, I'd already started moving.

Movement was a Shadarian's greatest asset. Our speed defied logic, broke men's minds long before our feet reached them. Ordinary men were born crawling; we were born sprinting.

Gilded flames collected around my feet and raced up my legs. I twisted in place, extending my leg and waiting until my foot spat across Camble's face, dislocating bone and knocking two or three teeth out with sickening crackles.

But a Shadarian hardly aimed for just the teeth. On impact, Camble's muscles locked, and his lifeless body sailed down into the dark.

The others gaped. Ret nearly pissed himself. "How could you—"

"His real name was Cetoran." I readjusted the black scarf wound about my neck, Ignis fading into pulsing afterglow. "An assassin working for the Noda." I'd known about Camble's real identity since our last raid. I'd known he was going to try to kill me at some point, but I just hadn't thought it would be this soon. *Never underestimate the quiet ones, I guess.*

"He was going to betray everyone, *idiota*," I said, and turned my back on the pit.

Nico moved to get up in my face. "Mercs don't go kicking other mercs off cliffs."

That pried a cold laugh from my throat. "If you wanna play Navigator, go piss in a dragon's den." I raised my fire before carrying on. "But don't come crying when you're missing a leg and half your face is on fire."

The steps gradually grew sturdier, then wider as the scattered pits were replaced with iron floors bearing engravings. Marble columns made way for walls connected by steel flaps and rusty cogs.

Nico looked over the machinery, skin pale in the light of his orange Ignis. When I reached the floor and took my first step onto the engravings, a soft whirring began, freezing him in place.

Ret's silhouette glowed brown as he tapped into Ignis. "What'd you do?!"

"'Touch the floor, head for the door,'" I recited before striding across the patterns to peer through one of the narrow slots in the walls into the temple vault.

The red light humming at the end of the darkness was unmistakably my destination: identical to the descriptions of the temple that I'd received earlier from the Shrouded Men. It was understandable why the other mercs wouldn't necessarily believe me. The Shrouded had little respect for the criminal underworld and would tear their bandaged faces off before revealing archival information to a merc.

But I'd once belonged to another group as well, and the Shrouded *always* told them the truth. By bringing my hated past life up, I'd received the most accurate intel I'd ever been given.

"Head for the *what*?" Ret said.

"The Shrouded Men," I said, frowning. "That's what they told me."

"Then let's—"

"No. The ticking is a countdown." I followed the edges of the walls to the slots they were placed in on the ground. Enhancing my vision with Ignis, I spotted the same grooves up near the ceiling. The doors could be slid open.

I turned on the three of them. "Who's going to attack me once I've got the map?"

Their silence was fittingly deeper than Camble's. They couldn't possibly think that I was that stupid. Of course I knew that Camble was an assassin. Of course they were *all* assassins. The Jackals were too smart not to send them.

"Responde la pregunta."

Nico worked his mouth. Ret stared bug-eyed. Then Lee did an awkward shuffle and raised his hand slowly.

"Wait, what do you mean the map?" Ret said. "I thought—"

"Shut up and help me with this door," I told Lee, lifting my scarf so it masked my nose and mouth. A Shadarian tic for when times got tough, and the only way I could keep Lee's betrayal from nipping at me. I'd liked him early on. "I suppose your Ignis isn't too weak."

"What's that supposed to mean?" Ret stammered as Lee brushed by him.

Lee took up position on the opposite side, avoiding eye contact, and allowed Ignis to overtake him. Gray-blue light trailed down his arms, turning his irises the same color. He'd always been the best Ignis user of the three.

My shoes scraped against the floor as I pulled back on the door frame in unison with Lee. The assassin grunted noisily, but I moved in silence, listening for a dark click. When my side of the wall crept to a halt, I found it.

"That it?" Lee said, wiping his brow.

I pulled my black suit jacket around me, squinting into the shadows.

Nico stared. "We gotta go down *there*?"

"Then stay here," I said, already entering. "But that ticking isn't going anywhere."

Only a couple of steps in, I realized that the hall was more of an in-between aisle passing through a series of smaller ones. The perpendicular aisles were identical—black-brick vaults that emerged into church-like steeples—and sitting within the center of each was a silky translucent pod.

I glanced down three more of the aisles on my way to the red light to make sure the pods were what I thought they were. They glowed a sickly pink, punctured by black cords that trailed off into the darkness. Each of them quivered, but only Ignis-enhanced Shadarian eyes detected the movement. Probably for the best.

An anxious hum escaped Nico's throat. "Are those moving?"

Tick-tick-tick, the shadows replied. I lit another flame of Ignis.

The assassins clearly didn't know what to expect. Lords, they'd thought we were actually about to find the Talisman *here*. But I was more than familiar with the machine that the light stemmed from. I'd left Anders's mercenary band in search of it, paying unbelievable amounts to Whisperers for more information. It had been years.

And now I'm finally here.

Striding past the last six pods, I entered the main vault. Lee followed close behind, nearly bumping into me when I jerked to a stop.

Plastered to the wall was a red rectangle set into a black base, and sticking out of it at hand height was a thin keyboard.

I extinguished Ignis, freeing my hands. After smashing a button on the side, the screen flickered on, displaying paragraphs of strange lettering. I immediately identified it as the Dark Tongue, a dead language from a darker age, embedded in a piece of dark technology.

My fingers flew across the keys. The sentences were structured thickly, their accent marks crude. To Lee, it probably looked like the kind of tongue bats conversed in. It came to me just as easily as Shadarian and Common Archengardian.

A few quick clicks and I was in. Lee pointed out a cluster of folders in the left corner. I found them faster and was barreling through their contents before he opened his mouth.

"This—"

"Not now."

"Can I get a word in?"

I narrowed my eyes.

"What *is* this, Murta?" Lee said. "Where's the Ka?"

"Not here."

"You brought us all this way—?"

"For the map. You honestly thought we'd find a Talisman right away?"

"Fine." Lee shook with anger. So the Jackals wouldn't allow him to kill me until I found the Kardem Ka. That almost made me laugh, dreaming of what that mistake would eventually cost them. What I'd eventually do to them.

"Then where's the map?" Lee added.

"Aquí."

The screen of folders was replaced with a single image—a network of spiraling red lines: a thousand different passages buried deep within the gorges of East Khronera.

"The Eastern Strip," Lee said. "That's where the Ka is."

I pointed out the dotted black lines weaving in and out of the gorges. "And that's the only path that gets us there. There's still the northern path to take into consideration. The map cuts off."

"So we're just supposed to memorize all this?"

One of the black cords attached to the side of the machine gave a soft shudder. I picked it up, examining the end. It was cylindrical around the base but ended in a sharp point.

Dread crept up my spine. I smothered it with rage. Shadarians didn't feel dread; they seized it by the throat and slaughtered it.

Gripping the cord in one hand, I loosened my scarf and pulled down the collar of my crimson dress shirt. Lee was right. Memorization of such intricate pathways was impossible, even for a trained mind like mine.

But if memorization was out of the question, then there was only one other alternative.

My body went rigid the moment I stabbed the probe into my neck.

Even with years of my life spent training my body to deal with pain, living and dying and living again, I knew I'd never be ready for the feeling. I'd had all kinds of weapons shoved into me—spears, broadswords, knives, even got shot a couple times—but the cord was by far the coldest. It felt sickly. My soul felt contaminated.

"Putting the map into my brain," I said when Lee shrieked. "This is the only way to completely memorize it." On the screen, a white bar began to fill up.

"The ticking's gotten louder," Ret yelled across the hall. "Why's it louder?"

I watched the bar fill to 43 percent, then pause.

"He's almost done," Lee lied.

"Don't remove it," I gritted through clenched teeth when Lee looked like he was about to yank out the cord. It was about to be the last thing on his mind. "Get ready to run."

Sirens howled from the depths of the vault. The screen's red light pulsed, sending light flickering across the darkness. Through the shafts of red and the pain racing through my body, I saw the end of the hall and lifted a shaking finger toward it.

The walls we'd strained to open were closing.

Lee sprinted for them, taking Nico with him and screaming. Ret followed, screaming louder, but I only heard the sharp whine of technology.

The map sprinted across my mind, imprinting itself into memory. I saw the right way, the *true* way that would take me directly to the Kardem Ka, but the path still ended before the north. I had to take in the map's entirety and piece it together with what I already knew of the Strip.

So even after all the searching I'd done, this still wouldn't be enough.

Black technology tugged at my soul, dark chemicals racing down my spine, twisting my mind in two. I wanted out, but couldn't. Not if I wanted the Ka. *Not if I want* them.

Peering through flickering eyelids, I jerked my pounding head toward the screen.

59%.

The pods opened before I could shout. The liquid spilled out through holes punctured by white spikes made of bone and mechanical mess. Unsettling half-made faces of tissue and metal pressed themselves up against the clear shells, wiggling through the holes.

67%.

"Time to go, Shadarian!" Nico said. He and Ret held on to the walls, trying to prevent them from closing.

I felt for Ignis to still the writhing darkness within me. It was like trying to hold back a tsunami with nothing but my hands, but I had to let it hit me. I had to allow its information to filter. If I didn't, one of the Talismans would be forever lost to me.

One of the pods splattered open. Something tumbled out.

"We can't keep this door open!"

Two more pods broke. A third followed. A fourth. The white beasts scuttled across the metal, slipping in the leaking liquid. Something wet touched the toe of my shoe, and I kicked it with a foot engulfed in flames, but it was only the water from the pods. Tapping into Ignis made my eyes sting in their sockets, and I almost blacked out when the cord gave an electrical surge. The machine had literally told me, *You do nothing unless I tell you.*

78%.

My skull vibrated, throwing me in and out of consciousness until the only sliver of thought in my brain was a scowling jackal head set with a golden collar and orange eyes. My end goal and endgame. The banner all my roads led to.

Metallic howls filled the vault as their pale owners galloped toward the doors. They were like hairless dogs. Demonic, spidery things ironically resembling albino jackals without eyes. Their makers had a twisted sense of humor.

Ret and Nico screamed, rising over the creatures' shrieks, but everything was silenced by Lee stepping forward and flinging gray-blue spheres of Ignis into the tangle of thrashing limbs.

I peered through flickering eyelids in astonishment.

There'd been a time when Lee had been terrified of fighting—a time I remembered well from previous missions—but as he faced down the creatures, he seemed to become a different person. The mist of fear that typically clouded him had given way to thunderous determination. His clumsy, disheveled movements turned fierce and fleet.

And then I knew.

Though I'd refused to join them at night for talks around the fire, choosing instead to man the perimeter, I'd heard from Nico what had attracted Lee to become an assassin, and later, a mercenary. I'd heard who and what he took inspiration from.

And now, it made perfect sense why he'd practically begged me to bring him along. Now, it made sense why the assassin seemed so reluctant to kill.

Though Lee was a greedy bastard, he had Ignis, and that meant in the quiet moments, he looked to the Code. Though Ret and Nico saw the Kardem Ka as a way to make money, Lee knew that finding it was bigger than them, more important than money.

So, for the time being, he had put aside his greed to *protect*. In mind and body, he was still an assassin for hire. But in spirit, he became a Navigator.

Damn him.

85%.

The pod closest to me split down the middle. The translucent material cracked instead of bleeding out, and the thing resting within it merely stepped out of the hardened puddle.

Mierda.

The creature galloped toward me.

93%.

"Lee," I hissed.

The last section of the map filtered into my memory slowly. The cord sent pulses down my spine, making my body twitch as I tried to harness Ignis. Movement made the map load longer, and the creature only gained speed.

One of Lee's gray-blue spheres finally flew up through the shafts of shadows, passing over the beasts in the center of the hall. It hit the ground ten feet away from the one running at me, missing.

I closed my eyes. Something hot dribbled onto my face. The smell of rotting flesh and stinking machinery felt inches from my nostrils. The jackal symbol branded into my mind seared my brain . . .

99%.

Enough.

My hand shot outward, seizing the creature by the mangled throat and squeezing the life from its hollow lungs. Gears, springs, and chunks of flesh flew everywhere. The beast bucked, but I held on coldly, eyes blurring between the last bits of code and the gnarled face trying to bite me. Then the code switched off.

100%.

The cord whipped out of my neck, taking fragments of bone and blood with it. I stumbled but hung on to the creature. Its wicked tail cut through my jacket, leaving a long scar across my arm. It tried lashing at me again, but I caught the end of it with my claws and burst into flames. The creature became a screaming torch.

Instead of surging in on the hall, the creatures fled back to their destroyed pods. My gold inferno sent them clambering over one another. They turned away from their burning brothers, fleeing my black-sun eyes and the hell I rained from them.

After tearing my way to Lee, I found him twisted up on the floor, limbs mashed into the metal. He twitched, yet still managed to offer a blue flame using his spirit. It exited his heart and floated up into the darkness before my face.

Lee couldn't speak, his windpipe crushed, but the offering and bright-blue flicker in his agony-filled eyes spoke for itself: *Though I'm not a Navigator, I wish to die like one.*

I reluctantly honored his dying wish. I burned a quick, painless hole through his heart and watched the last trickles of blue Ignis fade up toward the ceiling.

"SHADARIAN!" Ret wailed, and the creatures leapt forward to devour Lee's remains.

I sprint-hobbled to the doors. Nico was missing fingers, orange Ignis fizzling from their bloodied stumps. Ret lifted his eyes, but only one was intact.

"Close it," I said once I was through.

Nico sank to his knees, weeping. As the doors rumbled closed, shutting us off from the smacking sounds that the creatures made as they feasted, Ret seized me by the shoulders. "No, they're . . ."

Something white stepped out of the cavern shadows, metal teeth dripping with saliva. My heart sank.

The creatures, *dozens* of them, filled the room. They crawled out of every crevice, dripping their foam on every patch of stone . . . except the narrow stairway.

A half mile of running up stairs with multiple wounds, surrounded by monsters. A regular human didn't stand a chance. A Shadarian with fire in his veins might.

"Can you keep up?"

"Keep . . . up?" Nico repeated.

"The map is first priority. I can't save you."

"W-what do you mean?! You have to—"

One of the creatures dropped from the ceiling. I demolished its face with a kick to the jaw. Even without Ignis, the flesh split under my shoe, sending shock waves through the metal underneath. I danced backward, possibly with a broken toe.

"I'm a merc, not a Navigator," I snarled. "And an *actual* merc at that. Now: Can you keep up?"

"Nico's missing fingers and I'm missing an eye!" Ret screamed. "And these white things are EVERY—"

Half of the creatures pounced on the injured assassins while the other half scrambled to snap at my legs. The first group hit their mark; the second missed.

I hurtled up the staircase, trying not to focus on the pounding in my neck, the foot that worsened with every step . . . or Ret's bloodcurdling scream.

Even now, I could save them. If I wanted to, I could.

Sharp metal suddenly pinned me against the rock wall. My eyes sparked out of control, illuminating the passage in brief flashes. Ignis sputtered in my hands, but my claws wouldn't come. The pain felt fixed into my very soul, a searing black burn that refused to heal, and more looked to be coming if the swinging spike hovering over my head was what I thought it was.

Without using Ignis to enhance my reflexes, I dodged its tail. The spike sank into the stone, and before it could come dislodged, I body-slammed the creature into the wall. Its scream was muffled as it ate rock. When its tail finally escaped, it thrashed about the enclosed space. Nothing punctured, but the scrapes piled up. Tiny methodical scrapes, like the scars etched into my mind, splitting memory in two . . .

I kicked the *puto* through the wall with a bellow.

Natural light exploded into view. The intrusion of something so pure in a place tainted with such darkness took me aback. At first, I cowered away from it, then realized that the halfway-destroyed creature I'd used as a battering ram to get through the rock squealed in an attempt to escape.

I threw myself into the crevice, aiming through the limbs toward the light. Pale liquid spurted out of the monster's tattered back. Its head went flying backward and pieces of its tail were crushed in the tight area as I turned the crevice into a fiery tunnel of Ignis, then burst into open air.

I welcomed the wind and wetness of the jungle. Chunks of grass engulfed my vision, creating a blurry forest around me. Every wound I owned was hit a hundred times over with the endless spinning of the world of Archengard around me.

As long as it gets me away from the temple.

Open air again, then water. I blinked in confusion before calming.

I'd fallen into a river. The coldness of the liquid as I swallowed some didn't bother me. It carried me away from the temple.

Blood seeped out from the hole in my neck, Ignis seeped out from the scar in my spirit, and my mind slipped into the void. No matter. I had the map.

And in a week, I'd have the Kardem Ka.

In the river's current, I felt Ignis working to fix my wounds. In the current, I felt fragments of hope, of knowing that I was one step closer to recovering a Talisman. One step closer to beating the group that pulled all the strings . . .

The jackal symbol carved into my memory ruptured across my eyes, making my brain seesaw. The stream nearly unclasped the gold necklace I wore tucked under my collar, almost identical to the one worn by the jackal. A necklace, that when removed, would uncover a bottomless well of chaos. A screaming dark thing trapped inside me.

Let go, a voice rasped within me—one of their voices. *Unleash it. Bask in the blood.*

I reached blindly for something that wasn't there, looking to the golden spark of my spirit and finding only dark fragments floating away from me, like the last bits of Ignis leaving Lee's body.

The water extinguished the flame, setting the necklace securely around me. The cold metal falling against my neck sent me into a dream where the Dragon Lords all convened around my lifeless body and forgave me for my sins.

But even then, that was still too little.

CHAPTER 2

Enoch

Over the barks of thunder, the old man's voice somehow rang louder. "Are you quite certain that you want to do this, lad? There's no shame in turning back now, lad. No shame whatsoever . . . Lad?"

I began winding the white tape around my fists. When a scar of lightning charioted across the dark sky, I felt my spirit ride with it, illuminating the wild grin I wore. The old man cringed so far back that he bumped into his son, who sailed the rowboat out into the Grand Sea.

The weather was hideous for an evening off the coast of an unnamed mining village, but according to the old man, it was the only time "it" ever swam near the surface. The only time anyone had ever come close enough to pick the bastard's nostrils was during a storm, and from the constant shuddering of the boat, clearly the old man and his son had little faith regardless. They were terrified.

Unsurprisingly, I was ecstatic.

The rain picked up until it stung my eyes. The old man muttered a drawn-out prayer that made my head ache. His son rowed faster, digging the wood into the waves, and sat rooted to the seat in front of me, refusing to look at the bubbling sea.

I finished binding my left fist, ripping clean the last line of tape with my teeth. "Where's he hiding?"

The old man placed a wrinkled hand to his brow to keep the rain from pelting his pale eyes. "Pardon, lad . . . *He?*"

"She?" I tried again. "It? Where's the beast off sleeping?"

"Father, this is the most immature child I've ever encountered," the son said. "You enlisted this fool to kill the Serpent of Besping?"

Pausing mid-strip of my shirt, I frowned through a white sleeve. "I'm twenty years, bruv. Fools have to be somewhere under that, I should think."

That seemed to set the son off even more, though I couldn't place why. The two ended up in a shouting match, something about a dead wife that had been drowned by the creature I hunted. They grew serious. I hastened to reassure them.

"Not to worry." I tightened my green bandana, throwing my soaked shirt down into the boat. "She shall be avenged once I set my sights on the snake."

The son spun around, rowers and all. One of the wooden boards would've taken my head off if I hadn't had world-class head movement.

"That's just the thing, *pirate*. My mother wasn't some Ignis-using scallywag looking to make a quick buck, and she shouldn't be avenged by one."

"We prefer the term 'swashbuckler,'" I said. "Honest mistake. But for the record, I've never sought to waste my life."

"So I guess there's no need for us to pay you, then?"

"Arman—" the man started.

I held up a taped fist, a warning. "Money hasn't a fragment to do with it."

"Then either you do this for fame," Arman said, "or you're just downright insane."

I swayed in the rocking boat to keep my balance, then shimmied past the son to reach the helm. "No bloke's ever seen meself and insanity in the same room, so you might be on the right route there." I pounded my fists together and grabbed for Ignis.

My spirit lifted out of me to surround my body in an emerald-green aura. It started within my heart, a spiral galaxy of controlled fire, then swept outward, stilling my racing heartbeat and quivering veins.

I swept Ignis-infused eyes over the thrashing waves. No sign of anything yet. The creature still seemed entranced in its slumber, unaware of the handsome bloke sailing above it looking for a fight. Or perhaps it had taken a more predatory approach and watched. Maybe this was more of a mind game than the exchange of blows I'd prepared for.

Ignis evaporated from me—a power I'd been told was incredibly rare, yet still had no idea how to use. I hit things hard and glowed green. Weird markings, like the swirls and symbols left on the interior of sea caves I used to venture into, appeared on my skin. There wasn't much else to my Ignis ability besides deep concentration and an out-of-body feeling, like I knew the thing I was hitting inside and out. If I concentrated really hard, I could feel individual spirits, but only on a good day.

Today isn't a good day.

"Well?" Arman said.

I never took my eyes off of the waves. "Patience is said to be a virtue, bruv. Don't worry, I wouldn't know either. But it's been a while since I've taken on a job like this."

A lie. I'd fought everything between crabs and chimeras. *And on good days.*

"Don't you just conjure fire down into the water and kill it?"

"Rubbish. I don't 'conjure' shite. My Ignis doesn't allow me to throw projectiles. No two Ignis abilities are alike, bruv."

"So what *do* you do?"

I'd been lucky to grow up in the heart of the Light Isles where Ignis users were common. Arman was from the far western isles, where blokes like me were far scarcer, making him all the more susceptible to the lies that the Government fed people. His comments ventured close to downright discriminatory. They clouded my mind with the cardinal sin of all swashes: doubt.

But in times of doubt, I recalled why I did this. I recalled the one who had made it possible for a damaged, dying bloke to resurrect himself and never doubt again.

His name was the Leviathan.

My chest instinctively swelled at the thought of the legendary Navigator at the helm of a ship, gripping his white-fire sword, white-gold coat and bandana billowing behind him.

Out of all the great Navigators, the Leviathan was the greatest. Most people didn't even know that his Ignis could only be filtered through weapons, meaning that without the Sword, he was practically Ignis-less. Under the banner of the Brotherhood, he'd gone from quest to quest, solving every problem every Navigator before him had deemed unsolvable, showing everyone that Ignis wasn't something to be reviled, but admired.

But then the hunt for the Sacred Heart had happened, a quest which even his limitless perseverance had failed to conquer. Supposedly, the failure had crushed him, but he never stopped looking. Always keeping faith, never giving in to doubt despite knowing he might fail spectacularly.

To say I felt a great deal of kinship with him was an understatement.

This is my Sacred Heart, I thought, spotting a flash of silver scales in the deep. *This is my losing battle that I can win.*

I'll win it for the Leviathan.

Bulbous red eyes crackled with their own lightning in the sea. Thick serpentine skin skimmed past the boat, carving directly under us then spinning back around toward the helm. Razor-sharp back fins emerged. The son shouted, the old man's mutterings rose to a moan, and I forced Ignis to enter my fists.

Immortal, I think. Immortal, I become.

In the boxing ring, everything cleared. The screaming audience, pacing referee, and ring ropes made from knotted vines all dematerialized. Poof, gone. All that mattered was my opponent. All I heard was the controlled, quiet beating of my heart.

Fighting a monster was a lot like boxing; timing and belief were key.

The sea serpent sprung out of the waves in a death roll, launching itself directly at us in an attempt to crush the boat. What it clearly hadn't expected was someone standing at its helm.

My immediate instinct was to charge up my fist, but my timing was off. I was nervous and had underestimated the serpent's speed. At the rate the creature was going, it'd crush the whole boat if I missed. Better to take the fight down to the water for Arman's sake. Better to take the road that the Leviathan would take and fly into danger like a wild banshee.

Wait, my mind screamed. *That's not—*

Transferring Ignis into my shoulders before my brain could drop anchor, I shot out of the boat as a green comet, slamming into the serpent's thick chest.

—a bright idea.

The serpent lurched backward in surprise. My arms barely wrapped around its chest, and I felt as though I'd body-slammed a galleon, but the Ignis coursing through my veins did its job. I tackled the serpent back into the ocean.

My mistake materialized almost immediately. In the roaring darkness that raced around me, I was scraped from every angle. Trying to fight a sea serpent in the sea was such a bloody stupid idea. Like trying to take on a dragon in a flying contest, but now I could say I'd done both.

With Ignis, I could at least move somewhat freely underwater—much quicker than an Ignis-less person—but the serpent was in its natural habitat. It was everywhere at once, winding its slick, steely body around my torso.

I squirmed for a plan. Green Fire Fist wouldn't work underwater—fire was in its name—unless I *connected* with something.

There was that word again. The old Ignis users I'd spoken to among the Light Isles, hoping to leech off some of their knowledge, claimed my ability had nothing to do with fighting and everything to do with "connecting."

How was punching hard a form of connection? How was evening out my breathing so I could last longer in a fight associated with connection? What was I connecting to?

I pried an arm loose, blasting the serpent's coils with a grueling left hook of Ignis. The rock-hard layer of scale and muscle relaxed slightly, emerald particles clinging to it. I tasted blood in the water, but the creature's underside, pressing directly into my body, began to hum with red electricity. I could already feel the sparks racing up my spine.

Oh, bugger.

I punched the creature in the neck as hard as I could but sacrificed precious energy better spent elsewhere. A wave of pain engulfed my arm, and the serpent just continued to vibrate, dragging me deeper and deeper into the dark ocean.

It would electrocute me, then take me to its lair to feast.

I was going to get *mauled* by a giant snake.

Green light fled my body in reverse raindrops. I yelled for them to come back, but that just wasted more air. I reached for the particles of Ignis, willing them to return to me, but that was folly. Ignis rested within. I could call on it anytime I wanted, but sometimes it chose not to answer.

Sometimes, Ignis chose to die inside me.

Connect.

I threw my eyes closed.

Connect with the serpent. Place your spirit in it . . .

The sea serpent let out a sudden scream and began to unwind itself from my body, as if provoked by something unseen. But before speeding away, it released the buildup of electricity crackling against its scales.

Crimson lightning knifed through me. I writhed in white-hot pain, felt colder than I'd ever felt before, then lay still.

Water pouring in everywhere, I found my mind harkening back to Arman somewhere up above. Arman and his hate. Hate piling on top of me all my life, no matter where I lived, no matter where I went. From city streets to back alleys to dirty boxing rings.

I already felt the fish nipping at my wounds, snapping at one another to get a go at me. Even they couldn't connect. They'd rather fight one another for bits of blood and food.

They were the world.

Connect . . .

Something rough lay beneath me. It was flat, but my body sank into it. The ground seemed to breathe. I peeked my eyes open just to snap them shut when I saw red light glowing in the darkness.

I've been eaten.

Bits of water sprayed across my face, making me cringe against what I assumed was the stomach of the sea serpent. The material shifted with me, though, and the spray came with the familiar sound of waves crashing against rocks. Wind followed, tossing my hair.

"I recommend not moving too much," a low voice called from behind me.

It's bloody talking, the irrational side of my mind screamed. *It's—*

"Shut up," I scolded myself, squeezing the sifting material beneath me—sand, not skin—and opening my eyes.

The multicolored corridors of the night sky met me. The sand belonged to a long winding beach, and the red light was the warm glow of a fire.

I tilted my head back carefully. The fire was unnaturally crimson and stood straight as a pillar. It didn't swim about the air and waver naturally. It remained rooted in place.

Ignis.

"Rise slowly." The voice came from behind the fire. "Don't try and—"

I shot up and instantly regretted it. Everything I owned turned fiery, and I lay back down with a barely contained howl. It hurt, *bad*, but when my back slammed against the sand once more, a sickened laugh escaped me.

I'd gone through my Burning—the moment a user harnesses Ignis for the first time—relatively late in life. And ever since then, every time I accessed Ignis, I felt like I was somehow losing more of it.

Ignis was dying in me. I felt severed from it. Laughing and moving was the only way to remotely cope. If I stayed in one place for too long and indulged in the pain, I might never get up again. I might return to the version of me that had almost succumbed to the cruelty that Archengard was capable of producing. The cruelty I knew so well.

Sitting up with mild discomfort, I rose to my feet. My chest gave a pained response, but I ignored it, half hobbling over to the pillar of red fire.

Walk it off. Think immortal.

But I couldn't. The pain raced down my legs, turning my bones to rum.

Which I'd kill for a barrel of right now. I had to grit my teeth just to stay upright. I felt more than mortal.

"Pretending the pain doesn't exist is pointless," the voice said.

"You're pointless."

A snort.

Clutching my throbbing arm, I slowed to a stop and glared through the flames. Sitting atop a piece of driftwood was a figure in a brown hooded cloak covered in jagged black markings. I squinted. Only a hand was visible, weaving red lines through the air that formed into the flame column.

Their other hand suddenly emerged from the cloak, gesturing at a second piece of driftwood across from it. "Please. I have extra clothes."

"Don't need extra clothes." I eyed their Ignis ability with jealousy.

"On the contrary, you're in need of much more than just clothes."

I took a cautious seat before examining myself from toes to chest. "I'm alive."

"Yes."

"You saved me?"

"I did."

"Why?"

"Why not?"

That was a rubbish response. "But I dunno you."

The hood tilted. "And therefore that means I shouldn't have done so?"

"I had it under control."

"And I'm one of the Dragon Lords."

I averted my gaze from the figure's flames, dragging memories under the surface. Ignis-created or regular flames, fire only made my chest feel as though it were being filled with cement. Made me harken back to the bloodstained cement, the spinning core of a fire beam heating up above me.

"Where I'm from, blokes only look out for themselves," I said.

"So you would've rather accepted death than be saved?"

"If that's what life wants." I began to ferociously scrape the sand from my legs. "We're all slaves to it one bloody way or another."

The fire darkened.

"Your heart isn't in what you say," the figure said.

"How do you know? It's *my* life."

"Did you not just refer to yourself as a slave to it?"

"I—"

"And what would you say if someone gave you the tools to take the life you so desperately yearn for into your own hands? What if I were to tell you that you could live the life you want *and* reach the full potential of your Ignis? To hone it for the right reasons?"

I paused. "I'd say that's impossible. Ignis can only accomplish so many things. I almost died because mine didn't work when I needed it."

"Because you lack the proper instruction. Perhaps even the proper purpose."

I thrust out my fists. "I don't even know how to use this shite. I thought I could just wallop people, but now blokes are telling me I have to 'connect' first. How's that make sense?"

The figure folded their hands. "I've spoken with many men who know of Light Eyes Amon, from the isles you've crossed to the mud pits you fight in. They say he's wicked fast, wicked stubborn, and harder than hell to hit. They say that when he does get hit, he's even harder to hit again. They say he's typically in a bar, drinking himself into a coma . . ."

I felt my fists tighten over time until I saw them turning pale as bone in my lap.

"But they also say," the figure said, "that once in a while, he'll forsake his beloved boxing rings and bars. That once in a while, he'll be seen taking on eight-armed demons with nothing but his fists. And that when he does embark on these crusades of heroism, he'll sometimes don a white-and-gold jacket and bandana. He'll sometimes be mistaken as the reincarnation of a certain friend of mine.

"What they say most of all, Light Eyes, is that above every swashbuckler and Ignis user, he takes inspiration from the Leviathan of the Navigational Brotherhood the most."

The pounding that erupted within me wasn't the fear-induced drumming that had filled me as the serpent dragged me to its lair, but the staccato thunder of revelation. Of possibility.

I saw the figure's red Ignis ability and marking-engulfed robe in a new, familiar light.

"You're Barco Reyveth," I whispered.

"I am."

"You're recruiting me to be a Navigator?"

"From what it sounds like, you already are one."

A false life flashed before my eyes, one where I stood at the helm of a massive galleon just like the Leviathan. One where I extended my hands and Ignis exploded from my fingertips. A life where I was truly free, where I made sure *no one* was held down like I'd been ever again.

Sparks from the column snatched me from my dream.

I shook myself slowly. "I'm not a Navigator."

Barco withdrew his hood, revealing slick brown hair, eyebrows etched from granite, and blazing Ignis-infused eyes. A face I knew all too well from village library archives and many a night spent collecting as much information about him as I could.

"You're a swashbuckler, born and bred," Barco said. "You fight the uphill battle to protect the unprotected, braving danger before decision, sacrificing your body for others. And you have an impressive Ignis ability you're still learning. That's the most basic definition of a Navigator there is."

"I'm not a Navigator because I have no interest in the politics of Archengard. Neither side of the War concerns me."

"The whole point of the Brotherhood is that we don't take sides."

"But you try to stop them from fighting. You try to keep the peace. Well, I don't care if they fight. They can tear themselves to bloody bits and bones for all I care. I'm a swash, not some neon knight. I save people and fight monsters because I want to, not because I feel obligated to follow some honor code."

"Even a swashbuckler cannot ignore the world around him."

I closed my mouth.

Truth be told, I thought about the Perpetual War every day. I was *incredibly* concerned about it. Ignis users were being dragged into it continuously, enslaved by the Noda and blackmailed into service by the Archengardian Government.

And the effect that the War had on Archengard was even more concerning. I stuck more to the outlandish kingdoms—far away from the technologically advanced megacities that made up the Government and their neon steel skylines—but every other village I passed was on fire. The War had made its way to the lands that wanted nothing to do with it. Even the Light Isles, out in the middle of the Grand Sea strewn between the two great continents, weren't safe anymore. After all, they were smack dab between the two warring factions.

And worse: I'd heard rumors of who led the Noda. A secret cabal of Ignis users who didn't use their Ignis to create and protect, like the Brotherhood did, but to destroy.

The Jackals.

Barco was right. It was impossible for someone to adventure across Archengard and not see what was happening now. These were the darkest of times. Careers like swashes and adventurers, and even the more roguish occupations, like treasure hunters and mercenaries, were steadily dying out, replaced with soldiers. Serve the Government or be enslaved by the Noda. The choice of every Ignis user.

But there's always another choice, I thought. *And it's sitting right in front of you.*

Finally, Barco just nodded. "Then again, perhaps you're right. You might hold the resume of a Navigator, but you're clearly not one. Very well. I shall honor your refusal."

This is what you've wanted your whole life.

Sand literally slipping through my fingers, I stood abruptly. Bugger the pain. "If I wanted to, I could be a Navigator."

"You could not," Barco said plainly.

"Watch me."

"I'm watching."

"I *can* be a Navigator."

"Have you forgotten your own words so soon?"

"'Immortal, I think. Immortal, I become.'"

Caught in the middle of extinguishing Ignis, Barco stiffened. "What did you say?"

"Those are my own words." My body shook as I spoke. "It means—"

"I understand its meaning." After drawing his hands back within his cloak,

Barco let the crimson fire die slowly, watching the column deteriorate. "You think like him, you know that?" He seemed to be half laughing to himself. Amusement twinkled in his eyes. "But a High Navigator cannot guide a recruit to Carbonek. The journey—if you seek it—must be completed on your own."

I nearly gasped. "I seek it."

"Do you?"

"I swear on—"

"The Code isn't something you may swear upon yet."

"Then what am I missing? Please tell me."

Barco stood slowly, striding over. He withdrew a card from his cloak, its front emblazoned with a simple symbol: a triangle with a circle suspended over its topmost point and an arc hanging above the circle.

The mountain-rainbow-sun.

I accepted the card with shivering hands and traced the symbol, recalling nights alone among twisted skyscrapers and blackened streets. Nights spent nursing my wounds, waiting for the smoke-filled skies to clear during that rare hour after midnight, when all the stars revealed themselves and my dark, destroyed world finally lit up.

The constellation of the Leviathan had strode across the sky, and under it, I'd drawn the symbol Barco had just handed me over and over on small sheets of crumbled paper, whispering stories to myself, quiet enough for no one to hear but loud enough for me to feel every word with my tongue. Loud enough for the stars I traced and the stories I spoke to brand themselves into my very spirit.

When I finally looked up from the card, Barco was already halfway across the beach.

I flipped it over and found a set of scrawled coordinates.

"*Wait!*" I screamed, stuffing the card away. "What am I missing?" I chased after him. "What more do I need to learn?"

Barco's black boots scuffed to a halt in the sand. I paused some ten yards behind him.

"That Navigators aren't born to walk through life, but to help others run."

Barco's shadow glittered in the blue moonlight, burning brighter than the stars watching us converse; I'd watched them in turn in a ruined city, wondering if I'd ever have what it took to sail among them. To sail with the Leviathan.

"And how you go about doing that is entirely up to you," he said. "Individually, or *collectively*."

CHAPTER 3

Jezna

The town of Hecton burned. I only blocked out the screams with the ritual of orders I'd ingrained into my mind.

Observe with purpose.

I scanned the flames that devoured the remnants of what had once been wooden cottages. A small village along the coast of the continent of Khronera. Another one of the many innocent, unadvanced regions of the world that longed for simpler times. Times that were not these.

I spotted steaming blood in the fire, charred bodies among them.

Listen to nature.

I finally let myself hear the screams. They were distant and small, but painful enough to drive a spike of iron through my chest.

How could I have been so late to such a slaughter? How could a knight have failed so terribly at protecting those in need?

One, I pleaded silently. *Just one. If I can aid just one . . .*

My gaze locked on to a moving shape in the distance, returning the last and most important of Macín's ritual orders to me.

Save a soul.

I tapped into Ignis. The aqua-colored energy surrounded my armor, enhancing all senses. As I trampled in the direction of the shape, the flames spread out before me. Water-like energy spread from my gauntleted hands, sending fire sulking back into shadow. It carved me a river for a path.

Walking through the fire, I searched for the wounded, my sight enhanced. With Ignis, I peeled back the layers of the world and saw the flames dancing inside people: the souls they possessed. But none of the bodies I passed bore flames anymore. The fire was all around them, not in them.

I wanted to fall to my knees and scream.

But a knight did neither. They observed, listened, then saved.

I'd journeyed across sea and sand, traversed across the warring continents of Khronera and Narthes, and witnessed firsthand the duel between their opposing governments for too long.

The Noda controlled all of Narthes under an empire that had been up and running since the War's inception, but the Government, who owned every inch of

Khronera and still claimed ownership of the entire world, refused to let them walk away so soon. High Chancellor Veres was notoriously known for his iron will.

The violence that had escalated from their conflict was carnivorous, but it had already been fought for twenty years. Perhaps both sides figured why stop now? Perhaps both sides voyeuristically *relished* this.

In my time as a knight, I'd seen far bloodier violence through the slit of my helmet, but for some reason, the burning village I'd arrived too late to at least attempt to save cemented itself within me the deepest. It wasn't a sign that one side was finally beginning to win, but that the Perpetual War truly would be fought perpetually.

What's the point? I thought, stepping over the tattered fabric of a white G on a blue field—the Archengardian Government's flag. *Everyone has forgotten how the War even began.*

I turned back toward my destination and saw the shape move again.

"Hello?" My own voice alarmed me. It sounded so afraid. The other knights—my Brothers—had always spoken with such fearlessness. Even the most mundane of conversations between them had been tactical duels. They'd been so eloquent. And I was so . . . not. "Are you—?"

A disturbing moan escaped the shape. I began to make out human features, and when I focused Ignis, I saw a tiny flicker of flame burning inside it.

Save a soul.

I rushed the rest of the way, passing the ragged but still-standing Nodan flag of silver stars on a purple field before springing to a stop.

The shape was a boy, and though he was still a yard away from me, I'd almost stepped on the bottom half of his body. His legs had been severed.

And worse: When I looked into his agony-engulfed eyes, I saw flickers of bright yellow flame. An Ignis user.

"Please . . ." He reached for me.

I knelt at his side, shaking. "It's okay. Shh. I will . . ." What could I say? What could I promise him? My water could heal small cuts, not stitch severed limbs back together.

"No," the boy said, sweat pouring down his forehead. He blinked for an eternity, then slowly reached bloodied fingers into the pockets of his military jacket. A soldier. "Listen."

I nodded.

"We were transporting the artifact back to the Government," the soldier said. "The Noda got word of it . . ." He sifted about the pocket before withdrawing a gleaming turquoise prism. It looked like glass, but its interior swirled with trapped cosmic flame. Ignis. "I know my place. I know what people . . . like us . . . are supposed to do . . ."

Tears began to slip from his eyes. "But . . . *they* came. They were here." He shook his head, fingers clamping around the prism. "I could take on twenty Nodan soldiers, no sweat . . . But *them*? How does anyone stand a chance?

"We were set up. Because *they* knew. You have to tell the Brotherhood." He started to sob, voice quaking. "The Jackals were here. And they weren't supposed to be. It wasn't even what they were looking for."

I felt a black hole widen inside me.

"We Ignis-using soldiers pay the price. We're the smokescreen. Our superiors told everyone we were transporting the Sacred Heart." He looked like he wanted to crush the prism, his fingers clenched around it so tightly. "But this isn't the Heart. This is just another artifact, not a Talisman." He looked up at the sky. "It was all a lie."

I didn't know what to say.

"Take it." He suddenly thrust the artifact at me. I stood, stunned. "And destroy it. Or keep it. Or . . ." His eyes grew distant. "Give it to those that will protect it."

The artifact slipped from between his fingers. I caught it as his hand hit the ground.

I kneeled by his side for another minute, staring down at the glittering artifact in my hands. Two words cycled through me endlessly, bringing shade and horror to a night darker than a dungeon cell.

The Jackals.

I would never know. I would never know if the dark cabal rumored to rule the Noda had been here. And silently, some ashamed, childish part of my spirit would thank myself for arriving late to the battle.

So I made my way back through the flames to a lonesome hill overlooking the devastation, wondering how I could prevent something like it from occurring again.

It was a miserable sight. Other flames—purple, white, and blue—still dotted the village. Then, as their users breathed their last breaths, their Ignis slowly festered out with them.

The remnants of the last buildings began to crumble. What had once been a peaceful village was consumed by the natural flame—a reminder that even Ignis fell to the elements of Archengard—but the fires of Ignis continued to dance in my memory.

Is this really what Archengard has come to? How am I supposed to save it? Chivalry is all but dead. How can I keep defending a world like this one?

How can I find balance on a scale where both sides threaten to break?

I watched the artifact hum in my palm. The Dragon Lords were worshipped for granting certain humans the ability to use Ignis, but I held nothing but animosity toward them. If they were so wise, then why hadn't they foreseen that the human race would violate their powers as opposed to finding greater peace with them?

And why hadn't they granted *me* Ignis initially?

I eyed the stars angrily, then tilted my head when I picked up the faint roar of a great engine. I pocketed the artifact within my gray battle-skirt, turning toward the sound and tapping into Ignis. Through my enhanced senses, I realized that the engine emitted from a much smaller machine than a mile-long battle cruiser.

Already in the process of landing, the lowly crab cruiser unfolded the four mechanical limbs that gave it its name, approaching a section of grass a hundred feet away from me. Drawn onto its sides were spray-painted dragons and a familiar symbol: the mountain-rainbow-sun.

Navigators.

Releasing Ignis, I turned back to the village, disgusted.

The cruiser's legs dug into the ground, and when the side doors slid open, two men and one woman stepped out, all wearing well-tailored suits.

Suits, particularly a vest and tie, were considered the "uniform" of the Brotherhood. The color of the shirt or tie one chose to wear was supposed to match with the color that their Ignis manifested, akin to how a knight wore the surcoat and color of their Order.

Like everything the Brotherhood did, they'd taken what had been the Chivalric Order's and made it their own. Made it worse.

Yet Macín had seen something in them. Something greater than flesh and blood and suits and Ignis. Something . . . balanced.

Eyeing the head Navigator, a dark-skinned woman in a black suit jacket and purple dress shirt, I weighed my options. They were only here for the artifact. I just hoped that the flames did their job and reminded them of their failure.

On the far side of the village, I saw two more crab cruisers emerge out of the night, racing for a group of stumbling figures that had seemed to walk straight out of the flames. One of them, carrying a limp figure across their back, glowed brown with Ignis. When the cruisers touched down, he fell to his knees halfway there and wrapped the limp arms around his body. Those at his side moved to help him ease the body—what was clearly a dead Navigator—into the cruiser.

I looked at the female Navigator. Darkness was written on the taut skin around her eyes. She wasn't going to forget this anytime soon.

"You and the Brotherhood have crossed paths on several occasions now," she said, surprising me. "A suit of silver god armor. A watcher of the War. A knight."

"There are no knights left." I stared back at the village coldly. "That much is clear."

"Oh?"

"Don't you think a massacre like this would've been prevented if I had brethren left to call upon? I'm the last of what's left."

"There are others in the Hills of Nymia. The Cartorian Order, I've heard."

"I've been to the Hills. They are dead. I'm the *last* of what's left."

"To many, the Brotherhood are viewed as the only ones keeping chivalry alive."

Macín used to say that. He was wrong. "Chivalry isn't just about honor and protection, but following through on them."

"I see. Then, if you will, permit me a last request and we'll be on our way."

But he also used to say that knights and Navigators are both after the same thing: peace.

I reluctantly reached down into the pouch of my battle-skirt. "I suppose this is it?"

She accepted the artifact with a polite nod. "That's the fourth time we owe you."

"Fifth."

"You are quite good at this, you know."

"I was the youngest of the Tolkkyan Order of knights. I go where the War goes and attempt to stop it." I paused. "At least I attempt."

The woman ignored the slight. She seemed used to my discontent, as if it were merely another day for a Navigator. "Where did you recover the artifact?"

The memory stung, but the water calmed me. I thought about the river I used to visit as a little girl, where Macín always practiced his swordplay with Junia. Where Bebel would sit sharpening his broadsword with a stone, grumbling about how "Ignis never needed sharpening, but iron needed it every other hour." In my mind, I returned to the moss-covered rocks and sat on the flat stones next to them, listening to the water's gentle lapping as opposed to the crackling inferno before me.

"An Ignis-using Governmental soldier gave it to me," I said. "He has passed on. And in his last uttered breath, he requested I hand this to the Brotherhood." I made sure to state the next sentence slowly. "And inform them that the Jackals were here."

The two male Navigators standing next to the woman stirred.

The woman just stared back at me, then turned her irises violet. I tensed, uncomfortable with being studied by an Ignis user. I tried to hide my secret by acting more human—standing a little straighter, breathing more normally. I tried to return to my mind river, but by then, the woman's eyes had already returned to normal.

"Some among the Brotherhood would rather believe them to be legends," she said.

I looked around in disbelief. "I was told they weren't even here for the artifact. A Governmental official planted the idea that their soldiers were carrying a Talisman with them: the Sacred Heart."

"Then the Government are even greater fools than we thought." When sparks of fire settled down upon her shoulders, the woman swept them away. "The Sacred Heart has been hidden for a thousand years. Not even the Leviathan could find it. And I knew him."

I was surprised by such a revelation. The Leviathan had been hailed as the greatest Navigator of all time. To think this Navigator had known him . . .

She glanced back at me, pain lacing her face. "Just as I knew the Navigators that fought beside him. I trained many of them, you see."

I studied the woman, finally *seeing* her for the first time.

"I am High Navigator Daria Deckara," she said, inclining her head. "The Brotherhood is grateful for your assistance, and we respect those who keep closely to a code similar to our own. We could use someone of your talents. Navigating Archengard with nothing but a suit of armor and the stars is difficult. As is keeping chivalry alive."

The world seemed to spin faster, returning me to simpler times.

It had been a year since I gave up my search for Carbonek, since I came to the conclusion that the Brotherhood's fabled base was too well hidden. And that maybe I didn't deserve to find it.

It had been two years since I realized that the only way to honor Macín and Bebel and Junia's memory was to seek out the organization Macín had said was the reason he founded the Tolkkyan Order to begin with.

It had been three years since I gained Ignis.

And four years since I failed to save even a single soul, and watched the Tolkkyan Order perish because of it.

Finding Carbonek was impossible, but *joining* the Brotherhood?

"That's out of the question," I said. There was so much Daria didn't know. So much I couldn't share with anyone. Just living in Carbonek would make my stomach turn. If I had one. "I'm a knight. You expect me to align with pirates and thieves?"

"Is there anything wrong with souls that seek to be free?"

"Freedom must be earned."

"Freedom is a right. Freedom is an honor. I would've thought a Tolkkyan knight would understand."

She's right.

But the idea that freedom was a right, that everyone deserved to be protected, killed my brothers.

"How can those without honor or organization protect Archengard?"

"Ignis should be used for good, should it not? Those who manifest Ignis bear hearts forged in the Lords' flames."

I eyed the burning village. "Yes. That is evident."

"You expect us to interfere with the War?"

"I expect you to do something."

"If we fought the way we once did, we would be no better than those we protect others from. The Brotherhood isn't a force, but an ideology. You don't even have to be an Ignis user to join."

I stood in silence, her words rolling over me. I'd never heard a Navigator say that you didn't need Ignis to be one. That seemed almost blasphemous. Could I really have been one before I broke the laws of nature? Before the Lords cursed me?

"Find the balance," Macín had always said, whether he was teaching me how to hold a sword, how to catch a fish, or merely to wish water from a well. "If a knight is out of balance with the world around them, something must change: the world or the knight."

"The War benefits no one," I said. "Both sides commit atrocities such as this. I've been to both continents. There's fire and darkness here on Khronera as much as there is across the sea on Narthes."

"Then perhaps become part of the water that will one day put out the flame?" Daria said.

"You don't understand. I am . . ." I struggled to say the words. I never had until now. "I am cursed. The Lords didn't bless me."

Surprisingly, Daria didn't go back on her word and denounce me.

Even more surprisingly, she smiled.

"We are all cursed among the Brotherhood, child. Cursed to protect a world that doesn't want our protection. Cursed to uphold a code that no one but us abides by. You see, we are not so different from one another after all."

A million different paths my life could've chosen to take, and yet, I'd ended up here.

The Dragon Lords continue to curse me.

Joining the Brotherhood would be penance. Painful. I was a knight, not a Navigator.

But if what Daria said was true, if the Brotherhood's own code was so close to the Chivalric Code that even Ignis-less people could join . . .

And I couldn't just forget the day Macín had taken the Tolkkyan banner off the tree so I could see the golden fleur-de-lis that I'd come to take pride in, then flipped it to reveal that it was nothing but an upside-down mountain-rainbow-sun.

"The other Chivalric Orders burned themselves to the ground," he'd said then. "They did not truly understand that to protect Archengard, one must become part of a whole. The Brotherhood understands this—and the Tolkkyan Order is the last true Order to stand. Because we understand the Brotherhood."

I bowed my head.

Must the world change if this is what it's become? I thought, watching the farthest cruisers, those that had just picked up the wounded, weeping Navigators, lift back up toward the stars. *Or must I?*

CHAPTER 4

Prince

I shoved the magenta sunglasses up the bridge of my nose, trying to look as threatening as possible. The leather jacket helped—and the backpack full of Aestus pistols, stun guns, and everything in between did wonders—but all anyone ever seemed to see when they looked at me was my height and sunglasses.

"Those pink?" one of the treasure hunters I'd met mere moments ago called across the circle. A few of the tall ones scattered between us cackled. They weren't even that tall by Archengardian standards. I was just shorter than snail shit.

"Magenta, actually," I said, but the hunter was too distant to hear. I could try yelling, but that would set the Big Kahuna off immediately. Being the youngest of the group—and likely the youngest dude to ever be independently contracted by the Corbin Criminal Underworld—I was already on thin ice. How I'd managed to convince the three-hundred-pound crime lord to haul me along for the ride was still a blur.

Fifteen treasure hunters in total stood in a gigantic circle surrounding the rickety shack. Each man agitatedly scuffed their shoes on the dusty rock and kept their hands at their sides, preparing to harness Ignis when the situation called for it. Kahuna had scavenged all of Archengard for the Talisman, prepared the raid himself, and gathered the best Ignis-using treasure hunters together.

But I had no Ignis to call upon, and instead prepared to whip one of the guns off my back.

That turned out to be an excruciatingly long preparation period.

Practically praying for pixies to fly out of the ground, I had just dozed off when a tumbleweed hit me square in the face.

I danced around. To my left and positioned behind our circle, I saw Kahuna shaking his gigantic head from the driver's seat of his turner. It ran on Aestus—as all vehicles and weapons did—but was an older, antique model. I'd helped the freaking tub of lard swindle it from a seller two years ago.

Well, this is just a time and a half. After finally prying the ball of dust and twigs off of my face, I threw it to the wind, then held a sideways thumbs-up in Kahuna's direction. "I'm good."

The huge man grumbled and held up a fat fist. We began to take slow steps toward the shack, the turner's big black wheels rolling forward.

The closer we grew to the building, the faster I felt the adrenaline rush approaching. In the heat of action, anything could happen. Sometimes, I'd be able to pull off random feats of otherworldly awesomeness. Other times, I'd fall flat on my face. My legendary bad luck. Kahuna saw it only as an inconvenience, but I found it more akin to slapstick. It was funny when I failed. Sometimes you won, sometimes you took a big fat L and went home.

But Kahuna didn't like losing. If the Talisman slipped between his fingers . . . well, it never had. He had big freaking fingers.

"Bret!" Kahuna bellowed from the turner, hoisting himself up into the roofless air. The whole vehicle quaked when he did. "Get your ass out here before we blow your house up!"

I frowned. *That's a little much.*

Unsurprisingly, Bret didn't answer. The door to the shack remained shut and nothing new passed in front of the windows outside of dirty curtains.

Squirming internally, I peeked over at Kahuna. He held up a fist once more.

At first, no one moved. Things could go sideways real quick in our line of business, and no one wanted to be the first one through the door. Treasure hunters were cowards through and through.

But not me. I'm the son of a Navigator.

I took a step forward. *That wasn't so bad.* So I started to walk.

Every treasure hunter head snapped toward me, then swiftly followed. Being outclassed by an Ignis-less nineteen-year-old probably seemed like a fate worse than death, but long before the fifteen of us reached the porch, the roar of an engine belched out from the house and a dusty turner smashed through the entire front side.

I barely dodged the flying door with a panicked screech and watched the other hunters lunge in opposite directions to avoid being hit.

Chaos ensued. Bret was making a getaway with the Talisman, and from the look of his house, he had no plans of returning.

"CATCH 'EM!" Kahuna said, nearly crashing his turner into three hunters before taking a sharp U-turn in my direction. "START SHOOTIN', PRINCE!"

Still reeling from my near-death-by-door experience, I spun and removed the first weapon my hand found—a purse pistol.

"You've got machine guns, yet you're using that?!" Kahuna said, slamming on the brakes before he hit me.

I looked down at the weapon, then out across the desert at Bret's escaping turner.

Take the impossible shot, Prince, Father's voice called, and I listened, the world around me whirling away.

Father had called it the abyss. A place of complete and total darkness. A place of peace. Where a man went to focus entirely on his task, to reach deep down into the black and pull something out. The place where man went to conquer his fears.

Closing one eye before thrusting the gun out in front of me, I delved deep into the abyss, focusing entirely on suffocating my bad luck and removing the chaotic desert around me. The hot wind disappeared; Kahuna's screams faded. I squeezed the trigger, the spark caught, and one of the turner's wheels was punctured by an arrow of Aestus. A sniper-level shot.

The tire fluttered off, making Bret spin out of control. The turner kept going, but now that it was missing a tire, he was doomed.

Kahuna stared open-mouthed as I climbed into the front seat and pushed on his knee, forcing his meaty foot to slam down on the accelerator and send us rocketing off.

The chase—if one could even call it that—was hysterically anticlimactic. Bret screamed at his turner to go faster as Kahuna and I sped forward at thrice the speed.

"Do figure-eights to make him feel like he's winning," I said.

"Shouldn't you be shooting?!" Kahuna said.

I pulled a bazooka out of my bag. The Aestus rocket struck the ground a good thirty feet away from Bret's turner, but it caused enough of an explosion to make the rear fly up into the air.

Kahuna tried to wallop me, but I dropped a pistol by accident and ducked to pick it up. Sometimes bad luck saved my ass.

"You missed on purpose!"

"I'm not gonna *kill* him!" I checked to see how much Aestus I had left before the weapon needed to recharge. I was good for another two minutes or so of firefighting.

"Now's not the time for that Navigator bullshit!"

I paused. "Who said this had anything to do with Navigators?"

We were gaining on Bret, practically bumping into his rear.

"Everything you do has to do with Navigators," Kahuna shouted. "And if you're so concerned about his life, then why were you shooting him?"

I handed Kahuna the empty bazooka, standing in my seat. "Please hold."

"Wha—"

And summoning my best Leviathan impression, I bellowed, "*Fortuna Favet Fortibus*" as I threw myself from our turner and landed in the back of Bret's.

His driving turned chaotic in an attempt to shake me off. Kahuna barked orders behind me, but it was pretty difficult to hear when I was being whipped around.

Guns are weighing you down, my mind calculated in Father's voice again as I fought to climb into the backseat. *Free some—*

"Prince?!" Bret glanced over his shoulder.

A cluster of fleet-footed memories returned to me. I felt a hole in my chest begin to take shape. Bret and I hadn't been super tight, but we'd gone on multiple missions with one another. We'd shared drinks, told stories . . .

We've both lost our fathers.

I didn't like many treasure hunters, but those that I did, I'd always considered friends.

Standing with one foot on the turner's trunk and the other in the back seats, I removed my sunglasses so he could see my eyes.

"The hell are you doing, Bret?" I asked, gripping the seats when the turner gave a sudden jerk to the right. The burst wheel was doing its job.

"I need the Talisman," Bret said. "The Noda will pay me a fortune. My family will never go hungry again."

"You're gonna sell it to the Jackals?" I asked, trying to hide the fear from my voice. "It's a *Talisman*, dude! You wanna help them win the War?!"

"This isn't about the War! I don't care if Archengard tears itself apart!"

"How can your family live happily if there's nowhere to freaking live?"

"The Brotherhood won't give me anything for it!"

"That's the whole point!" I said, just as Kahuna rammed his turner into ours.

The impact sent me flying into the front seat, where we began to scuffle. Bret's Ignis ability barely worked and was only good for cooking, making it a fair fight between us, but I had no interest in blowing his brains out.

"I. Don't. Want. To. Do. This. BRET!"

I messily ducked around Bret's jabs, smacking him with the butt of my pistol but trying not to open him up too bad. I was a shit boxer. Never tried, never wanted to. And the turner just went in circles; Bret's hands constantly slipped away, so he let it take itself where it wanted to. Kahuna tried to take out the other wheels with brutal sideswipes, but my bad luck made him miss every time.

"You. Might. Have. To!" Bret pulled out some moves of his own from his sitting position and ended up almost launching me through the windshield. He paused before doing so, hand wrapped around my throat.

I looked into his eyes with cold anger. "Do it, scumbag. Show me that you're just as much of a self-centered thief as the rest of them."

To Bret's credit, he kept his grip locked tight, but then his gaze shifted beyond me and his eyes widened.

"Get back!" he shouted, throwing me into the back seat before gripping the steering wheel with both hands. Weapons flying all around me, I caught my stun gun and tunnel gun but watched as all the rest scattered.

Oh.

We plummeted down a ditch, a *really* big ditch, which turned out to be the gorge we had all passed on our way to ambush Bret, but solid ground arrived first, shedding light on a small landing right before the massive drop.

We teetered on the edge, glowing silver liquid leaking out of the damaged turner. I started freaking out. The longer that Aestus leaked out, the greater the chance of a spark catching. The whole thing would go up in flames and take us with it.

A flash of red light down in the driver's-side compartment sent me scrambling back from the possible start of an explosion, but Bret dove headfirst.

The Talisman!

I yanked him back by the collar. "That belongs with the Brotherhood!"

Bret's punch flattened me. I'd *never* expected such a focused feat of anger from him.

Reeling back as Bret rummaged through the compartment, I blinked away stars, but before I could elbow him in retaliation, Bret shoved the Talisman in my face.

Without my sunglasses, I was nearly blinded.

The Kardem Ka was the brightest, most stunning artifact I'd ever laid nearly fried eyes upon. The fact that a hand-sized ruby emitted such light and contained such astronomical amounts of Ignis was ridiculous to contemplate. It was frightening . . . and alluring. Especially for an Ignis-less dude like me. Part of me craved that power, just like Bret. Part of me was that two-bit thief I knew myself to be deep down.

But when the crimson light slammed into me, I retreated. Unfortunately, there was nowhere else to go. Either I returned to Kahuna empty-handed, stole the Ka, or stayed in the turner and died. I chose the middle option and held a pistol up to Bret's forehead. He froze, right fist grasping the Ka.

"The turner's on the brink of collapse," I said, blinking rapidly. "Don't make me do this." I'd always had a steady hand—blacksmithing did that to a dude—but this time, there was a visible shake to my grip.

Bret saw straight through me. "Use it, Larocque. You don't have Ignis. You need the Ka more than anyone."

"I don't."

"Then you're a fool."

"You're fighting for the wrong cause."

"Better to die for a cause you believe in than submit to one that means nothing."

"The Brotherhood *isn't* nothing!"

Sparks erupted out of the corner of my vision, but I remained locked on Bret's collar. His brow furrowed, then the engine exploded.

I only had enough time to kick up off the trunk and grasp the ledge with my left hand, holding Bret in the other. Years of metalworking around a forge paid off, but I was slipping fast, and the Ka had flown out of Bret's hand during the explosion. The Talisman now lay within the blazing inferno that had been the turner.

"I'm slipping!" I said.

Bret continued to twiddle his fingers through the air in an attempt to somehow make the Ka fly toward him. The only thing his Ignis would allow him to do was cook it.

"Bret!"

He finally looked up, eyes wide. "You got a grappling gun?"

"Not unless you wanna go look around in the gorge, and if you keep pulling weight, that might happen!"

"I can almost . . . reach it . . . !"

"It's like thirty feet down!"

"I CAN REACH IT!"

This was the Craving, the moment of overbearing avarice that Father had said took over whenever someone became too fixated on an Ignis-infused artifact and forsook the world around them.

And this wasn't just another artifact that some ancient Ignis user had placed a bit of its power in—it was a Tintagen Talisman. One of the five beacons Father had died searching for.

I felt a finger come loose from the ledge. I winced and tried to harness whatever strength might've still lay sleeping in the abyss—the strength Father had taught me to seize whenever I was afraid—but nothing came to the forefront. An Ignis-less boy could only do so much.

Talk to him, Father's voice whispered. *Just be cool.*

"Look, I like treasure just as much as you do," I said. "But it's not worth your life! Your family—"

"My family will be stuck living in the slums unless I give the Ka to the Noda!"

"I can help you! I've got money! You know you always could've asked, right?"

Bret's face contorted in the light of the wreckage and the Kardem Ka sitting within it. "I . . . You think Kahuna will give me another chance? He'll kill me!"

"I won't let him. The prize isn't worth obtaining if the cost is your own humanity. The hunted shouldn't be more important than the hunter. Look at me, dude." Bret did. "I don't even have Ignis. I . . . don't have a father anymore. But this isn't—"

A shuriken of dark orange energy carved a path directly through his forehead.

Bret's hand slipped through my fingers. When his body hit the flaming wreckage, the damaged turner bent then sailed off into the gorge, Kardem Ka included. I watched it all.

The moment replayed itself for an eternity in my mind, and when I looked up at the Big Kahuna standing on the edge, the man's silhouette burned with orange Ignis.

He offered me a beefy hand. "That went better than—"

I didn't think, just spat in his face and scaled the rest of the ledge, blinking back tears of frustration.

That was two men now that I'd watched die right in front of me for the sake of the game. Twice I'd been unable to save someone, unable to get through to them and remind them that the game shouldn't matter. Not more than your own life.

And it seemed that everyone I'd ever cared about was always dying for it. Because at the end of the day, they chose not to feel fear.

But fear's good. Sometimes you should just run away. Sometimes, that saves your life.

"Where's the Ka?" Kahuna said, wiping his face. "I'll ignore that gesture if . . ."

I turned my back to him, beginning the long walk out of the desert.

"Where do you think you're going?"

Focusing on the abyss and its soothing emptiness was the only thing that kept me from screaming as I looked back. "I quit."

Kahuna blinked twice, then began to heave with laughter.

"I'm serious. Sift through the remains for the Talisman on your own."

"So that's it, then?" he asked. "You're retiring? I thought you knew what this life entailed. I thought your father—"

"I know what this life entails. Father knew, too. But what you constantly get wrong is that it somehow entails killing. You think betrayal and murder are part of treasure hunting. They're not. So I'm done watching men die for you. I hope I never see your fat ass ever again."

"Then what will you do now? What awaits a thief with nowhere else to go, no land to call home? No family?"

I found myself looking to the east, an instinctive tic I had noticed Father had. It felt right in a way. Nostalgic. My internal compass pointed in that direction. Not toward the gloomy continent of Narthes, but the upper coast of Khronera. Toward the emerald sky isles that were said to float there, and the black-and-gold manor that Father had sworn lay hidden in their midst. A realm separate from the world, full of endless and eternal possibility. A blazing beacon in a sea of war and shadow.

A land of fearlessness and friendship and honor, Father's voice resonated through me.

My hands suddenly began to fiddle with the right sleeve of my leather jacket. And when I peeled back the hem, the set of scrawled coordinates stared back at me under a drawn symbol: a mountain with a sun above its peak and a rainbow encircling the sun.

In the past, where my fingers had shook as they traced the secret message Father had left me, now they moved with meticulous accuracy. They understood.

"I've always had somewhere I can go." I dropped my hand, still feeling Bret's clenched in mine. "I've just been too scared to."

Realization dawned in Kahuna's eyes. "But you're an Ordinary!" he shouted, beginning to shake with cruel laughter once more. "Ignis-less! What do you think you'll do at Carbonek, if such a place even exists? You'll have the whole world against you!"

Reaching into the inside pocket of my leather jacket, I removed the magenta sunglasses—Father's sunglasses.

What Kahuna didn't understand was I was no stranger to the world's Aestus and bullets flying at me.

I didn't need reminders of how alone I was, how alone I'd be even in a place like the Brotherhood's fabled home. I had the abyss, and when I walked within it, even bad luck trembled with fear.

"Whaddaya know." I slid the sunglasses back onto my face. "That's how it feels already."

When I was far enough out of the desert that patches of crabgrass began to spring up under my shoes, a tumbleweed missed me by five feet. I tilted my head and watched it go before turning my back on the setting suns.

Ten minutes later, I felt an overwhelming flutter of happiness, like that same tumbleweed had just rolled over Kahuna's turner windshield and smacked him in the face.

A boy could dream.

CHAPTER 5

Murta

I hacked water from my lungs, then sprang immediately upward. The world spun from being swept down the river for so long, but an unsteady Shadarian was more balanced than the most agile of warriors. And I still had a strong enough hold on Ignis to turn my hands into claws.

Whoever had pulled me to shore would be distracted if not intimidated by my immediacy. It gave my brain time to get back up and moving. Everything was still so blurry. Every part of me ached, especially the wound in my neck. I wouldn't be able to make it far, and if whoever pulled me to shore was a fellow Shadarian . . .

My vision returned slowly, revealing pieces of the silhouette standing before me. A light gray three-piece suit appeared first, followed by tufts of blond hair sticking out from under an ugly flat cap. Definitely not a Shadarian.

Wait a minute.

When I locked eyes with the boy's agitated umber-brown irises, the air between us might as well have been set on fire.

"Out of all the bastards we could've saved," Lariat Tollo started.

I forsook Ignis for the first time in my life; my bare knuckles meeting his cheekbone was far more satisfying.

Larry went down like the sack of shit he was, but got a foot underneath and brought me down with him. If I hadn't just had multiple near-death experiences stacked on top of one another, I could've easily stepped out of the way, but instead, Larry *actually* tripped me.

We scuffled in the grass next to the river, using every limb to make each other feel as much discomfort as possible. Not nearly wounded enough to forget a decade of training, I got the mount almost immediately and prepared to wail on him, but familiar hands hoisted me up by the armpits and threw me off.

Few men had the ability to do that to me, though one stood above all others.

"Knock it off, both of you," the thrower said. But Biassis Ondenecro only stated and expected others to follow. And everyone did.

Except me.

I ripped my gaze from Larry's icy scowl to Biassis's warm blue eyes. The olive-skinned Navigator wore only an unbuttoned dress shirt with red-and-white thorn-covered vine patterning, sacred symbols of the Ondenecro tribe. It seemed like the older he grew, the less clothes he wore, always wanting to reveal more of his meticulously built abdominal region. He vexed me greatly.

"I thought," I began icily, "that I was crystal clear when I said, 'Leave me the hell alone.'"

Larry stood, wiping off grass. "You spout so much nonsense all the time that it's hard to figure out what's actually meant to be taken seriously."

"Coming from someone who's only at Carbonek because of who he knows? *Eres gracioso.*"

"And you're just one to talk about being at Carbonek, aren't you?"

"Larry," Biassis said, "if you can't have a friendly conversation, leave."

"Don't bother." I squeezed water from my scarf, then quickly wound it back around my neck before their eyes could flick down to my necklace. "I was just going."

"Hold on, bro—"

"I'm not your 'bro.' If I was, you would've honored my resignation."

"Banishment," Larry corrected.

Biassis crossed his arms. "We have for three years. And never mind that we just saved your life. You're welcome, I guess."

"I was fine."

"Your neck says otherwise. Barco sent us out here looking for the same thing as you." He paused. "We know about—"

"Spare me another speech." I put my face inches from his. "And if you think I'll come *back* just so you can download the map from my brain, I'll tell you what everyone told me." I held up bloodstained middle fingers.

The satisfaction at getting to do that to Biassis Ondenecro, the supposed golden boy of my generation, almost slid a smirk out of me as I moved to retreat to the rendezvous point.

But the reaction I'd expected never came. Biassis showed no anger, no frustration.

I glanced over my shoulder, studying my ex-colleague's expression. He didn't look angry at all. Just . . . hurt.

"Fine," he said. "You want the truth?"

Larry hissed.

My neck flared in pain, as if beckoning me to walk away, but something greater than pain kept me rooted.

"The map is part of it," Biassis said. "I won't deny that. You know it belongs with the Brotherhood. If the Noda were to get their hands on the Ka . . ."

"I know what would happen," I said. "I don't know if that's much worse than it rotting forever in Carbonek."

"Then what did you plan on doing with it, oh wise and powerful Dark One?" Larry asked. "Wield it for yourself?"

"As long as it's kept out of the Jackals' hands."

Larry threw his arms in the air. "Here he goes again. 'Ass, let's leave him to his conspiracies."

"No," Biassis said. "We're not leaving again. I don't turn my back on other Navigators. Even exiled ones." His jaw set stubbornly. "Murta, what does the Kardem Ka have to do with the Jackals?"

"Absolutely nothing," Larry said. "The Jackals are just an old rumor. The boogeymen of the Brotherhood. No one fears them except rookies."

Biassis lifted an eyebrow. "You feared them."

"That's a pile of rubbish—"

"You know about the Tintagen Talismans?" I spoke directly to Biassis.

"Hektor let the secret slip one day," Larry said. "They're the strongest artifacts on Archengard. So what? We specialize in retaining Ignis-infused artifacts."

"Then you know why it's important that I find the Ka." I lifted my chin. "And especially the Sacred Heart."

"And the Karnocolix is held by the Brotherhood," Biassis added. "As should the rest of the Talismans."

I wanted to kick him. Did he think this a game? Another foolish quest? The Talismans contained enough Ignis to wipe out entire countries. To blow up the suns, even. A world-ending power brewed in their bodies, a trapped Ignis that had been stored for centuries.

"The Karnocolix gathers dust," I said. "If the Brotherhood ever seizes the rest of the Talismans, they'll never use them." I made sure my next words reverberated around the clearing. "And then the Jackals will seize them and *burn* Archengard to its core."

Larry continued to mutter under his breath, but Biassis stared in silence. I let my warning waft through the air. The wound in my neck screamed, but not nearly as much as my head. My mind was a thunderstorm, flashing between images of Lee bleeding out on the temple floor and the jackal head cemented somewhere in memory. And with the jackal head came the voices. Voices trapped inside me that never stopped whispering.

Finally, Biassis said, "So that's what you've done with your time away? You're hunting the Jackals?"

I didn't reply.

And later I'd regret the hell out of it.

Biassis got that familiar twinkle in his cat's eyes that meant he knew something I didn't. Or that he was about to win an argument.

"You've spent all your time away from the Brotherhood hunting the supposed sworn enemies of the Brotherhood?"

I glowered. "That's not what I'm here for."

"And this isn't what we're here for."

"What is it you're trying to say?"

"This is such a terrible idea," Larry said.

My heart began to race. "No," I forced out before any other emotions got the better of me. Before Lee's silent, pained eyes looking up at me flashed through me again. "Not in the . . ." I trailed off. *"Why?"*

"Because Barco asked us to help with recruiting," Biassis said. "With the War picking up, we're particularly short on good Ignis users. And Barco asked for names. A few were tossed around, nothing really stuck . . . so I brought up your name. Mads flipped. So did Larry."

"Course I bloody did."

"But Barco agreed."

I shook my head. "I'm not coming back."

"This is a second chance," Biassis pleaded. "The War escalates with every passing hour. Ignis users die every day. The Archengardian Government thinks that the only way to win is to 'recruit' more. Have you seen the kinds of things they make Ignis users do out there? How they treat them?"

Only too well.

"We gotta stick together. The Brotherhood's the only option for people like us."

"Chasing rainbows isn't an option," I said. "I've seen the effects of the War firsthand. Connection won't sew Archengard's wounds shut. It needs a steady hand and a steadier tool. It needs fire to cauterize it. The Brotherhood won't stop the bleeding—I will."

"'Ignis doesn't make the Navigator,'" Biassis recited. "'The Navigator makes Ignis.' And if I recall correctly, there was a time where you enjoyed chasing rainbows just as much as the next Nav. Or have you forgotten those memories, too?"

I was suddenly fresh out of comebacks.

"Who knows, maybe you'll actually find a squad this time around." Biassis shrugged. "It's a hell of a lot easier to save the world in numbers than it is on your own."

CHAPTER 6

Enoch

I squinted against the twin suns blasting my eyeballs before striding out onto the airship deck. The wind rushed through the clouds, nearly stealing my bandana. Tightening it, I promptly told the wind precisely what it should do with an airship deck and precisely where it should stick it, then set off to find the captain.

My wounds from the sea serpent had closed, yet the pain persisted. I was limping lightly and still bore cuts from where the scales had clipped me. My ribs throbbed and the wound on my back—a grim reminder of my past life—never stopped tingling. There was always pain for me, a never-ending cycle of half-heals and scars.

I could take the pain. It went away after a while. But the crew's irritation was as persistent as a peacock.

Every crewman I passed on my way threw me the same scowl, as if my very existence were a burden. Any time they spotted my soot-stained green-and-black boxing jacket, their content expressions flattened.

"Damned swashes," they muttered, like I was some bloody boogeyman. Then again, they were a strictly legal air-shipment crew. They'd probably been ambushed and held at Ignis-point by blokes sporting personalities, powers, and bandanas similar to mine. They might've even heard rumors about twenty-year-old Light Eyes Amon, taken one look at my orange irises, and assumed the worst.

Yea, I'm Light Eyes! I wanted to squawk out from the metal crow's nest. *But I'm off to be a Navigator now! You won't get to shit on me like seagulls then!*

"Oi." I strolled up to one of the younger-looking crewmen. "Where's your captain at? Wanted to see me at nine, right?"

The man looked terrified that he'd even been addressed. "The captain?"

"Nay, the Leviathan."

"The L-Leviathan?!"

"No! I was being . . . Lords, do they mentally starve you lot up here?"

"It ain't nine, *pirate*." An older crewman with wispy gray hair hobbled over. "It be twelve in the afternoon."

My stomach lurched. "Is it now?" *Lazy arse.* "Must've slipped by me. That ale down there is good stuff."

I sped up, rounding the great mast and glancing over the starboard side at the clouds. For all the enclosed quarters, foul weather, and lack of luxury that came with life aboard an airship, the scenery was drop-dead brilliant.

The clouds swam by in mountains of white mist, and the airship weaved in and out of their maze. Archengard's surface stretched out around us in every direction, and from the height we were at, nothing blocked the twin suns. Tanten's gold and Rolarns's green light threw itself off everything, giving the clouds a sparkling tint. I glanced down at my chest: Maybe with time and exposure, I'd start to sparkle, too.

At the helm, I found the captain, a tall man with dark skin and an eastern accent that identified him as a Northern Narthesian, hailing from Nodan-occupied territory. He was far from home, but his brightly colored robes made up of crisscrossing patterns and silky fabrics were undoubtedly from there. He was brave to wear such in Eastern Khronera, stowed quite firmly in the flames of the Archengardian Government. Not that I gave a shite, being a Light Isles lad and all.

"Oh," he said. "It's you."

"Try not to wet yourself with excitement. Seen anything?"

"We've been sailing over mountains and plains since leaving White Town. Pretty soon, we'll hit the coast and be out over the Grand Sea." He pocketed the golden telescope he'd been twiddling between his fingers. "These coordinates you've given me can't possibly be real. I mean, they're real coordinates, but they lead to nowhere."

"How many miles need we sprint still?"

"Two."

I nodded. "Then take us lower."

"Lower will see us run into those mountains I spoke of."

"Your helmsman's done a fine enough job of ducking and weaving through clouds."

"You're the one trying to be a *Navigator*, right?" The captain said the word with several different emotions. Anger, annoyance, disgust, superstition. Maybe even a bit of fear. "Shouldn't you be the one *navigating* us through this wasteland?"

"There's a difference between navigators and Navigators with a capital 'N,' bruv."

The captain shook his head. "You're seriously going to make me do this for an old legend?"

I reached into my jacket and pulled out a stack of brown dollars, my earnings from the last five boxing matches. "*I'm* not making you do anything."

He pursed his lips, then spat off the side of the ship. "Below the clouds! Same course!"

"Lords save the economy," I said.

A few crewmen grunted their disapproval, especially after having just tied the lines down, but the sails were unraveled further, forcing the airship to gain speed. Beneath the floorboards, I felt the rumblings of its core.

The ship began to drop, the burning core causing the hull to gain weight, and plummeted through the clouds at an increasingly faster rate.

"Lighten the load!" the captain said.

The rumbling ended, like the core had been switched off, and the light bounciness that accompanied airship sailing returned. I did a few hops in place as the crewmen adjusted the lines accordingly.

We sailed below the clouds, the captain's hands gripped behind his back. I swayed in place, watching the white peel back. When we emerged into a passage of green-topped mountains and scattered pieces of floating rock, my swaying stopped. The captain's hands unclenched.

Pieces of flora-covered terrain levitated directly off the sides of mountains, some of them spinning slowly while others lay dormant, clinging to their places of origin.

I gaped. The silence that resonated behind me implied that the crew had taken to staring as well.

The captain gripped the metal railing. "A sky garden. Unbelievable."

I fidgeted with anticipation. Floating isles were direct causations of Ignis. The more Ignis that rested in one place, the more the land began to float and act "unnatural." And the coordinates Barco had given me were teeming with it.

The clouds dispersed the deeper down the passage we flew, until the sky was decorated a heavenly sunshine blue. The floating isles became even more numerous, boulders growing into grassy plateaus with brooks trickling off the sides, floating higher off the sides of the mountains. The helmsman had to maneuver the airship around a few as they began to scrape the port side.

"This shouldn't be here." The captain fumbled with the charts he kept folded in his coat pocket. "On no map does it say a sky garden should be here . . ."

"Another fairy tale?"

He tore his face from the charts to glare at me. He wasn't completely swayed yet, but when the mountains disappeared and the ship slipped into a vast field—a place that had to dwarf every valley that had been etched into Archengard's surface—he dropped the charts.

Situated at the tail end of the green field was the largest structure I'd ever seen.

The grand manor was part chateau, part castle. A perfect collision of two opposing types of architecture. The walls extended out of the central building for at least a mile, and there were towers, courtyards, and gardens galore. Everything was erected from black marble but gleamed with gold trimming. Window sills and balconies glistened brilliant gold, as did the grand gates that wound about the front.

Fear, discomfort, and all emotions in between ran rampant through the crew. Some froze. The majority stumbled belowdecks with curses.

None of them had expected me to be *right.*

"It's real," the captain said.

The airship loomed near the valley floor. Heart battering my chest, I tore my eyes away from the manor to the emerald fields dancing softly in the wind around it. My path to Carbonek.

As if reading my thoughts, the captain glanced around at the nearly vacant deck. "You can walk the rest of the way. The crew is spooked."

I lifted my eyebrows. "But don't you want . . ."

"To see it? Aye, I see it. Loud and clear. But although I'm an ally of Ignis users, that doesn't mean I'm an ally of Navigators. I still earn my pay from the Government. I willingly brought you here, but if the Government knew . . ." He placed the edge of his hand against his throat. "I thank the Brotherhood for not choosing a side, but whether I like it or not, *I'm* on a side. You must leave now, Light Eyes. It was a pleasure doing business with you."

Rather than accept his handshake, I handed him the stack of brown dollars. "Pleasure was all mine, Cap'n. Without you, I wouldn't be here . . . Till we, er, meet again?"

The captain studied the currency, glancing between it and Carbonek. He went back and forth more than once, considered, then handed back the dollars with a sad wince. "I believe the phrase you're looking for is *Ra'lenv Ro'drac.*"

I stared confusedly. "Pardon?"

"It's Old Draconic. The Navigator's farewell."

"What's it mean?"

"In Common Archengard: Till the rainbow's end."

Winnings stored once more in my jacket, the captain's words elevating my emotions, I jumped off the final iron wrung of the ladder onto the grass. The airship took off immediately afterward, and I turned to watch it sail back down the clouded path, wind blowing off of it back toward me. With the wind came the realization that there was no turning back.

Not that I wanted to anyway.

"Till the rainbow's end," I said, feeling the words before watching them whisk away. I turned toward Carbonek. *Let's start at the beginning, then.*

CHAPTER 7

Enoch

Outside, Carbonek was a masterful feat of craftsmanship. Within, you *felt* it. The black walls were engraved with briar forests, crystal castles, and monstrous creatures—some of which I'd traded blows with once in a purple moon. The high ceiling was held up by marble columns, and the Nightguards, Carbonek's armored Ignis-using guardians, stood with their backs to them in burnt-orange armor.

Though the manor itself was a beaut, the root of Carbonek's beauty lay within its people. Packs of young Navigators walked the halls. The colorful entourage made me think of a modernized version of the many courtly kingdoms I'd visited, only instead of vassals clothed in the colors of their liege lords, Navigators wore colors correlating to their Ignis abilities.

I noticed that some carried strange objects in their palms—artifacts—while others wore backpacks and looked as though they'd just returned from strenuous journeys. They were all so different, too. Carbonek was a concoction of cultures and styles. The only thing I noticed that they all had in common was that no one was alone.

Navigational squadrons, I thought, watching a few glance me up and down, then cock their heads down the hall before giving me a thumbs-up, as if to say, "Best o' luck." It was obvious I was a recruit. *Probably rookies from their age, too.*

Among the perpendicular corridors, I saw some middle-aged Navigators, veterans paying me little mind. They hustled about with the boldness of those who had been doing this for a long time. Probably some since before the War began.

They're probably heading out on quests right now . . .

I paused mid-thought. Moving down a hall adjacent to me, heading in the same direction, was another boy that looked my age, one who moved with incredible purpose. Rather than take everything in, as I'd taken to doing, he stalked without even looking up, the ends of his black suit jacket flying behind him. He wore a crimson dress shirt, a black tie, and a black vest over both. Curiously, a black scarf was wound about his neck, and he kept it fixed over the lower half of his face. The short black-brown mohawk atop his head resembled a jagged arrow.

He looks barking grim.

Unlike the Navigators who had pointed me toward the throne room—where all recruits went on the day they were to be inducted—those who saw the dark boy coming fled, and before I debated picking up the pace to stay in line with him, he was gone in blur of black and gold.

I tried not to dwell on him too much. The great marble doors to the throne room loomed ahead, flanked by four Nightguards, and it took all I had not to start jumping up and down.

The Council. I get to meet the bloody Council. Hektor and Daria and Eleri, and maybe I'll get to see Barco again, and—

I nearly seized the Nightguard standing closest to me.

"Is he here?" I asked, much louder than I'd anticipated. "The Leviathan?!"

The Nightguard's eyes flicked down at me with annoyance, then he and his brethren seized the two great handles fixed to the double doors and pried them open.

Guess I'll find out.

The throne room was the jewel in the crown of Carbonek, lined completely with multicolored stained-glass windows depicting scenes from the Brotherhood's legendary history. Columns along the walls sparkled with gems carved to resemble stars, and wide buttresses soared up to the crystal ceiling, which spiraled like turning galaxies. A red-and-gold throne stood against the back wall, a great stained-glass rose window beaming the light of the twin suns down on top of it, and at the sight of the throne, I felt my chest swell with pride.

A throne that had sat empty since Carbonek's construction. A throne that would never seat anyone. It was symbolic of the Brotherhood's purpose: to protect and preserve as a great king would, but to never sit upon the throne. Because Navigators didn't rule: they were down in the dirt and muck with those that needed it. They were adventuring across Archengard, solving problems and leading by example.

Even though he could've sat upon it, I thought, *the Leviathan or his best friend, Mathias, could've seized the throne.* I began to walk forward, my dirty boxing shoes seeming so foreign in a place as spotless and divine as this one. I moved toward the center, until I was surrounded by the stained-glass walls, eyes sucking in every detail, recalling the stories and songs that had kept me alive most nights. That had kept me going. *But they never did. Even with all that power, they never took it. Never gave in to what the Brotherhood could become should it forsake the Code.*

Among the walls, I spotted Adam Evenstar, Talen Vento, and Rebecca Newblood—the three founders—standing atop an emerald hill, speaking to a group of fellow Ignis users and founding the Brotherhood. It had been Newblood who coined the phrase "Navigators."

I spotted the legendary Dresden Roberts sailing his famed ship, the *Torrential Tempest*, through the Seventeen Storms, black Ignis swirling all about him.

And beyond that, I spotted a white-coated figure brandishing a flaming white sword, back to back with a black-coated figure who summoned crimson lightning from the skies.

This is where I make it happen. I stopped before the depiction of the Leviathan and Mathias Flint, the two greatest Navigators who ever lived. *This is where I end the pain and never look back. Where I forget the fire, the darkness, and learn to start—*

The great doors closed behind me, causing me to spin.

Three other figures stood in the throne room, all of us seemingly having realized at the exact same moment that none of us were alone.

Er . . .

I tried to find something to say, something witty to hopefully strike up conversation, but no words came out. I was too surprised to even speak.

The first figure that stood out to me was a knight. They wore a thick suit of silver-blue armor—a relic of the ancient time before the Brotherhood existed—and seemed to barely move at all. They stood rigidly up against the left wall closest to the doors, as though half debating rapping on the doors and requesting the Nightguards let them out. I'd initially thought they were just an empty suit of armor until their gauntleted fingers closed into tense fists.

A knight was indeed a strange sight. All the old Orders of Khronera were extinct, or so I'd heard. Yet the next figure was even stranger.

He had to be at least two years younger than me, mayhaps more given how incredibly short he was, and wore a worn leather jacket over his skinny build. His brown hair was spiked into ferocious mountain peaks, and strangest of all, a pair of pink sunglasses hid his eyes. Unlike the knight who never moved, this bloke couldn't stop moving, always either tapping his foot or humming to himself.

Then came the third figure, leaning up against a crystal column at just the point where he was half hidden in its shadow, and I realized it was the dark boy from before. He looked the most like a Navigator out of all of us, yet there was something so *un*-Navigational about him. Mayhaps it was the way his dark solemn eyes drifted about the throne room, studying everything, or the relaxed but incredibly tense posture he held. I'd fought blokes like him before in the ring. His relaxation was an act.

Kind of a good-looking bloke, though, if I'm being honest . . .

The short boy stepped forward, coughing noisily. "Uh, is there a bathroom somewhere?"

As soon as he spoke, the boy seemed to shrink in size, his leather shoulder pads practically swallowing his whole head, and in the raging silence, the four of us watched each other, gauging how the others should act or respond to such a bewildering first question.

"You're here to be a Navigator, aren't you?" the knight eventually spoke, surprising me with both their assertiveness and the fact that the voice that echoed out of the great armored helm was feminine. *Make that a knightess. Bloody badarse.* "Shouldn't you be able to 'navigate' your way in search of one?"

The short boy's face flared as pink as his sunglasses, and to hopefully save him from further embarrassment, I finally stepped in.

"Oi." I waved all of their attention to me, jogging over to them so I didn't have to shout across the room. "That's not entirely what navigating's about, innit? The name's a little misleading, I suppose." I cracked my knuckles, a nervous habit. "Navs don't really direct routes and chart courses for airships. It's more about charting the course of the future of Archengard. Helping countries and cities and kingdoms all come closer to the Brotherhood's vision of what this world could be." I smiled at the short boy. "And sorry, bruv. Not sure where the loo's to be found."

"You're insufferably optimistic."

It took me a while to realize that it was the dark boy who had spoken. He didn't move from his place up against the column, and his scarf hid his mouth. Yet that dismal drawl, as oddly warm as it was icy, couldn't have come from anyone other than him.

"Pardon?" I said. Because I honestly hadn't heard him that well the first time.

"Your faith in the Brotherhood is misplaced."

"A bold statement coming from a lad currently in Carbonek. And, mind you, one that's completely decked out in Navigator attire."

"Carbonek is just a building. The Brotherhood has a lot more to answer for. You talk of charting courses for the future of Archengard. You talk about a world of peace and adventure, of green hills and blue skies." He crossed his arms over his chest. "Well, get off your airship, *swashbuckler*. The Perpetual War rages on." His dark eyes embedded themselves in me. "And the Brotherhood hides away in Carbonek."

My hands curled into fists, my legs already wanting to start shuffling, like I was back in the boxing ring. But instead of blowing my chance at becoming a Navigator by knocking someone out on the first day, I let my hands come unclenched and faced the bastard.

"Swashes are supposed to make natural Navs, I've heard," I said politely. "*Mercenaries*, on the other hand, not so much." The way he pushed off of the column slightly let me know I'd hit the nail on the head.

"You assume a lot about me."

"Bloody hard to assume what's right there. You've been standing there scowling like you're confined to a cell with a trio of lunatics."

"That's putting things lightly, *amigo*."

"Put things darkly, then. I thought those that came to Carbonek would want to be here, not be scrambling for a way out."

"None of this is new to me. The stained glass, the stories . . ." He shook his head. "You all come in here with these dreams of grandeur, thinking you can save

Archengard and stop the Perpetual War. You look to and base all your ideals off of fools, like the Leviathan.

"You might be a swash, but that doesn't mean you're ready to be a Navigator. That doesn't mean you've dealt with the Brotherhood's pathetic ideology of neutrality."

I took another step forward at that. No one criticized the Leviathan to my face and got to just keep standing there. "Then why're you here if you hate the Brotherhood so bloody much? Answer me that."

"Because *I* was recruited," the dark boy growled, causing my eyebrows to lift. "Because the Brotherhood needs more Ignis users like me." He finally emerged from the shadows, unveiling tan skin and swirling brown eyes like dying embers. His scarf fell from around his nose and finally revealed his whole face to me, a handsome face hardened into iron. Almost statuesque in its beauty and focus. "Because even without Ignis, I'd still be a better warrior than every Nav in Carbonek. Now why are *you* here, pretty boy?"

My whole body locked up. My stomach turned. Flames were in the dark boy's eyes. Flames that made me numb, that shuddered great heaving gasps from my chest instead of ordinary breaths. Flames that held me down, made me scream and wail until my voice was lost. Those flames that had scarred my back, that had uttered the exact same words beneath a much darker sky, among concrete and ruin. And in this place of promise and hope, so far from the dark city I'd escaped, I was reminded that I'd never be free from the fire. Not—

"I was recruited, too," the knight suddenly said, and the dark boy turned his head to glare in her direction. Freeing me from the flames. "By Daria."

I eyed her gratefully, rubbing my shoulder to make sure I wasn't shaking. I wasn't. "Me too, actually." Then found it within me to smirk just a little when the dark boy's steely gaze returned to me, laced with shock. "But by Barco Reyveth."

The short boy, whose shoulders had once more begun to steadily crawl up toward his neck, popped back up. "Whoa. Seriously?"

"Aye." I shrugged. "Said I was basically already a Nav."

The look of sheer astonishment on the face of the dark boy made me want to start doing a Light Isles jig. *That's what happens when you underestimate a swash.*

"You must be an amazing swashbuckler, then," sunglasses lad said, creeping toward me a little. I liked him. He seemed honest.

"I'm all right." I inspected my dirty nails nonchalantly to keep showing the dark boy I didn't fear him—or anything for that matter. "Fought a sea serpent before I got here, you know."

Sunglasses lad sighed. "You wouldn't believe what I was doing before I got here."

"Bet ya five hundred brown dollars mine was wilder. And scalier."

"I'll raise you all ten hundred," the knight said, sounding tired.

"Nope," sunglasses lad said. "The freaking Kardem Ka slipped right through my fingers. Literally."

The dark boy, who'd gone back to leaning against the column, slipped and fell. *"Qué?!"*

The double doors opened once more, and in stepped an assembly of colorfully suited men and women. They moved past us steadily, speaking with one another jovially, until coming to a stop just before the throne. They formed a ring facing us, then a familiar man stepped out of their ranks, his brown cloak billowing around him. He beckoned us forward.

"Approach, inductees."

Barco wore his dark robes, jagged black lines slipping up and down them. His slick brown hair was combed back, and his silver-gray eyes moved between the four of us until falling on me. They softened, and I received a gentle nod.

All doubt I had felt before fled me. I beamed back. *I'm here. And I'm ready.*

As the four of us approached—the knight clanking all the way, sunglasses lad practically tiptoeing, the dark boy lingering toward the back, and me practically skipping—the Nightguards closed the doors.

We formed a line before the High Council of Carbonek. I'd only ever seen their faces staring up from the drawings and photographs stored in books kept by the Light Library. *And now, they're right in front of me.*

I easily identified the dark-skinned woman wearing a purple dress shirt and black suit jacket as Daria Deckara, the Peacekeeper of the Night Desert.

The light-skinned man in a black suit and blue dress shirt at her side made my heart skip a few beats. I'd idolized Hektor CinCarde as a child. Still did.

An older woman in a sparkling red dress with blond hair and pale skin was Eleri Emeres, one of the most influential Navigators in Brotherhood history. Whereas her brethren—the Leviathan and Mathias—had mainly been skilled combatants, she'd specialized in peaceful negotiation and healing.

Next to her glowered the Major General in his dark gray suit. His Ignis ability was a tornado, having been efficient in the early days of the War.

And then there was Barco, the Lord of a Thousand Flames, one of the all-time greats.

"Carbonek stands before these inductees," Barco said. "Is Carbonek ready to induct them?"

"Ayes" echoed throughout the arc of High Navigators, though I could've sworn I heard a muttered "Nay" from the shadows of the throne behind them.

Before I could set off in search of it, Barco's voice rose throughout the hall, as if to drown it out.

"Archengard grows older and wars are continuously waged, yet the Navigational Brotherhood stands. Because we're the one constant: the one true servant of Archengard and its people. Even as the world eats itself around us, we heal it.

Even as the storm closes in from every side, we sail through it. Not because we choose to, but because we have to.

"Ignis was given to many of us by the Dragon Lords for a reason, and for those without Ignis, the skill and understanding of the Lords have been given to you. These aren't tools that should be wasted, but built for good. The Brotherhood are the architects. After the Lords' passing many millennia ago, we've been all that stands between our world and those that would see it plunged into carnage. We are, in many ways, the Dragon Lords' heirs."

"If you seek a clan of warriors, the front gates are open," Eleri said sternly. "The Code states that the Brotherhood doesn't fight."

"And so," Daria said, "as those who came before you did—as we did—you four have navigated your way to Carbonek. High Navigators, let us recite the Three Laws of the Code."

"Law One," Eleri said. "Never use Ignis for evil or destruction. Protect all people, countries, and cultures equally. Judge as a Navigator should judge: fair and unbiased. Fight as a Navigator should fight: to protect and preserve."

"Law Two," Hektor said. "Master your fate. Your spirit, like the stars, is free. Use that freedom to grant others it."

"And Law Three," Barco said. "Never betray the trust of your brethren. Place them and the connections you hold before everything."

"Jezna Caelius." Hektor turned toward the knight. "You were recruited because of your skill at collecting Ignis-infused artifacts. Although there's always been tension between the last Chivalric Orders and the Brotherhood, we hold nothing but respect for the orders—especially the Tolkkyan Order."

Barco gestured toward the sunglasses lad. "Dante Larocque, Jr., you weren't recruited at all, but your arrival is welcomed. You are Ignis-less, but you are also the only son of Dante Larocque, Sr., a colleague of ours."

"It's, uh, Prince." He shook softly. "Father only ever called me Prince. Always hated the 'junior' label."

"Enoch Amon," Hektor said, making me jump before I got caught up in that fact about Prince. *Here we go.* "I suppose saving people from airship wreckages basically guarantees you a seat here. And it was hard not to be a bit interested when word of a strapping young lad taking on Captain Blizerburn the Bad in a fist fight—and *winning*—reached us."

Don't cry, bugger. Don't bloody cry.

"Thanks," I blurted. "Er, sir." I thought I was done, then added, "Blizerburn was a pillock."

Then Barco turned toward the dark bloke.

The room got cold. Every expression worn by a High Navigator no longer looked content, but angrily poised. Though none of them seemed aimed at me, it was terrifying just being within their vicinity.

"Murta Kaster," Barco said. "You're a skilled combatant, arguably the best we've seen at your age. And above everything else, you're a survivor. But that doesn't mean you have nothing left to prove." His gray eyes betrayed little emotion, but there was a wariness there that I hadn't seen before. "Prove to us that you can keep the Code."

My eyebrows raised to the point that I thought they might lift off my forehead.

Was it possible that this Murta fellow had somehow already been a Navigator and was being brought back? Was that something that could even be done? Was that why he was so familiar with the Brotherhood and already wore a suit?

"You wouldn't be in this room if we didn't want you here," Hektor assured us all. "There're traits of a Navigator in each of your professions. Knights aid, treasure hunters recover, mercenaries protect, swashbucklers rescue."

"But Navigators do each of those every day," Eleri said. "Whether it be aiding those affected by the Perpetual War, recovering Ignis-infused artifacts, protecting cities, and exploring the unknown parts of Archengard. This may seem like a steep endeavor, but no Navigator is alone. The Brotherhood isn't defined by the deeds of its individuals but by the strength of its squads. All working together to bring Archengard closer to the peace that we all know it can one day achieve."

"At first, your arrivals were completely coincidental," Barco said. "And I won't deny that we were hesitant. But like many of the inductees that have all arrived through chance, your unique skill sets have convinced us. The four of you will begin as a Navigational squadron-in-training."

We froze.

What?!

I'd always pictured my squad made up of fellow swashes, bright-eyed lads with fearless attitudes and fiery personas. How could these three be my squad?

Yeah, the sunglasses lad was all right, but the knight was a little too posh, and the dark bloke was the last person I'd ever want to be in a squad with. And Barco had said the sunglasses lad was bloody Ignis-less! The Council thought *we* could work together? Just because we all ended up in the throne room at the same time?

"As Navigators-in-training," Barco said coolly, "you have an obligation to set the standard for the Navigators you may become. For now, you are trainees. Only through skill and spirit may you move beyond that title. Only by passing the Trials and keeping to the Code may you become a true—"

"It takes more than just skill and spirit," a voice erupted out of the shadows. "More than yer own individualistic qualities."

I frowned, recalling the "nay" I'd heard from before.

Another High Navigator was outside of the line standing before us. His accent was thick and familiar, definitely from the Light Isles. I'd picked up traces of one, but whoever the man was, he'd been born and raised there.

He slowly stepped into the light, illuminating a gray suit jacket over a gray vest, white dress shirt, and black tie. It was boringly plain, so unlike the vibrant colors and patterns among the younger Navigators and Council members. The man's face remained hidden, but his tousled hair looked blond enough to be white, an ugly pale color that reminded me of ice.

"Kaleo, please," Barco said, but was silenced with a pale hand engulfed in scars from palm to fingernail—so many that they looked like gloves.

"You wanna know what I see when I eye the four o' ya?" he asked, making Prince flinch. "Wasted potential. Wasted on yerselves, not on others. You might've convinced yerselves that deep down you do what you do out of the goodness of yer hearts, but that doesn't mean you actually do it. And it don't make you Navs-in-training. Not even close."

He stepped fully out of the shadows, revealing a face torn with the same tiny white scars as the ones on his hands—and amethyst-colored eyes. Yet when he emerged, I felt an unsettled stirring. I couldn't place where I'd seen him, but something about his features rang faintly familiar.

"I read your files," Kaleo said. "Other High Navs might've been impressed, but I wasn't." He strolled up to Jezna. "Jezna Caelius: a knight who gained Ignis using an artifact. Bugger whatever Order you came from." He moved on to Prince, towering over the boy despite the hunch in his posture. "Prince Larocque: an Ignis-less petty thief from the Corbin Criminal Underworld."

He marched over to me, though I raised my sails in preparation to weather the storm.

"Enoch Amon," he said, foul-smelling spit flying across my face. "Mud-pit brawler, drunkard, has an Ignis ability that barely works . . . and Murta Kaster." He snorted as if that alone was self-explanatory. "You'll be lucky if we even let you begin the Trials."

The four of us studied one another, our lives thrown open for all to see. We'd barely known each other for an hour, yet now knew too much. It was mental. It felt wrong.

Gained Ignis using an artifact? I thought, watching Jezna sway. Even under the emotionless features of her armor, she conveyed astronomical discomfort.

A petty thief? I glanced over at Prince, a child that who to be at least a year younger than me, who stared at his hands.

And Murta Kaster.

"Are you kidding me?" Prince finally said, glowering around the ring of quiet High Navigators. "I mean, really? That's how this is gonna go? Isn't this supposed to be the Leviathan's stomping ground? Where's he at?! We wanna speak to the freaking Leviathan!"

Though I was shocked into silence at the outburst, I agreed with Prince's every word. He had bollocks to say that in front of the Council, and I wanted to see the Leviathan, too. He'd instill us with the kind of hope that this Kaleo bastard could never dream of.

But Kaleo's face fell like ash from the curdling remains of a volcano. Something seemed to change in him, a flicker of fury that spoke of a far greater tempest than the one that had just smashed into us.

Barco swiftly stepped in front of him. "The Leviathan is on a quest at the moment. And I can assure you that you will be given a chance to go through the Trials. No matter what other High Navigators may say."

Summoning my courage, I stepped forward to take Prince's place, trying to peer around Barco's cloak at the old bloke.

Fine. This was the squad that the Council threw me? Bring it on.

If this Kaleo really thought that I was nothing more than a drunken boxer, then so be it.

"Doesn't matter," I said. "We're gonna pass the Trials with flying colors. None of us will fail it."

"Your confidence is well-placed," Barco said. "But the Trials are not something that may be easily passed. These are miniature quests. Advanced preparation for when—*if*—you and your squad ever make it to the field. Do you understand?"

Nods all around. I nodded the fiercest.

"The Trials begin the moment you set foot in this manor. And they don't end until a High Navigator says they've ended and confirms you as an official squad. You'll begin the Trials under our guidance. There'll be days where you'll shadow one of us. Days where you'll strike out on your own. Navigational training is fluid: every squad has their own way of doing things. I'd suggest you figure out yours, or you *will* fail.

"And remember: one of you already has."

Before I could make off with assumptions, he clapped his hands twice, sparks of red Ignis flying from them.

"Now go rest up. You've all just arrived here, but the real quest lies ahead. Deal the cards you've been dealt. I'll expect you in Training Hall B by noon tomorrow."

Then, seemingly as an afterthought: "We'll see what kind of immortality you have then."

CHAPTER 8

Kaleo

The High Navigators didn't so much as spare me a glance as they crept from the throne room. They pretended I wasn't even there. That the old crippled bloke in the corner was just a shadow. Specks of dust that glittered in the suns but disappeared in the dark.

And as they crept away, I wanted to chase after them, roaring.

How could they be so blind? How could they say "aye," every last one of them, to the likes of Murta Kaster? Had they forgotten what transpired the last time? Were they so quick to forgive and forget the sins we'd all committed?

Not me. I'd never forget. So I began to recite their names in my mind, as I did every night after pulling my carcass of a body into bed.

Janne. Sasha. Champ. Kyrus. Malie. Tyson. Erika. Tandra.

Them and dozens more. Hundreds. All Navs I'd lost to the War. All Navs I'd *failed.* Never mind those that turned their backs on the Code completely.

Those names I won't recite. Ever.

I felt the shadow of the throne on top of me like a mountain on my back. I might've been selected Grand High Navigator by the rest of the Council, but I was the last person on Archengard who deserved to sit in the throne. Every last one of them had kneeled before me, sworn that only I could lead the Brotherhood, that only I had the capacity to heal it—and now they'd stabbed me in the back.

How could they recruit another batch without my knowledge? After all those who had forsaken the Code, how could they even fathom re-recruiting Murta Kaster, to say nothing of Dante's Ignis-less son, a knight, and . . .

A crack finally appeared in the dam I'd built myself over the years, sending the ball in my throat smoldering up to the surface, a single fiery tear slipping into my bared teeth.

Those eyes. They were *his* eyes.

And when he'd looked at me, repelled my rage straight back into my face . . .

No emotion. No pain.

I took a seat on the first step of the throne, the aching joints in my knees exclaiming with a few dangerous pops. I stared at the floor beneath my boots, instinctively picking out the flecks of blood decorating their edges. No matter how hard I scrubbed, they never all went away. I'd finally stopped after five years.

"Why're you still here?"

Barco slid out from behind a column. "The Grand High Navigator can't keep turning away every recruit we bring him."

"And why the hell not?"

"I understand that you fear—"

"I slayed fear and ate it afterward."

"Maybe so. But we cannot ignore the Brotherhood's dwindling ranks."

"I haven't ignored shite. I let you take on Ben Sedes and Squad 324. I let Hektor take on Biassis and Squad 326."

"Yet you refused to designate either of them as 327."

"A number that means nothing now. Archengard *despises* us. The Government tries to enlist us, the Noda tries to enslave us, and the rest that can't pick a side just want us gone."

"Carbonek exists for a reason."

"But Murta Kaster doesn't belong here."

"That doesn't mean we should turn our backs a second time. He was closer to finding the Kardem Ka than any of us. You don't find the Talismans unless they want to be found. The Brotherhood needs a mind like him."

"Then admit your mistake and say you didn't send Biassis—"

"Are we not at fault, Kal?"

I stammered.

"Murta only lost control because he didn't receive the proper guidance from us," Barco said. "We neglected him out of fear. That he might be like those that came before. He possesses one of the strongest Ignis abilities I've ever seen, and we treated him as an outcast. He must be taught connection."

"Connection," I repeated. "May as well be the Dark Tongue. No one has any idea what it bloody means anymore."

"Enoch knows."

I ground my teeth until they hurt. "Leave me."

"There are things you'd be interested in knowing about the other three."

"I know enough. The knight's a relic, Dante's boy will meet the same end as his father if he's got no Ignis, and the swashbuckler's been punched too many times in the head."

"That swashbuckler"—Barco stepped toward me—"bears an Ignis ability that's more valuable to the Brotherhood than twenty Murtas."

I didn't move. How could I when Barco got going? He was a whole squad unto himself.

"Do you think I recruited him just for his appearance?" he continued. "I've been all over the Light Isles. They speak of him like some emerald phoenix. Just like the Southern Kingdoms—where they still cling to the old ways of life—tell tales of the last Tolkkyan knight. Just like the criminal underworld of Archengard speaks of an Ignis-less ionsmith. Just like the dark hills of West Khronera whispers of a lone mercenary who stalks black souls in the night: El Cazador de Sombra. If you'd just give them a chance, Kal . . ."

"Nay."

But Barco refused to give in. "Daria picked Jezna because she's a knight. Dante always said he was planning on sending his son here. Biassis brought back one who we'd considered the most promising recruit in years . . . and I found the next Leviathan."

I prepared to throw myself full force behind the mightiest tirade Archengard had ever witnessed, then I remembered.

A time before the Perpetual War, before the Brotherhood turned themselves into warriors just to flee in fear when the world needed us most.

A time when I hadn't seen the pillars of smoke rising up off the black sand like gargantuan columns in a cavernous catacomb. A time when I hadn't seen graves and burial mounds and crooked crags bearing tattered flags everywhere I went, but young men. Four boys full of life, four faces I recognized.

One was a face I had seen looking back at me from a mirror—a face I might've worn in some bolder, brighter age—and the other three were beside me once again. Not dead. Not defeated. Not fallen. But alive, *together*.

Instead of cursing Barco, I sank into a puddle at the foot of the throne. Because he was one of the faces, and so was I. And the other two were dead.

Never again.

"Leave me," I whispered.

This time, he did.

CHAPTER 9

Jezna

Night fell over the valley fast. By seven in the evening, Archengard's blue moon Aldrisno was already in the sky, and we were led to our quarters by a female Navigator with silver hair and a lime-green suit. Located in the Rookies Tower in the same vicinity as other new trainees, our living space consisted of three rooms: a common area and two shared bedrooms connected by twin staircases on opposite sides.

I cringed. Each bedroom contained two beds, meaning we had a decision to make, and at the moment, no one seemed in the mood to make any. It had been a little over an hour, and I already sought to leave. Daria had barely said a word throughout the entire initiation process. And then Kaleo, the man who made me realize I could hold so much animosity toward someone that I'd contemplate going back on everything I'd ever sworn upon as a knight. He might as well have ripped off my armor. He might as well have told them all what I was, what cruel fate had befallen me.

How? I wanted to scream as the four of us did slow, silent circles around the common room in the firelight. *How did he know? Did Daria tell him?*

If I had eyes, I would've squeezed them shut. But I didn't, so I let the memories roll through me. The world changed, and a knight had two options: change it or change because of it. Right now, I was having a hard time doing either. It was a lot easier to just never step in a stream to begin with rather than fight against it or let it take you. Right now, all I could think about was how wrong Macín had been about the Brotherhood.

I took a heavy seat in an armchair.

"Bright idea." Enoch sank into the seat across from me, his expression souring. "Does anyone know who that bastard was?"

"I say we beat the crap outta him," Prince said, flipping himself up onto the couch after messily boxing the air. Enoch laughed at the display.

What fools, I thought incredulously. That they could be so carefree at a time like this . . .

"You plan on beating him with your bare hands, Ordinary?" Murta said from up against the right wall, using the slur for Ignis-less individuals. "That'd be a sight to see."

Prince rose, but Enoch gently pushed him back into his seat.

"So?" he asked. "Didn't you hear what Barco said? His father was a Navigator." He looked back at Prince. "Dante Larocque, right?"

Prince kept his gaze lowered at Murta but answered Enoch with honesty. "Yeah. Father was a Nav. And he didn't need freaking Ignis to be one."

"So it runs in the family," Murta said.

"We'll see just how much of an ass you wanna be once they give me back my guns."

"Guns?" asked Enoch.

Prince deflated back onto the couch with a sigh. "I . . . can't use Ignis, yeah. But I make up for it with Aestus."

"Aestus?" Enoch sat up, interested. "Like the glowy element that looks like Ignis, but isn't? The man-made one?"

Prince nodded. "If that's how you wanna look at it, then sure. It's a liquid compound. Runs through most vehicles and ships. Some of the cities use it to power all of their stuff, too." He looked suddenly uncomfortable. "I've been working with Aestus for as long as I can remember. I'm an ionsmith, I guess. I make Aestus-powered firearms."

Enoch's face lit up. "You don't have Ignis but you can do all that?"

Prince looked appalled by Enoch's reaction. "I guess I can."

I kept silent. I despised Aestus—the glowing chemical whose invention had drastically changed certain parts of Archengard—and thus, despised those who utilized it. Archengard had been better off without it a century ago and was worse off now because of it.

I was comfortable with a tilled field and a cottage. I had ridden horses in my youth and knew how to care for them. Megacities full of vehicles and skyscrapers had never intrigued me. It disgusted me that the old world, a world of simplicity, had since given way to one of steely complexity and strange new technologies. I missed wooden and brick villages with cobblestone roads. I missed castles.

"Ignis never goes away," Murta said, flinching me back to reality. "Once your guns are done, they're done."

"Is that so?" Prince said. "'Cause it sounded like *you* went away for a bit. It sounded like you failed the Trials the first time. So what's your Ignis ability, Scarfy?"

"You wouldn't believe me if I told you."

The fireplace wasn't enough to snuff out the cold that suddenly overtook the space, just like in the throne room. A dark wind seemed to follow the younger man, but the darkness that poured out of him was ancient and much more daunting. Like he'd seen more violence in five sun cycles than I had in my full twenty-two.

"Which category is it?" I finally asked, intrigued.

Murta stared. "I don't necessarily think you need to know, Ignis stealer."

I doused my anger. Anger was the path to foolishness, and a knight always kept a level head. That had been one of the first things the Tolkkyan Order taught. Back when I'd first stumbled upon their lair in the glade and Bebel had come flying at me with his sword, only to be stopped by Macín.

"No matter how fiercely the fire burns," Macín had said, "come the rain, it will all be extinguished in the end. Best never to strike the flame to begin with."

"Fine." Bebel had shrugged. "But it'll be cold as balls at night."

"Pardon, gents," Enoch said. "What's a category, and why should we care?"

"The four categories of Ignis classification," Murta said. "You were recruited for your Ignis ability, weren't you? How've you never heard of them?"

"All I do is punch, fight monsters, and engage in flamboyant adventures of passion and bravado, bugger."

"I'm envious as hell," Prince said.

"Why, thank you." Enoch looked back at Murta. "My point being: I never needed to know about them."

I studied the swashbuckler. The more I did, the more I began to hear a certain knight I'd known in his cadence, and that unnerved me. Enoch was nothing like Macín, nor deserved to be respected like I'd treated Macín. A swashbuckler was almost the furthest one could get from a knight. Though not as far as a thief.

But if there was one thing that Enoch had that no one else in Carbonek seemed to, it was Macín's kindness. He stood up against Murta, looked at me without the prejudice of everyone I'd met so far, and had even sworn at the Council.

For the time being, it appeared I had an ally.

"Every Ignis ability can be classified as either Practical, Conflicted, Elemental, or Transformative," I explained to him. "Practical pertaining to everyday uses, Conflicted to combat uses, Elemental to elemental manipulation, and Transformative to the transformation of one's body or spirit. Make sense?"

Enoch scratched his head. "Sure. What's yours?"

I tensed, though Enoch's question was honest. I could talk about my Ignis ability without delving deep into the details. *Without explaining my curse.*

"Elemental." I extended my palm, conjuring a swirling orb of glowing water.

Enoch whistled. "Wicked." And in a stunning blaze of emerald light, his left fist caught fire.

I watched the green flame dance. "Do you know which category it falls under?"

Enoch was still staring at his fist, as if surprised he'd even managed to harness Ignis. "Elemental?"

"Doubt it," Murta said. "It'd be more akin to natural fire. Not bright green."

I warily turned toward him, thinking for a moment that I'd seen Bebel sharpening his sword in his place. "And what about you?"

He held up his right arm.

From his fingertips to an inch just above his elbow, Murta's hand became a set of gnarled claws made of overlapping obsidian scales. Gold sparks danced around them.

"Transformative." Murta's arm returned to normalcy and wrapped back around his chest in seconds.

"That's—" I began.

"None of your concern."

We fell back into silence. Partially because though I was interested in Murta's Ignis ability, I was too afraid to ask any more questions. A knight didn't fear anything, but it was best to be cautious around mercenaries. And this dark boy was definitely one.

Maybe Enoch reminded me of Macín, but Murta and Bebel was a stretch. Bebel had been gruff in a jolly way. His armor had been the strongest of the Order's, but that also meant he'd been the slowest. He'd laughed at misfortune and cursed like a swashbuckler, but it had all been done to lift others up around him.

Bebel had been a knight caught in an endless hyperbolic banter with the world around him. Murta looked like he wanted to slaughter it.

"Lovely talk," Enoch said to Murta, then glanced around the room. "Er, do we really happen to be stuck in this boring-arse room on our first day in Carbonek?"

"It's night," I reminded him. "Barco seemed quite assertive that we get to bed before beginning the Trials tomorrow. And I, for one, think he's right."

"That's a load of dung." Enoch stood, stretching. "We just arrived, and now we're supposed to zonk off? I don't need rest. I need action!"

Prince leapt to his feet. "I like the way you're thinking. How do they expect us to just sit around and sleep? I joined this shit so I'd never have to sleep again!"

I protested, but Enoch and Prince were already scheming. Their minds seemed almost linked in chaos.

Another thing that annoyed me about Navigators: their unwillingness to listen to reason or follow orders. Few knights ever joined the Brotherhood—with Talen Vento being the only one of importance—but swashes, thieves, and the like were said to join every day, all as unruly as the last.

"But don't you think—" I tried.

"Sometimes," Enoch said. "When it occurs to me. But if you suppose I'm just willing to take the beating that Kaleo bugger delivered us, then pitch yourself overboard. Real Navs like the Leviathan prided themselves on telling authority to go wank themselves. So why shouldn't we do the same?"

"Because we're trainees!" I found myself sputtering, furious with myself for thinking this boy had anything in common with the knight who had taken me in. For thinking I'd find anything other than distress and disorder here. "We cannot just wander around Carbonek!"

"Come on, mate. It's not like we're nabbin' anything. Just going out for a brief strut around the corridors. When's the Code ever said a trainee couldn't do that?"

"And you just know *so* much about the Code," Murta said.

"Does anything sensible ever escape your mouth?" Enoch asked.

Smoke began to sizzle up from his nostrils. "Try me."

"Don't think I'd like the taste very much." Enoch raised his fists. "You'll love mine, though." But instead of igniting, they remained normal. He kept them raised despite the slight widening of his eyes.

"You'd be a fool to try and fight me," Murta said. "You're no Leviathan yet."

"And you're no Mathias. So what happened to you? Didn't become a Nav the first time?"

"Hardly. I was held back."

"Might I ask by whom?"

"The same fools Mathias was held back by: the Council."

"I suppose that's the reason you despise them so much."

"And you don't?"

"I don't."

"Then you're denser than I thought. They're a pack of hypocrites. Kaleo is proof."

Enoch was a glassblower shaping a stained-glass window. At first, it was difficult to uncover the pattern he wove, for there was such intricacy poured into it, but once I seized the secret of his art, the masterpiece was unveiled in all its splendor.

"The Council's a pack of hypocrites and fools," Enoch said, tapping his chin, "yet you listen to them so assertively?"

This one might not have been the brightest, but he undoubtedly had a way with words.

Murta's hand was already on the door handle.

CHAPTER 10

Enoch

So what's your story?"

"Murder."

"Heh. Wicked. You gotta be a merc, right?"

"For a time."

"Why?"

"Why do you think?"

"The money?"

"You're telling me you're a swashbuckler just because you like it?"

"Well, why else would I?"

Murta looked away with a slow shake of his head.

I followed, flabbergasted. There was little fun in being a merc. I'd tried for a week. The Corbin Criminal Underworld had a monopoly on all of them, and I'd never worked well with their lot. The Light Isles were for free men. Working for the underworld was the same as working for the Government or the Noda. You were just another soldier.

With those claws, he probably excelled at that.

Even under his vest, Murta's back muscles stood out. He was so much more imposing than the Navigators we passed throughout the halls. Though his clothes were a Navigator's, he still stood out among them. There was something . . . well, spooky about him.

I watched him uneasily. Coupling his spookiness with his scarf, accent, the short mohawk his earth-brown hair had been clipped in, and the odd language he spoke . . .

Murta suddenly shoved right through me back the way we'd come. "Four Nightguards up ahead. We'll take a shortcut."

"Where are we even going?" Jezna asked.

"There's a storage area in the corridor under the North Tower," Murta said. "Always wanted to check it out."

I looked back at Prince, who shrugged. I figured I would've been the one leading. Carbonek was huge, we had a lot of exploring to do, and neither Prince nor I had any plans of turning in for the night.

But then Murta had taken the lead, and we were off to find this storage area. And from how briskly he moved, he was a man on a mission.

We passed among pillars, ducking in and out of hallways whenever a Nightguard appeared. It seemed Murta assumed that if one recognized him, they'd alert Barco. It was ridiculously fun for me, though Jezna didn't appear to share in my enthusiasm. Her armor was loud. I thought about asking why she wouldn't show us what she looked like, but then Murta cursed in his native tongue, and I recalled where it stemmed from.

I sprinted after him into the next corridor, one full of Navigators playing rounds of board-based games. Among the seated Navigators stood marble statues of famed Navigators from the past. A group of four blokes played Castle-King-Horse at a table directly under Adam Evenstar's crotch.

"Shadarian," I hissed in Murta's ear. "That's what you're speaking. You're a Shadarian?"

He spun on me, shadows spilling out of his eyes. "If you say one more word, I'll tear your tongue out through your neck." He was already halfway across the corridor by the time I blinked.

Prince emerged at my side. "The hell did you say to him?"

"He's a Shadarian," I said. "A shadow warrior from the west. I knew I'd heard that language before."

"A freaking cornfield ninja? What's he doing this far from a Sanctum?"

"Dunno." I frowned. "Haven't the faintest idea."

Jezna popped up from behind the statue of Adam Evenstar, scaring Prince half to death. "I assumed he was. It's been a long time since I've encountered one."

It had been long since I'd encountered one, too. A Shadarian in the Brotherhood? Unthinkable. Not only did they never leave their Sanctum—and those who deserted their Sanctum were hunted to death by the rest of their clan—but they despised Ignis users. Shadarians were the cause of multiple Ignis user lynchings. The idea that one of them would flee the only life they'd ever known to become a Navigator of all things was admirable but unsettling. The idea of an Ignis-using Shadarian was beyond so.

"Watch out, Enoch," Jezna suddenly said.

We stood under an archway facing the main hall. There were so many Navigators bristling about that it would've been impossible for the Nightguards to pick us out. Even Jezna's armor blended in. Whereas the corridors we'd passed through had been full of relaxing Navigators, the main hall seemed to be a runway.

Squads piled in from out of the night, covered in soot, dirt, sand, and some missing pieces of clothing altogether. Like those from before, there were backpacks and artifacts, but now there was an even greater variety. I spotted some holding small creatures in their arms, as if nursing them, others pulling great sacks of objects, and some just tackling one another all the way to the unloading bays located on both sides of the throne room.

Seconds later, the humming of an Aestus engine came rumbling down the hall. A sleek vehicle crept by us, wicked inscriptions etched into its sides, lines throughout it pulsing with purple Aestus. There was no roof, revealing a squad of three girls and two boys loudly conversing. We watched their turner rumble down the hall and out of sight.

A tender yearning began to slow burn inside me.

I wish I had a squad like that, I thought, then remembered what Barco had said.

Deal the cards you've been dealt.

Easy for him to say, when his squadmates had been Mathias and the Leviathan. I liked Prince, but Jezna didn't seem like she wanted to be here. And then . . .

I became aware of the empty spot next to me.

Prince looked around. "The spook ditched us?"

"Looks like it," I said numbly.

"I *loathe* him."

"He is somewhat . . . unlikeable," Jezna added.

"Unlikeable?" Prince said. "There ain't a nick of likability in him! No wonder he's a Shadarian. I hear they drain their children's tears at birth."

"That's uncalled for," Jezna said.

Prince turned back to the parade of squads. "You get what I mean. We can't be stuck with him."

"Doubt you're gonna get out of that since Barco made us a squad," I said, feeling worse by the minute.

"How're *we* a squad?!" Prince thrust his arms out at our section of the hall, now taken up by an Aestus-powered vehicle that looked like the bastard son of a turner and a steamboat. Its wheels alone were four feet tall and its center was occupied by what looked like three squads all packed together. I spotted a few dusty rag-wearing individuals among them.

People they'd saved, I realized. Probably straight from the War.

The slow burn I'd been feeling transformed into something scalding. The Trials were what every inductee dreamed of passing—the path to becoming a *true* Navigator—and the Leviathan and Barco's squad had passed them in under two weeks. The shortest training period in recorded history. And then they'd gone on to become the greatest squad ever.

I was beyond determined to aim for somewhere around there, but how could I with an Ignis-less thief, a prissy knight, and a Shadarian?

To make matters worse, younger squads started popping up. One in particular only contained three lads, but they looked around my age and were carrying a big black cube between them. I eyed them depressingly.

One was my height with pale skin, hazel eyes, and a fluffy red mullet kind of like mine. He wore a white zip-up hooded sweatshirt over his lithe form, and a white shirt with a blue-black tie under it.

The two lads assisting him couldn't have been more different, though. One was shorter than Prince and wore a brown vest over a wrinkly white dress shirt. A mane of freckles peppered his small nose, and his ruffled brown hair danced mindlessly whenever he shifted, but the last lad seemed to be doing most of the heavy lifting. He was tall with black hair, a forest-green suit jacket over his muscular torso, and two dark stripes of eye black across his cheeks.

The three of them grunted as they heaved the cube down the hall, and as I watched—now curiously—I noticed that the cube bore red lines along its six faces that glowed menacingly.

An imprisonment box!

They might not have been riding a vehicle down the center of Carbonek, but whoever this struggling squad was, they had to at least be pretty bloody important. Only a select few imprisonment boxes were left in the world. Using one required a ridiculous amount of skill and patience. The Leviathan had supposedly trapped a demon in one.

But the more I watched the three Navigators, the more obvious it became that they weren't anywhere near the Leviathan. Not to say I would've been any better, but the longer they carried the box, the lower it seemed to slope in their hands until the short boy was having to do an awkward side shuffle.

"Slipping!" I heard him cry, and in response, the tall fellow lunged low, gathering his corner under his arms.

Except he underestimated his own strength and lifted the box so high that it completely flew out of the short boy's hands.

"Whoops."

"You bastard!"

The lad with the mullet scrambled to save the unmanned end, but by that point, the box was already tumbling toward the floor. When it landed, the top burst open and a hurricane of black energy exploded across the hall.

CHAPTER 11

Murta

I'd been slowly making my way in the direction of the storage area, somewhere I thought I might be able to find information on where the Karnocolix—one of the five Tintagen Talismans—was supposedly being kept, when the sound of a large object being dropped echoed down the corridor I'd just entered. It was followed by the rushing sound of a tidal wave.

I'd heard a lot of strange things living in Carbonek three years prior, but this didn't sound like anything I'd ever heard.

Rushing back the way I'd come, I looked down the main hall.

I had just enough time to think *I turn away for two seconds*— before a midnight comet swept toward me and my instincts kicked into overdrive.

Rolling out of the way, I watched the unnatural substance impact against the throne room doors, then unfurl itself into a plume of twisting shapes. Within the cloud of black smoke, a hundred different limbs attempted to take shape in a disturbing concoction. Only when the limbs turned into eight writhing ones did I finally tense.

The legs became serrated torturers' blades, and, suspended within the darkness of its raging body, eight crimson eyes flickered open.

A Skrill stood across the way from me inside Carbonek.

The hall erupted into chaos. Nightguards sprung from their posts, sending spurts of Ignis up at the monstrous black creature, but the Skrill just let out a piercing scream that drove icicles into my spine—and charged them. Though their armor might've protected them against Ignis-oriented attacks, the Skrill was made of another energy entirely and smashed through their phalanx. Nightguards sailed into columns, and when they were completely cleared, the Skrill focused its eight crimson eyes at the next person closest to it: me.

Given the option between sprinting back into the manor and having Barco find a way to blame me for the multiple walls that the Skrill broke down, or sprinting down the hall toward the other Navigators, I chose the latter.

Maybe there, I'll find who let this damned thing out. Then feed them to it.

Skrill were endangered to the point that they'd become legend. The energy that made up their bodies wasn't Ignis, but a darker, much older substance. No one knew what it was. That made them immensely difficult to kill.

Now that I thought about it, I didn't think anyone ever had. My Shadarian clan definitely hadn't taught me how to kill one, which was concerning.

As far as I knew, Skrills couldn't be killed, and for that reason they'd been hunted by the Jackals. The rest of this creature's brethren were probably locked away in some deep dungeon cell, only to be pulled out if the War called for it. By the demented group that kept them chained to a post. Just like the post they had my mind chained to.

So in a way, I realized, the Skrill and I were alike.

Focus on the task.

I began seizing Ignis-infused artifacts from their pedestals about the halls, but none did a speck of destruction. Eventually, I just got tired and flung the fabled Shield of Mon Gaijer up at the Skrill's face.

Where's the Sword of the Leviathan when you need it?! Although the legendary curved blade could only ever be wielded by the Leviathan—it was said anyone who touched its hilt who wasn't the Leviathan would pass straight through it—I was up for anything at the moment.

Anything? one of the dark voices that rested within me said.

I nearly stopped sprinting.

There was, of course, one option far more tempting than all the others. One that tore through darkness like the Skrill before devouring it whole.

But the last time I resorted to that—

A Navigational thunder turner smashed straight into the creature. It was so obnoxiously surprising that I slowed and watched.

The Aestus-powered vehicle belched bright Ignis-like fire from its engine, the Navigators in the driver's seat flinging meteors of actual Ignis from their fists at the Skrill's face. The creature gave a resounding screech that shook the manor, then dug its legs into the floor, but the enormous thunder turner held.

I recalled with a flicker of faint amusement how desperately Biassis had wanted us to invest in one.

Navigators began to empty out of the manor from all sides, starting out in dozens, then quickly converting into hundreds. The hall came alive with roars and yells as Ignis collided with the Skrill in a cataclysmic rainbow. It was actually kind of impressive. And I immediately felt ashamed that I'd once again contemplated letting what slumbered inside me out in Carbonek.

Then the Skrill's smoky body seemed to harden, and its eyes glowed with malice.

Thrust by the creature, the thunder turner went flying back into the crowd of Navigators, quickly carving a path as those nearly run over by it spun out of the way. It didn't look like anyone was hurt, but some were definitely stunned. And the Skrill instantly began to rampage.

The fabled Navigational bravery seemed to dwindle out then. The majority fled back into the halls, calling for the High Navigators, searching for artifacts that were capable of capturing a Skrill. They knew how foolish it was to try and take on one that had just been released.

But some Navigators stuck around, silhouettes burning with Ignis.

One in particular, I noticed, wore a familiar white hoodie and raised a bow made of churning blue Ignis up at the Skrill's head from several feet across the hall.

Loc, I thought. *Mierda.*

Though a part of me wanted to simply watch with pleasure as Carbonek was turned upside down by someone else for once, something else hinted that this was my time to redeem myself. This was how I could win them back.

So I prepared to sprint *at* the Skrill as opposed to away, and ran face-first into a dark-green suit jacket.

I swung my head, preparing to curse whoever had been stupid enough to run into me, then I saw that the Navigator wore eye black beneath smoldering Ignis-infused eyes.

Maddox—seemingly in the process of making his way around the Skrill to attack its ass—squinted like he couldn't wrap his finger around my face. When that finger wrapped itself into a fist and swung toward my face, I figured he'd remembered.

"No 'Nice to see you again?'" I asked, ducking behind a column. Unlike Larry, who hadn't used Ignis when we'd scuffled outside the temple, Maddox's fist appeared encased in a cinder block of forest-green Ignis, taking a chunk out of the column I hid behind.

He rushed after me, thick eyebrows lowered with fury. *A look I'm very much deserving of.* "Fuck off."

"If you'd survey your surroundings once in a while," I growled, "you'd see that I'm actually trying to help—"

The tidal wave sound hit again. I leapt back, thinking the Skrill had decided to become a cloud again, before an *actual* tidal wave, glistening an unnatural aqua-blue, hurled into me and Maddox.

I thrashed against the waves, but it spun us around the backside of the Skrill, dropping us directly where Jezna stood behind a column, gauntlets curdling with the same material. Before she could bring us to a stop, I used the momentum of the makeshift river to launch myself at the blond boy next to her.

"What did you do?!"

"Get off me, bugger!" Enoch slapped my arms away. "Why're you assuming I'm at fault here?"

I stood, shoving him back down to push myself up, then another familiar face—Cowlin, Maddox's disheveled partner in crime—rushed toward us.

"We may or may not have released the spider," he said.

I spun on Maddox. "YOU—"

The Skrill swiped at us with one of its enormous legs. We all ducked, Jezna being the first up. She smashed her palms together, then extended them, and the tidal wave rose out of her once more. It spread up toward the ceiling of the hall, creating a wall between us and the Skrill.

"Save a soul," I thought I heard her whisper.

At least someone knows how to act.

"There's cover over here!" Jezna called toward Loc, still out in the middle of the hall with blue Ignis swarming off of his arms. He scrambled over.

"You're bleeding!" Cowlin said, tending to Loc's arm immediately. The gash wasn't huge, but still big enough to be a concern.

Loc shook him off, but his shoulders were quaking. "S'fine. I'll visit the healers and be patched up in no time . . ." His eyes finally met mine, and the anger that erupted there made my heart sink. "What're you doing here?"

"Dying." Maddox threw another fist at me, but he never made impact. The Skrill had finally wedged its way through Jezna's wall and brought down one of the columns.

Cowlin screamed as the marble plummeted toward him, but Maddox was at his side in an instant, Ignis surrounding him, Cowlin, and Loc so that they were suddenly stored inside a giant Ignis-created mecha that grew until it was the size of the Skrill. The column clanged measly off of the growing armor, sending the remaining Navigators scrambling.

Within the mecha, Maddox fixed his footing and raised his fists, Loc and Cowlin positioned behind him as though in the backseat of a turner. The mecha mirrored Maddox's gestures in tandem, facing the Skrill.

The creature studied the imposing enemy before changing its tune—scuttling up onto the wall above us and throwing itself into the Ignis armor with a screech. Maddox's mecha went smashing into one of the neighboring halls, and the Skrill rushed in after him, leaving us hidden behind the fallen pillar.

Without thinking, I placed a hand on the marble to leap after the beast, but a boxer's jacket flew into my face.

I spun in bewilderment to see Enoch taking off his clothes.

"Wha . . . ?"

Enoch threw his shirt off next, revealing his tanned body. He didn't have as many abs as I had, but I was deeply unsettled that he had some.

"Why are you stripping?!" I asked.

"Why aren't you?" Enoch replied.

When he turned around to slip off his pants, my eyes locked on a massive circle scar that took up the entirety of his back. A white sun. The skin had healed over everything, but it was of a far paler color than the rest of his body. What had caused the scar . . . and how much pain had it caused him?

I felt my face heat up. "Do you even know what that thing is?"

"Giant spider."

Ignoring that Enoch was now in nothing but black underwear, I spun him so we were face-to-face.

"That's a Skrill," I said. "An unkillable creature that the Shrouded Men claim to be foreign to Archengard. I don't even know how to kill one, so what makes you think a stupid swash can? And why the hell are you in your underwear?!"

Prince's face fell with devastation. "We're so screwed."

"Like hell we are." Enoch jumped to get a glimpse of the rampaging monster on the other side of the pillar, then said the unfathomable: "I can take it."

He's batshit insane.

"HOW?" Prince asked.

"That's a terrible idea," Jezna said. "I've heard stories of these creatures . . . Murta is right. We aren't aiding our cause by sticking around. We should go find Barco and Daria. And besides, you're one man."

At that, Enoch surprisingly seemed to take in his surroundings. I would've given years of my life to know what he was thinking at that moment. But instead of caving in on himself, Enoch only glanced around at the dazed Navigators decorating the archways and clenched his fists. A dangerous fire lit up in his bright orange eyes.

"Can't believe I'm saying this," he said. "But we need to fight it together. If we all attack it at once, we might stand a chance. Might even be able to beat it."

Not this again. Barco claimed we were a squad, but that was idiocy. Just because we'd all ended up in the throne room at the same time didn't mean we could work together.

What Enoch was proposing wasn't the Shadarian way . . .

Memories of my first few days in Carbonek filtering back into me—days spent beside Biassis, Loc, and Maddox when they'd all looked at me with respect rather than anger—I leaned against the column warily. "Your proof being . . . ?"

"Blackheart Bay," Enoch said. "Mathias didn't just win it for the Brotherhood on his own. He had the help of the rest of Squad 327. The Brotherhood survived because Mathias, Barco, and the Leviathan stood together." His words were only accented by the frustrated belches that emitted from the Skrill as it attempted to pierce Maddox's armor. "And it might be useful if we did the same."

I wanted to laugh with malice. No one thought like that anymore. Thinking in terms of unification was illogical. Nothing ever came of it. Not on Archengard.

But as if instilled with newfound purpose, Prince dug around in the inside pocket of his leather jacket and whipped out a small silver cylinder. When he pressed a button on the bottom, it extended outward, the metal reworking itself until it resembled a gun the size of his arm. When he cocked it, the muzzle glowed purple white.

"I want one," Enoch said.

"It'll take a year to make," Prince said. "Gotta sneak it past the Nightguards somehow."

"Can you provide cover?"

Prince frowned. "Why?"

"That thing the three Navigators were carrying was an imprisonment box." Enoch pointed at a black shape laying open some hundred feet away from us. "And if I'm not mistaken, that's it right there. I can get the Skrill into it if I have cover."

I was astonished that Enoch even knew what an imprisonment box was, let alone that from the sound of what he'd said, Loc, Maddox, and Cowlin had found one.

If that's the case, then it means the War is close . . . They're *close.*

Prince poked his head up over the column, watching the Skrill through the scope of his weapon. "It's fast as hell."

Enoch's irises turned emerald, trickles of Ignis beginning to crackle around his naked shoulders. Green symbols and swirls sprang up along his arms and face until they covered his entire body. I'd never seen anything like it.

"But there's a pattern to its movements," he said. "A fighting style. And I read fighting styles for a living. Jezna, how about another one of those water walls?"

"I can do that," she said.

I watched closely. Enoch was right: The Skrill did move with a pattern. It paced back and forth almost rhythmically, attacking Maddox's Ignis armor at certain moments, then going back to attacking other Navigators scattered around it. Pieces of marble flipped up all around where its dark legs dug. Now and then, it would snatch up a few with its pinchers and munch away.

As long as we don't end up like that marble. "And where do I fit into this?" I asked, shelving thoughts of where the Skrill had come from for now.

"Battering ram," Enoch said.

I didn't like the idea of joining forces with these fools. Not one bit.

Either that or I bring the entire manor down on top of us. Either join them or face another three years of hatred.

"If it gets out of Carbonek," I said, "I'm taking matters into my own hands."

Enoch nodded. "Deal."

"Hang on!" Prince said. "How do we fit it back in the box?"

The green energy snipping at Enoch's skin intensified. He looked . . . anxious. He was trying to be determined, but his uncertainty was written in the unnatural way his Ignis snapped at him. Something just didn't seem right about the way he used it.

"I'll handle that," Enoch said. "For now . . . let's carpe diem this shite."

And despite never having worked together—despite us seemingly never working with *anyone* outside of ourselves—we carried out the plan.

Though my mind remained situated behind the column, my body flipped over the marble, spinning to avoid the Skrill's leg.

Why am I doing this? I thought as I charged toward a monster I had no idea how to injure, defending a Navigator who had attacked me twice. *Why am I taking orders from a swashbuckler?*

For a short, unsettling second, my spirit felt as though it'd been separated from my body and somehow filtered into the boy behind me. For a second, I felt as though the actions I took weren't dictated by me, but someone else. A puppeteer making my spirit move, willing my mind to act even when I disagreed with its actions . . .

Possessing me.

At the thought, I faltered and was struck by one of the Skrill's legs. Channeling my rage into action, I grabbed it with my claws and threw myself toward its rearing head with a roar. Instead of channeling Ignis down into my legs, I let the fire convert my body into a pyre.

Gold sparks exploded across the hall as I sank my claws into the Skrill's face. Its skin was nothing like skin, instead made up of a pure, coursing darkness, but my claws could cut through everything. Even darkness from another planet.

As I tore bits of shadow away, the Skrill thrashed, but I sustained my grip, swinging to and fro in an attempt to make my way up to its back.

Something glimmered off to the right, and blasts of pink Aestus answered, taking the Skrill in the underside. I spotted Prince, gun in hand.

So he's not completely useless—

A bolt of green lightning nearly toppled me. The Skrill flew into a frenzy and eagerly tried to chase it.

"Stay put," I said, throwing Ignis into my right foot. Unhooking my claws from the creature's body, I twisted in midair until the Skrill's demonic head was right in line with my leg, then threw a spinning roundhouse that sent it flying back into the main hall. Enough to hurt it, but not enough to crash it into the rest of the manor.

You're welcome, Ḅarco.

"Hurt," however, seemed to be relative. The Skrill was no longer going after Enoch, but it appeared only irritated as opposed to injured. Maybe I *should've* kicked it through the wall.

Prince fired a few more spasms of Aestus, snagging up its attention. A wave of Jezna's water responded, blocking the beast off. The tips of its legs appeared through the barrier every few seconds as it scampered to escape, but stayed stuck. Off to the side, Jezna fell to a knee, arms outstretched.

"Any day, Noc!" Prince said.

I ripped my gaze back toward Enoch, whose glowing hands lurched the imprisonment box onto its side and pried back the lid. "Lead it over here!"

I spotted the shakiness in his legs from fifty feet away.

"Are you out of your mind?!" I yelled.

"Just get it over here!" Enoch's left fist burst into flame when he raised it. The symbols along his body crackled. "We've got one bloody shot at this!"

"What's your plan?!" I asked.

Enoch shook his head.

If he fails, he's dead. He knows it.

Unless . . .

Enoch looked terrifyingly determined, but not like someone who faced death. I'd looked into the eyes of many men on the brink of it. The fear was always there. And the look on Enoch's face didn't feel like a fear of death so much as what would happen if he kept on *living.*

The Skrill dove straight through the water and came out the other end screaming.

I cracked my neck tiredly. *Well, we're screwed either way. Either die to the Skrill or to the Council.*

Eight eyes narrowing slightly, the Skrill seemed surprised that I'd deliberately launched myself at it but never slowed.

I didn't either.

We met in a clash of black and gold, the beast barreling into me and me digging my flaming claws into its face for one final beatdown. We sped toward Enoch and the box, neither one letting up on our assault. I basked in the violence, forgetting the startled Navigators we flew over. I basked in the onslaught, ripping, tearing, screaming. *Loving* the carnage.

Why couldn't it have just been the Skrill and me out in the fields? Why couldn't we settle our score and decide who was the strongest without the interference—

"MOVE!" Enoch said.

I unhooked myself from the Skrill—almost sadly—and dropped to the floor. The darkness blew toward Enoch with unhinged hunger, and Enoch held up his fist, Ignis spilling out of it. He didn't charge, just remained in place.

Punch it. Come on.

Enoch's outline fuzzed, as though he were a holographic image, but he didn't move.

PUNCH IT!

Then he dropped his fist and threw his arms outward in an embrace.

Enoch disappeared; his body faded into sparks of green light, which flew into the creature, turning the midnight currents a blazing emerald.

I stared in disbelief.

The Skrill's darkness spun in and out of itself. The green fought the red, overtaking each other until one side of the Skrill's body was black and red, and the other was black and green. The Skrill's eyes switched between both colors, screeching up at the ceiling in an attempt to overthrow whatever had taken control of its body, and when it looked back down at the floor, I saw a contorted face screaming within it. I saw Enoch screaming inside.

Possession. That was his Ignis ability.

And he'd just possessed a Skrill.

"Help him, Scarfy!" Prince shrieked from the other side of the writhing mound. "Get him out of there!"

"How do you expect me to do that, Junior?!" I asked, panic rising in my voice as I watched the Skrill—Enoch—spasm between forms. "I can't—"

"Lords, children," a gravelly voice emerged from the second-floor balconies. "We leave you alone for an hour . . ."

I jerked my head upward, but the figure that the voice belonged to had already leapt from the balcony. The burning sword in their hands carved downward in a wicked arc, forcing me to throw up my arms or be blinded.

At first, I thought the figure was attacking us, but a human siding with a Skrill was odd, especially when that human wasn't a Jackal.

Especially when that human wielded the Sword of the Leviathan.

Regardless of the light scorching my face, my eyes snapped open.

The Sword split the roiling darkness in two. Red and green were separated; the hurricane of black and red returned to the imprisonment box, and the green exploded outward in a shower of sparks, spiraling in place until it formed back into Enoch, shivering in his underwear. Using the tip of the Sword, the figure snapped the lid of the box closed and kicked it away with a dress shoe.

Enoch knelt on the wet floor, chest rising and falling with the panic of one who'd stood on the precipice of death, or perhaps a fate worse than that. His entire body twitched.

Slowly, he lifted his gaze. First, at me with horror-stricken eyes that annoyingly tugged at my heartstrings, then at the newcomer who had saved him.

When he saw what the figure held, he stood at once, fear and pain replaced with venerated disbelief.

"What in the hell," Kaleo asked, "are you damned trainees doing out at this hour?"

CHAPTER 12

Prince

Having seen Enoch jump inside a giant spider then get stuck in it, I figured I'd now seen the strangest things that Archengard had to offer me. And depressingly, I thought I'd lost another person that I'd grown close to. After mere hours this time.

A minute later, Kaleo had freed him with the Sword of the Leviathan.

Nuh-uh. I shook my head until I saw stars. *Nope.*

Murta just stared at Kaleo, his tan face taking on a ghostly tint.

"I thought Barco was understood when he said you four were to be resting back in your quarters," Kaleo said, sheathing the Sword like it disgusted him. The white light that illuminated the whole hall was snuffed out. "If not gone from this place."

"You're *him* . . ." Enoch said at a ragged whisper before rising to an exclamatory shout. "You're HIM?"

Glaring, Kaleo unhooked the sheath from his belt and pitched the Sword across the hall. I watched it clatter with alarm.

"Haven't a clue what you're on about. You're delusional. Now would you put some bloody clothes on?"

"'Only the Leviathan may wield the White Flame,'" Enoch recited, still very much in his underwear. "*Only* the Leviathan— And you look just like him! Lords, I don't know how I didn't see it!"

"You know exactly how. Because I'm not him. Just a tired old Nav that needs to be getting his much-needed sleep, as should the rest of you dung-filled buggers. Why in the Lords are you still here anyway? I thought I told you—"

But Enoch and I were long gone. Enoch, who'd clearly idolized the Leviathan since his youth, tried to ask a hundred different questions while staggering back into his pants, and I, who fondly remembered Father's stories, asked just as many.

"Did you ever find the Sacred Heart?" Enoch said.

"Do you remember fighting beside Dante Larocque?" I asked.

"How many monsters have you slain with the Sword?"

"I—" Kaleo tried.

"What was Mathias like?"

"How did—"

"I AM NOT THE LEVIATHAN!"

Kaleo's deafening roar made the Skrill's screams feeble in comparison.

I clamped my mouth shut. Enoch looked sick to his stomach as he slipped back into his jacket. Everyone stood in silence, afraid to move in case we caught fire. We looked to be in what Father would've called "deep, dark shit."

Kaleo stalked up to one of the ruined stained-glass windows, examining its shattered frame with a mixture of colossal fury and anguish. He stared at it for several silent seconds before muttering, "Not anymore."

Without warning, he spun in his boots and strode toward us so quickly that I almost screamed—because the freaking Leviathan looked like he was about to wear my skin as a coat—but then he stopped mere feet in front of us.

His black-pit pupils and the amethyst irises that ringed them passed over Jezna, making her visibly shiver; went to me, who met them with a measly glare despite nearly crumbling under it; carried on to Murta, staring at the ground; then ended on Enoch, who clutched the sides of his jacket with white knuckles.

Kaleo glanced between us for a decade or two before turning to the rest of the hall, still scattered with Navigators.

"I want everyone except these shite-brained trainees back to their quarters immediately. Level-four Navs, too. Don't give me that look, bugger. If I see a single one of you crab-kissin' bastards peeping about within the next five seconds, I swear to the bloody Lords and their draconic children, I'll take the Sword to every last one of your miserable carcasses—"

By the time he reached "crab-kissing," everyone—even the three Navigators who had dropped the imprisonment box—had fled.

We were alone with the Leviathan.

He turned back to us stiffly, and I chewed my lip in preparation for the scolding of a lifetime . . . but then his shoulders slumped.

"Now that we have some privacy . . ." He massaged the hand that had gripped the Sword. "I wanted to tell you that I didn't just arrive here. In fact, I've been watching since before Loc, Maddox, and Cowlin dropped the imprisonment box. I, er, might've followed you from the Rookies Tower."

Never mind how he'd snuck up on us. I was pissed now. "But the Skrill almost—"

"The Skrill wouldn't have done shite. We're Navigators, not them Governmental fools. Navs know how to take care of one another. I should've intervened sooner, but I needed to be certain."

He gestured around at the ruined hall. "This isn't something that's happened just this once, you know. Monsters escape and start roaming about the manor every other day. Back before the War, Champ and I used to challenge waricorns for fun . . ." He chuckled miserably.

Then the misery trickled away, leaving him melancholic.

"But no trainees have ever lasted as long as the four of you did against a Skrill," he said. "A tired, old, and still very sleepy Skrill, but a Skrill nonetheless. And for that, I suppose I have to commend you."

Kaleo eased himself down onto the overturned column with a wince, the joints in his knees cracking. "You four have never met one another until the throne room, aye? That's mental. That's what it is. Downright mental."

"What do you mean?" Jezna said.

"Lords, knight! Need I spell it out? It means I gave you too hard a time." He shook his head in bewilderment. "Heh. First time against a bloody Skrill . . . Maybe you will find a High Nav to train you after all."

"Can you?" Enoch said.

All heads spun toward him. I could only gape.

Kaleo looked back at the broken window in horror. He seemed so different from the man in the throne room. Not angry and decrepit—merely tired and torn. "I cannot. My teaching days are . . ."

But as he drifted off, his eyes drifted over to where Murta stood.

A silent conversation occurred between them. One that spoke volumes without words.

Murta had been a Navigator once. Or at least gotten close. I was sure of that now. Had Kaleo been at fault for his removal and failure? That'd explain Murta's hatred of the Council. That'd explain a lot of things about the way he acted.

Ten seconds into their "conversation," Kaleo broke off and settled his gaze on Enoch. And this time, there wasn't any tiredness or remorse in him.

There was hope.

"One month," he said. "I'll guide you through the Trials for one month. I'll teach you how to be a real squad. And after that, I'm really going to retire."

Enoch swayed in place. I could tell that it took every inch of his being to keep from screaming. I already felt the whoops welling deep in my throat, threatening to turn into Father's bombastic war cries.

"Now scurry back to your dorm. Barco expects you in Training Hall B by noon tomorrow, right? Belay that. I want you in the hangar by eight a.m. You heard me. Stop moping. I can see you doing it internally. No cries, no lies, no alibis."

Holy shit, he said the thing.

"Sir, yes, sir, Lord Leviathan, sir," I said, my mind heading in the direction of the Rookies Tower, but my feet staying firmly stuck to the floor beneath me. "Absolutely. You have a good night. Thank—"

Kaleo extended an arm. A column of white fire rocketed into the air from across the hall, sending a glowing object spinning back into his open palm. The light—a glittering crystal hilt—spun, and when Kaleo caught it, glimpses of the heavens slid out from where the Sword had almost slipped out of its sheath.

No one moved. No one did anything except watch Kaleo stare down at the weapon that had forever cemented his name in history . . .

"That's an order, trainees," he snapped, sending me scampering, Enoch hot on my heels. We bid him farewell several more times, then raced up the stairs.

Once we stood in the dark glow of the upper hall's candlelight, now completely empty of Navigators, Enoch and I seized each other by the shoulders.

"Did that . . . ?"

"DID IT?!"

I staggered dizzily. "Kaleo's the Leviathan? And he wants to train *us*?"

"I did have my suspicions at first," Jezna said. "It was awfully hard to miss the similarities. Light Isles accent, blond hair, purple eyes . . ."

"He's got the Leviathan's eyes, but his attitude sure isn't," I said. "That ain't the guy that went around preaching '*Fortuna Favet Fortibus.*' What do you think? Noc?"

When I glanced over, he was occupied with watching a dark shape slink through the columns across the corridor, then disappear down another hall.

"Another Skrill?" I asked.

Enoch shook his head. "Murta."

I spun. He was right. Where the Shadarian should've stood lay open air.

He'd ditched us for a freaking storage room again.

"Moving on." I clapped my hands together happily. "Who remembers how to get back up to the tower? 'Cause I couldn't to save my life."

CHAPTER 13

Enoch

The darkness dug its pinchers into me. They dug out my eyes, pushing smoke into my skull. Tendrils pried open my rib cage, ripping the skin clean off the bone. Eight crimson eyes leered over me before becoming one with me. They belched the infernal sounds they'd made while I was trapped inside, then re-formed into . . .

Gold eyes and black claws.

"*Connect with this*," they said.

Murta stood on my arms so I was pinned, and reached down through splintered ribs and the mess of tissue to grab my heart with those demented claws. I writhed beneath him, pleading. I grasped for Ignis, for any hope of connection.

And when Murta squeezed my heart and his claws caught fire—

I shot up out of bed and hit my head on the slanted ceiling.

Ow.

Vision blurred, I sat up slower this time, gave the wall the finger, and clutched my pillow until the blurriness passed. But the nightmares didn't.

I studied my shaking, sweaty hands and tried not to think about the time I'd looked down at them and seen eight legs. I ran twitching fingers through my messy hair, remembering when I was nothing but black smoke.

Punch 'em away, I ordered my mind, forcing my legs out of bed. *Think immortal. Box those bad dreams back to bed. You're training with the Leviathan today. You're—*

I froze mid-stride toward the dresser.

I'm training with the Leviathan today.

And the darkness fled me.

Skrill and the like could eff off. I wasn't a walking corpse like I'd been in Serapharus, the black city I'd spent all of my childhood in. Fear no longer meant a thing to me.

Here, I'd be trained by the best of the best—the Navigator I idolized. With the Leviathan as a mentor, I could've just been guaranteed eight epic quests or a seat on the Council or . . .

Or things could go horribly wrong. Just like last night. You could be just as mental as Murta says you are.

I stared at the vacant bed that was supposed to be his.

Last night, Prince had been the only one to blatantly refuse sleeping with him, but from the way Jezna shuffled whenever she was put in an uncomfortable situation, I'd "happily" accepted Murta as my roommate. For now.

How could I explain to him that I'd only lightly possessed them during the fight with the Skrill? How did I tell him that I'd accidentally persuaded him to act?

How do I explain my Ignis ability to anyone?

A thunderous rap at the door jump-started me to get changed. I slipped back into my jacket.

"Noc!" Prince said from the other side. "It's seven a.m., bro! Let's get breakfast before the Trials!"

"On the move," I said, snatching my bandana off the door handle.

Prince grimaced when I stepped out onto the staircase. "Whoa. You look like you were run over by—"

Jezna elbowed him in the ribs.

"How was your rest, Enoch?" she asked calmly.

I gestured for us to head down. "Suppose I've had better."

"Murta's still missing?"

"He never came back up."

"We're about to start the Trials and Scarfy thinks he can go sauntering off?" Prince said. "That's got Shadarian written all over it."

"No," Jezna said as we descended the spiral staircase. "That has *Murta* written all over it."

"Who happens to be a Shadarian."

"I don't like them as much as you do, but that doesn't mean that they're all evil."

I shook my head to clear away the images of my blood dripping from black claws holding my pulsing heart . . .

Prince gestured around at the passing Navigators wildly. "If Shadarians were on these stairs with us right now, they'd kill everyone here. You wanna know why? A) We're too modern. B) We're wearing modern clothes. C) We're in CARBONEK. And D) EVERYONE HERE'S A FREAKING IGNIS USER EXCEPT ME!"

Everyone on the stairs paused at practically the same moment and watched us with confused expressions. Two blokes in black suits and blue ties that looked my age even tried to trip Prince.

"Pink glasses," one of them said. "Nice."

"THEY'RE MAGENTA," Prince roared.

Carbonek was under construction when we returned to the hall we'd turned into a war zone. Navigators with levitation-based Ignis abilities were surveying the movement of debris to the front entrance. I saw the column we'd hid behind already in-flight, five glowing Navigators positioned beneath it. Those with construction-based abilities had also already begun rebuilding. Goggles fixed to their faces, they bent over long tables, pounding away with their fiery Ignis. I saw one bloke with a literal orange blacksmithing hammer as his Ignis ability. He had a great blond beard to go with it.

Some of the tension I'd felt from before fled me. Kaleo hadn't been lying when he'd said that multiple creatures had escaped in Carbonek. From the way the Navigators efficiently worked, it was clear that the manor had taken a lot of damage in its lifetime. Our destination was no exemption.

The dining abbey was stored away on the left side of Carbonek and occupied a vast chamber that had clearly once been a training room. Nicks covered the wall and the wooden floor was littered with white scrapes, but it excited me more than any room before it. The stories that surrounded the Brotherhood could fill up the Grand Sea, but much of it was stored in paintings and books. Here, I could actually see the changing of the times and how the Brotherhood had changed with them.

The scars in the floor weren't ghastly; they were the markings of a Navigator's growth. The splinters of wood weren't displays of old age and messiness, but history and hard work. The dining abbey's disorganization—the long oak tables shoved into the tight hall swarming with people—represented the very best of the Brotherhood: its ability to remain. To take dents and overcome.

Jezna hesitated in the archway. "It's very . . . different."

"It's brilliant," I said.

"As long as the grub's good." Prince eyed the stone windows that allowed the cooks to slip plates in and out of the kitchen. "Father said they get half of it from the Light Isles. Love me some crab."

As he shot off to try cutting into the line, Jezna and I found seats at the vacant end of what was clearly the rookies' table. Those sitting toward the front looked younger and hulloed when Jezna and I took our seats. Most of their eyes hovered on Jezna's armor, but everyone stuck to their groups. The experienced Navigators toward the back mingled the most. There seemed to be a definite pecking order.

I chewed my lip, pondering how long it'd take to be accepted into that crowd and climb the ladder toward the back of the abbey, then began to chew harder when I noticed a number of squads looking at me.

Though they'd seemed lively at first, that had clearly been a mask. At Jezna's and my arrival, many of those masks had slipped, revealing uncertainty. I noticed bumps and bruises along some of their faces. Quite a few looked familiar from last night.

So the Skrill *had* taken a toll on them. Kaleo said Carbonek had been through a lot worse, but how many more dents could Carbonek take before it crumbled?

I kept my head low and away from the wary stares. Who knew how many had seen what I'd done to the Skrill. Who knew how many were preparing to scorn me, like the Olders had done on a daily basis back in Serapharus . . .

"Are they looking at us?" Jezna whispered beside me.

"Afraid not," someone said. "That would . . . er, probably be at us."

I looked up into the faces of the three male Navigators that had dropped the imprisonment box—the short boy, the muscular bloke, and the handsome red-haired lad. Each interested me, but the red-haired lad—the one who had spoken—snatched my attention the most. He wore his hoodie from before, but now, a glittering blue crystal hung from a thin black cord around his neck, and the way both he and it eyed me felt like a challenge just as much as an invitation of friendship.

He winced. "Mind if we join?"

"If you agree to fight me later," I said.

He eased into the seat across from me, eyes flicking about the dining abbey with caution. "First day in Carbonek and already picking fights with rookies?"

"Figured you owed me one after we took care of your dirty work last night."

"Yeah. Thanks for that . . ." He sighed. "Bloody useless, I was."

I tried to cheer him up. "Oi, I know a fellow swash when I hear one, bruv. You from the Light Isles?"

"Aye. Bounced around. Born somewhere around Fireroot, if you can believe it."

I whistled. "Myself, I set up shop around Agquei City." I flashed the Light Isles Combat Club patch sewn into the shoulder of my jacket. "I boxed for the Club."

His eyes lit up. "So that's why you did so well against the Skrill. Didn't see much, but the little I did was bloody impressive."

I rubbed the back of my neck. So he hadn't seen me possess the Skrill. Or else he'd have never asked to sit down.

"How'd you know it was our first day?" I asked to take my mind off things.

"Missing some squadmates, you are," the short boy said. "Figured since there's just two of you. And you're sitting awkwardly. Don't worry, we're still working things out, too. Only just got confirmed three months ago." He poked Jezna's armor, making her recoil with a curse. "Sorry. Never seen a real knight before. Had to make sure you're real, I did." He giggled.

"Confirmed?" I asked.

"The moment a trainee becomes a real Navigator," the red-haired Navigator said. "A rookie. After you pass the Trials, your squad gets to swear on the Code. Once that happens, you're confirmed and allowed to start questing for real. That's when you really get going."

"And you're confirmed?"

"Right-o. Locken Aldradeas." He extended a fist. "Just call me Loc."

"Enoch Amon." I returned the fist-bump. "Just call me Noc. The knight's Jezna Caelius. And our other mate . . ." I swiveled toward the buffet, trying to peer over heads. "Is fetching food, I think."

"Nononono, trainees don't eat yet! All the level-four Navs are up there right now! Lords, if they find out he's a trainee, they'll eat him alive."

"We'll definitely hear him if that happens."

"Level four," Jezna said. "Those would be the highest-ranked squads."

Loc nodded. "Everyone on this half of the hall is level one. You gotta go on at least three quests before you start moving toward the back. Meaning, we're stuck here until Kaleo can make up his mind what to do with us. And after last night, it'll be *eons.* Lords, we deserve to go straight back to the Trials. 'Ass is gonna kill us when he gets back."

"You lot have worked with Kaleo, too?" I asked.

"More like met him," the short boy said. "He's a cranky one. Bloody hates our squad, he does. Thinks we don't do enough." He shrugged. "He's right."

"And your squad is . . . ?"

The short boy crossed his arms, attempting to go back to back with Loc, but the other Navigator just hung his head.

"Navigational Squadron 326," Loc said depressingly. "Biassis, Larry, Loc, Maddox, and Cowlin."

"Biassis Ondenecro?" I asked. Talk of him was all over the Light Isles.

"*And* Lariat Tollo," the short boy said. "Can't forget him or he'll flip his lid faster than a teapot-goblin. I'm Cowlin Kayvindren. Unlike Larry, I don't care if you call me Cow." He slapped the tall bloke on the shoulder. "And this cathedral buttress is Maddox Gorza."

"Larry's a dick," Maddox said in a voice that might've echoed out of a mountain.

"Larry is indeed a dick," Loc said. "But he balances us out."

"The scale breaks every time."

"Cowlin and I are twenty, but 'Ass, Larry, and Mads are all twenty-one," Loc told me. "We're a little young to be grouped with some of the more experienced squads, but a Navs gotta shoot for the stars, aye? We ain't the smoothest squad, but we have a good time. So that's us. What about you?"

I was having too much fun watching the trio converse that when Loc turned to me, I froze. "We . . . don't really know what we're doing yet." *Definitely not having a good time.* "Barco made us a squad, but we don't even really know each other. We train with Kaleo in about—"

Loc almost fell out of his chair. "So when he made everyone leave . . . it was so he could *recruit* you?!"

I nodded silently.

"That's mental! Kaleo hasn't trained a squad since ever. Wow, he must've *really* taken a liking to you lot. I mean, you deserve it after saving our arses, but Kaleo doesn't like anyone. He's been trying to get Barco to take his place as Grand High Navigator for years, ever since Mathias died during the War."

That means Kaleo's the leader of the whole Brotherhood, I realized. *Of course he is. Only the Leviathan could be.*

"If that's the case," Cowlin said, "then you're bound to pass the Trials in weeks. And get some great quests. Hektor trained us and he's cool and all, but he ain't the Leviathan. No one here is."

"Quests," I said, heart warming. *That's right. That's why you're here. Not to worry about if you're not good enough. Before you know it, you'll be out there protecting people, too.* "You've gotta have been on loads of 'em already."

Maddox's scowl deepened the closer I came to asking the question, whereas Cowlin's grin only broadened.

"Oh, sure," Cowlin said. "Our first, we were sent out to wrangle a skydrake that was stealing roofs from a town a few miles south of Licht City. We all ended up in an outhouse at one point—don't you dare ask why—when the skydrake came by. Decided it wanted to make the thing part of its hoard up on a mountain, it did. So off we flew. Rather traumatic experience for Larry, Loc, and Brother, but 'Ass and I had the time of our lives."

Loc shivered. "I'm a scallywag through and through, but only up until we start flying. After that, I'll see myself out. I value the ground beneath my feet."

Maddox coughed.

"Oh. I guess we escaped and fought the dragon, too." Loc smiled slyly.

"You turned right around and *fought* it?" I asked.

"It was mostly 'Ass and Brother." Cowlin smiled up at Maddox, who continued to glare at everything other than the boy at his side.

"And the Skrill? How'd you wrangle that?"

All the energy that had been bubbling between the three boys snapped out of existence. I felt terrible the moment I asked, but it was clear from the way Loc's face set that I was going to get an answer whether I wanted it anymore or not.

"Biassis and Larry had been off hunting a powerful artifact for at least a week prior," he began quietly, "so Barco put us three on food duty. All rookies cycle through it. Someone's gotta get the food for the dining abbey somehow. They grow all the herbs and vegetables in the hanging gardens on the fourth floor, but all meat's traded with neighboring villages. We drove one of the Brotherhood's vehicles to Kanbrik, the city that Carbonek gets all its chickens from . . ."

Loc's handsome features wrenched.

"But Kanbrik was in ruins. We had no idea how it happened. People were scattered everywhere, and there was a terrible humming that echoed around us. Almost drove me mad. Wanted to rip my ears off . . . We traced the humming to an abandoned barn a few paces across the battlefield." He inhaled. "And inside, we found that bloody box."

I let his story roll through me, then said, "It's from the War."

"Impossible," Jezna said. "No mortal could keep such a creature under control in battle. Not even Nodan Ignis hunters. That would take Ignis and power *far* beyond—"

"We couldn't tell if the Skrill was used in the battle." Though Loc was in Carbonek, he looked around uneasily. "But from the cargo stacked along with it, it *definitely* looked like it was being transported across the Grand Sea back over to the Noda."

"We didn't dig too deep into answers," Cowlin said. "Honestly, I didn't even want to bring it back with us. Sorta knew if we had to drag it all the way back that something was gonna happen, I did. Barco told us this morning that we should've just left it and called ahead anyway . . . but leaving it seemed so much worse. We drove to just outside Carbonek, but break down, the turner did. Something about the random pulses that the box kept letting out. So we'd been carrying it for a mile before we, uh, dropped it."

Maddox shrugged. "We beat it."

"With help from these blokes." Some life finally settled back into Loc's face. "Without 'em, our arses would be on the first crab cruiser out of here."

"It's called the Brotherhood, right?" I asked. "A Nav's gotta help another Nav out. And you lot were doing a hell of a better job than we were." I looked at Maddox. "What even was that Ignis ability? Some type of armor?"

Maddox just stared.

Cowlin laughed. "Doesn't say much, Brother does. He's a bit shy." Maddox walloped him in the head in response. Cowlin popped back up with a wince. "Heh. A real powerhouse, though."

"Sounds familiar to us," I said. "Our other, er, mate has got a crazy powerful Ignis ability. He did most of the fighting against the Skrill."

Loc's face surprisingly darkened again. "Murta."

My stomach flipped, suddenly recalling the way Murta and Maddox had grappled with one another. "Mayhaps?" I winced.

"Don't feel bad," Loc said. "Not your fault Barco shoved him into your squad. Biassis recruited him again anyway—rather stupidly—but he shadowed our squad a few years back.

"At one point, he was one of the best recruits ever. A prodigy. He was literally days away from being confirmed."

"What happened, then?" Jezna said. "We haven't received a straightforward answer."

"There's . . ." Loc drifted off after he and Cowlin looked at one another. "A lot of reasons. First—and I know this sounds a little prejudiced—he's a Shadarian. According to the Chronicler, he's the only Shadarian to have ever joined the Brotherhood. I think everyone's always been a little unsettled by that alone, especially since they, you know, *kill* Navigators for sport. But the main reason is what he did during his last few weeks here." He eyed Maddox. "You wanna take the reins?"

"Good riddance," was all Maddox said.

Cowlin smacked him across the chest playfully. "Go back to being a brick wall."

"I like bricks," said Maddox. "Fun to throw."

"It has something to do with his Ignis ability, right?" Jezna said.

"He can't control it," Loc said. "He disappears completely and . . . the Other takes over."

I tried to calm the nervous turning in my stomach but failed spectacularly at the way everyone at the table shivered.

Loc stared at the tabletop. "He's hurt a lot of people with that Ignis ability. If Barco hadn't stopped him, I honestly don't know if Mads and thirty other Navs would be here."

Suddenly, the way Maddox had thrown himself at Murta made perfect sense.

Maddox glowered at me. "Good riddance."

"But he's back now!" Cowlin said. "And he's got Noc and Jezebel to help him out, he does."

"Jezna," Jezna coughed.

Cowlin shrugged. "And who knows, maybe the merc life humbled him. If Biassis brought him back, he's probably changed."

I thought about Murta's duel with the Skrill. The claws, flames, and devastating kicks. It was mind-blowing that he'd said his ability was Transformative, not Conflicted. Barco had been right. Murta *was* the fiercest fighter I'd ever seen.

"He seemed to be in control from what I saw," I said. "I didn't see this Other—"

Maddox, who'd been glaring about the dining abbey again, suddenly tensed. "Black claws," he said. "Black soul." His eyes narrowed. *"Gold breath."*

I looked past him to see what he'd been staring at and froze. Within the shadows of one of the rounded archways that made up the right wall of the abbey, Murta leaned against a column, arms crossed. He tapped his wrist angrily.

"Bloody hell." I glanced up at the clock face on the wall that read 7:50 a.m. "Jezna, we gotta go. Fetch Prince." I nodded at the three rookies. "Sorry, lads. Let's hang out again sometime. Maybe throw some fists in a friendly fashion."

"Love to," Loc said, but he wasn't smiling anymore.

I shot off across the hall.

"Apologies," I said when I was next to Murta. "I forgot—"

"We're due in the hangar." He spun back the way he'd come. "Let's get this over with."

CHAPTER 14

Murta

Kaleo steered us down the twists in the tunnel, scarred hands exchanging positions. There was a ferocity to his movements. Both ship and High Navigator seemed strung together, movements executed as one. They seemed familiar with one another.

We sailed down the cavernous rapids with such speed that more than once, I felt my hands tighten around the metal rail in front of me, wondering when the lurching of the deck beneath my feet would end. The ship's hull scraped against the metal, making me tense, then the light threw itself into us and the Grand Sea was everywhere.

I didn't pay attention to the inhale of delight that escaped Enoch or how seeing Kaleo among the endless blue was like being transported back in time to when the world still admired Navigators. A Shadarian didn't care about things like that. He kept his focus forward, his destination the only set path.

Rather than gape stupidly around at the sea, like Prince, I glared behind us up at Carbonek.

This is a waste of time. I won't find a Talisman out here.

When the humming of the core below deck began to dwindle away, the ship slowing to a drift, Kaleo finally spoke up. "Figured we'd spend the first day of the Trials out here. You get good experience, I get to ride the waves again . . ." He paused. "In fact, this is the exact spot Cahis Cor took my squad out to on our first day."

Enoch, who stood at Kaleo's side, looked up at him. Whatever light had been sucked out of him during his possession of the Skrill seemed replenished tenfold.

"Cahis Cor," he said. "He trained more than half of the Brotherhood at one point, right?"

"That he did." Kaleo adjusted the wheel to the left. "Barco, Champ, Mathias, and I among those. A mighty fine trainer, he was. Cahis backed us at every turn, even at his own expense. He never stopped believing in the Code. Fought like a firedrake, but was a masterful negotiator. He had Ignis beyond a Nav's dreams, but he knew when to use it and when to shake hands. Whereas most High Navs preferred to operate from within Carbonek, Cahis was always striking out, checking on the most mundane of things, making sure Archengardians were just being good to one another."

Kaleo gestured to the northeast. "One thing he saw as crucial to a Navigator's duty was the establishment of trade routes, especially between the less technologically advanced segments of Archengard. Created at least a hundred of 'em in his lifetime. That's because he was always building bridges of connection.

"This route we're checking on is a simple shipping route between the cities of Nothomathos and Kanbrik. Twin towns on opposite sides of Peniel Valley, the sky garden Carbonek rests within. Like many of the nations within Archengard, they've refused to move with the times. Advanced technology and Aestus is something they shun, not celebrate."

Prince tensed, mumbling something under his breath.

Kaleo failed to notice. "There was a time long ago where no one hated one another more than the Nothomathos Princes and the Kanbrik Elders. Carbonek's an equal distance between 'em and acted as a sort of neutral ground. Both cities staked claims to one another's resources, but Cahis struck up a truce between them by founding this trade route.

"Every fifth day of every month, Nothomathos and Kanbrik send their trade vessels out to greet one another. Every fifth day, I sail out to meet them—just as Cahis did until his death—and every fifth day, the two cities barter goods with one another under the eyes of Carbonek.

"Because *this* is what we should be. Not warriors. Not fighters."

I saw the point of the lesson—who wouldn't with Kaleo waving the damned thing in our faces?—but that didn't mean it was right.

If I had one of the Talismans back then, their "century-long" conflict would've been over a century ago.

"Hang on," Prince said. "Our first official test in the Trials is to . . . ?" He gaped, the enormous backpack, full of every firearm imaginable, making him look even sillier. "To watch people exchange fruit and rugs?!"

"To oversee," Kaleo corrected. "Not all navigating is protecting, young'un. The 'preserving' part of the Code's just as important. Why bother protecting something if it ain't built to survive? Those guns of yours—and this Ignis of mine—might give us arse-kicking advantages, but more conflicts have been solved through sitting arses down and talking than any bullet, blast, or blade."

Kaleo scoured the sea in search of the ships. "And that is what today's Trial is about."

"That's boring," Prince muttered.

"Don't worry, bruv," Enoch said, light restored as quickly as it'd been doused. "I'm sure we'll get to see how those wicked guns work in no time."

A stab of jealousy shot through me, and my irritation only skyrocketed when I felt it. Shadarians didn't feel jealousy. I needed to get control of my emotions. They'd been spiraling out of control since—

Since being corralled with these three idiotas.

Fuming silently at the memory of Enoch and Jezna at the table with Loc, Maddox, and Cowlin, I slid to the back of the ship and leaned up against the iron siding. *Waste of time.*

Prince's hand had already started creeping up toward his bag. "Wanna see a few right now?"

Enoch looked at Kaleo, who shrugged. "We've got some time to kill before reaching the rendezvous point." He squinted into the distance. "And they both seem to be running a little late."

Prince was lightning quick on the draw. A massive gun appeared in his hands, snapped up, and was glowing, cocked, and fired off the side of the ship in the blink of an eye. The only signs that he'd actually fired the weapon were the magenta glow that darkened behind the barrel and the white smoke escaping off of a spot in the sea. I frowned at the feat.

Prince lifted his sunglasses. "How was that?"

Kaleo held out a hand. Prince nervously placed the gun into it.

"Aestus-powered," Kaleo said, letting both hands off the wheel to toss the weapon between them. "Not a speck of Ignis in it." He gazed down the barrel. "But fashioned well. Difficult to use. Even more difficult to upgrade, which you seem to have done consistently . . . Hm. I see Dante's fingerprints all over it."

Prince slid deep into longing. "Father taught me ionsmithing. He had a forge out back. Lots of good memories from that place."

"I suppose his hybridized style is how you craft all your weapons? I see the Government's influence in 'em."

"I use their prototype guns," Prince said defensively. "But mine are safer. They aren't meant to kill. Just stun."

"Stun someone enough times, their heart stops beating. All weapons are weapons for a reason. Just because they're perceived as being in the hands of 'the good' as opposed to 'the bad' doesn't make them any less so. You understand that, trainee?"

Kaleo never glanced in my direction, but his voice carried. The special emphasis he put on the words meant he wasn't just speaking to Prince, but to everyone. Especially me.

The Council doesn't just still distrust me, I realized. *They despise me.*

"I understand," Prince mumbled. "Must be fun having Ignis, huh?"

Kaleo handed the Aestus cannon back. "The same goes for Ignis. Always." Surprisingly, the High Navigator's brow softened. "And never think for a second that those who don't have it aren't as powerful as those who do."

"Right." Prince spat on the deck. "You all can incinerate people with your hands."

"Don't worry, bruv," Enoch said, right there to comfort him. "Ignis's wicked and all, but it's not everything."

Jezna appeared shaken by this assessment. "Then what's it mean to you?"

Enoch was silent for a moment. Clearly, he'd never even thought about it.

"Barco told me when we met that those who are able to harness Ignis have fire etched into their souls." Oddly, his shoulders shuddered at that. "But I've always seen Ignis as freedom. The means to accomplish whatever you desire. Maybe not now, maybe not soon, but someday. By honing your Ignis, you hone yourself."

Jezna didn't respond.

"Aye," Kaleo said. "No truer statement has been spoken. Too many Navs see Ignis as just power, but it isn't." Though he never looked in my direction, his words sliced at me like daggers. "It's the manifestation of your spirit. No two individuals are alike; the same applies to Ignis abilities. You might find similar colors and styles, but nothing directly identical. That individuality should be cherished. And no Ignis ability should ever be deemed useless." He smirked slightly. "I mean, look at mine. Can't do a damned thing without a weapon in hand . . ."

Kaleo's gaze locked on to a dark point in the distance. His fingers fell, scraping briefly against his belt. They lingered longer than they should've, searching for something that wasn't there. My eyes narrowed as they moved from Kaleo's waist, where the Sword had hung last night, to the strange speck across the water. And in the opposite direction, when I tapped into Ignis to strengthen my vision, I saw another speck approaching.

Prince cupped his hands to his eyes. "Those them?"

Kaleo didn't answer. Like Enoch moments before, I saw a similar concern flash across him.

Masts and sails began to appear, their specks growing. Glowing lines in the sides announced them as hyper-ships like ours, not mere fishing vessels. And their cores seemed to be working overtime, pushing them forward at thrice the normal speed.

I began to piece together what was happening. I'd been here before.

Both Nothomathos and Kanbrik weren't advanced cities, like those that made up the Government. Despite residing in Government-controlled territory, they lay on the precipice of being third world. Neither one had any access to the technology that Carbonek possessed, and here they were with hyper-ships powered by Aestus.

Here they were, two opposing factions, speeding toward one another at a rate unnecessary for a mere resource exchange.

"Kaleo," Enoch suddenly said. "What'd you say the names of the cities were again? Nothomathos and . . . What was the other one?"

Jezna raced to the edge of the upper deck, gazing out in the direction of the Kanbrik ship . . . *Ships*, I realized.

"Kanbrik, right?" Prince said. "Why?"

"Kanbrik . . ." Enoch repeated. "Loc said Kanbrik was where he found the imprisonment—" His sentence was cut short by the roar of a cannon.

A cannonball sped away from the Kanbrik ship, trailing sparks in its wake, and sank into the sea a yard away from the Nothomathos ship. Before Kaleo could shatter his silence with a roar, the Nothomathos ship was firing back with twice the number of cannonballs, a hundred feet in front of our bow.

We were in the middle of the Perpetual War.

Kaleo lunged for the great lever next to the wheel, pulling it back until the metal screamed. A dark clanking followed by a sudden splash and the whole ship jerking to a halt announced that he'd dropped the anchor.

Aqua Ignis swarmed around Jezna. "If they found the imprisonment box there, that means—"

"Kanbrik's joined the Noda." Kaleo whipped back the ends of his suit jacket to reveal five knife sheaths.

When he removed one, the curved blade glowed with the same white fire that the Sword was made of. Although his outline began to glow the same color, tendrils of flame seeping off of his shoulders, there was enormous pain in his eyes.

The Trial had been meant to be a display of peace, a reminder that not all conflict was solved with violence, but Archengard had defied him. The War had grown so great that not even the lands surrounding Carbonek were untouched by it. Not even the bridges Cahis Core had built could hold it.

And if Loc and Maddox recovered the imprisonment box from the outskirts of Kanbrik . . . then that means the Jackals are here in Khronera.

I tapped into Ignis, but Kaleo spun on us. "Stay on this ship. We're far enough out not to be struck by anything." His expression nearly splintered. "I'll handle this."

Enoch protested. "But we can—"

"STAY HERE!" Kaleo filled his empty hand with another knife. "The Trials are on hold! I will not have the War waged in Carbonek's backyard!"

I watched as the white aura surrounded him. Kaleo spun the fire knives in his hands before leaping off the deck and sprinting for the bow. White Ignis fled, leaving afterimages of his burning body, and when he reached the bow, he knelt low.

The white afterimages flew back into him, bubbling out from his heart in a multicolored foam, then, as Ignis exploded out of him, he vaulted off the ship. Kaleo sailed the sky in silence for two seconds before falling somewhere among the approaching Kanbrik ship.

Though the air was peppered with the whine of cannonfire, the deck aboard our hyper-ship fell still. No one moved, nor spoke, nor breathed loudly.

I eventually snorted.

Kaleo would take care of things, while we watched. And the Jackals clearly weren't here. A minor skirmish between unadvanced fishing cities hardly constituted as anything worth their time. They remained in the shadows. When they did choose to emerge into the light, it was with assured victory.

Among the Kanbrik hyper-ship, flashes of white light began to spring up, further emphasizing the two-facedness of the Code.

"All weapons are weapons for a reason," huh? Let's see him do this on his own, then.

But before I could saunter belowdecks to possibly catch a brief nap, Enoch strode up to the lever on the right side of the wheel and thrust it forward.

The rattle of a chain announced that the anchor was being raised.

I blew toward him. "WHAT IN THE SUNS—?!"

"The suns?" Enoch had both taped hands wrapped around the wheel, eyes focused on the distant flashes of white Ignis. "They won't do shite but keep burning up in the sky. But down here on Archengard, we've got the ability to move out of our orbits." He began to steer the ship around in the direction of Nothomathos. "'No cries, no lies, no alibis.'"

I didn't grab him like I had in the hall—I had no interest in touching him after seeing what he'd done to the Skrill—but I made damn certain that he knew I was there.

"The person you're trying to be is dead," I said. "And you can't cheat death more than once."

That wasn't necessarily true. I'd cheated death all my life, yet this blond boy—this insane swashbuckler from the drunken Light Isles—looked back at me with the abandonment of one who'd faced it as many times as I had.

"Watch me."

"What do you think you'll do when we ram into Nothomathos?!" I shouted. "Take on their entire crew?"

"He's right." Jezna appeared at Enoch's other side. "They'll pump us full of cannonballs by the time we come within reach of boarding them."

"Boarding?" Prince said. "You think four schmucks can take on a whole crew? Never mind that we'd be directly in the line of fire of a Nodan ship! They've got these crazy Aestus lasers that go haywire—"

"Three 'schmucks' and one Shadarian, puto," I said. "I could tear their ship in two in my sleep. And how do *you* know so much about Nodan weaponry?"

Prince's face paled. "What? I don't—"

A cannonball shot from the Nothomathos ship slammed into the water ten feet off the port side. Enoch immediately pulled us into a hard right, spinning the wheel until it struck the metal and bounced back. The deck swayed beneath us, sending Prince rolling. I dug my feet into the floor and stood my ground.

The two hyper-ships were within range now, less than a mile between one another. I didn't understand Enoch or Kaleo's logic. Why try to keep them from fighting? This wasn't the battle that dictated the course of the War. The real enemies were the Jackals, not Kanbrik Elders and Nothomathos Princes.

More cannonfire erupted, some angled directly at us. Luckily, our hyper-ship moved faster than Enoch's flow of logic, but insanely, it began to swing around the front of the ship, setting us directly in both lines of fire.

"Enoch—" Jezna started.

"Man the cannons, Prince!" Enoch said.

Prince looked at the cannonless deck, then down at the weapon in his hand.

"Aye-aye, dude!" he said, and after switching on the core, began to fire blasts of Aestus in the direction of the Nothomathos ship. I saw half of the figures hurrying about the deck leap out of the way from the Aestus now pelting their decks. The other half grabbed the weapons nearest to them—humongous broadswords.

"READY FOR BOARDING!" Enoch said, his right hand searching for the lever while his left hand steered us up against the ship.

I could hear the clanging of metal, smell the black powdery scents of Aestus and steel, and before I could shove the idiota off of the deck, he'd thrown down the lever again, plunging the anchor back into the Grand Sea.

Our hull being peppered with cannonfire from all directions, we were now left with no choice but to abandon ship . . . onto the enemy ship.

Stretching my legs twice in less than twelve hours? I readjusted my scarf before sending Ignis surging down into my legs. *Maybe coming back was worth it.*

CHAPTER 15

Jezna

Left with no other option but to fight, I prepared to step onto the enemy ship. Then I saw them.

Two Nothomathos Princes charged at me, their broadswords held in ferocious hanging guard stances. Yet their weapons might as well have been invisible. All I saw was their armor: massive, majestic hulks of iron covering their bodies from head to toe. Each of their faces masked by a gleaming silver helmet.

Not Princes, I realized. *Knights.*

More specifically, judging by the yellow N against a crimson field pinned to their chests, remnants of the once-mighty Nothom Order. Now, clearly reduced to fallen fishermen.

Though I'd tapped into Ignis, no Ignis emerged from my body. Instead, I was hit full force by one of their swords, and went crashing back down onto the deck. Through the world blurring and spinning around me, I saw the knight examine his now-crudely bent blade then attempt to bend it back into place.

"God armor," I heard his companion say, then take a humongous swipe at my leg. This did nothing as well, though it did send a spike of pain ringing through me. "Where did you come across such a substance, traitor?"

I fought to reach my feet, my mind slipping and sliding. "Traitor . . . ?" I barely mustered before a gauntleted fist collided with my helmet. It didn't dent at all. Instead, I stumbled backward, nearly crushing the steering wheel as I briefly leaned against it.

"Answer the question," the first knight said. Blasts of magenta Aestus and flashes of green erupted over his shoulder, but I felt no flashes of sympathy for their wielders. Right now, none of that mattered. Squads and Navigators-in-training weren't important.

Observe with purpose. "I'm a knight, just like you," I said, my voice sounding meek and childish. "We shouldn't be fighting with one another—"

"You came with the Navigators," the second knight bellowed, raking his sword against the side of the ship. Bits of wood and metal flew. Another cannonball, fired from the Kanbrik ship, exploded into the hull, shaking the deck. I went down on a knee again.

"You joined the Brotherhood," the knight stated.

"I haven't," I protested. "Never. I don't keep to their Code. I will always be a knight first. I . . . I'm the last of the Tolkkyan Order. My duty is to my Brothers. To Archengard."

The second knight stayed his swing, keeping his blade fixed to the sky. He inclined his head, helmet creaking noisily. "You swear upon the Chivalric Code?"

"I do."

The blade lowered. "Then help us." He took a slow step forward, as though reaching out for me. "Our land is under attack by Kanbrik, and Carbonek seeks to aid in their cause by keeping us from fighting. We are all alone. As knights always have been."

My head swam. My mind drifted. My heart twinged. All things I no longer possessed, but somehow still felt, pulsing inside me. I tried to speak. "I—"

"Help us heal the world," the first knight said. "Help us exterminate these Navigator fools and reinstate the Orders. The world will only heal if knights reign once more. The—"

There was a streak of black behind the knight, then a foot engulfed in golden flames collided with his chestplate, sending him flying off the ship into the Grand Sea.

Before his companion even realized what happened, he was flying in the opposite direction, propelled by the same flames.

I watched in astonishment, peering through the black smoke that slowly cleared to unveil a black-suited boy with gold eyes. He stood over me, his shadow somehow longer than the hyper-ship mast.

"Whose side are you on?" Then he stormed back over onto the Nothomathos ship.

I didn't stand for a long time. Just watched through my visor as the Shadarian carved through the knights, beating them senseless with flaming kicks and claw rakes. Armor and swords didn't stand a chance against someone—*something*—like him. They couldn't even take down the swashbuckler, who ducked and weaved around their sword strikes, knocking them back with a left fist surrounded by a crackling, messy green flame.

The knights were losing.

This isn't right. I stood. *It shouldn't be like this. The world can't change into . . . this.* All of me seemed to sway. Or maybe those were the steadily crumbling remains of the ship whose deck I remained rooted to.

The Chivalric Orders had once been Archengard's only protectors. Before the Brotherhood, before the War. Before the founding of the Archengardian Government and the formation of this new, mechanical world of Aestus.

But then Ignis was bestowed upon man, and suddenly, a new breed of protector was born. Adam Evenstar—nineteen years old at the time—befriended a brash knight named Talen Vento, then met a kind warrioress named Rebecca Newblood. And together, they'd created the Navigational Brotherhood.

Though the Orders had begun to adopt Ignis users into their ranks, it hadn't been enough. They'd splintered into factions. Broken themselves into bits and pieces before practically becoming extinct, kept alive only through knights like Macín.

Knights like the Nothom Order.

Truth be told, the Orders were dead. And those who had survived long after the Brotherhood took their place—those like the Tolkkis and the Nothoms—had all disintegrated.

The Tolkkis lived on in a cursed knight who had joined the Brotherhood out of guilt, while the Nothoms lived on in the heralded "Princes" who were beaten back by mere Navigational trainees.

Look what's become of us. The world changed. Too fast.

CHAPTER 16

Murta

I turned away from Jezna and kicked a sword out of an incoming knight's hand all in one motion. *Sloppy. Slow.* These weren't the skilled warriors that my Shadarian clan had trained me to take down with nothing but my own physicality and wit. A single Ignis-infused kick did the work of twenty moves. These "knights" were nothing but men in armor. Princes playing at being something worthy of engaging in combat.

Streaking across the deck, kicking knights into incapacitation, I felt myself rub shoulders with a boxing jacket more than once. As soon as I caught a glimpse of blond hair, it was gone in a flutter of green fire.

My judgment had been off. I'd left my battle with the Skrill thinking Jezna to be the most useful of this . . . group. Now, I wasn't so sure.

Annoyingly, having the Brotherhood's ship positioned in the center of the crossfire prevented many of Kanbrik's cannonballs from reaching the Nothomathos vessel. Enoch's plan, though something I'd originally interpreted as senile, had actually been . . . clever?

Ridiculous. Swashbucklers are stupid, not clever.

In the process of dodging a messy sword strike, a beam of magenta Aestus nearly took my head off, forcing me to dodge from the direction I was already dodging in.

Speaking of stupid, I thought, before coming face-to-face with Dante Larocque, Jr. Out of spite, I contemplated snapping those obnoxious sunglasses in half. Instead, I just shouted.

"Watch where you point that damned thing."

"How am I supposed to know where your face is gonna end up?" Prince said. "Recalculate your angle of trajectory better next time."

"I'll recalculate my angle of trajectory up your—"

A cannonball rocked the Nothomathos ship. We all swayed for a thunderous moment, with multiple pieces of debris and even a few knights spilling off the sides into the sea, then the ship righted itself, revealing the smoking Kanbrik ship in the distance.

So the cannonballs had finally gotten through the Brotherhood's ship positioned in front of us—Enoch's anchored wall. But judging from the angle that

Kanbrik had hit the Nothomathos ship, their cannonballs were on the move. They'd been fired past both ships, yet somehow hit the Nothomathos ship on the nose.

When I looked back at Prince, the agitation was gone from the boy's pale face. He looked terrified.

"They've got angle cannons?!"

I felt my heart sink. Jezna reemerging at my side sent it streaking back up into my lungs with a fury. I wasn't in the mood to deal with her at the moment. Not after seeing—and hearing—what she'd said to those knights.

"What . . ." Jezna's words were slurred with discomfort. "What are those?"

"Nodan weaponry," Prince said, scampering about the deck for some place to hide that wasn't taken up by dazed Nothomathos Princes or Enoch brawling with those that still stood. "Only the freakiest, nastiest cannons ever designed by man. They're enhanced with a weird kind of Aestus that allows them to zigzag at a ninety-degree angle from where they'd been zigzagging initially."

When Jezna just swayed confusingly, Prince said, "*They change course in mid-freaking-air.*"

A second cannonball—this one glowing a cobalt-blue rather than purple-pink—belched forth from the Kanbrik ship. It aimed for the empty air past the front of the Nothomathos ship, then, with a violent whine, paused and sped toward us with the same fury.

It smashed through the base of the mast.

The wood ripped free with a sickening crack, shards flying every which way. I dropped to the deck as a twisted piece flew over my head . . .

Then the remnants of the thirty-foot-high mast groaned, falling toward us.

Time stopped around me. Pathways bled from my blood spreading out as options born from my suffering as a Shadarian laid themselves bare. One arrived before all the others, propelled by a demonic voice from my past.

Use it.

The move was an unnamed power gifted to the creature living inside me. It allowed for movement from one point to another in a nanosecond. It also enabled the use of moving opposing points with it. This meant that if I wanted to exchange places with an item, or vice versa, I was more than capable of doing so. Anders, an old merc ally of mine, had named it "castling," after the move in Castle-King-Horse.

But although castling was the easiest of the options, it meant that I'd have to channel the Other for a nanosecond. And that was all the time it needed to seize control.

Power is granted to those for a reason, the voice said again. *Use it.*

But if I did, wouldn't I be putting everyone at risk?

Could I really face waking up with blood coating my claws once more? Could I really face another three years of banishment—of *hatred*?

I could hold the Other back. I had enough control to know how much Ignis I was capable enough of channeling before—

That's not the Navigator way, something in me said.

When had I ever followed "the Navigator way" to begin with?

The Brotherhood gave you a second chance. You asked Jezna whose side she was on. How about asking yourself?

Prince shouted, raising his arms to his face . . .

Left with no other option but to be flattened, I turned toward the looming shadow and chose the best course of action.

I let myself get hit in the face by a thirty-foot slab of steel and wood, clutched as much of it as I could with Ignis-infused arms, and suplexed it over my shoulder into the sea.

There were several terrifying moments involved in the process. At one point, when the mast was on my chest, grasped in my arms, I thought it might truly flatten us. Then, when that was proven incorrect and that my draconic strength had prevailed, a sharp pop made me think I'd snapped my back in two. But that was the edge of the deck shattering beneath me, which sent me and the broken mast spilling into the sea.

Submerged, the first emotion I felt was anger.

If Enoch hadn't been so stupid, I never would've been in this situation. But that was shortly replaced with the relief that my back was still working, if aching in agony. But even then, the anger returned, along with anxiety when I realized why I was underwater in the first place.

Avoiding fragments that continued to fly off of the ship and into the sea around me, I bolted up to the surface and emerged, spitting out particles of everything between sand and water. Wiping my eyes, I craned my neck.

Both hyper-ships were on fire, the pink-purple flames of Aestus and the bright orange-yellow of natural fire streaming from places in the hull where cannonballs had punctured. The gnarled stump of the Nothomathos mast burned, and near it knelt Jezna and Prince. They looked terrified, spirits strewn with as many holes as the ship.

But someone stood before them, somehow facing every which way at once. Somehow, he faced Nothomathos and Kanbrik with the same visceral intensity, the burning wreckage blazing around him so that he didn't look surrounded by fire, but one with it.

At first glance, I thought it was Kaleo.

Seizing hold of a passing shard of debris to keep me afloat, I watched as the ash-covered figure glanced between ships, fists clenched at his sides, then raised his arms the same way he'd done against the Skrill. Familiar green symbols began to spin about his body, streaks of emerald lightning shooting from shoulder to shoe.

His eyes were spiral galaxies, and I felt my blood freeze.

Who is *this boy?*

A single roar echoed up out of the Kanbrik ship, followed by the firing of a cannon. The cannonball sped across the sky, designed to locate its target with pinpoint accuracy and exterminate it. They were flawless weapons. I'd had to duck hundreds of them in my lifetime.

But instead of ducking, Enoch spun toward the cannonball. And instead of being blown to bits, his burning fist collided with the cannonball in a punch that sent emerald tongues of flame licking across the length of the ship.

The cannonball rocketed back the way it'd come as a newborn green comet, and although I couldn't see what it hit, yells and a resounding crash hinted at its precision.

Then the green fire that surrounded Enoch winked out, and he fell onto his face.

CHAPTER 17

Kaleo

By the time the Kanbrik and Nothomathos captains I'd brought back to Carbonek were being dealt with by Daria, the hyper-ships had been swept out of the bay, and the trainees had been escorted out of the hangar in the direction of the Navigational healers, I needed to sit my old arse down. A box of spare crab cruiser parts carried by two male Navigators sufficed. As they passed behind me, I took a seat. They shot me irritated looks until they saw who I was.

"Don't worry about it, lads." I waved them off. "I'll carry it the rest of the way. Just need to rest me bones a bit." When I saw Hektor, Barco, and the major general approaching, I added, "Be off, now."

Hektor gave me mere moments to recuperate. Mere moments to massage the soreness from my legs, silence the screams of pain echoing out of my spine, and scuff the fresh blood clean from my boots. I hadn't killed a soul—killing wasn't in a Navigator's vocabulary—but when men attacked, a man had to defend himself. Even hurting all over, even rusty with age, I'd gone easy on them. But it was still too hard.

The Kanbrik Elders had attacked with little fear or remembrance, like they had no idea who I was. Had they forgotten the white-coated, golden-haired boy who had visited them beside Cahis Cor thirty-some years ago? Did they really no longer remember that smiling lad?

No. Of course they didn't. In my conversation with their captains, I'd seen in the dark eyes of the High Elder that the Noda had ensnared another nation. Another section of Khronera had fallen to the ideology that poisoned the world. The Noda promised Kanbrik power, and the elders had acquiesced.

One day . . .

I lowered my flickering eyelids at the ground rather than the approaching trio that was just a reminder of all those days long ago when I could've actually done something.

"He *punched* a cannonball?" Hektor said.

"Let's not dwell on meaningless details," the major general said. "Kanbrik has become a Nodan nation, the first Khroneran city to declare itself such. Nothomathos has aligned with the Government in response. Carbonek is surrounded on all sides."

"Kanbrik is more village than city," Barco said. "And now, more ruins than village. They won't inspire any other Khroneran nations to join the Noda. This was just a skirmish."

"Skirmish?" the General repeated. "I had my boys investigate the ruins. That was a *battle*. The War knocks on our doorstep." He sucked in a violent breath. "We must prepare—"

"For what?" Hektor said. "Finish that sentence and you send us tumbling back into the War. Send us back to warriors instead of protectors."

"Warriors are what we need at the moment."

"Be silent, both of you," Barco said. "Kanbrik and Nothomathos's conflict didn't sprout up overnight. These are two ancient lands caught in a rapidly advancing world. They've been hoodwinked into thinking that joining the War will put an end to their problems when they were at each other's throats long beforehand."

"You misunderstand me," the general said icily. "It isn't the cities I'm concerned about, but their alignments. Are we to just forget that an imprisonment box was found by a Navigational squadron on the outskirts of Kanbrik? And that that same squad upended its contents inside Carbonek's walls?"

"That squad," Hektor said, coming the closest he'd ever come to a snarl, "did nothing other than what was asked of them. I'm incensed that a High Navigator ordered them to bring the imprisonment box here by themselves in the first place. The Council should've been transporting it, not having children drag it here."

"Navigators should be capable of transporting imprisonment boxes without need of us."

"They were down two squadmates!"

"I was down all my squadmates when I tore Admiral Dagus's stronghold to pieces during the War," the general replied. "Or does Mathias get the credit for that, too?"

"Lords, Reggie, can't you at least sympathize with them? This isn't something we can fix by turning Navs into soldiers again. This is *far* beyond Kanbrik and Nothomathos. Beyond even the Government and the Noda—"

"It's them," I said.

Silence fell. I didn't need to see to know they were all staring at me, Hektor with probably a great deal of panic, the major general with anger, and Barco with inquisition.

"Kal . . ." Hektor started.

"They're toying with us. This is all a game."

"Respectfully, I fear that you're in desperate need of sleep," Barco said. "You used a lot of Ignis—"

"Damn my Ignis."

Barco blinked, but I couldn't find it within myself to be the Charger of old and comfort him one more time.

"You think that box showing up when it did was an accident?" I asked. "You think Kanbrik and Nothomathos upending everything Cahis built right behind Carbonek was an accident? All this has been *planned*. ALL THIS HAS—"

Though I was old, I still had a firm enough grasp on my sanity to know when I was flying off the rails. I wrangled myself back to land, smoothing my mind over.

"Apologies."

"Don't apologize," Hektor said quietly. "Not you."

"I agree," the general said. "You aren't at fault for the War or the trickles that bleed over into Carbonek. You cannot hold sway over all of Archengard. And you cannot continue to jump to the conclusion that everything leads back to the Jackals."

"Shut it, both you buggers. What I meant to say was . . ." I looked at Barco. "You were right."

"I was?" Barco said.

"About giving the trainees a chance. Neither Kanbrik nor Nothomathos saw a protector in me—all the more the reason to retire—but when that orange-eyed swash punched that cannonball . . . it was like the whole bloody world stopped breathing. Nothomathos surrendered, and after I got a hold of the High Elder, every Kanbrik vessel swore up and down that they'd obey us. I'm not the reason they've agreed to begin talking peace: the trainees are.

"And after everything they did against the Skrill . . . They didn't stop it, but they sure as hell stalled it. Trainees stalled a Skrill on their very first day while veteran squads scampered around them."

I stared begrudgingly at Barco. "So, yeah. You were right. I'll teach the buggers how to be a squad. And pass the Trials."

"You need not have said anything other than 'a Charger charges with his fists, but a Sharpshooter shoots with his brain,'" Barco offered.

"How about I charge my fist into your brain?"

"That would be a sight to see." He paused. "But I'm in agreement that a number of happenings over the past week have been, shall I say, conveniently well-placed? The Kardem Ka seems to have disappeared again, too. Murta has the map, but who knows how much he'll share with us. Who knows if the map is even complete."

"I, um, just received a call from Biassis and Larry, too," Hektor said grimly. "They found two dead Shrouded Men. If the Noda is here on Khronera, then I think we can assume they're here for a reason."

I sat up like lightning. "The Sacred Heart?"

Barco frowned. "Unlikely. I've heard little from my spies, but I'll tell them to dig deeper. A creature escaping inside Carbonek is nothing out of the ordinary. A Skrill is cause for concern."

I went back to staring at the ground, remembered banners bearing the mountain-rainbow-sun being ripped to shreds by black jackals swimming about my eyes. "See that you do."

CHAPTER 18

Jezna

I stood outside the hangar archway, watching the Navigational healers lift the white stretcher Enoch lay upon and hurry him off to the healing branch. Careful to remain hidden, I watched two more healers exit, half carrying, half assisting the stumbling, shaken Prince, followed by Murta slipping off down the corridor and out of sight.

It wasn't until Barco emerged that I stepped out of the darkness.

"I must oversee the negotiations."

I was surprised by how easy it was to say it. Especially to someone like Barco. I'd almost just said nothing at all—better to try my luck with Hektor. Barco was too close to Kaleo. Too careful.

But even more surprisingly, the High Navigator whom fate had chosen to walk through the entrance I was perched behind didn't seem alarmed by my presence at all. In fact, he simply looked at me.

"I'm afraid not. This is a matter for High Navigators only."

"I'm a knight."

Barco said nothing. I took that as approval to continue.

"The arguments of Archengard will always be the matters of the Chivalric Orders. We were Archengard's first servants. I'll say nothing if you wish me to. I just . . ." Memories of people running away from a cracking dam spun across my eyes. Memories of seven armored figures standing in front of it, trying to hold back the waves with their Ignis. "I . . . *must* assist. In any way I can."

"I wonder," Barco said, "if this need comes from where you think it does."

"I'm sorry?"

"A knight seeks to aid Archengard? I can understand that. But a knight, now a Navigational trainee, that suddenly bears an interest in the Brotherhood because her knightly brethren are involved?" The unreadable expression that I'd interpreted as amused skepticism gave way to icy disappointment. "I might not have witnessed what took place out there, but I've been known to make startlingly accurate estimations.

"During the early days of the Perpetual War, Mathias didn't look to Kaleo for assistance in constructing battle plans, in reading our opponents' moves before they ever even contemplated making them. He looked to *me*. And I looked to the words of Talen Vento, a man that every Chivalric Order deemed 'the Traitor' following his founding of the organization I now help lead."

His cold gray eyes narrowed. "And because I've read the chivalric texts written by a man that followed the Chivalric Code so firmly that he left the Orders rather than stay aboard their sinking ship, I've come to see quite clearly when a knight decides to do something for their dying ideals rather than their dying world.

"And might I add, we no longer solve border skirmishes and broken trade routes with sword and stallion. We sit down and talk. Like civilized people."

"Then do so," I said, calming my shivering legs by stomping them into the stone. "Make your estimations and draw your battle plans. But know that I'm not another self-centered swash or mindless treasure hunter. You won't make me into Talen Vento. Navigators are nicknamed 'neon knights,' but never forget that for a time, there was no need for the 'neon.'"

Barco startlingly cracked a smirk, and long before my amazement trickled away, he began to walk down the hall. "Indeed. I won't make that mistake again. I won't be dealing with Nothomathos and Kanbrik for the moment, but I'll take you to Daria. You may observe."

When I didn't move, he turned with a lifted eyebrow. "If you step lively."

The negotiation chamber was located on the third floor, somewhere between the outdoor hanging gardens and the High Navigators' private quarters. It was a round room made of dark marble shaped like a basin with ten steps leading down to a flat floor. When Barco extended his hand for me to look within, I saw Daria on the island in the center. Seated all around her on stair-stepping benches were the Kanbrik Elders and Nothomathos Princes. Divided straight down the middle, all facing one another with fearsome scowls. A few Nightguards lined the upper benches—peacekeeping reinforcements.

I looked over at Barco to thank him, but he was already gone. So I clenched my fists and leaned against the archway, listening to the conversation below.

"—crossed the border two hundred years ago!" a tall red-caped knight bellowed. Probably the Lord Prince of Nothomathos, as he was the only one that stood on his side. The rest sat, stirring angrily around him. "Our dealings were supposed to be done at sea only! This all started because they proposed a return-to-land trade!"

"It's easier for us to traverse through White Town than through the Clauso Rapids," said an elderly white-and-gold-robed man, the only person on the Kanbrik side standing. The High Elder, and the clothing he and his fellow elders wore was light mail. A type of armor that appeared silky and light to the human eye, mainly worn by politicians in the Southern Kingdoms of Khronera.

By those that seek to appear friendly, I thought, watching the High Elder shrug in a sorrowful manner, *but are never slow to stab one another in the back.*

"So you sailed a whole fleet of Nodan hyper-ships through them?" the Lord Prince said. "Propositions of land trading were spurred behind your city's lust for our aqueducts!"

"So lend a few to them." Daria's calm voice broke through the chaos. "Every city would be far better off if they'd simply work with one another." She noticed me then, and gave a short but silent nod. I returned it cautiously, not wanting to attract attention.

"Impossible," the Lord Prince said. "Such coalition benefits no one. They sought our aqueducts, yet aligned with the Noda and built their own. Powered by Aestus. Though the Government bestowed us with a single hyper-ship, we Princes have never built our machinations with that unnatural substance. It kills Archengard. The old ways of life must be protected."

"The War kills Archengard," Daria responded. "Not advancement."

"The War will *free* Archengard. Kanbrik chose the side that will further shackle it."

"So you invaded their city in return?" Daria asked. "Burned it to the ground? For what cause?"

"For no cause," the High Elder said.

"For our cause!" The Lord Prince beat his chest with an iron fist. "That land once belonged to the Nothom Order! A castle made from crystal and gold was erected there by Sir Nothom Hacis himself!" He jabbed a finger at the elders. "They destroyed it, and the Government has promised us that they will rebuild it!"

Though I'd grown disgusted with their childlike bantering—especially coming from knights—something twinged inside of me.

A real-life castle.

Just the thought was enough to make me want to throw myself full force behind the Nothomathos Princes. Macín had said that a long time ago, the Tolkkis had a castle, too.

To think there was ever a time where knights protected Archengard from their mighty stone seats in the highlands, while people from all across the world flocked to them: creating cultures of color, creativity, and peace. To think there was ever a time where there weren't only a few ruins of the last great castles left, but hundreds of fully built ones. . . .

Both sides began to scream at one another, the High Elder and Lord Prince lost in the crowd. I watched the madness take hold of the room, Nightguards swiftly moving to get between them, then Daria's silhouette glowed purple and silence fell.

It seemed that every one of these elders and princes were Ignis-less. Daria was like a Dragon Lord compared to them. *I* held more power than all of them.

"In this manor," Daria said, "there will be order. I understand that things have gotten out of hand—"

"Out of hand?" the Lord Prince boomed. "Have you not stepped outside those damned golden gates? Have you not walked the walls of this world? The battlefields between countries? The blackened skies and burning bodies?"

"The only burned bodies we've walked among," the High Elder immediately said, his calculated persona slipping briefly into fiery rage, "are our own." He turned toward Daria. "High Navigator, you must not forget that while Nothomathos still stands, Kanbrik no longer does. Our days of listening to the Brotherhood are over. Because of the Perpetual War, our people have become nomads. They will never be able to return to their home. The ships are all that we have left—"

"Given to you by the Noda!" The Lord Prince whirled on Daria. "High Navigator, though this snake might play the part of the victim, the reason we took the fight to their home is because they've aligned themselves with the Jackals!"

Ignis swirled back into Daria's heart, leaving her eyes dark and emotionless. Void of any light. Void of hope.

I felt my insides stir, fear creeping up and down through my armor.

The Jackals again. And this time, Daria didn't seem to brush it off as she had when we'd first met. This was different.

"That is an unspeakable accusation," she said. "One that requires a great deal of evidence. So, do you have any?"

Though the High Elder protested in vain, the Lord Prince nodded almost stoically. "I've heard that an imprisonment box was recovered from Kanbrik recently. And that its contents were spilled recently in this very manor."

"There was, indeed, an imprisonment box in our possession," the High Elder said. "We did not, however, use it, nor did we know for certain what it was at the time. Someone from the Noda hierarchy must have planted it among us. High Navigator, you must understand. We don't even fully support the Noda to begin with. This is something that these armored murderers have shoved us into—"

"I swear upon the Chivalric Code," the Lord Prince announced. "I swear upon it, and as the stars are my witness, these vermin have had dealings with the Jackals. We all know who it is that truly leads the Noda."

"Your oath means nothing," the High Elder said. "You cannot swear upon a pile of ashes."

"I will swear upon anything that proves you guilty. This is about the disintegration of our world. An honest and good world." He shook his head defiantly before pointing at the elders again. "And you have betrayed it." Then, even eerier, he pointed at Daria. "While you do nothing about it."

The elders, though nowhere near as riled up as the Princes, seemed to be sustaining a smokescreen. There was something about this High Elder that wasn't right. Something in his glinting eyes and broad gestures. He was hiding something. By the stars, the Princes were *right* . . .

"Though we can confirm that an imprisonment box was taken from Kanbrik," Daria said, "that doesn't therefore confirm that Kanbrik is working with the Jackals."

The Lord Prince slammed the bench in front of him. "They lead the Noda—"

"The Noda is led by a clergy of princes," Daria stated. "The Jackals' involvement—make that *existence*—has yet to be proven. Conspiracies do not solve problems here: the truth will."

But that wasn't good enough. The Lord Prince and his men rose as a single mass, and the Lord Prince seemed to speak for all of them in that moment.

"So the Brotherhood would rather beat around the bush than admit that there's a darkness which they cannot contain? Very well. What Chancellor Veres speaks is the truth, then. The Brotherhood no longer represents Archengard. It no longer bears the ability to protect it.

"If you'd simply stepped outside, you would've witnessed the massacre that occurred out at sea. If you'd looked out the window at the world around you, you would've seen how the Kanbrik fleet of fifteen ships cornered our *single* ship on all sides, stormed through us until our hull split down the middle, then came aboard the wreckage, cutting and mutilating their way through every one of my Brothers—"

"That's a lie."

When everyone in the room turned to look at me, I realized that I'd said it.

The Lord Prince's armor shook. *"You dare . . . ?"*

"You swore on the Chivalric Code," I said, words pouring out of me before I could realize what saying them meant. "You swore. Yet you lied." *Just like I did.* "I was out on the Grand Sea when your Princes met the Kanbrik Elders. There was no slaughter. Only two sides pathetically pelting one another with cannonfire."

The knight closest to the Lord Prince pointed at me. "You would sell out your own—"

"Let her speak." Daria silenced all protest from the Nothomathos Princes, but I wasn't watching the High Navigator. My gaze hadn't left the Lord Prince and the armored figures all around him. "Go on, Jezna."

"That trade route was founded by High Navigator Cahis Core." My insides coiled and cramped up with every sentence I drove home. With every step I took in a direction I never contemplated I'd ever walk. "For peace. And though Kanbrik did arrive with a fleet, Nothomathos wasn't surrounded." I sucked in a breath. "Nothomathos attempted to drill through the Leviathan's vessel just the same as Kanbrik did.

"There are no victims here," I concluded. "Only bickering children. No. The only victim, if there is to be one . . . is Cahis Core's spirit."

"*TRAITOR!*" the Lord Prince said, but his cry was swallowed up in the sound of every Nothomathos Prince leaping to their feet and cursing. The elders immediately retorted with their own words, and havoc took hold of the room once more.

Daria remained rooted to her place in the middle, head bowed, strands of coal-black hair twisting down around her shoulders. The woman I'd originally viewed as an immovable mountain of stoicism briefly shattered, just as Kaleo had done when the first cannonballs sped across the Grand Sea.

Because this is what Archengard's become. Screaming mobs. Lines drawn. Boundaries built . . .

And the Brotherhood caught in the middle.

I staggered out of the archway and back down the hall, searching for the staircase that would get me back down to the first floor. Away from the claustrophobic room and the screaming Nothomathos Princes. Away from the mob.

Every one of them had stared at me through their dark eye slits. Every one had named me "traitor." And though my god armor was twenty-times stronger than their ordinary armor, their hatred had pierced straight through it.

And now I'm in the middle, too, I realized. *I've become Talen Vento.*

CHAPTER 19

Enoch

I woke under a whirl of colors. *Tapestries and pinned blankets? The healing branch, then.* I'd read about it and the Brotherhood's expert healers: Navigators trained to harness the fire within them to heal wounds, seal scars, and ease pain. I detected what was probably one of them standing over me.

I thought about jumping up with a manic shriek as a joke, then caught a glimpse of silver hair glowing with red Ignis.

"Oi, I know you."

Eleri Emeres let Ignis fade from her body but kept it sustained in her eyes. Though they and Barco's were a similar shade, Eleri's reminded me more of threads and fabric than Barco's rigid crystalline flames.

"Well, I'd be a little vexed if you didn't," she said. "Those that stormed the dark lands of Narthes during the early days of the Perpetual War aren't the only Navs, you know. In war, someone's always losing. With peace, everyone wins. If I'd been with you instead of Kal . . ." She shook her fists, but the Ignis in her eyes faded, revealing shards of sadness. "How're you feeling?"

I sat up with little pain. "Brilliant. Whatever you did, it worked."

"It better. I've been perfecting that ability for thirty years now. Usually I'd have one of my healers take care of you, but Kal said he wanted you ready to go immediately." She shook her head. "Stubborn bastard never did know when to lie down and get some proper healing. Always jumping from one quest to the next."

"Is he all right?" I asked, images from before I passed out swirling back into me. Ships, fire, cannonballs. "And what about the others?"

"All fine. Little Larocque had a few cuts, but he's back at it. Kanbrik and Nothomathos, on the other hand, still have a few kinks to work out. I handed things over to Barco. Think that knight of yours might've went with him."

Though everything surrounding the sea skirmish was a little fuzzy, I frowned. Jezna had seemed to lay back for the majority of it. And the blokes I'd been boxing had definitely looked like her on the outside. Did that have something to do with it?

Then I remembered the frequent streaks of black and gold that had swum around me, sometimes getting in my way, other times seeming to push me aside in order to go after even more knights. It had seemed starving for a fight.

"What about Murta?"

"Never saw him come in," Eleri said. "In fact, I haven't seen him since the induction ceremony."

I recalled the broken mast falling. How it had blocked out the suns, turning my confidence to ash.

But in a moment where I'd actually been faced with death, where I had no idea what to do, Murta had caught the mast and launched it over his shoulder into the sea. He'd saved us.

"You haven't?"

"If it was up to me, I would've made sure he was put with a squad that knew how to control him, not all newbies . . . Though, if it were up to me, he wouldn't be here at all." Eleri sighed. "But the Brotherhood takes in anyone and aids everyone. Even if it comes back to bite us in the ass."

She strode over to a pedestal with my boxer's jacket draped over it.

"Personally, I'd have kept you another day—especially after fighting a damn Skrill, too—but Kal wants you resuming the Trials. He'll be waiting in Training Hall A."

She handed me my jacket. "Hektor told me what you did out there. When you first showed up, I won't deny that I was skeptical to induct another blond-haired swash. But there might be the makings of a Nav in you yet."

I stood. "Always knew you were the brightest bloke on the Council."

"Don't patronize me." Eleri eyed me as I slid my arms through the sleeves. "And where'd you get a scar like that? A firedrake burn your back off?"

"Not exactly."

The path to Training Hall A was packed with people. I hurried, but that didn't stop me from noticing the bits of dust and rubble decorating the corridors in some places. It definitely didn't stop me from noticing a few squads throwing me cautious double takes. Last night seemed fresh in everyone's sunken faces and minds. Some had definitely seen what had happened or heard rumors of what Kaleo Ashai had said to the four trainees who had somehow stopped a rampaging Skrill dead in its tracks.

But I didn't stop it. I almost died. Just like I almost died on the hyper-ship . . .

At the thought, I felt a sudden soreness well in my left hand. I curled it into a fist and studied it. Eleri's healing had relieved my pain, but discomfort remained. I could almost feel the places where the bone had met iron. Where, somehow, I'd deflected a cannonball with nothing but my Ignis and my fist.

Running fingers over my bruised knuckles, I ignored the clusters of colorfully clothed people that strode by me in groups until a black-suited figure walking on his own passed. Recognizing his swiftness, I looked up. And for some witless reason, I called out to him.

Murta stopped, slowed, then turned. He was so natural in the heat of battle: Against the Skrill, he'd resembled a majestic skydrake in terms of fluidity. Whereas strolling about, his movements were jerky and awkward.

“Er, where you headed?” I asked, stepping out of the way so a squad of four female Navigators could blow by, chattering happily. I noticed that two wore sparkling dresses like Eleri, while the other two wore three-piece suits like Murta.

“Somewhere,” he said, seeming like he wanted nothing more than to resume his search for said somewhere. I almost let him.

Show some backbone, Noc. “Well, thanks.”

His lips tightened. “Qué?”

“For saving my arse. Everyone’s arse.” I gained more confidence. “That was seriously wicked what you did back there. Honest. You took the whole mast and just—” I began to mimic how he’d suplexed it, but he just walked away.

I watched him disappear down the hall, a lone shadow among a rainbow of squads.

What’d I say?

The fact that Murta seemed almost afraid to hold a conversation with me only propelled me to the Training Hall faster, where I found Kaleo sitting atop a great seven-foot boulder in the center of the room. He was picking at his boots broodingly, but when he heard my footsteps, he looked up, face softening. I stopped where I stood.

I couldn’t bloody take it anymore. Words I didn’t know I could say rushed out of me. Words I’d wanted to say since I was seven, since I was rotting in the dark gutters of Serapharus and using nothing but the stars and old stories to get me through the nights. Most of those stories had been about this man. The star patterns I’d traced had been of the constellation dedicated to him. For years, he’d been my only nightlight. And since arriving at Carbonek, I’d only gotten myself into trouble and made a fool of myself.

“I shouldn’t be standing here,” I said finally.

Astonishingly, Kaleo roared with laughter. “Look at me, boy! Am I anything close to who you had in mind? You think I can fight the way I used to? That I can even go back to being what they used to call me?”

His laughter withered away. “You can stand in front of me right well, lad. ’Tis I who shouldn’t have the right to stand before you.”

“That’s not true. You’re . . .” I stammered. “You’re the Leviathan!”

“Once, I was,” Kaleo said softly. “My name’s been cemented. Now, it’s time to cement yours.”

That was what I had wanted to hear more than anything.

This is my chance to learn from the Leviathan. My chance to become him.

I tightened my bandana. “Then teach me.”

“That’s more like it.” Kaleo hopped off the boulder, striding to the center of the room. “We resume the Trials right now. And I think we’d do best just getting everything out in the open. Your Ignis ability isn’t about power and boxing. It isn’t Conflicted; it’s Transformative.” He paused. “Do you know what you’re transforming every time?”

"My spirit," I said hollowly.

"Don't say it like that, lad. Now that you know it's Transformative, we start training like that. You were close to sedating the Skrill, you know that? Very close. And you probably would've beaten it if you'd kept going. That's because your Ignis ability deals with transforming your spirit, thus allowing you to either transfer parts of your spirit or your entire spirit."

I nodded reluctantly. "But I dunno how I . . . *possess* things. It sounds so messed up. When we were fighting the Skrill, I might've possessed Murta, too. I didn't go inside him like I did the Skrill, but I . . . persuaded him, I suppose." I shook my head. "How's that work? And how'd I punch that cannonball?!"

"All forms of life are vessels for you, lad," Kaleo said. "And not just life, but lifeless objects, too. It's my belief that you could possess the Rock of Sages just as well as you could me. Your spirit isn't possessing so much as connecting. And I believe that that connection is what allows you to do things like hit a cannonball coming at you full speed."

I stared at the giant boulder and imagined possessing it, *connecting* with it. I imagined placing my spirit within the darkness of its form. "How's that possible?"

"You can possess things and use your fighting moves," Kaleo said. "That means there's something you're missing. You're not using your ability properly because you're concentrating on two aspects. You need to be concentrating on one."

One.

I'd only ever thought of my Ignis ability as two different branches, not one whole. Not two sides of the same coin.

Maybe if I hadn't been so eager to find my Ignis after escaping Serapharus . . . maybe I'd have actually figured it out if I hadn't rushed the whole process.

"You're saying that when I use Green Fire Fist," I said, retracing the steps I'd taken in punching the cannonball. It hadn't felt real, like someone had taken over my body. "I'm possessing myself?"

"Your spirit is fluid," Kaleo said. "What you're doing is merely filtering and enhancing it into parts of your body. The disorientation you feel is because you don't have a strong enough grasp on what kind of a relationship an Ignis user should have with Ignis."

"What do you need me to do?"

Kaleo studied me. "Close your eyes. Ignis can be forced out, but it doesn't like it. You and your Ignis should be mates. Brothers. You must connect with it before you start connecting with other things. If you're trying to force Ignis out every time you tap into it, then you're doing something seriously wrong."

I almost opened my eyes. If that was the case, then I'd been a shite excuse of a brother.

"Them eyes better still be closed."

"Now that I'm in this sorry state, what next?"

"Think of Ignis like a spark. See it in your mind. Say hullo."

"Hullo," I said under my breath.

Remarkably, the spark brightened.

I jumped back. "What—"

"Keep your eyes closed!"

"They're bloody closed!"

"Then reach out to the spark. Tap it gently. The scrape of two pebbles in a world of darkness . . ." Kaleo hesitated. "Start in the shadow; that's when you'll need the light the most. Fan the spark . . . Now, transfer that spark into flame."

I did as instructed, reaching out to Ignis kindly instead of seizing control of it, and watched as the spark spread into a cool emerald flame. The rigid lightning from before was gone. This felt warmer. *Clearer.*

"It's . . ." I exhaled, allowing my mind to dance with the flame in the darkness. It was a beautiful feeling. Like good food and cold beer and all the things I'd come to love about my adopted home of the Light Isles. "I've never felt anything like this . . ."

"Stay focused on the flame. Allow it to grow. Don't force it—allow it. Gently . . . gently. Understand it as energy, the soul of a Dragon Lord, a fragment of a god. Brighten the flame, and with it, brighten the darkness."

I tightened my stomach muscles, earning a dry cackle from Kaleo. "Not like that."

"I'm trying."

"Try not to try so hard. It's easier when the gates are closed but not locked."

The mention of gates only forced me out faster. Gates made me think of great black ones. Of roaring entrances into wells of fire, of boys my age being dragged through them, screaming until their voices burnt inside their throats.

Fear built itself inside me before rushing up into my shoulders. I felt the weight bear down, pressing up against my back scar, then the darkness that had clawed at me in nightmares sprung forward to devour my spirit.

I gasped as the spark sputtered and died, opening my eyes. "It's gone."

"It's not." Kaleo brushed aside his jacket, unveiling the daggers from before. When he drew one from its sheath, the blade instantly turned into white fire, and his irises blazed with the same energy.

"Try once more," Kaleo said. "And allow me to give it a push."

I recalled the pain that he'd spoken of in terms of harnessing his own Ignis and the stories I'd read of the times when he was forced to fend for himself without the Sword.

"But you said—"

"—I wasn't as good as I used to be. Not that I couldn't."

The darkness overwhelmed me. I didn't want to go back down there. I didn't want to see those eyes again, to drown in my own melted body, just as I'd nearly drowned in the furnaces of Serapharus. But that wasn't thinking immortal.

"I need to be able to do this myself," I said. "Or else I'll never be able to do it at all. Especially when I'm out there."

"Foolish words," Kaleo said. "Sometimes help from another Nav is exactly what you need. Your ability deals with connection, doesn't it?"

I cautiously tiptoed back into the darkness, reimagining the spark with greater care. This time, when I closed my eyes and concentrated, the green came without a flicker of vulnerability. My confidence swelled.

"I don't accept it," I said, "but I'll let you help."

"Then locate my spirit."

The rush of color that infiltrated the darkness nearly sent my flame spiraling off into the shadows, but I held fast and focused. During a match, I focused on my opponent to the point that I saw nothing but them. I was just applying the same rules to locating Kaleo's spirit.

In the world of Ignis that blazed around me, having been peeled back before my closed eyes by my own Ignis, I saw Archengard as it was supposed to be seen.

Ignis sprung out around me in vortexes, and when I looked at Kaleo's silhouette, I saw his spirit: a gleaming white flame. I was back in the ring, only this time there wasn't just one option straight ahead, but two.

Threads of Ignis peeled off of me and raced toward Kaleo, creating one strand of green energy—the path of possession—and a second strand that fixed itself in the center of the white flame, creating what looked almost like a target. A means of attack.

I'd been granted both options by my Ignis, and now, neither one of them felt off. By embracing my ability as one, I'd opened up two different paths.

"Now redirect it."

The white fire went out in a flash as Kaleo sheathed the knife. At once, the darkness returned, and I was forced to welcome it again. I saw spots, dancing white-hot ones that tried to burn me.

Burn.

I stumbled blindly. The strands of Ignis that had connected me to Kaleo were severed now, their lines snipped by scissors of shadow.

"Focus on the stone," Kaleo commanded. "Find the spirit of all things!"

"First you want me to connect with Ignis, now you want me to connect with a bloody rock?!" I asked, still reeling. Everything spun.

"Nay!" Kaleo said. "I want you to get faster! You punched the cannonball because if you hadn't, you'd have died. You need to be able to punch the cannonball ten times over—in your sleep! If you spend all your energy on just one person, then how do you expect to be able to take on two? Two hundred?"

"When am I ever gonna be fighting two hundred people?"

"I took on two hundred thousand by my twenty-second sun cycle!"

I hissed, caught between calming and trying to get control of Ignis, but the green energy spasmed angrily. Like the beam of fire that had nearly split my back in two.

Don't think about—

Through the darkness, I saw the outline of the Rock sitting in the center of the hall, but nothing else. It refused to reveal its flame. I had zero connection with it.

"You wanna move mountains, don't ya?" Kaleo's shouts conjured images of the pack of Olders holding me down. With every shout, the deeper the beam of fire sank into my back until I felt my spinal cord blackening. Until I remembered what had brought me to it in the first place and the mistake I'd made.

I'd believed in connection.

"You wanna break rocks between your fingers?"

Stop.

"You wanna feel Archengard rise up around you when you call upon it?"

Stop!

"I was moving mountains by the time—"

"STOP!"

Instead of releasing Ignis, I thrust it out of me. The pressure that had been building up inside me was finally expelled in a soft supernova. I felt myself briefly lifted off of the ground, then collapsed in front of the Rock, the last bits of my Ignis shooting up toward the ceiling. Pebbles of marble spilled around me in the aftermath, a pattering rock rain in volcanic silence.

"I'm sorry," I said.

Kaleo shook himself, looking up at the ceiling. "It's all right. I'll fix it—"

"Not . . . for the ceiling."

Feeling for Ignis, I returned empty-handed. The source lay dormant.

That should've broken me—it probably would've broken anyone other than me—but I merely looked up at the stone.

The Rock of Sages had served as the punching bag for thousands of Navigators over the years. There was every scar and scrape imaginable among its surface. Some of those scrapes had probably been created by Adam Evenstar, Dresden Roberts . . . and I knew for a fact that one of the great white ones had been delivered by the man standing before me.

Each of them had beat at the Rock until their scar was etched upon it. Each of them had refused to quit until their mark was made.

"Before I accept help from anyone," I said, shadow and flame converging in my eyes so I had tunnel vision, "I need to be able to do this myself."

"That individualistic nonsense is what got us in this Perpetual War mess," Kaleo said. "Don't you be falling for it, too."

I dug the roll of tape out of my pocket, then threw off my jacket. As I began to wind the white strands around my fists, Kaleo hovered behind me. I ignored him.

Kaleo hadn't grown up on the streets of Serapharus. He'd been born in the Light Isles. He hadn't seen how hopeless connection truly was.

Before there was any connection, there first had to be zero fear. If I wasn't yet thinking immortal, then connection would only fail me.

Again.

It didn't just go one way, but two. The connector could connect to the connected, but if the connector wasn't yet connected with itself . . .

I tied off the last fist with my teeth before stripping my shirt. Wisps of air running across my back wound usually made me shiver, but this time, I felt nothing.

Kaleo wanted me moving mountains and punching cannonballs in my sleep?

So be it.

CHAPTER 20

Prince

"How're you feeling?"

I dabbed the skin just above my right eye, once home to a nasty cut I'd received during the sea battle, now smooth and scarless. My fingers fell to my sides.

"Um, fine." I blinked up at the Navigator, a blond boy in a white dress shirt with an indigo tie, not much older than me. "How'd you do that?"

"Just a few taps here and there," he said. "I'm one of Eleri's healers. As much as Navs are always getting injured, there's gotta be a group there ready to heal them, right?" He raised a hand surrounded with indigo light.

Ignis, I brooded. This wasn't fiery like Enoch's and Murta's, but thin and silky. Nothing like the violent spasms of Aestus I was used to.

"Uh-huh." I looked around the dark space full of multicolored curtains and banners. "Well, am I healed? 'Cause I'm in the middle of the freaking Trials and—"

A female Navigator threw back the curtain closest to me. I'd already seen her in the throne room—though I'd been far more focused on not pissing myself then—but here and now, I could safely say that Eleri Emeres was the woman of my dreams.

"The Trials," she grumbled. "That's all I hear from any Nav that looks under twelve. Why's everyone so concerned about the Trials? I remember back when all a Nav needed was a squad and a brain. Now we got Skrill running around, hyper-ships fighting in Carbonek's backyard, and trainees punching bloody cannonballs!"

I worked my jaw to come up with something smooth, but all I ended up saying was, "I look *twelve*?!"

Eleri begrudgingly let me leave thirty minutes later after concluding that I was fully healed, and pointed me in the direction of the exit.

"Don't know how soon your whole squad's to resume everything," she said, "but the blond one's with Kal in Training Hall A, I got no clue where the Shadarian's off roaming, and the knight was in Training Hall B, last I saw her. Pick your poison, I guess."

I turned to leave in a daze, but not before one of her pale hands gripped my shoulder. There was none of the ferocity her voice displayed in it. Just a kind of . . . familiarity.

I gawked at her.

"If Mathias was still here, he would've given your father a proper funeral," she said. "Dante was a good dude. Reckless, but good. I was sorry to hear about him."

I just swallowed and left as fast as humanly possible.

Better to run from nothing than look back and see a ghost following you.

When I got to Training Hall A, Enoch and Kaleo were gone, and I didn't have any interest in hunting for Murta, so I strolled into Training Hall B and found Jezna.

The hall was crowded to the point I wanted to go back to the tower, but Jezna refused any time I asked. Even with Navigators running rampant throughout the space, despite being on the receiving end of numerous uncomfortable glances—probably still from our tango with the Skrill—she seemed transfixed on practicing her Ignis ability.

She also didn't say a single freaking word to me.

The incident out at sea hadn't just affected Enoch. It was getting to the high and mighty knight, too.

But not to me, I fumed, staring down at the guns spread out around me.

Unlike Jezna—or any other Ignis user, for that matter—I didn't need to practice my aim. I'd never really needed to, though that didn't mean I didn't have to clean and rewire.

Sifting through my leather jacket for a wrench, I watched Jezna dance her Ignis through the air. Despite the suit of armor that clanked with every movement, she was actually pretty graceful. At least when using Ignis. The aqua energy dripped from her armor, but when she spun it through the air, it seemed more solid than water. Though clearly liquid, it seemed laced with something stronger than any steel I'd ever worked with at the forge.

I looked up from my work. "It's not water, is it?"

The helmet jerked toward me robotically. Ignis flew back into Jezna's armor and faded. "What do you mean?"

"It's a different color," I said, feeling my mood lighten at having finally been acknowledged. "And harder. If I was dumber than I am, I'd probably say it looked like it came from inside *you*, not your spirit."

"It appears that way due to my armor."

"Hrm. Do you ever change out of it? I haven't seen an inch of your skin." I backtracked quickly. "That sounded waaay worse out loud. All I meant was that I've never actually seen you. Like, your face. In fact, I've seen as little of you as I've seen of those nutty knights back there on the hyper-ship."

"A knight remains in armor at all times."

"What about for shits? Eats? Sleeps? What if you get an itch?"

Jezna tapped back into Ignis. "You soil chivalry with your baseless questions. Of course a knight may relieve oneself in private. But a knight must wear armor every other moment. Even when they're off duty. Only a knight is never off duty. Do you require further explanation?"

"You answered it." I put my palms up before jamming a pair of scissors into the core of my cannon. "Sheesh."

Jezna let go of Ignis again and walked over. "That's wrong." Her massive shoulders hunched in disgust. "Weapons should be given greater care. I've witnessed Nodan soldiers do similar things with their bulletswords . . . It's cruel. It's violating the weapon."

"Not to me." I fished the snipped shrapnel out of the core. "I'm healing it more than violating it. Quicker and easier this way, anyway." *This ain't the days of chivalry anymore. I don't got time to clean a sword. Nor make out with it.*

"There will come a time where you'll run out of wires to snip."

"But until that day comes, I'll just keep on snipping." I gestured over to my backpack slumped up against the wall. "I've got dozens. They're not hard to make. Check 'em out, if you'd like."

Jezna observed silently, and I went back to work, Eleri's words still spinning through me.

I always found that the deeper I went into a gun, the calmer I became, as if delving into its core was some profound quest. Journeying into the weapon's parts, networking them, then fixing what was wrong with them. I was giving them a sliver of me. Father had shown me how to do it. It wasn't a ritual I liked to have disturbed.

"You've made every one of these?" Jezna said.

My fingers coiled around the barrel of the cannon as I was shoved from my trance, but I blew out the emotion. The knight and I did have one thing in common, if what Kaleo had revealed about her was true.

Except I never found a way to grant myself Ignis using an artifact. I'm forever stuck with my plain old Ignis-less self.

"Kinda. I add bits and pieces to the already-made models. Remake 'em sometimes."

Jezna examined the ones closest to her: an Aestus-grenade launcher and a sniper rifle. "These contain parts from all ends of Archengard."

I braced for impact.

"What you said on the ship about Nodan weaponry . . . You use Nodan weapons."

"All right. So I lived in Narthes, home of the Noda. *Only* as a treasure hunter. The first chance to get out of there that came about, I took it. I hate that country and how they hunted people like Father, but that doesn't mean I won't use their weapons. It gives me an advantage. The only reason my cannon was able to do damage to the Nothomathos ship was because it's got Nodan tech in it. The Government uses a type of Aestus covering that's easily affected by the Nodan branch."

"Using weapons your father fought against seems—"

"I get it. But I'm making them safer. See?" I showed her the rounded muzzle of the cannon, a signature design of the Government. The Noda's were more triangular. More jagged. "They've got Governmental technology in them, too." I took to ferociously scrubbing the outer core with a rag. "It's no longer the Noda's. It's mine. And it means that no matter which side I come face-to-face with, I'll be able to fight 'em all."

And it means I'll be ready when those bastards come for me like they came for Father. And this time, I won't fall prey to fear either.

Jezna's battle-skirt rustled as a male Navigator practiced his wind-like yellow Ignis ability close by. Her "chivalric" tone was maddening for someone like me. Chivalry was just an excuse to be snooty. Those who still followed the Chivalric Code only followed it for bragging purposes. You shouldn't need to be all stoic to be a good person. Good people could be chaotic. Good people could be treasure hunters.

Right when I'd finally begun to get back into the swing of things, so that I swam about the abyss happily, humming some of Father's old songs, Jezna crossed her arms. "That is dishonorable."

Father's bleeding corpse flashed across my sunglasses.

Rage I'd kept controlled for a good chunk of my life was thrust to the forefront of my mind before escaping out my mouth.

"Dishonorable?" I stood, casting the cannon down with more force than I'd meant to. "That's something I'd recommend *never* accusing me of again, Your Knightliness."

"You imply that a thief knows more about honor than a knight?"

"I'm implying that you don't know shit about me. I'm not a thief and I'm not dishonorable. Hypocritical of you to call me either, too."

One look at her shaking form was all I needed to know that I'd gone too far.

No. I don't regret saying it.

Jezna had insulted me, and worse, she'd insulted Father. Claiming that I was dishonorable after all the years I'd spent searching for his killers, for why they'd killed him . . .

Honor and the abyss were the only things I still had.

"C'mon," I said. "Say something to that. You keep calling me a thief, but who's the real thief? Who stole Ignis—?"

Jezna marched past me at a pace that defied the size of her armor, and exited the hall through a side arch. She never said another word; that was the worst part.

The silent treatment again.

"Yeah, and stay out there!" I said. After glaring around the room of blinking Navigators, I plopped back down.

Freaking knights. No wonder they went extinct.

CHAPTER 21

Murta

Second-floor staircase. Turn left. Turn right. Through the arch. Behind the shrine dedicated to Bartholomew Norcus.

I repeated everything before stepping onto the staircase, simultaneously stepping back into memory.

Three years ago, I'd walked the same route, unsure of where I was going, knowing solely that a map of the Carbonek underground would only do a Navigator good if he was in Carbonek, not being forced out.

It had been my last act among the Brotherhood: making sure the map was secreted away and not in the hands of some Noda-sympathizing puto or weak-minded High Navigator.

If it isn't still there, though . . .

I reached the top of the staircase and turned left, ignoring the way squads spread out around me. I ignored the pygmy dragons that flew among some of them, beating their tiny wings and trumpeting in my direction, as though to sound the alarm that one of their darker, larger cousins stalked among them.

Because one does, one of the voices rasped within me. I ignored it, too.

Squads and their pygmy dragons might fear me, but it was only because I was willing to do what so many of them wouldn't. I'd fight the Skrill. I'd catch the mast. I'd become what they all feared if it meant securing victory, and now, I'd find the Talisman stored within Carbonek.

On my way to the arch that would take me to Bartholomew Norcus's shrine—one of twenty shrines dedicated to legendary Navigators throughout Carbonek—I passed the enormous entryway to Training Hall A. Expecting to see the Rock of Sages sitting triumphantly undisturbed as it had three years ago, I instead saw that it was being attacked ferociously.

By Enoch.

He looked miserable: blond hair matted, chest drenched with sweat. The green markings coated his body, blinking agitatedly, and boxing tape hung loosely from his fists as he pounded away. Every punch sent spurts of Ignis around the hall, and he was constantly switching stances, messily moving his feet, stepping through piles of discarded bloodstained tape.

I snorted when I spotted the sloppiness of his form, but frowned at the white strands. There had to be at least over a hundred. How long had he pushed himself? How long could he push himself before deciding to throw in the towel?

Sooner than later, I figured, making myself comfortable.

I waited ten minutes, eyes flicking between the immovable, unchangeable Rock of Sages and the silent, sweaty swashbuckler. Enoch never slowed his assault, throwing combination after combination.

And he never stopped channeling Ignis. Even when the green markings dispersed from his skin and his fists no longer resembled flames, his outline continued to glow.

He wasn't stopping.

What's he doing?! I strode into the hall. It was far too painful to watch him throw kicks like that.

"*Detener*," I said over the thunderclaps. "Stop."

Enoch continued to punch, face taut with intensity.

"Hey. Idiota. I'm talking to you. What are . . . ?"

When Enoch swiveled to send a right hook into the Rock, I saw his irises. They glowed green, but violent black cracks had begun to consume them.

"Stop using Ignis!" I shoved him to the floor. "You're Breaking!"

Enoch tried to stand, but when he let go of Ignis, the black scars in his eyes shattered, and he collapsed. A grunt of pain escaped him as he squeezed his eyes shut.

I shook my head. "You have no idea what just happened, do you?"

"Bollocks." Enoch sat up numbly, massaging his eyes. "I almost broke it."

"You didn't break *caca*, except your eyes. You kick like a drunken scarecrow and your punches aren't focused enough. Who taught you to fight?"

"I did." Enoch stood on wobbly legs, but the fire in his orange eyes never changed. Even dilated and murky, they still glowed. "And what do you mean I was breaking?"

"Breaking. Capital B. Ignis had begun to destroy your eyes. It happens when someone holds on to Ignis for too long. Or over-exudes it."

"Good to know. But what've I done to be graced with your presence?" Enoch spat with the accuracy of one that had done lots of spitting. The glob landed inches off my shoes.

"Because if you get out on your first quest and fight like that"—I stepped over the spit—"you'll fall flat on your face again. Hasn't anyone ever told you how to fight with Ignis properly?"

The mention of quests seemed to restore some sanity to Enoch, if he'd had any to begin with. Color slowly returned to his face.

"I didn't realize there was a right or wrong way."

"Clearly." I eyed his bleeding knuckles. "Bandage those up. And don't do it half-ass."

Walking over to where his jacket lay on the other side of the Rock, Enoch removed the last bits of tape and began to wrap his fists suspiciously. I studied the Rock. It hadn't moved. Nor had it obtained a single fresh mark.

"Lords, were you even hitting it?"

"I've been at it all bloody morning."

"You can't go that long without fully understanding how to combine Ignis with technique. It's idiotic and unhealthy."

"Technique?"

"The proper way of fighting with Ignis. And there is a proper way. What you're doing is just . . ." I flailed my arms.

Enoch snorted with amusement.

"Get in your stance," I ordered.

When Enoch was situated in one place and not always moving about, he actually had a decent open stance. Right foot forward, left foot back due to being a southpaw, and fists positioned at equal lengths. The only issue: The forwardness in his posture meant he led more with his knuckles as opposed to with his feet. On top of that, he clenched his fists to an almost unnatural point. He wasn't afraid to get hurt in the ring; that much was clear. He was insanely reckless.

I stepped forward and began to maneuver his fingers. "Not that tight. Ignis needs to be able to move about."

Enoch's hands slowly came unclenched as he allowed me to shift and change them. He refused harshly at first, then slowly relented until the strain in his muscles surrendered completely.

My fingertips lingered. Enoch's palms were warm from punching but disturbingly cold between the crevices. He smelled exotic. The deeper I went into closing his fists properly, the harder it became to tear myself away. The longer I held on to his hands, the harder it became to breathe, the faster I felt my heart race until it was flitting about in ways it never had before . . .

Enoch sucked in a staggered breath, unsettled. That sprung me from my daze.

"Loosen up more around the middle," I said, quickly removing my hands and pointing down at his naked waist. *No need to go touching that, too.* "You should be more focused on your lower body. You don't want to be so tense all the time; Ignis shouldn't be tense. You can be firm in your striking, but it should feel natural. Ignis will assist you."

From the doubtful but anxious look Enoch gave me, I knew he was probably going back through every fight he'd ever fought in his head.

"Now show me some punches."

Enoch turned toward me, fists up.

I scowled. "On the Rock."

The smirk that flew across his face enraged me, but Enoch was already going to town.

His technique, though sloppy when he grew tired, held together firmly. Firmer than most mercenaries. Having to focus on the sustainment of two fists as opposed to one had robbed him of the maximum power he was seemingly used to, but he divvied it up well.

All things considered, Enoch was fantastic. Suddenly, it made perfect sense why he'd dedicated his life to fighting monsters, pirates, and other underground boxers. There was an art to his fighting. The only glaring issue was his blind determination; he never let off the gas, not even for a second. He got sloppier over time from using so much energy at once.

"No need to go that fast," I said. "Slow it down. Lords, hombre, you plan on lying in bed for a week?"

"It's Ignis, not me," Enoch said between low hisses that boxers made when punching.

That means he's been "possessing" his body to make himself faster for the past two minutes, I realized. *His control's improved immensely.*

"Then Kaleo's help is working," I noted, irritated.

Enoch finally paused, gazing through the bottom of his bandana. "He didn't help as much as you'd think."

"Really? I'm *so* surprised."

"Trained with him before, have you?"

"Barco. None of them know what to do with the talents they've been given."

Enoch halted mid-jab. "Oi, was that a compliment?"

"Show me some kicks."

Enoch switched to his legs on the fly, holstering his fists closer to his face and instantly becoming lighter on his feet. I nodded approvingly but scowled when he bounced from foot to foot like a boxer. His first kick made me wince.

"That'll do."

Enoch fell still. "Something wrong?"

"Definitely. Try this for me. Try actually kicking. Not with the sole of your shoe."

"What's a good kick, then?"

Pouring Ignis into my leg, I head-kicked the Rock. Gold sparks sizzled off of it.

Enoch stared down at his legs and mimicked the move slowly, stumbling his way through before losing balance near the end. "Blimey. Doesn't it hurt?"

"Not if you know what you're doing."

"Well, I don't, and prefer my fists. I'm not a kicker."

I stared at the Rock. Biassis had suggested we put our mark on it during my first go-around. Something about "cementing us among the greats." Ridiculous. Each of us had gone at it individually until we'd had more bruises than the squads that came back from War-dealings. Biassis, Larry, and I just hadn't meshed well.

"I'm assuming you swore to Kaleo that you wouldn't leave this room until you split the Rock in two?"

"Something like that. If that's what it takes."

"The Rock is unbreakable. I've seen Kaleo take a swing at it with the Sword. The damned thing didn't move." I slowly ran my fingers over the many dents in its surface. Biassis, Larry, and my marks hadn't remained, but maybe they weren't meant to. "I can, however, help you add one of these to it."

Enoch looked taken aback.

I found a flat, untouched section on the Rock, right next to a great black canyon that belonged to Mathias.

"To make a dent," I said, "you need to have a constant barrage of force. Not just full of punches but different techniques. The Rock doesn't like taking the same amount of pressure all the time. You have to convince it to make a dent. Not just try and force it. That's why Biassis and Larry failed."

Something about that made Enoch stir. "We could . . . I suppose, trade off." He stepped forward and held up a burning fist. "Put Ignis in one of your legs."

I nodded, flames engulfing my right leg. "So if I kick . . ." I struck the Rock with my Ignis-infused foot and sprung back, allowing Enoch to slide through and take my place.

"Then I wallop . . ." Enoch smashed the same smoldering spot with his fist, then moved so I could kick again.

The process worked, but it was slow, and the burning mark we'd created on the Rock cooled every millisecond that one of us wasn't hitting it.

"We're not fast enough," I said.

Enoch held his knees and panted. "How do we get fast enough?"

Digging back through my mind, through memories I'd actually tried to forget, I recalled a similar session Anders and I had designed during our nightmarish days on the battlefield. The two of us were Government-bought mercenaries at the time and the fighting technique we'd created had been what Anders called "Rolling Chaos," named after another Castle-King-Horse move. As silly as it had been, the move was entirely focused on hitting the same point on an enemy over and over until they broke. It was designed to smash through Nodan phalanxes.

It was designed to utilize connection.

"This is ridiculous . . ." I watched the bright spot on the Rock fade. "But go back to back."

Enoch lowered his fists. "Pardon?"

Shoving Enoch behind me before I could change my mind, I held my arms out backwards. "Link your arms through mine."

Enoch hesitated.

"The longer we stand here doing nothing, the faster the Rock cools."

Enoch linked his arms through so that we were locked back to back.

"*Bueno.* Now, I'm going to kick the Rock, then flip you over."

"Pardon?"

"So you need to hold on, push off with me, then be ready to let go so you can punch."

"Pardon?!"

"And after that, be ready to link arms again and flip me over. And stay linked after you flip me. I don't need my hands."

"Hold on! What's this supposed to do besides bloody confuse me?"

"Build up momentum," I said, careful to keep Ignis situated in my legs as opposed to running through my upper body. I didn't want to burn Enoch . . .

I paused, as if awoken from a clouded daze.

Why did I care so much all of a sudden? Why was I collaborating with Enoch?

And why the hell was I back to back—

Shaking away the doubt, I kicked the Rock with Ignis. Enoch yelped as he was tugged along for the ride, and allowed himself to be dragged. When I dug my feet into the ground and prepared to launch Enoch over my back, he scrambled to his feet.

"Too slow."

"I know, I know!" Enoch propelled himself off the ground and backwards rolled across my spine. I easily let go when I was supposed to, but Enoch still clung to my arms and got stuck halfway down, somewhere around my neck and head.

"You can let go now!"

"Apologies!" Enoch shook himself loose, forcing a faint pop out of my back.

When his feet touched the ground, his fist instantly slammed into the spot. Enoch backed into me quicker than expected, and we linked arms once more. He scuffled briefly, accidentally grabbing me by the wrists, but once linked, he dug in his heels and shoved me over him.

I rolled lightning fast, snapping my arms back in before he could get them jammed, and kicked the Rock again.

We fell into the process until the set of moves became a chain of conjoined motions. Punch. Link. Roll. Kick. Roll. Punch. The warm spot on the Rock brightened with each resounding blow, and the faster we went, the hotter the surface grew, becoming more malleable.

"Don't stop," I said when I felt Enoch's pace slow.

He grunted an affirmative and sped back up, landing an impressive punch that sent ripples of gooseflesh down my back. We were making good time, working together to the point that the Rock no longer felt us as two separate attackers, but as a solitary figure. We were convincing it.

I pushed us. Rolling over each other's backs turned into practically flipping over one another, and every time our arms relinked, we held firmly up to the point of release. The Rock grew hot under our touches—I felt its warmth through my shoe—but Enoch refused to stop. He looked and sounded as though he could've gone on for hours.

I blinked away the sparks that shot out from my foot's contact with the Rock. "Almost . . ."

"Ten more," Enoch said.

Punch. Link. Roll. Kick. Roll. Punch. Link. Roll. Kick.

Faster and faster, until the wound in the Rock dripped with molten flame. My foot and Enoch's fist became the same limb. Our bodies became each other's bodies, and the gold Ignis pooling off of me collided with Enoch's green Ignis to form a vortex of churning energy.

In that instant, I saw Enoch's mind—felt his mind in my own—and released myself to the swelling determination rioting through both of us. In that moment, we became one.

I gave the Rock of Sages an extra-hard kick before sending Enoch over my back.

He rolled through, half side-flipping over me, and exploded his fist into the wound. The emerald energy bit into the Rock, as it had into the cannonball, and pushed it back a few inches, sending shards of green-gold fire rippling up and down.

Ignis dispersed from Enoch's fist as he swayed tiredly. Panting softly, I peered through the smoke at the Rock, searching.

Though small in comparison to the dents from the past five hundred or so years, our mark was still there, a pale scar among a labyrinth of craters. We'd done it.

Enoch wiped sweat from his bandana and looked back at me.

Not bad, swash. I nodded. *Not bad at—*

Thunderous applause echoed from the other side of the hall. I spun, all contentment dashed against a jagged rock. I felt it all spill out around me.

"Bravo!" Kaleo hurried out from under an archway, shaking his head. "And to think that the two of you were so set on being mortal enemies! At first I thought what happened on the hyper-ship might've been a fluke . . . but Lords, young'uns! You marked the Rock of Sages! In my book, you just passed at least three of the Trials!"

Whatever I'd been feeling, it was gone now.

I didn't feel enlightened or empowered; I felt violated.

Jaw trembling, I stared down at my hands. "What did you do to me?"

"Me?" Kaleo sounded proud. The happiest he'd ever been with me in the same room. "I've only been an observer! You did all that yourself, Kaster!" No, he was beaming. I'd never even thought he could look at me like that . . . "You found—"

"I found *nothing*."

The gold necklace hummed beneath my scarf, reminding me why I could never connect with another soul again. Not until I healed this curse.

I turned toward Enoch.

You.

Before he could utter a syllable, my foot cracked across his face—Ignis-less and dull, but with my strength thrown behind it.

Enoch dropped to the floor, and I made sure my shadow loomed over him so that he never forgot my next words.

"Don't. Ever. Do. That. Again."

CHAPTER 22

Prince

You know what? I squinted up at the fifty-foot-long stained-glass depiction of the Dragon Lords using their final flames to grant the human race Ignis. *This place is actually kinda dusty.*

Whoever was in charge of cleaning Carbonek's windows hadn't done a very good job. A layer of brown dust coated the whole top section of the window, masking lime-green Lord Draconus of the Universe in a cloud of haze.

Luckily, I felt no connection toward magical flying lizards, so I slid my bag of weapons further up onto my shoulders and waltzed on down to the next window.

I didn't recall what the next window was. Or the next.

I didn't recall any of them. That was because while I walked, I walked in the abyss. I didn't see Carbonek around me anymore. How could I? After all Jezna had said? After all the looks I'd been getting from Navs who knew I was Ignis-less, that could guess based on my guns? After everywhere I went seeing nothing but Ignis?

The abyss was the only place where it all just went away. There wasn't any Ignis in the abyss. There wasn't anyone.

Although, at times, I could hear Father and his songs.

He had built the abyss for me, and without it, what did I have? My guns? They were made through my time there. When I had to think, to build, I dove into that dark place and brought something out with me. Archengard and its stupid Lords had failed me since day one. The abyss never had.

Now that Father's gone, the abyss is the only connection I'll ever need. No matter what a bunch of stuffy old dudes say. The knight's a nut, and the Shadarian's just an asshole.

I blinked slowly, my eyes having drifted away from the stained-glass window of Talen Vento and settled on a figure standing in the shadows of a column. My right hand instinctively shot for my backpack, but instead of attacking, the figure just slid deeper into the blackness.

I dropped my hand. "I can still freaking see you." I hesitated. "Get your ass out here, Scarfy. You and I got some talkin' to do."

Barco Reyveth stepped into the light.

Oh.

My mouth began to form a hundred syllables at once but only succeeded in producing a squeak. After I'd flogged my brain into raw pulp, I struck a sorry salute.

"Holy moly, High Navigator Barco, I'm so freaking sorry, I thought you were that spooky Shadarian dude, and I promise that I'll never say anything like that ever again, and if you don't believe me—well, I'd honestly understand that—but—"

"Do you like the windows?"

"Huh?"

Barco moved to stand at my side. "The stained glass. They're quite extraordinary."

I pivoted, following his gray-eyed gaze. Talen Vento had never really appealed to me. He'd been a knight of the Hotsporent Order before becoming one of the three founders of the Brotherhood, and because of that, was generally despised throughout history by both knights and Navs. Knights hated him because he'd betrayed them, while Navs viewed him as a knightly dropout. Father had respected Vento, but only ever told me stories and sang songs about Adam Evenstar, the father of the Code.

And Talen's turquoise-and-silver god armor reminded me too much of Jezna.

"It's all right, I guess."

"The ionsmith thinks he can do a better job than Carbonek's finest glassblowers?"

"Course not." I'd tried glassblowing for a week. The results hadn't been pretty. "I just don't see why Vento needs such a huge window. Everyone and their mother knows he's one of the best . . ."

"I suppose that makes you an Evenstar follower, then?"

I nodded.

"He has a whole wall to himself along the east side. There's a window for every great Navigator that has traversed these halls . . ." Barco began to walk in the opposite direction. "So if you'd like to see your father's, follow me."

I practically tripped over his cloak.

Not long after entering a hall perpendicular to the one I'd wandered into, Barco stopped before another window. In contrast to the one dedicated to Vento, it was a lot smaller, but still towered close to thirty-five feet. And instead of an armored figure stoically clutching the hilt of a broadsword, the violet, pale, and black glass depicted a man with brown-black hair in a leather jacket, magenta sunglasses hiding what I knew to be twinkling green eyes.

Unlike the other windows, there were no flame-like depictions of Ignis roaring around him. Instead, he held a gatling gun up on one shoulder and carried a sniper rifle in the other.

Though it was just a stupid little window covered in dust and surrounded by much larger, much cooler windows, I felt an overwhelming pressure build up behind my eyes.

I sniffled. "Tell me about him."

"Dante was one of the best Sharpshooters the Brotherhood ever had," Barco said. "A stubborn man, but one who lived and breathed the Code. He was one of the many reasons why our time was such an incredible time to be a Navigator . . . and one of the many reasons why it was so hard to see that glorious age shelved so early by the Perpetual War."

Father had seldom spoken of the early days of the War, when the Brotherhood had acted as elite fighters for the Government. I knew that he'd been involved somehow, but I'd never pried too deep. Any time it was brought up, he'd always sunk into sadness. And I'd hated seeing him sad.

"He fought well?"

"You must know, Prince, that I speak only the truth."

"Then speak it. Please."

"I'm afraid you won't want me to."

"Tell me."

Barco closed his eyes. "Although Dante was called 'the Fearless Forger' for his seemingly impenetrable courageousness, he was deeply afraid of dying. The fear of death is nothing new to Navigators; we're a legacy-chasing folk as it is. We all want to be remembered, but Dante was more afraid of being lost to the winds of time than anyone.

"That's why I had his window erected larger than it should be. His window was to be only twenty feet tall. I had the glassblowers add the extra fifteen feet." He paused. "I figured that despite lacking Ignis, he deserved a shrine befit for a Dragon Lord. It's very rare that an Ignis-less Navigator spends more time saving Ignis users than himself."

When he looked down at me, I saw sorrow etched into his tight features.

"The rest of Dante's squad perished during the War. He left the Brotherhood immediately. Despite his brilliance when it came to firearms, Dante was firmly against killing. The Fearless Forger was a façade: his attempt to live up to the Ignis-using legends that his brethren became. But in many ways, that was why he was such a good Navigator. He didn't need Ignis.

"He was a skilled thinker, a brilliant Sharpshooter. And an even better friend."

I wiped my nose on the sleeve of my jacket, the same sleeve I'd wiped my nose on at age eight when Father told me that he was going away for a while. That I was to make myself food and put myself to bed at night while he went off on what was to be his final quest. The quest for what he said had been one of the powerful artifacts on Archengard: a Tintagen Talisman.

I wiped my nose, dove into the abyss, and returned.

"Barco," I said, "what's the Obsidian Obelisk?"

He stopped stone dead. For a moment, I thought that he might've actually *been* dead. Barco was always still as the grave compared to the always-twitching Kaleo, but here he was, even stiller than that.

"Why do you ask?"

"Because Father died looking for it."

And as quick as the darkness had crawled across Barco's face, it was gone, replaced with solemn warmth. "Then it sounds like he continued being the Fearless Forger until his dying day . . . Can you take up his mantle?"

CHAPTER 23

Jezna

Fresh air. Somewhere outside.

After several minutes of searching, I relocated the throne room and retraced my steps to the front gates. Two Nightguards stood on opposite ends of the entrance. Pausing between them, I couldn't help but feel that they surveyed me, internally scoffing at my armor. To them, I was nothing but a relic of an age that many Navigators would've been fine with forgetting. An age before the Brotherhood had existed.

I remembered how Macín used to sit with me beside the river and clean his sword, helmet tilted low. I remembered, during one of our many philosophical discussions, him saying, "We may be the last, but that does not mean we just let the ways of the Orders die." He'd point at the tip of his glistening helmet. "These are our faces. Not this flesh beneath. The metal is our promise—that our bond to Archengard is stronger than steel."

"Our honor needs no face, because we're *all* capable of finding the balance."

Though the sight of the sky garden through the golden gates stilled some of my anxiety, it wasn't enough. My legs shook under the stare of the Nightguards.

Not here. Back to my river.

I turned and bolted back through the entrance, beyond the Nightguards into one of the intersecting corridors. For a knight that prided herself on being a *real* navigator—one that dealt with the navigation of landscapes instead of anything Brotherhood-oriented—it was a serious navigational error. The corridor was packed with rookies and veterans alike.

The younger ones merely glanced my way with interest, but the older ones slowed, raising irritated eyebrows.

A hundred years after the last knights declared their Orders dissolved, and the Brotherhood still harbored disdain. Some part of them appeared to believe that if the Chivalric Code was to return, it would remove the Navigator's Code. Of course, such ponderance was fear-driven, but I wasn't entirely opposed to it either.

Yet these Navigators were different. They watched me, not just with the frustration of someone who couldn't comprehend what they were seeing, but with fixed hatred. There was a deeper resentment than that of the Navigator-versus-knight complex.

I turned down a less-crowded hall as fast as possible. Could it be that they knew my secret, too?

Kaleo knows I am cursed. He could've told them.

But Kaleo was so much different now than he'd been in the throne room. No matter how hard I wanted to believe it, I couldn't picture the Kaleo that had leapt off our ship telling people that I'd obtained Ignis by unnatural means.

Daria recognized me when we first met. Others must be able to as well.

I nearly ran over a short boy with slick brown hair in a maroon dress shirt.

"My sincerest apologies . . ." I tried to right the child without touching him but succeeded only in scaring him away. This caused a ripple effect, and the hall was cleared of everyone in moments.

Fresh air, my mind pleaded, longing for the green hills and blue brooks of Anamana. For Macín and the rest of my departed Brothers . . .

I let the halls take me where they wanted, moving quickly, armor squeaking. It was best to keep the pace and pray for a pathway to the outside rather than slow down and deal with the consequences—the eyes that seemed to always be on me.

The thief, I concluded angrily.

He was the one that had told everyone. Enoch would never and Murta didn't like anyone, but Prince had a big mouth and little filter. All the glares I'd received over the past few hours were the product of his simplemindedness. He'd let my secret slip and—

"Knight," a male voice called. "Face me."

Nervousness slipped into fear, which quickly curdled into faint anger. Did this man think me a fool? That I was some court jester, never to have jousted or dueled?

I ignored his command. "That wouldn't be wise."

"And why's that?" another voice asked.

I turned, coming face-to-face with a group of seven middle-aged Navigators—five men, two women—all dressed in multicolored suits and vests. The voices had come from the two men who stood at the front. One wore a dirty brown suit jacket and the other a black suit jacket over a seaweed-green dress shirt.

All of their eyes glowed with Ignis.

According to the Chivalric Code, a knight didn't attack unless attacked. Provocation wasn't grounds for entering combat, though facing a group of Ignis users was something else entirely. This was no longer the mere man I'd thought I was being heckled by, but a small mob.

A handful of times in the Perpetual War, I'd found myself surrounded and alone. I could duel my opponents one on one, but groups were different. There were only so many angles you could see in armor, after all. That was why there had been Orders. Knights fought in groups, not alone.

Yet Macín said he founded the Tolkkyan Order as an alternative to the way things were—he founded it based upon these fools standing before me.

"Who recruited you?" the brown Navigator asked.

"Daria," I said.

"She and Lance are High Navs by default. Neither one fought during the War."

"I was instructed by Daria that Carbonek was a haven from the War. Is this not it? Is this not where Ignis users seek refuge from a world that seeks to enslave them?"

"You'd be one to search for such a thing. After all the Navs *you've* left behind."

That gave me great reason to pause. When I spoke next, it was in a much lower, far weaker tone. "Where did we cross paths?"

"Hecton."

They're the Navigators I saw.

The battle I'd arrived at too late to save anyone. Where I'd been handed the prism artifact by the dying Ignis user, told that the Jackals had returned, and first met Daria.

There'd been deaths on both the Government and the Nodan side, but these Navigators had somehow been caught in the crossfire, too. Whether it'd been their mission to keep the peace or recover the artifact, it didn't matter anymore. The truth was, as a knight, I'd failed to save them.

There'd just been too many souls to save. The only reason I didn't recall the situation in as painful a light as those facing me did was because it had just been another night in the War. Another battle.

Another river to cross.

"If I'd been able to," I said sorrowfully, "I would've assisted them."

Just like you assisted Kanbrik? Nothomathos?

"Bullshit!" the brown Navigator said. "You would've fought them, too!"

"And now you think you can join us?" the green Navigator asked. "A knight?!"

With every bellowed word, the group crept closer, until I could see the swirling of Ignis in their eyes. They really did mean to attack. They were willing to defile everything they'd ever sworn upon just to get revenge for their fallen brethren.

Honorable . . . but also the exact opposite. They were the reason I'd been reluctant to come to Carbonek to begin with.

Macín had been wrong. All Navigators were the same. They preached about collectivism while isolating others. They spoke about "spirits of fire" and burned everything in their wake. They built palaces of peace held up by pillars of violence. They only protected and preserved if it was in their interest.

Connection, as Archengard around me had proven, as the death of my Brothers had proven, was a lie.

I stood my ground, tapping into Ignis. A knight didn't attack until attacked. And a Tolkkyan knight definitely didn't run.

"That armor taints this place!"

"Cast it off!"

"Knights can never be Navs!"

I'm sorry, Brothers, I thought, and the aqua flames spread up around my chest and shoulders until I was bathed in them. *But my attempts to quell this world have failed. I must—*

From the other side of the hall, located up on the eastern balconies, a meteor of pink fire streaked through the air with pinpoint accuracy, nailing the brown Navigator in the dress shoes.

It was so sudden and alarming that my Ignis winked out. Luckily, all of their Ignis had been extinguished as well, all except the brown Navigator. Still glowing, he paused, looked down at his flaming shoes, and roared.

In response, eight more meteors soared the length of the hall and attached themselves to six more pairs of dress shoes until every one of the Navigators' feet was on fire. Those toward the back were smart; they turned and fled for their lives, scuffing their shoes in an attempt to kick the strange material off of them. The others followed with purple faces and wails.

I watched the procession prance away with disjointed focus. I was too high-strung, too exhausted to feel any relief or humor toward what had happened. What I did feel, though, was immediate recognition.

The fire that had stuck itself to the Navigators' shoes was identical to the fire shot out of the Nodan Ignis hunters' terrifying cannons: an unnatural man-made flame that attached itself to one's flesh and ate away.

Except the fire that had saved me hadn't eaten through anything. It had been harmless. A mere distraction.

When I glanced up at the balconies, I found their black-and-white marble basins barren. Whoever had fired the Aestus was gone.

CHAPTER 24

Enoch

My fault. All my bloody fault.

Kaleo rushed to my side, but I slapped his hand away, lurching to my knees.

"You two need to get it together for the sake of the rest of your squad. And don't be in a rush to rise. You just got kicked by a Shadarian—"

I jumped to my feet, hiding the pain that laced my jaw. I was tired of people rushing to my aid. I knew how to take a punch. No one had helped me in Serapharus. I hadn't needed anyone's help in the Light Isles.

"For the rest of 'my' squad?" I asked. "How are he and I supposed to be a squad?! You said so in the throne room!"

"And I took it back, didn't I? I said you had the potential. You don't just go to sleep one night and wake up a squad the next. You don't just be a trainee one day and become a full-fledged Navigator the next!"

"You did."

Kaleo closed his mouth abruptly but shook himself, gesturing at the Rock. "You still have a lot of work to do, but look what you can do when you work together! That's a dent, not a crinkle!"

His words were better saved for the Rock.

I tugged my jacket back around my still-smoking shoulders.

"The first time I fully possessed something," I said, "I almost got trapped in it. The second time, when I didn't even mean to, I messed with Murta . . . I can't keep trying to connect when I clearly can't. It's bloody hopeless."

"Hopeless. You know what was hopeless?" Kaleo slapped my chest, harmlessly but hard, startling me from my sorrow. "Rescuing Mathias from the Black Cells. How do you think I did that, hrm?"

Now, it was my turn to close my mouth. The veins in Kaleo's forehead bulged, sweat prickling his brow.

"How do you think I honed an Ignis ability that didn't manifest in me until I was sixteen, huh? How do you think I convinced the Council to even let me in Carbonek?!"

He slapped my chest again. I took a shocked step back.

"You think I gave up on hope?" he shouted. "That I looked Champ, Barc, and Matty in the eyes and said, 'Well, since we can't beat the Bastion together and not one High Nav on the Council wants us to be a squad, I guess we might as well disband'?"

"You can't compare our squads!" I said, my voice rising. "From the get-go, you had Barco, Champ, and Mathias bloody Flint at your back! You lucked out on the squad that the Council gave you. Who'd the Council give me?!"

"Who you were meant to be put with. Just as you were meant to have that Ignis ability! Did you not see the mark that you and the Shadarian made?"

"And you don't see the marks you and Mathias made all on your own?" That finally shut him up. "How can you ask me to connect with someone that doesn't want to connect?!" I turned away furiously. "I don't need a squad, and I don't need connection."

I felt Kaleo's hand brush my shoulder. "Where are you going?"

I stomped toward the archway. "The Bastion. If I can't beat it with my squad, I'll beat it on my own."

"Why would you attempt such a foolish—"

"Because it's what you would do."

I left Kaleo and the bloodied bandages surrounding the Rock in a ruinous graveyard.

The moment I stepped out into the hall, I blocked the path of a passing squad of four boys. I must've looked terrifying—all bruised, sweaty, and bleeding from my hands—because their eyes widened.

"Oi, where's the bloody Bastion?" I demanded.

"The Bastion?" one of them said.

"Didn't hear me the first time, did you? Where is it?"

"Right up that staircase. On the second floor. Should be real easy to find . . . You running it?"

I glanced over my shoulder, already on the second step. "Suppose I am."

Another one snorted. "You and what squad, trainee? I haven't seen no Navs strolling about wearing boxing jackets. Haven't even got a suit yet, have you? Blimey, you can't be planning on running it by yourself?" He began to laugh, but I'd already reached the landing and was scaling the second set of stairs.

If this was Serapharus, I would've broken his nose in twelve places . . . Though I might've ended up possessing him instead. Then I'd just be punching myself.

Ignis enraged me. I just wanted to use Green Fire Fist, not all the shite that came with it. I didn't want to be able to manipulate those around me. I didn't want to connect. I just wanted to box, to swashbuckle.

"Why's that so difficult to ask for?" I shouted, earning a stupefied expression from a passing female Navigator. I glared at her, then paused.

I bloody needed that pause.

I can't hate my own Ignis, I realized, brushing by her with a somewhat sincere nod. *I have to at least try to be friends with it . . . But then how am I supposed to get blokes like Murta to accept me? How am I supposed to get the* world *to connect?*

The Shadarian's touch still lingered on my hands. His caramel scent still hung in the air around me. He'd been so intimidating for so long, then suddenly, at a touch, I'd felt . . . comforted by him. And that deep comfort had unsettled me beyond words.

Those emotions . . . I wasn't supposed to feel those. I shouldn't have let him help me—build up my confidence just to tear it all down. That was what the Olders had done to me in Serapharus. Those emotions had almost gotten me killed. Connection was a lost cause in this world. What had once thrived now lay dull and dead . . .

"—bloody ridiculous that you're making me do it by myself!"

I slowed next to a vacant hallway and listened.

"Pardon my Archengardian, but the Skrill was easier than this game of grab-arse!"

The frantic voice rang familiar; the mechanical churning that accompanied it didn't. The voice shrieked to hysterical crescendos, dimmed, then was replaced by the churning. Scattered curses became a constant, and after a moment of slow recognition, I peeled off down the hall and into an archway glowing with light.

I emerged onto a balcony overlooking a vast room similar to the training halls, but instead of a wide-open space, the room was a mazelike jungle-gym.

The Bastion: the legendary obstacle course that had tortured squads for decades.

Rocks and boulders, grass and moss, streams and rivers, and even parts of what looked like an abandoned temple lay meshed together along its width. Parts of it spun and shifted, the stairs leading up to the temple roof constantly switching places and forcing the bloke running up to it to jump about.

He gained speed, nearing the green jewel situated at the top, then a thick log climactically erupted out of the wall and knocked him off the side into the lake. He screeched before slamming spread-eagle into the water. Cowlin's cackle erupted from directly under the balcony.

I quickly descended the stairs to watch Loc emerge from the pond shore, hoodie plastered to his chest. It was only after he resurfaced that the machinery stopped, the platforms falling back into place.

"You, my friend"—Loc pointed a dripping finger at the Navigator rolling around on the floor—"are the designated Charger from now on."

"Fine by me." Cowlin hopped to his feet. "Let's trade positions this round. If you dare."

"Pfft. That'd be a sight to behold."

"I'm staying Shield," Maddox said, standing beside Cowlin.

Cowlin punched him in the shoulder. "You're only saying that so you don't have to swim, Brother."

Maddox shrugged. "Water sucks."

Loc finally spotted me making my way down the stairs and waved.

"Look who's back," he said, shaking water from his red hair and fishing around his hoodie to withdraw his crystal necklace. "The mighty Skrill slayer. How'd—" His lips parted slightly in astonishment. "Whoa."

"Aye?" I said.

"What happened to your face?" Cowlin said, bounding over and inspecting me. "Got a grapefruit on your jaw, you do!"

I dabbed at the welt. "Er, fell in the shower. Slippery floors. S'all right." I changed the subject. "So this is the Bastion?"

"Aye," Loc said, eyes still slightly narrowed. "It's like a third training hall, but when you hit the other two, they don't hit back. A while back, High Navigator Jesper Krantes imbued the room with his Ignis ability so that it'd be the ultimate challenge for trainees."

I remembered Jesper from many of my books. He'd been obsessed with preparing the next generation of Navigators. He'd helped train Mathias Flint . . . and the Leviathan.

"Is that what makes it move?" I asked, uppercutting thoughts of Kaleo from my head.

"Got a mind of its own, it does," Cowlin said. "Did you see Loc go flying?"

Loc's eyes glowed blue, his crystal pulsing strangely with them. "My Ignis's only good for being Sharpshooter, not the bloody Charger!"

I realized with a start that I didn't know what any of their abilities were. Loc generously held up an arm. The three-foot-long bow made of electric-blue Ignis he'd used against the Skrill materialized in his hand, the energy used to form it springing out from his soul.

"It's a Conflicted ability," he said, "but that also means I can't use it on the Bastion. The room's already been rebuilt at least a hundred different times, and the major general's been cracking down on Conflicted users ever since the last time."

"Suppose you tell me what last time was." I said.

Loc's face fell. "Murta."

I touched my chin instinctively, flinching against the cold wrath that had slammed into me and the gold eyes from my dreams, then realized that all three Navigators' eyes were on me.

"You've gotta be kidding me," Loc said.

"It's not what you think!" I protested. "It . . . it was my fault."

"'Ass brings him back to Carbonek and he does *this*?!"

"It was my fault! He didn't even use Ignis!" I trailed off. "We were just practicing, and my ability . . . I accidentally used it on him. Somehow." I shook my head angrily. "Like I said, my fault. I was bloody stupid."

Cowlin tilted his head. "And your ability is what, exactly?"

I squirmed. "Connecting, Kaleo says. I don't even know anymore. I can transform my spirit inside me, but somehow also transfer it into others."

"Like possession?!" Cowlin asked.

"It's disturbing, I know. Can't believe you didn't see me go inside the Skrill."

"No, that's awesome! Think of all you could do!" Cowlin set to brainstorming immediately. "You could possess enemies in the middle of the battle, run 'em off a cliff, then exit their body to safety! Or you could take over monsters and wreck everything! Can you possess objects, too?"

"I tried. We mainly worked on connecting with my own ability."

"How'd that go?"

"Getting better at sustaining Ignis for longer, I suppose."

Loc cocked his head back toward the Bastion. "Then you think you can hang with us?"

Though the plan had originally been for me to run it by myself, my excitement swelled, filtering fragments of that infamous swashbuckler cockiness back into me. Being around rookie Navigators did wonders. Especially Loc. "Hang?" I repeated, tapping his crystal competitively. "I can do more than hang, bruv."

Though a steely shadow crossed Loc's hazel eyes moments after I touched the blue jewelry, it dispersed even quicker. "Oh, can you now? Usually we only run the Bastion with three since Larry and 'Ass are always bustling about, but we'll switch everyone around and give it a go if you'd like. How's that sound?"

"Sounds wicked." I nodded eagerly. "When do we get started?"

Cowlin poked my jacket. "After we get you lookin' like a real Nav, we do."

CHAPTER 25

Prince

Bad luck followed some fellas to the ends of Archengard. I knew for certain that I was among their ranks.

It had lurked over Father his whole life, following him from Narthes to Khronera and back again. It'd even latched onto me after his death.

"If your luck is so bad," I'd asked one night when he wandered in through the creaky oak door, bandaged up and bleeding, "why don't you just give up?"

His reply hadn't been what I'd expected.

"That's the secret, isn't it, little prince?" Father had replied. Always "little prince." Never Junior. "You gotta find something to counter it. In my case, I found the great spirit of honor. In this life of criminals and mercs and all kinds of thieving lot, having bad luck and no Ignis puts you at a disadvantage. So you just gotta put honor before everything. As my old pal the Leviathan used to say: No cryin', no lyin', no alibi'n. Something like that. And as the Brotherhood used to say . . ."

He'd toast his glass of ale to the dripping candles. "Til the rainbow's end!"

The memories hit hard, even after so many years. Especially after seeing that stained-glass window, seeing him again.

Father was right. Honor was the last thing I had, and for that reason, I had to put it before everything. Even before my pride. It would be the thing I fought for, the thing I died for if I had to.

Though it'd be nice not to die yet, bad luck. Still got fathers to avenge and Obsidian Obelisks to find, right?

Training Hall A was empty when I slunk back into it. It was that rare part of the late afternoon where I could actually focus without interruptions, where everyone was either gorging themselves on a late lunch or heading out on a quest. From what it seemed like, the grind never stopped for most Navs.

Letting my fingers roam free, I lost myself in my work, shifting between the ring of weapons scattered around me and the tools in my lap. Metal and light collected as one, spiraling me into the abyss where I worked.

What was I thinking? I was suddenly aware of my rapidly working hands almost ripping out the wrong wire in my flamethrower. That would've been disastrous.

But nowhere near as disastrous if Kaleo had seen me . . . Lords, those dudes probably went straight to the Council. That fire won't fade for another twenty minutes. In

T-minus two minutes, I'll be packing my bags and sent straight back to Narthes. Back to Father's grave. And my bad luck will follow me there.

I'll be forced to start over. Without anyone. *All over again—*

A figure stepped through one of the archways located along the sides of the hall. In seconds, I had the flamethrower's burned wires replaced, its core scrubbed off, and the whole weapon locked and loaded. A squeeze of the trigger and the south side of the hall would've become a bonfire.

But when I looked over the weapon, it wasn't the Navigators I'd attacked. It was Jezna.

Honestly, I would've rather had it be the Navigators.

Switching the weapon off, I slumped back down at the center of the weapons ring and got back to work.

Jezna took her time walking over. She moved more stoically than before, as if intimidated. Nah, definitely not that. She was chill now because she was trying to hide that she owed me. She was mad as hell; the rigidness of her movements reeked of it. The slow trudge was done out of anger. She wasn't here to express her gratitude, to say—

"Thank you."

A wire flew up out of the core of the flamethrower, smacking me in the face. I cursed and shoved it away, making sure it was tightened before snapping the compartment shut. When I looked back up, Jezna stood beside me.

"Oh." I quickly scooted away from her, bringing as many guns as I could gather with me. "No clue what you're on about. Why're you here?"

"You wouldn't have exclaimed 'Oh' if you didn't know what I was thanking you for," she said.

"I exclaimed 'Oh' because I didn't see you come in."

"You pointed a flamethrower at me."

"Hm. Don't recall that. Must've been that tiny-ass helmet vision. Imagine having to look through a mailbox slot to see."

Jezna seemed to accept the strangeness of the situation and—to my enormous irritation—decided she'd keep standing in place.

"Didn't realize you'd become a Nightguard," I said.

"You aren't going to acknowledge what you did, are you?"

A simple question, with a much simpler answer.

I picked up my stun gun and began to toy with its barrel. "Nope." Just giving my hands something to do besides shake. When Father was out hunting for the Obelisk, the only thing that had soothed me had been working in the forge, just touching the tools he'd kept there. "That'd be dishonorable."

Jezna's silence no longer felt forced, but content. That kinda freaked me out a little. I moved the conversation forward.

"Not all Navigators are like that."

"What makes you so sure?"

"Because Kaleo isn't, and Father sure wasn't. Those asshats weren't Navs. They aren't getting stained-glass windows any time soon."

She looked up at me. "'Wasn't?'"

I chewed my lip. "He's dead."

"I had no idea."

"S'fine." I exhaled deeply, but it came out all staccato. I'd never realized an exhale could have that many periods in it. "Everyone kicks the bucket someday, right? And besides, he was asking for it. Lunatic stuck his nose in too many wasps' nests."

Jezna was quiet for a moment, as though she were deep in the process of remembering something. She looked like me when I dove into the abyss. "We are in the same boat."

This time, I looked up at her.

"My . . . Brothers died, too," she said.

"The Tolkkyan Order?" I remembered.

"Yes. They were my only family. I never knew anyone other than them. When no one else wanted me, they took me in. No one wanted an Ignis-less child in Anamana. No one wanted . . . weakness."

"So you never even knew your parents?"

"No."

I swallowed. "Father wouldn't have cared. He would've taken you in."

Jezna shuffled awkwardly. "I . . ." She shook her head. "Nevertheless, those were confirmed Navigators. And you still attacked them."

"No, I didn't."

"If Kaleo asks, you'll say the same thing? Even when they show him the Aestus still attached to their shoes?"

I said nothing.

"Which gun was that?"

"Sticky gun," I said under my breath.

She chuckled. It was weirdly refreshing to hear such a human sound escape her. "Is that really what you call it?"

"Sticky-fire gun, to be exact. I nabbed a bunch of the pieces from Shade's Bay. There's a lot of Nodan tech in here you can't get anymore. Unless you, like, loot a battlefield or . . ."

I drifted off. I'd gotten good at reading Jezna's armor. The distaste that returned to her posture was immediate.

So that was it, then. Part of her still resented me for the life I'd chosen. And knights could *never* be anything other than mere acquaintances with thieves.

I turned back to my guns—to the abyss. "All right, fine. Just don't call me a thief . . . Weakness or not, I'm not the one that stole Ignis."

She went rigid, identical to the stance she took when channeling Ignis. Again, I thought she might attack me; the Lords knew she could. Her Ignis ability was more than capable of drowning me before I could fire one of my guns . . .

Only instead of attacking, Jezna bowed her head.

"I needed it. Stars above, I needed it. Because without it . . . I'm nothing."

The words poured out of her. They seemed pent up inside. I listened.

"As a Tolkkyan knight sworn to the Chivalric Code, as the *last* knight of the Tolkkyan Order sworn to protect every corner and crevice of Archengard . . . Can you imagine bearing the greatest weakness known to man? Can you imagine not having Ignis?"

"I can."

"And I commend you for that."

I studied the helmet's dark slit, searching for eyes—anything that I could identify her by. I ended up empty-handed but shrugged anyway. "Oh, shush now. No need to drop your chivalric ways. A knight shouldn't commend a lowly treasure hunter."

Jezna took a seat next to me. "Perhaps, for the time being, I can make an exception."

CHAPTER 26

Enoch

I smoothed down my clothes. "How's it looking?"

I'd told Cowlin that I had to wear my green-and-black high-tops—dress shoes weren't good for boxing—but everything else had been sent back up to my room. Instead of baggy gray sweatpants, I'd been given tight-fitting black dress pants. Instead of a plain T-shirt, I wore a bright green dress shirt, and in exchange for my jacket, I'd donned a black vest and double-knotted tie.

My first Navigational uniform.

"Well?"

"Bloody marvelous," Loc said, making my heart soar.

"You like it?" Cowlin asked.

I adjusted the sleeve cuffs. "Kinda itchy."

"Get used to it, you will. You were right about keeping your old shoes, though. Really puts it all together. And Navigational suits are more flexible than regular dress clothes. Shouldn't inhibit your movements at all. Since you're a boxer, I had them give you a vest instead of a jacket. Should make your punches a lot smoother, it should."

I spun my arms to test the fabric. They held firmly, but also provided just as much movement as Cowlin had said they would. Truly a wicked feat of tailorship. It'd almost be a shame to strip them during battle.

Loc tapped his crystal. "You ready?"

I fetched a roll of boxing tape from my pocket. "Let's carpe diem this shite."

"I call dibs on that phrase next go-around," Cowlin said.

The course began on a ledge of rock looking out over the entire room. Etched into the flat surface was a giant circle with the mountain-rainbow-sun at its center. Maddox was the first one to step into it. Cowlin followed, then Loc.

After gingerly stepping over the line, I looked out at the Bastion. There were two main pathways stretching right and left. Each led up to the top of the temple where the green jewel sat. The room actually looked pretty peaceful. When it wasn't trying to squash or toss someone into the lake in the middle.

"I'm assuming Jesper's ability goes into effect the second one of us leaves this circle," I said over my shoulder, careful to hide the anxiety I felt leaking into my voice. Loc's laid-back personality stilled it.

"Aye." Blue Ignis rose off his shoulders. "You know the squad positions?"

"Er, refresh me."

"Don't stress, mate. A squad has to be able to work together to the point that their moves are in sync. Need to know each other's minds in and out. That can obviously be pretty difficult, so designated positions help. That way everyone's contributing to the whole."

He sounds like Kaleo, I thought glumly, but undid my collar and listened.

"You can be Charger," Loc said. "They're the main man. The one that goes for the jewel. It's a match made in heaven for us swashes." He pointed up at the jewel. "You think you can get up there?"

I traced the pathways, reading them like an opponent. Sure enough, I found weaknesses—the right path looked shorter despite it being farther away—but a lot of its strengths were hidden.

"I know so," I said. I'd taken down more than one stealthy opponent in my lifetime. Sometimes, the more closed off they were, the more afraid they'd be in the heat of the moment. "What about you blokes?"

"I'm Sharpshooter," Loc said. "Usually occupied by someone with an Ignis ability capable of launching projectiles. Cover fire for the Charger. Meaning that I'll be attacking the Bastion and trying to prevent it from flinging you into the lake."

"What about what the major general said?"

"There are designated hit points. Most of the things that come out of the walls can be hit and sent back into them, but watch out. Hit a wrong hit point and you're technically disqualified."

I frowned. I hated rules, especially ones that kept me from using my fists. What good was an obstacle course if you couldn't pound your way through it?

"I'm Driver," Cowlin said as a hundred little moving points of bright orange energy materialized in the air around him. "Take up the rear and keep things moving, I do. My Ignis allows me to create these cute little critters . . . but that's about it, so I'm just here for moral support!" He threw me a thumbs-up, which the fireflies flocked to.

"Shield." Maddox pointed at himself. "I carve the path." Rivers of dark-green Ignis snaked their way down his shoulders. "Loc?"

"Right." Loc scuffed his shoes against the stone. "Noc?"

I didn't hear him, caught by the realization.

That was exactly how we'd fought the Skrill. Unknowingly, we'd acted as a full-fledged Navigational squadron. Jezna had been the Driver, Prince the Sharpshooter, Murta the Shield, and I the Charger. Everything had run perfectly . . . up until I'd been tasked with finishing it.

Then it had all come crashing down.

"Noc?"

"Apologies . . ." I tightened my bandana. "Ready when you are." *Immortal, I think . . .*

A dark mist engulfed me. At first, I was alarmed by its sudden intrusion, but then it grew somewhat comforting. It was black but with an elegant blue hue around the edges. I fought briefly against it, then quickly calmed. And as I calmed, I heard it whisper, "Good."

Now it felt wonderful, like all my worries had just been bled dry. Like Seraphal-rus had never happened, like I hadn't been punched by . . .

Murta.

The Shadarian's presence wafted around me, clenching down on my spirit. I suddenly felt unbearably afraid, terrified that he was hovering over me in the mist, preparing to dig out my entrails with those claws.

But then, just as quickly as the mist came, it dispersed. There was the memory of the moments before he'd lashed out. The dry-as-a-desert kindness—but kindness nonetheless. The comedic snorts. The beauty that came out of his golden Ignis rather than the overwhelming darkness. The firm but gentle touch of his hands sifting through my fingers . . .

"GO!"

I stumbled the first few steps and was the last one to leave the circle. Loc's voice rang in my ears and Maddox sped by me, rising up off the ground as the green mecha he'd used against the Skrill surrounded him, but my mind still lingered on Murta and the mist, not the growing size of Maddox's Ignis armor.

"Get moving!" Loc said, and the Bastion began to turn.

Utilizing the technique Kaleo had taught me, asking Ignis politely but prodding with anticipation, the energy turned my eyes green before consuming my outline. The markings swiftly followed.

I felt alive again. The freedom of being a swashbuckler, the pride of being a Navigational trainee, and the joy of being an Ignis user all rushed back into me. Once more, all I saw was my opponent: the jewel sitting atop the temple. Nothing else—not Murta, not the dark mist—mattered.

But the moment I leapt out onto the Bastion, the jewel disappeared behind a storm of stone. The Bastion held nothing back: a marble beam that exited out of the rock wall nearly took my head off before I'd even set foot onto the main path, and other obstacles followed, including the cobblestone beneath my feet attempting to latch on to me.

The bloody hell . . . ?!

Through the smashing columns and twisting passages, I saw Maddox's armor turn back to look for me, but I was being battered from every angle, unable to find the correct passage, nor run in a straight line. The Bastion spun me in circles.

"Does this usually happen?" I asked between spurts of breath, concentrating on keeping Ignis dispersed throughout my body.

"Not usually." Maddox sounded bored.

"Not ever!" Cowlin said, a few of his orange fireflies fluttering around my eyes. They didn't do anything other than just disorient me more. "You sure you haven't run the Bastion before? It's acting like it remembers you!"

"Why would it remember me?"

I was going too fast to hear an answer, and finally found myself breezing by Maddox into a mess of vines.

Bollocks!

I backtracked, was nearly turned into a green pancake after a massive glowing boot plowed by me, and dodged a chunk of rock that almost blew my face off. A second piece unfixed itself from the wall and flew at me, but a spray of blue arrows blew it into rubble.

Loc no longer stood in the starting circle, but charged down the path, brandishing his bow. I threw him a grateful thumbs-up before getting hit by a rolling log.

"Watch out," Maddox said.

I'm done being a punching bag.

Before the Bastion got another chance to wail on me, I used my backward momentum to throw myself over the log, tapping back into Ignis and sprinting after Maddox.

The temple roared around us, further verifying that without Ignis I would've been screwed. Embracing myself as the driver as opposed to the vehicle, I allowed Ignis to take hold of my instincts, to *possess* my brain and heighten my senses. The attacks the Bastion threw at me—though great in number—became predictable. Like all fighters, I noticed the pattern within its randomness until the attacks grew slower. And the jewel grew closer.

"We're closing in!" I said.

"Wrong." Maddox sucker-punched a moving column so hard that it got stuck in the stone. Just before he did, I spotted a red target painted on it—a hit point. "Follow."

Dodging three blocks of rock that surged out of the narrow passage then balancing on the edge, I rolled up against the wall of the temple. Maddox, Ignis armor shrinking around him to fit, attempted to squeeze through the dark opening, but vines from the briar patch latched onto his legs and dragged him out. He went roaring past me in the opposite direction.

Connect, I recalled, and prepared to lunge after him, but found Loc barreling toward me.

"Into the temple!" He shoved me through the opening and up the granite stairs toward the sides of the temple roof.

"But Maddox and Cowlin—" I protested.

"No."

I stopped running. Though Loc and I were of similar height and age, what had just escaped his mouth sounded like a demonic rasp. And when I looked back at Loc, he towered over me, all of him hanging in the shadows, save for his pale face illuminated above the light of his crystal.

His crystal.

He spun it between two fingers so that the light revolved slowly, making my eyes spin with it. And the more the crystal spun, the more the dark mist condensed around me again.

"That isn't what you want to do," Loc said, sounding nothing like Loc. His Light Isles accent had been dropped completely. "You want to go for the jewel yourself."

I blinked, but that did nothing to dispel the mist that swarmed around me. Part of me wanted so desperately to sink into it, just let all the pain go and listen, but the other part struggled. The part that had survived Serapharus and Skrill and everything in between fought.

"Loc . . ." I said. "What're you talking about? A squad—"

"—means nothing. Kaleo won't tell you, but I will." His eyes were no longer hazel, but blue. And not the bright blue of his Ignis, but blue threaded with darkness. Threaded with so many distorted colors, that there might've been traces of neon pink in them. "His squad, the legendary 327, passed the Bastion on their first attempt. But days before that, Mathias beat the Bastion on his own. It wasn't the Leviathan that conquered it, but his Shield.

"The man you dream of becoming is a lie. Though the entire Council would have you believe that they're innocent, the Brotherhood itself is a *lie*."

The mist had grown so great that as soon as the words left Loc's lips, I forgot them, though they settled somewhere deep inside me. I found myself forgetting, but also agreeing. I liked this strange mist. Exploration and curiosity were built into a swash's blood.

But still, some spark of me fought.

"I dunno what you've been eating," I said, feeling the floor spin beneath me. Seeing Loc's horrific eyes spin with it. "But you're lookin' a little pale, bruv. What're you on ab—"

"Go for the jewel. Show me your power."

This no longer had anything to do with the Bastion. This wasn't Jesper or anything Navigator-oriented. This was all Loc.

"Loc, why're you—"

The crystal's light shone so suddenly bright that I thought my eyes might melt in their sockets. Had I blinked at all in the past minute?

I was transfixed, unable to look away. I'd heard stories about swashes that became so fixated on the treasure that when they found it, they went insane from it. Was that what was happening to me?

No. Treasure had never meant anything to me. This wasn't—

Yet the mist pushed me harder, and as I tried to tear away, Loc's commands rebounded every which way inside me.

"Let me in, fool," he said, making my knees wobble, my spirit shake . . .

And then I was happy. The happiest I'd ever felt. Mist danced about me, but it was refreshing and led me where it wanted, giving me little shoves along the way. It was *helping*.

I cocked my head up at the jewel and shrugged. "See you at the top," I said, then began to sprint up the slope. Maddox blocked my path.

"WHAT," was all the mecha said.

"Bugger off, Maddox!" I turned and leapt out of the way of five boulders that plummeted out of the ceiling. Maddox just threw them into the lake.

"Shield!" he said, pointing at himself. "Charge!" He pointed at me. "Get it?! Cowlin's back at the start. So he doesn't get hurt. Who knows where Loc is." He jabbed an enormous finger made of Ignis at my chest, and within the imposing body of the mecha, I saw Maddox's glower of rage. "*You* forsook them. You struck out on your own. Every individual must be the best version of themself before being the best version of their squad!"

I was stunned by his words. Not just because it was the most I'd ever heard Maddox say but that the mist was surrounding me once more, and before I could comprehend what I was doing, I was walking toward him.

"I can handle this!"

"Can't." Maddox turned his back to me. When six rocks unscrewed themselves and dropped, he raised his fists of light. "We—"

I slid between his armor's massive legs in desperation, leaping through a gap in the boulders before they could come any closer. I pounded up the side of the temple.

"FOOL!" Maddox said, but I was long gone.

Not stopping. Not when I'm this close . . . Kaleo wouldn't stop—

My Ignis was snuffed out.

The elated feeling that had filled me for the past minute was blown out; all the mist that had swarmed about me disappeared. My eyes, no longer blazing with Ignis, shifted up from the jewel to the windows suspended high above the temple, disturbingly drawn there. All lay dark except for one window flickering with a strange golden light.

More accurately, golden eyes.

And then I was flying off the side of the temple. A column made of a material slightly softer than stone rammed into my shoulder, sending me tumbling. I yelled wordlessly, grasping for the jewel and the disappearing temple as they both faded from my vision, then hit the water with a wet splatter.

When I emerged, Cowlin and Loc were standing on the stone beach at the bottom of the starting circle's mound.

"I haven't seen a Charger move that fast since Biassis!" Cowlin said. "Scared you were actually gonna do it for a second, I was!"

I stared at my dripping hands. "I don't understand." When I glanced back up at the windows, the gold was gone. No afterglow. No weird mist.

"What'd you think happened?" Loc asked, fidgeting with his hoodie as he carefully—almost confusingly—stuffed his crystal away. My eyes flicked toward it, but only for a moment. I felt like there was something I should've remembered about it, but I didn't remember anything. Just the mist. Where had it come from?

"You got too engrossed in the moment," Loc said. "Happens to the best of us. You see that you're so close to getting to the top that you lose control. You get reckless. But most importantly . . ." He pointed back at the lake, and I swiveled to see Maddox striding through the water. "You forget about your squadmates."

"Carpe diem, my ass," Maddox said.

I chewed the inside of my cheek to keep from screaming.

Of course Jesper had designed the Bastion to utilize teamwork. Of course I'd been oblivious to it. Loc, Cowlin, and Maddox worked so well together, and I didn't work well with anyone. They might as well have had a scorpion in my place; they probably would've had more connection with it.

"Stop scowling, mate." Loc ruffled my hair. "No one ever gets it on the first try. Hasn't happened since 327 ran it—Mathias and Kaleo's squad way back when. Even with Biassis and Larry, we still never win."

"But you've won before, right?"

"One time. But it was hard. You only have to beat it once." Loc eyed me attentively, drawing his crystal back out from under his hoodie and twirling it between his lithe fingers. Its blue light flickered in my peripheral vision.

"I'll tell ya what," he said. "Why don't you meet me sometime tomorrow? We can work on things then. Maybe get some sparring sessions going—"

"I appreciate everything, gents," I interrupted. "And mayhaps I'll take you up on that offer, Loc. But at the moment . . ." I glared up at the windows, water dripping down my hair onto my face. I didn't blink them away, even when they dripped so much that my eyes stung. "Something else needs *dire* addressing."

CHAPTER 27

Enoch

Let the Lords come between a wet, wounded swashbuckler and the bloke he's pissed at," the Light Isles saying went. "For there will be a bloody big mess if they don't."

Well, I was wet. I suppose my pride was wounded. And I was definitely pissed.

I zigzagged between corridors. Every painting reached out to me. Every sequence displaying an event that took place somewhere in Navigational history reminded me of my failure to do what Loc, Maddox, and Cowlin had done. My squad was split down the middle. My squad wasn't even a squad.

But there was *one* bloke that consistently tried to sabotage us. One bloke who shouldn't have even been invited back to Carbonek.

Trailing water from the Bastion, I descended the staircase to the main hall. I asked everyone willing enough to look me in the eye if they'd seen Murta. And I kept asking until I got an answer from a squad of rookies, who claimed they'd seen him enter the Rookies Tower.

So he's hiding. He knew I'd never look for him there.

I threw open the door to our common room so hard that it snapped against the wall.

Murta sat on the couch, sifting through pages of a brown leather-bound book. When he jerked his head upward to see me, the book fell to the floor. I was up in his face before he reached full height.

"What were you doing above the Bastion? And you better give me a good answer because I'm about out of patience when it comes to dealing with your sorry arse."

"I go where I please," Murta said. "And ever since I destroyed that room, I've stayed away from it. So I wasn't there."

"I saw you in the window!"

"You saw me because you wanted to see me."

"I saw you because you punched me! I saw you in my dreams tearing out my organs because every time I try to get close to you, every time I try to act like a real Navigator, you cast me aside!"

Murta's eyes narrowed. "Have you ever thought that maybe it's because I don't like you? Has that ever crossed your rum-soaked mind?"

My eyes slid over to green, but Murta's claws slid out faster.

He had me pressed against the wall, the gnarled things pricking my neck in a shorter time than it took me to blink. Few swashes drew their swords faster.

I looked up from the claws, expecting to see triumph plastered onto Murta's face . . . and found only terror.

I watched through Ignis-infused eyes as Murta's golden spirit quivered nervously inside him, and on the outside, he visibly shook. It was almost too unfathomable to believe.

I held up my hands in disbelief. Murta dropped his claws, but his violent breathing never went down. He was almost out of breath.

"What the bloody hell was that?" I asked, watching him head for the door. "Murta, what—"

"I'm going for a walk."

I blocked the exit. "Rubbish. I want answers. Why'd you look like you were afraid of me?"

"I'm not afraid of you," he sputtered.

"Yes, you are!"

"You're seeing what you want to see!"

"You're denying what's right in front of you!" I snarled.

"Fine, you want answers?! What answers are there besides the fact that the four of us aren't meant to be Navigators?! *We suck!* The knight doesn't want to be here, Junior doesn't have Ignis, you have no clue what you're doing, and not a single person in this manor wants me here! I don't want to be here! I don't want to be squadmates with you!"

My stomach throbbed with every word he hammered home.

"And trust me when I say," he finished coldly, voice falling back to a mutter, "that you definitely don't want to be squadmates with me."

I moved to place my hands on his shoulders. "That's—"

He tried kneeing me in the chest, but I'd grown wiser since our first skirmish. Using the technique we'd practiced, I tapped into Ignis to make myself faster, slipped over his head, and somersaulted over his back. Murta launched a spinning back elbow at my face, but I rolled out of the way, not wanting to engage him in physical combat . . . or accidentally possess him again.

"Why do you act like this?" I asked as he rose to his feet, twitching with rage. "You won't even sleep in the same bloody room! Why're you such a bastard to every . . ."

I shut up.

That look . . .

Murta's expression was the hollow stare of giant scorpions and chimeras. His tense but forward posture was the stance that beasts took when they felt their lives were threatened. The aura seeping off of him screamed *inhuman.*

So this is how it ends. Death by ex-Navigator in the place where all Navigators are made. Nice goin', Noc. You might as well have stayed in Serapharus.

"I can't keep fighting you," I forced out. "And I'm bloody sorry that I possessed you." To show him that I spoke the truth, I formed my hands into a triangle and pressed them against my heart—the Navigator's Vow. "And I swear on the Code that I'll never possess you again."

The darkness didn't disperse immediately. It threatened to grow into something greater, possibly angrier. Murta swayed in place, eyes flicking about. Something shattered in his face, unveiling whatever rested behind the walls he threw up . . .

Then he flung open the door and began to descend the staircase.

"Follow me."

I lingered on the carpet, but the longer I waited, the farther away he grew. Stomach turning, I sped after him.

Murta slowed just enough when rounding corners for me to catch a glimpse of the back of his suit jacket and know which passage to take. He took me down staircases made of black stone and empty hallways shrouded in dark curtains—places in Carbonek I didn't think most Navigators knew about.

At one point we took so many steps down a spiral staircase that I thought we'd eventually reach Archengard's core, yet we pressed on into Carbonek's bleak underbelly.

The archways grew gothic as opposed to their rounded forms aboveground. I recognized the oak banisters of several wine cellars and the iron doors of vaults. Murta, however, entered none of them. He continued down the same path.

Why's he bringing me here? I shivered in the dark space. *He can't be planning on . . . ?*

Far too familiar with the stories of Shadarians slaughtering Navigators, I contemplated fleeing, but then Murta paused before a wide cylindrical room. I followed him through the thick walls and down the iron steps to the landing.

Every step sent another bead of sweat trickling down my forehead. Murta's silence shook me to my core, and when he pressed a button on a vertical slab set into the curved wall, I couldn't cork the sharp inhale that escaped me.

The wall turned, revealing the contraption stored behind it. The machine was horrifying: a mess of steel restraints, bars, and pipes. Clearly inspired by a crucifix. The location of the person's arms were held outward, and around the place where their head rested, a ring of iron was tilted backwards.

At a loss for words, I resorted to unintelligible stammering.

"You wanted to know why I don't sleep in the same room as you?" Murta said. "Why I'm always gone at night? This is my assigned bed."

"Assigned?" I repeated stupidly.

Murta pulled the scarf clear of his neck, loosened his tie, and unbuttoned the first two buttons of his dress shirt, revealing a gold chain necklace strung around his neck. If he hadn't revealed it in such a cautious manner, I would've assumed it was just another piece of Shadarian jewelry. Only now that I was completely focused on it, I could see that instead of sparkling in the blue torchlight, the necklace sucked it in. Instead of reflecting light, the gold devoured it.

"This chain can never be disconnected," he said. "It does its best to keep what rests inside me trapped, but it's still just a piece of metal."

He looked up at the machine. "I'm restless at night. Sometimes, I forget about the necklace. Something in me tries to remove it . . . So I sleep in this thing. It sedates me. Keeps everyone above safe."

It hurt so much more than a fist.

"But when I'm down here," Murta said, "thinking about all the *mierda* going on across Archengard, I get even more restless. I start thinking about removing the chain when I'm awake." He turned halfway toward me. "And removing it would mean obliterating everyone that gets in my way . . . And I do mean everyone. Even innocent lives."

"I'm sorry," I said. What else was there to say? I looked up at the machine and shuddered. "How many know you have to do this?"

"Barco designed it. The whole Council knows. A few squads here and there."

His claws. His fire. The scales . . . Maddox saying, "Gold breath . . ."

"You turn into a dragon," I said.

Murta tensed.

"That's why everyone's so afraid of you. That's why your Ignis ability's Transformative."

"Not just a dragon," Murta answered emotionlessly. "A shadedrake."

The hair on the back of my neck sprung straight up. Shadedrakes were the nightmarish black dragons that dwelled in vast underground caverns and roamed the ruined cities of northern Narthes. They feasted on entire populations, hunted mountain beasts, and could grow to be the size of a skyscraper. They were . . .

"The most violent species there is," Murta said. "A mindless monster worse than any Nodan soldier or Ignis hunter. And it lives in a Shadarian of all people.

"If this chain around my neck disconnects, if I were to have my mind taken from me and possessed . . . there'd be no telling what would happen. There'd be no telling what *it* would do."

Murta redid his collar, hiding the chain and rewinding the scarf around his neck. Throughout the whole process, he kept his eyes on the machine.

He looked devastated, a boy spent living his life in a small black box. Alone and afraid of the world around him. Afraid that somehow, when he finally did emerge from that box, the world would be afraid of him.

But I know how it feels. I've lived inside that box, too.

"You know what?" I asked, facing him so he knew I wasn't afraid. "I don't care. Not even if you do turn into a dragon . . . Kaleo said being a Navigator is about trust. Trust as a whole." I took a step forward. "*We* need to trust one another, and honestly, after everything you've said to me just now, I trust you a lot more than I did. And that's the truth, bruv."

Murta's jaw came unclenched. The brow above his earth-brown irises started to lighten and curve upward in shock, sparking emotion I'd never seen from him.

But just when I felt as though I'd finally broken through that black box of his, that my determination had held out and I'd won the match, Murta's brow flattened back into a grim stare.

"The suit looks good on you," he said, conjuring a golden flame between his claws and stalking off into the shadows.

CHAPTER 28

Murta

I tried to stay focused as I walked the black-brick halls, searching the vault numbers with Ignis-infused eyes. I tried—

Why did I tell him?! WHY?!

The Carbonek basement became the pits of my Shadarian Sanctum. The jagged arches became men in sweeping cloaks with pointed hoods. As I searched, eyes flicking frantically down at the map I'd hidden away three years ago, they surrounded me. The jackal head seared my eyes until I couldn't see the map.

Escaping was always futile. They were in me, and you didn't escape the demons that slumbered inside. Not unless you sought out their source, then slaughtered them.

What good are claws if you don't slice a few throats with them? one of the voices whispered out of the shade. *What good is . . .*

Though I could feel the Other writhing inside me, I shoved it deep below. The voices receded. The chains that bound the creature rattled, but I resumed my search anyway.

It wouldn't have me today. Not if I kept fighting.

Vault 879 . . . 880 . . . 881 . . .

Each round door was identical to the last. And the map was severely faded. This was harder than it had originally seemed.

Before I even began to pinpoint where exactly the Talisman was being held, I needed to get a hold of Barco's notes. I needed to know for certain where it was, what guarded it . . . and whatever else the Council was hiding about the remaining Talismans and the Jackals. That had been the mission from the beginning.

Barco was head of Brotherhood intelligence. If anyone knew anything, he did. Uncovering those secrets was worth a lot more than being exiled again. Even if it meant never seeing Enoch again . . .

I shook my head. He was nothing but another brainwashed fool. Another recruit Kaleo and the Council thought they could feed their lies to . . .

But if so, then why had I gone to such lengths to help him lately? Why did I feel like he'd barely possessed me? That, instead, I'd willingly aided him and just been looking for another excuse? And why did I feel like he was smarter and of greater value than everyone else in Carbonek?

Because you still care, a dark voice mocked. *You're weak.*

"Go to hell," I said.

I'd played by the Brotherhood's rules for too long. I'd tried. I really had. And nothing had worked. Their ways were hopeless, and "weak" wasn't in my vocabulary.

This was the only way.

Torches became far less frequent. The 900s moved into the 1000s, and the more I focused on their numbers, the faster the voices fled.

Yes. The mission. That was all I needed. *Focus and something to focus on.*

After my encounter with Biassis and Larry in Jameronjag Jungle, I'd stopped in White Town on my way to Carbonek. Among the airship docks and marble streets, I hadn't been recognized. Just another wannabe Navigator passing through. Most had been too drunk to pick out a Shadarian, making it all the easier for me to find Gerald Lazabar, an older Navigator who had been exiled for starting one too many dining abbey brawls.

Lazabar was a gambler who seemed destined to live out the remainder of his days drinking about White Town. But I'd learned from my short time in Biassis's squad that even the biggest of fools had tricks up their sleeves. And those who knew their Navigational history would've known that despite his soiled reputation, Lazabar had once been a close colleague of Barco.

A few rounds of blackjack, nine drinks, and one or two exchanged coins later, and I'd pried out of the mustachioed man some of the most coveted information in all of Carbonek.

If one could somehow find a way into Carbonek, somehow find its underbelly, and then somehow navigate their way among the hundreds of thousands of vaults . . . they'd find a secret passage in Vault 1200 that led directly into Barco's private archives.

Now I stood outside Vault 1200.

Well, I thought, pocketing the map. *Here goes nothing.*

I inserted two claws into the keyhole and began to work, sparks spraying outward. It took a good two minutes of tampering before the vault let out a hiss, smoke began to escape from the sides, and the door sprang open slowly. I brushed my claws against my pants before throwing it wide. My Ignis-infused eyes searched, identifying dark silhouettes as wooden crates and sheets.

I set to work at once. Unlike the idiotas above, when it was time to move, you moved. No wasting time.

I scanned the ceiling. If there really was a trapdoor, it wouldn't be noticeable. Barco was the most careful of the Council, once called the Shadow of the Leviathan. Kaleo had been the beacon, charging into quests without thought. Barco and Mathias had been responsible for all the behind-the-scenes work. They'd drawn up the battle plans during the Perpetual War.

Knowing that, it almost made finding the trapdoor easier. As a merc, you learned how to think like different people, and Barco's caution was easy to slip into. If there was to be a trapdoor, it wouldn't be out in the open. It wouldn't be in the corners of the room, as most would assume it to be.

I swung my eyes about the domed, dark ceiling.

In fact, it wouldn't even be in the ceiling.

I started moving boxes, then took to stomping my dress shoes into the tile floor, searching for a hollow sound. Well into the process, a spindly black spider crawled out from under one of the sheets I'd thrown around and began to make its way up my leg. I incinerated it with a golden fireball. No more spiders fucked with me.

I kept moving around, stomping well into the evening, cursing as each stone hurt my right foot more and more, until finally, the dull thud became a light thwack.

I poured a tsunami of Ignis into my foot and smashed it through the stone. The material broke, splinters of marble sprinkling downward to a tight crawl space. I took a knee, jamming my head into the tight darkness.

The passage snaked to the right and rose upward. And from thirty feet away, I could make out the steel rungs of a ladder.

Glaring at the jungle of cobwebs, I sucked in a breath and lowered myself into the space, reigniting the part of my brain that had been trained to survive in most spaces that the bravest of men would've gone mad in.

I was down there for an hour.

Though I figured that crawling horizontally would've been the worst part, the real pain was the climb. It felt like it went on for a hundred sun cycles. Multiple rungs snapped when I grabbed them, pieces of black metal scraped away with my hands, spitting into my eyes, and by the time my head finally hit marble, I was draped in curtains of cobwebs.

For a moment, I was so flustered, so ready to escape the crawlspace that I almost just turned my left hand back into claws and raked straight through the tile. Then I paused.

Barco could be up there right now. I'd only ever visited his quarters once . . . The day I was exiled. I remembered that they weren't very big and how close the padlocked door had been to the archway that led off to his chambers. If I did happen to be directly under his study, he might be sleeping the next room over.

Then the best course of action was stealth.

My hand curled into a dark draconic fist, and I began to press up on the tile. Slowly, I added more pressure until the stone above me groaned softly. The tile pissed particles, but still I held Ignis, pushing the stone higher until my burden lightened and I could see the interior of a dark office.

I immediately shoved the tile up onto the floor—foolishly—but I was too damn excited. After whipping my Ignis-infused gaze about the room, I scurried up out of the crawlspace.

It was dark, so I lit a torch along the wall, then turned toward the room.

The walls were lined with rows of leather-bound books and piles of worn paper. There was *a lot*. But I had to start somewhere.

It was long and brutal. And the longer it went on, the more frustrated I became. By the time I located legal documents, I was livid.

Had I really thought that it would be that easy? That there'd be a great glowing box marked secrets I could search through? This was beginning to look like a multiday task, not the ten-minute infiltration I'd expected.

No. I'm not climbing back up that tunnel.

Though I'd never considered myself a Navigator, sneaking into Barco's chambers also carried with it a wrongness. That just made me more livid. I was a merc—a raider. I'd snuck in and stolen a lot worse than a bunch of crusty old papers. I'd committed far worse acts than . . .

A jingling emitted from the door, followed by the turning of a key.

My speed saved my *culo*. Before the door swung open, I'd already extinguished the torch with my claws, covered the tunnel with the tile, and leapt into the darkness of the room to hide behind a bookshelf. Careful to make sure the rest of me was hidden, I peered with one eye through a narrow shaft between shelves.

Someone stepped into the room, moving to light the three torches . . . but their Ignis wasn't red like Barco's. It was blue.

Loc?!

The figure that entered had their hands stuffed into the pockets of a white-hooded sweatshirt. And sure enough, the eyes set within the boyish freckles glowed a dark blue . . . the same color as the crystal that he withdrew from around his neck.

MURTA.

Shadows leapt forward, devouring my vision. My mind suddenly went haywire, spasming between forgotten memories that flew by so fast that I didn't catch any. Except *one*.

The image of a black crystal dangling above me from around a faceless hooded figure's neck.

Light returned. I calmed my rampant breathing, rapidly blinking away sunspots and the afterimage of the black crystal . . . now replaced with Loc's blue crystal.

What . . . ? I curled my hands into fists to keep them from shaking, closing my eyes in an attempt to still muscles I'd once wielded divine control over. *What's happening to me?*

Loc stalked toward the bookcase.

I crept backward, but he stopped at the front as opposed to coming around back. He looked down at the crystal expectantly.

I narrowed my eyes. I'd never seen Loc wear jewelry . . . let alone a crystal like that.

And what was he doing here? The Sharpshooter of Squad 326 had always played by the rules. The only way he'd be here was if he'd been directly ordered to. And Barco wasn't Squad 326's mentor, Hektor was. It seemed unlikely that Hektor would've asked Loc to enter one of the most secretive locations in Carbonek. Especially after the Skrill incident.

Surprises continued to spring up. Loc let the crystal fall back against his chest before opening one of the drawers and beginning to rummage. But he didn't scramble about like I had. He moved with meticulous understanding, as though he'd searched this room a thousand times before. And after maneuvering myself enough to get a glimpse of his face through the books and holograms, I saw that under his hood, Loc's blue eyes were unblinking orbs. The crystal pulsed perfectly in time with the Ignis glowing in his fixed irises.

What in the twin suns is going on? I craned my neck but failed to claim a better view.

And then Loc was leaving.

I sprang up, poking my head around the back to see him stuff a piece of paper in his sweatshirt pouch and extinguish the torches by sucking the Ignis back into his hand. Part of me almost demanded what he was doing here, but I kept quiet, watching as he closed and locked the door behind him.

I counted five minutes in the darkness, then lit the center torch and stormed to the same section of the shelf Loc had removed the sheet from.

There were descriptions of lesser-known artifacts and annals, but nothing on the Tintagen Talismans. And nothing on the Jackals.

I searched the room for another hour without interruption.

Not a damned thing.

CHAPTER 29

Enoch

I picked at my toast. Prince was on his third plate, gobbling his food like a starved chimera. Jezna just stared at the table. She never ate. And across the table, Loc eyed me worriedly, but I wasn't paying attention to him or the reason we'd all been stuffed into the dining abbey so late at night: to witness the peace treaty between Nothomathos and Kanbrik.

Escorted by Eleri, her ruby dress discarded for black dress pants and a red suit jacket emblazoned with dark markings, the Nothomathos Princes marched in, glancing around the abbey through their metal helmets. Jezna sank lower in her seat.

After Eleri had situated them at the head of the hall to the left, Barco entered—brown cloak replaced with a brown-and-black suit engulfed in similar markings—with the Kanbrik Elders all in a line behind him. They moved with a gracefulness that the knights lacked.

"Go ahead," I said, shoving my plate in Loc's direction. "I'm not hungry."

When he shook his head, his crystal danced a rapid jig.

"I don't want it, but you should," he said. "A Nav's gotta eat. Part of helping out Ignis is making sure you're taking care of yourself." He glanced between us. "Are you all okay?"

"I'm not sure," Jezna said. "Enoch hasn't said much."

Because you wouldn't believe what I'd say.

"What's there to say?" Prince said through bits of bacon. "Scarfy punched Noc in the face and now Noc's upset! *I'm* upset! Shouldn't Scarfy be kicked out?"

"He's not getting kicked out," I said. "He's fine."

"Which is why I'm *really* upset," Prince replied.

"I must confess to my confusion as well, Enoch," Jezna said. "If there's to be a weak link—"

"There's no weak link because we're not a squad," I said. "And if we were, Murta wouldn't be it."

Out of the corner of my eye, I saw Prince stop eating in hurt surprise, but I just tightened my fists.

"Lies," Maddox said.

I spun on him. "I'm right well sorry about what happened last time, but this time is different. The Council forces him to sleep in the tunnels. He's *protecting* us."

Shoulders shaking, I finally looked at Prince and Jezna. I'd never been one for keeping things bottled up, especially when they got to me.

"Murta doesn't sleep in the tower because the Council forces him to sleep beneath the manor in a device that . . . that keeps him from turning into a shade-drake. That's his Ignis ability. His necklace contains it."

Prince choked on a piece of bacon and hacked it up onto his plate. After chasing the remainder down with a chalice of sparkling grape juice, he stared wild-eyed. "We're livin' with a *shadow dragon*?"

"His claws . . ." Jezna said. "Of course. That's why his ability is Transformative."

"Yeah, well, that shadow dragon gave us all a good scare once." Loc gripped his crystal like it irritated him. "And now he's going around punching people? Sorry, Noc. No way. First chance I get, I'm talking to Hektor."

"Here, here," Prince said.

"Same," Maddox said.

"You're all missing the bloody point!" My shouts drew the attention of other trainees at the table—even a few Kanbrik Elders glanced over in passing—but I didn't give a harpy's arse. "He clearly still wants to live in Carbonek, or else he wouldn't sleep in that thing . . . Now, I know everything he says is the bloody opposite, but part of him still wants to be part of the Brotherhood. I know, 'cause I caught a glimpse of it last night."

Prince poked his food quietly, no longer wolfing down chunks at a time. Jezna closed and unclosed her metallic palms, taking shaky breaths in through her helmet.

"He's walking through life shackled by his own Ignis ability," I said, letting my spirit do the talking. "He thinks he has to act that way and put up a façade because this is how we treat him. Everyone treats him like an animal."

When the elders reached the head so that they were face-to-face with the knights, Barco stood between them and addressed the abbey.

"Today marks a historic event for all of our lives," he announced. "Today, the warring cities of Nothomathos and Kanbrik put aside their disdain, make peace, and leave the Perpetual War that kills Archengard. And as many countries have done before them, such acts of peace have been completed from within Carbonek's walls. Let us celebrate this joyous day."

Nervous applause answered him. It sounded like most Navigators were on board, but not nearly enough. Loc, Maddox, and Cowlin didn't do anything.

"Doesn't seem right, something does," Cowlin said, surveying the rigid postures of the knights and the smiles of the elders as the two parties exchanged rigid handshakes. Shortly after, something must have been taken the wrong way, because someone shoved someone, and suddenly, an elder was on their arse.

Curses erupted out of the group of elders as they attempted to charge the knights, but Barco and Eleri were between them, red Ignis circling around both of their silhouettes. Before either one of them could open their mouths, what looked to be the High Elder stepped forward, pale eyes an inferno of hate.

"'A joyous day,' you call it," he said. "There will never be a day more joyous than the day I finally see Nothomathos in flames. You want to mediate peace between our nations, do you?" He pointed at Barco and Eleri. "Even now, you yell for peace but stand between us, ready to fight. The Archengard you long for is gone: *you* killed it. This isn't the time for standing on the sidelines; you must choose a side. And whereas the Government promises endless servitude, the Noda promises strength for *all* men."

This caused an enormous stir, especially among the knights, and even among some Navigators sitting closest to them, but Barco sent a column of hardened flame up into the air to silence everyone. He exchanged places with Eleri, facing down the elders with red eyes. A few of the ones behind the High Elder took anxious steps back.

"Even after the negotiations we set up," Barco said, "after the accords *you* agreed to, you still say this?"

"How could we not?" the High Elder said. "If you'd seen what has become of our city and people, you'd never swear upon a code again. You'd never seek solace in peace if your world was on fire."

"Your city is on fire because you put your trust in the Noda," Barco said. The abbey seemed to darken around him, until the only thing to focus on in the entire hall were his curdling crimson eyes. "Never forget that the Brotherhood fought in the War at the very beginning. Never forget that I fought from one end of Narthes to the other. And in the end, every city, state, and speck of the Noda was on fire. Such is the way of War."

"Kanbrik is on fire because the Government destroyed it!" the High Elder cried. "Because the Brotherhood failed to protect it. For centuries, we've traded with Carbonek. For centuries, we've served you." He shook with fury. "Yet when we needed you most, you did *nothing*. You neglected to aid us."

"He's right, you know," I said.

Cowlin gawked at me. "Who?"

"Murta. He's right about the Brotherhood." I felt myself settle back into the dark blue mist, like it had never left me. It led me where it wanted, and I liked it. It felt right. "They're the ones that cast him out in the first place."

Maddox smacked the tabletop—hard. "You weren't there when the Other took his place. You know not of the darkness." It was the most I'd ever heard him say.

"And that therefore means the Brotherhood should keep turning him away? Just like they turned away Kanbrik?" Fury built in me. When I blinked for just a second, the sleek walls of Carbonek became the bloodstained cement sides of a factory. "Like they turn a blind eye to Serapharus? If they'd fight, they could heal these places! They could save *everyone*—"

"Enoch, please calm down," Jezna said. "It's bad enough that this is happening. We—"

But I was standing now, mind completely entrenched in the mist, and the abbey was in chaos. No longer did the scrapes along the floor look like the hard work of becoming a Navigator and overcoming obstacles. They were the scars of an organization caving in on itself. Murta and Kanbrik were as much proof as the scars in the abbey: The Brotherhood had failed both of them. Rather than uphold the Code, they'd force-fed Murta and Kanbrik their own ideals, their own path of righteousness.

Even when they can't follow it themselves.

"This is how you want to instruct your Navigators?" The High Elder gestured out at the abbey. "That there's no way but the Brotherhood's way? Are you not dedicated to protecting and preserving all of Archengard? You speak such words, but at the same time, seize artifacts from countries. I walked your halls! I saw your artifacts! You don't protect Archengard: You hoard it, then claim it's whole."

He's right, the mist chided inside me. *He's right.*

And then, even as I stood, preparing to rally to the Kanbrik Elders' sides, I thought:

He's wrong.

It's not about walking the path of righteousness. It's about trying.

All the other voices in the abbey—the curses, roars, and howls—fled me, so all that I heard was the High Elder screaming.

"Archengard doesn't need to be healed. It needs to be ripped in half! The Brotherhood has failed Archengard for far too long. Failed to do what should've been done!"

He paused, and in that pause, it felt as though a thousand black holes opened up. It was as though the air had suddenly become flammable, and the elder's next words set it on fire.

"And where the Brotherhood has failed," he said, almost softly, yet somehow heard above the entire abbey, "*another* has succeeded."

The mist tugged at my spirit, trying to blow me off course yet again but not enough to stop me from sprinting down the path between tables, shoving through the crowd of Navigators, and slamming Green Fire Fist straight into the High Elder's face.

Pieces of teeth flew from his mouth as he went flying, but I didn't stop.

I sped after him, the mist completely drained from me. I no longer felt controlled or manipulated, but that just made everything feel so much worse. The pain of all the stupid decisions I'd made since arriving hurled into me, forcing me after the High Elder, Ignis whirring in my eyes, emerald light consuming everything at once . . .

This time, I was toppled. My head hit someone's knee, my arms went flying, and I landed on my arse in exactly the same way that the elder had. But instead of staring up at more elders, I came face-to-face with two young men.

Both glowed with Ignis—pale red-white and sparkling silver—though the one with the red ability let theirs dwindle out and helped me up with strong but gentle hands. He hadn't even had to try to stop me to begin with: I'd just ran into him.

Bright-blue eyes, a handsome but chiseled face, olive skin, black spiky hair, and a white dress shirt emblazoned with jagged red and gray lines revealed themselves. The shirt was unbuttoned to reveal the most impressive set of abdominal muscles I'd ever seen. He was so well-built that even with my experience, I would've been a little iffy to go toe to toe with him in the ring.

"Man, I leave for a couple of days . . ." He sounded more amused than angry, if anyone could've at a moment like this. "I'm not one to go around telling a Nav what they can and can't do, but punching a High Elder has gotta be up on the Can't list. Lemme guess: Enoch, right?"

I looked between the writhing knights and elders, and the calm Navigator that had helped me stand. "Er, yeah. Suppose so."

"And I suppose I'm Biassis Ondenecro. Now what's all the commotion about?"

So that was him. The determined, broad-shouldered treasure hunter that Hektor had supposedly scooped up from the Stormbred Mountains in the Midlands of Khronera and turned into the most promising Navigator of his generation.

And here he finally was. We'd only just met, and I already knew that it was going to be him. It had to be him. Who else had I seen around my age that looked like they were already a High Navigator? Who else carried themself with the confidence that he did?

"What's it look like?" someone asked behind him. "You brought that fiend Kaster back and the whole place goes to hell."

Biassis turned, revealing the Navigator with him: a pale boy with his arms crossed over the chest of his cement-colored three-piece suit. His face was a glare of resentment and his hair was blonder than mine, platinum tufts snaking out from under a white athletic hat.

"A Navigator is his own compass, Larry," Biassis said. "But if you're really—"

"Murta's not a fiend," I said.

Larry frowned. "A thought to consider thoroughly: Fasten your trap when the adults are talking. Especially those here to clean up your mess."

All rational thought deteriorated. I walked up to him until we were chest to chest. "Pardon my bollocks, but kindly bugger off."

Larry stepped inward. "Cheeky bastard, this one."

"As much as I'd love to see Larry get his teeth kicked in," Biassis said, slinking between us, "now isn't the time—"

"ENOUGH!" The High Elder emerged out of the mass of bodies, his gaze firmly fixed on me. "You seek to stop me from speaking the truth, boy?" Though he was in a crazed rage, his right hand slithered into his cloak pocket and withdrew a glittering bracelet. A white crystal was attached to it.

Just like Loc's . . .

"You seek to halt *their* will?" The High Elder raised the crystal to the ceiling. "Their legacy? Do you know who deserves this world, who all must kneel before?"

Barco surged toward him. "I order you to end this—"

"Only the Jackals!" the elder screamed, and the crystal exploded.

A ball of fire consumed him, burning straight through his bones, but from the ferocity of the explosion, it should've taken us all with it. But it hadn't.

Eleri had thrown herself at the High Elder, and woven a ball of ruby Ignis around the crystal so that the full blast was contained within her conjured cocoon.

Yet when the dust cleared and the abbey lay in shock, staring at a pile of unscathed, empty light mail rather than the roaring High Elder, I saw that half of Eleri's face seemed to hang on by a thread. She staggered to the ground.

Barco began barking orders immediately, instructing Biassis to oversee the knights and elders' movement to outside Carbonek and having Larry help him get Eleri to the healing branch as fast as possible.

All my fault.

I remained rooted to the ground at the helm of the chaos, Eleri's burned face and the white crystal racing around me. Becoming blue.

I watched Barco and Larry wrap the wounded High Navigator's arms around their shoulders, and before hurrying off, saw Barco flash me a disappointed . . . possibly frightened look. Then his eyes moved beyond me to the western balconies high above.

A gray-suited blond figure turned his back to me and wandered out of sight. My stomach dropped.

I can't do this.

Though across the abbey I could see Prince and Jezna fighting to get to me—though I could see Cowlin yelling my name and Loc nervously stuffing his crystal out of sight—I peeled off through an archway and sprinted for the tower.

I can't connect.

CHAPTER 30

Murta

"I need a book on crystals."

The sound of a quill being dropped back into its inkwell echoed out from the rounded archway. Several seconds later, the yellow-and-blue candlelight illuminated a robed silhouette, then Lance Maximillian stood before me.

He was one of the few High Navigators who hadn't fought in the War, instead obtaining an internship with the Chronicler in the Carbonek archives. After the old Chronicler died, Lance had taken over.

Like Barco, he wore clothes from an older age—great billowing robes made of blue and black satin, puffed lace around the shoulders, and a wide black judge's hat. He looked ridiculous, and he might've caught on to what I was thinking, because his eyes narrowed.

"Murta Kaster." He had a sandpapery voice. "It's been long since I last saw you stalk these hallowed halls. They do, indeed, all return to the Code in the end."

I chose to ignore his comment for the sake of desperation. *I'll kick his teeth in one day.* "I need a book. On crystals."

Lance lifted both eyebrows. "Crystals? You're bound to find plenty out in the valley. A treasure hunter's dream."

"All I need is a book on them . . . And not the ones that you can just find anywhere."

"What did you have in mind?"

The line I walked was razor thin. Reveal too much, he'd send me on my way before reporting me to the rest of the Council. Too little, and he might give me a book on mineralogy.

"I'm looking more in the artifact direction."

That answer seemed to satisfy Lance. After producing a golden key from his sleeve then lifting a hand so a dark blue flame appeared at its center, he led me down the winding archival tunnels into a bronze vault lined with bookshelves. The round area went up for at least a hundred feet with crisscrossing ladders. Seated in the center was a little desk.

After a second of searching, Lance pulled out a massive book from the second shelf. He set it down on the desk. "Happy reading." The end of his blue robes snaked around the corner, leaving me alone.

For hours, I found nothing. Nothing but rocks and boring descriptions. I plunged through every crystal known to man and found nothing outside of the ordinary.

I'm wasting my time. I should still be searching for the Talisman.

But I couldn't get Loc out of mind. His wide white eyes, and the crystal that'd hung around his neck. He hadn't looked in control of his movements . . . like he was being manipulated.

When I closed my eyes and indulged in the darkness within, sometimes I saw red lines everywhere. Bright crimson things, like spider's silk, all winding around the world. Moving everything. Puppeteering. They felt connected to the voices, and the voices felt connected to whatever was going on.

Something was up with that crystal.

And if my brief glimpses of memory could be believed, something connected that crystal to . . .

I arrived at a section on known crystal artifacts and rubbed my eyes to seep some concentration into me. I'd shaped my Shadarian mind to single out the most important information, to sift through long paragraphs with barely a thought and find what I needed. But nothing stood out until the seventy-fifth stanza:

Though it can be said for many other minerals, certain rare crystals were known to be weaponized by powerful dark Ignis users. This was an art known as "splicing."

Navigator Haedrin "Harrenous" Nester experimented with crystals and discovered that splicing could be replicated without Ignis. Further experimentation was overseen by Mathias Flint during the Perpetual War, in order to turn them into weapons for the Brotherhood.

These manipulated crystals weren't Ignis-containing artifacts, but containers of the soul, enabling whoever controlled the crystal to control whoever wore it. Splicing has since been decreed a violation of the Code.

I reread the passage three more times just to make sure I had everything.

Containers of the soul . . . my mind whispered, then the glass shattered.

I felt my body lock and almost surge into a seizure, but then the slivers of memory began to cut against my brain. I threw myself at them, gathering up as many pieces as I could catch before they sliced my hands into ribbons.

That black crystal over my head again. A black hood, and within its depths, tattered eyes that screamed in the darkness, dissecting me.

Then a twisted dark tower disappearing from view as I sprinted into the night, hands and feet tearing through briar patches. Crystals chasing me.

Howling jackals chasing me.

I kicked the desk over. The candle I'd lit went out with a hiss and the book went tumbling. I scooped it up and stomped the rest of the candle into wax before it could set fire to anything, pretending that it was the sickly, broken eyes.

In the aftermath, stirred only by the wind rushing down through the archives, I breathed in and out, then lifted a hand to sift under my scarf and locate the necklace. It was freezing to touch, but still there. I was safe.

But Loc isn't. Not if that crystal is what I think it is.

I hurried off to find Lance.

"I need another book."

He looked up. "The book I gave you wasn't good enough?"

"I need one on the Jackals."

"You . . . you *what*?"

"Either that or Haedrin Nester's notes on crystals. If you still have them."

"*Haedrin Nester*?" Lance's jaw opened and closed on repeat. "Where . . . did you hear that name?"

"In the book you gave me. It said she worked with Mathias. Do you know where her notes—"

"*No*," Lance said. "There is *nothing* on the Jackals here. Do not speak of such darkness."

I narrowed my eyes. "If you think I'm like the other sheep, that I don't know the things I'm not supposed to know, then you must not have heard what I've been up to since I left. You don't have anything on the Jackals? Fine. Then where can I find Harrenous—"

"You cannot find Haedrin because she's no longer alive," Lance snarled. "And you cannot find her notes because they're restricted reading. Only a referral from a High Navigator may grant you access."

"Then I'll get one," I said, and left the library.

Passing glowering, panicked Navigators in the gilded halls, I thought about what my next course of action should be. The most obvious was infiltration. I couldn't rely on anyone here.

You can rely on Enoch, something foolish in me said, making me almost miss the dark voices. *You told him your secret. You trusted him—*

No. That had been irrational emotion: If this had to do with the Jackals, then I needed to be alone. Enoch . . . would just get in the way. The mission was the only focus. While I was investigating Loc's crystal, I could probably figure out where the Karnocolix was located, too. There had to be a book somewhere in the library that revealed where it was being kept, or at least speculated. Possibly among Dresden Roberts's original blueprints for Carbonek or Mathias's old notes.

So infiltration, then. Alone. Tonight, when Lance fell asleep at his desk, I'd sneak into the library and—

"Murta!"

I stopped, surprised to hear my name as opposed to "Shadarian." Let alone actually being addressed.

I tensed as I turned, expecting a possible ambush from one of the older Navigators. But it was Jezna.

She was out of breath when she reached me, so I seized hold of the situation. "You're still here? After Nothomathos, I figured you'd be long gone by now."

Jezna shook her head ferociously. "Weren't you in the dining abbey? Did you not just see—"

"Shadarians can go for days without food. I don't have time—"

"Listen." The franticness in her voice made me pause. "Kanbrik and Nothomathos were supposed to make peace, but one of the elders started yelling about the Brotherhood and . . . Enoch started agreeing, then he got up and punched him and . . ."

I listened to her story with a great deal of irritation and skepticism. But the longer she went on for, the more shocked I grew.

"It didn't make any sense," she said. "But then the elder had a crystal with him and lifted it above his head. He tried to kill us all, but Eleri stopped the blast." She looked around the empty hall frantically. "Loc has an identical crystal, and it's messing with Enoch. I saw something happen before he attacked the elder. Something in his eyes. Like a blue mist was pushing him."

I almost seized her by the shoulders. "You saw this happen? You saw Loc's crystal manipulating Enoch?" The fury in my voice startled me just as much as it did her. Jezna had to breathe deeply to get anything else out.

"Upon my honor as a . . . That's exactly what I'm saying. In the dining abbey, it seemed like he was fighting with his own mind."

A cold fist clenched around my heart.

"And after it happened," Jezna said, "Enoch ran off somewhere. I've no idea where he is. Barco and Daria haven't left the healing branch since Eleri got injured, and they're refusing to see anyone. I couldn't find any other High Navigators."

I blinked, utterly stupefied. "So you came to me?"

Jezna hunched her shoulders. "I suppose I did."

Impossible. Not just that the knight I'd heard say she'd align with Nothomathos over the Brotherhood would somehow do a complete turnaround, but that she'd come to me, when I'd given her nothing but disdain.

"Don't play games with me," I said, feeling my lip curl in disgust. "What do you think you're doing?"

But Jezna didn't turn away or scorn me.

"Choosing a side," she said.

CHAPTER 31

Enoch

Enoch.

My eyes snapped open.

The mist was everywhere, blanketing my bedroom so that when I sat up, I was in a cloud.

Bright blue threaded with black, the color of Loc's crystal and the only thing that seemed to be on my mind now. Even when I fell asleep, the mist was still there, shimmering in the corners of my mind. And here the mist was again, just as I'd woken up. It trailed out from my bed, seeping under the door.

Though Ignis pulsed nervously inside me, throwing brief green markings across my arms, I threw on my suit, forsaking the tie. No time to tie it. Especially when there were fae to fetch. The mist bore a curious resemblance to the little creatures that you could see swimming about the Khroneran coast from the western Light Isles. And when they were all together, pulsing and prancing, they'd resembled a mist of light.

Excited to see such a sight again, I slid out the door into the common room. The mist was there, too, sizzling around the fireplace where, if I'd been in a sorrier state than the one I was in, I might've sworn that a pair of blue and pink eyes watched me from the darkness.

Enoch.

Yeah, yeah, I thought. *On the move, mate.*

For a moment, I thought the mist was going to beckon me into the fireplace, but then it curved off toward the door.

I met not a soul on my stroll down the Rookies Tower. It was the dead of night, and no one seemed to be awake. Barco had most definitely instilled strict guidelines following the dining abbey incident. Either that or everyone was incredibly shaken from what happened to Eleri.

And I was fumbling about the manor, following a ribbon of fog.

Enoch.

The whisper sounded like Loc, but it had an older, huskier ring toward the end.

The mist guided me down vacant halls like it knew where the Nightguards were. I didn't need to hide behind columns. I strolled about like I owned the bloody place and eventually came to a peculiar-looking corridor that came to a dead end.

The ceiling stooped low, curving and undulating to form numerous archways made from white-and-black marble. Flower architecture spun out of the stone, intricately etched into it, and through the jungle of arches I saw a solid wall made of black-and-gold interlocking stone.

Loc stood up against it, crystal in hand.

"Enoch," he chided in tandem with the whisper, then the blue ribbon was gone, slithering back into the crystal.

"Morning, Loc," I said. "Bit early to be out, innit?"

"Right-o." Loc continued to twirl the crystal. "But they say a Nav's awake during the day and alive at night."

I looked around. "Where are we?"

"The Draconic Arches. One of the oldest parts of the manor. Made by dragons." He smoothed a hand along a meticulously carved column, almost longingly. "Look at the craftsmanship. It'd be impossible for a mere man to create such a thing. Especially a man living in as weak of a time as Dresden Roberts's Age."

That irritated me. Dresden Roberts was a legend. He'd drawn up the blueprints for Carbonek, then enlisted dragons to build it. But the crystal around Loc's neck spun, the mist closed in, and I calmed.

"But the remarkable thing about these halls," Loc continued, "is that some of them were destroyed near the end of Roberts's Age . . . Meaning some of these arches were created by Navigators. But where do the draconic designs end and the human copies begin? It's impossible to know—because the power we hold inside of us *is* the power of the Lords. Is the fire of dragons. And the Navigators who came to Carbonek during the next age picked up where the dragons left off and made Carbonek better."

Despite the light radiating from his crystal, Loc's face fell into shadow. "A powerful Navigator named Lucian finished the Draconic Arches with his Ignis ability. And Carbonek was better, stronger, because of it." He turned to face me, sounding nothing like the swash I'd met in the dining abbey. "Will you follow in Lucian's footsteps? Will you create wonders such as these arches? Will you create the change necessary to survive?"

The mist grew so dense around me that I hesitated, but only for a moment. Then I dove in headfirst.

"You bet your arse," I said. "Now, what're we doing parked up against this lovely wall?"

Loc looked up at it. "We're going to run the Bastion."

My eyebrows shot up. "Now?"

"Why not? You want to beat it, don't you?"

"Yeah . . ." I muttered. "But what about Cowlin and Maddox? We need them, don't we?"

"We don't. I was thinking the other day that maybe we might stand a better chance of passing if just the two of us run it. *Alone.* That's what you originally wanted, right? How's that sound?"

It sounded like bloody hogwash. Hadn't Loc been the one who stressed connection between squadmates? Hadn't Loc pointed out during the first time I ran the Bastion that I'd failed because I'd forsaken Maddox? Because I'd left my position as Charger and struck out on my own? What was with this sudden change?

"Sounds brilliant," I said, then glanced up at the wall. "But this isn't the Bastion."

"It is. Just not the one you might be expecting." Loc extended his left arm, pulling back his right. The blue bow appeared in his hands, an arrow of fire set in place and drawn back in his right hand. But this time, something was different. The blue energy was clearly Ignis, but it looked almost sickly. There were trickles of a darker material in its light. A material so black that it looked to be holes in reality, patches of the world that the human eye couldn't see. And when Loc loosed the arrow, it collided with the wall and the darkness spread.

The gold-and-black designs withered, the entire wall falling away to reveal a long granite passageway.

"Another hallway?" I gasped.

Loc dispersed his bow. "This is where you come in."

"I do?"

"I did some Sharpshooting. Now it's time for you to do some Charging. We gotta move fast, though. Ready?"

And suddenly, I was back in the Bastion. The mist cleared just enough for me to feel Ignis, and I saw that the hallway was covered in traps akin to those I'd already faced. I saw the multicolored Ignis of different Navigators that had placed their abilities around the hall, and behind me, the blue flame of Loc's spirit, demented darkness curdling within it. I moved to inquire about it . . .

"Ready?" Loc repeated slowly.

"Always." I took off down the hall.

I wasn't known for being the most agile swash in the world, but I'd learned how to move with a spring in my step and be light on my feet from Serapharus. Thieving was a hard business, and I'd hated doing it to the point that I'd sworn once I had enough money, I'd never do it again. But thieving did teach you things about ways and walls. Like how to scale one while dodging. Or how to run up its side, then leap to one close by and slide down. And all these things I'd perfected after I became a full-fledged swashbuckler.

As metal and rock, air and water all spun around me, I raced through them. With Ignis coursing through me, I felt myself become an emerald blur speeding through trap after trap. By filtering my spirit into every crevice of my body—possessing myself—I felt my physical form shift and reshape, allowing me to dodge and move easier. I felt . . . *immortal.*

"Oi, Loc?" I called. "What about them hit points?"

"There are none!" I heard him say. "So have at it!"

No hit points? That means—!

When two blocks of rock collided together in an attempt to flatten me, I poured every ounce of Ignis into my left fist and threw it. The rocks burst, leaving my knuckles stinging but freeing up the passage.

I became a tempest. Rock broke beneath my fists, water parted as I slipped by it, and earth crumbled. There wasn't an element that could touch me without being broken first, and the more there was, the happier I grew. The harder the attacks came, the higher my spirit soared. The more the mist began to dwindle away and I began to feel like myself again—

A wall of fire erupted up out of the ground.

No.

I scrambled back, heart moving from pounding with excitement to quaking with sudden waves of childlike fear.

Lords, the flames were humongous. A monstrosity that pried horrific screams from my memory. My screams. Unlike the earth, water, and air, the fire devoured everything. There was no escape from the fire. I knew more than anyone.

I screamed, shielding my face from the flames, feeling the scar on my back prickle with the discomfort of a thousand needles . . .

Then Loc was at my side, summoning his bow and sending a blue arrow piercing through the fire. The flames retreated nimbly, creating a great ring of empty space. And there hadn't been a speck of darkness in his Ignis this time.

For the first time since seeing him fight the Skrill, Loc looked luminous again. Like the lad I'd fallen for like a boulder pushed off of a cliff.

Then the crystal pulsed and the mist returned.

"One more room," Loc promised, eyes mad with swirling blue-and-pink fire. Where was the pink coming from? "One more room and you've won."

When I shook my head, the world shook with me. Something was bloody wrong. Something I couldn't . . .

I reached my feet, clutching my head as the swirl of colors strobed behind my eyes. "No." I felt Loc's words travel through my ears down to my spirit. "*We* will have won."

With that one word, the mist began to dissolve. And this time, it looked gone for good. When I went to think for myself, it didn't try to push me in another direction.

This time, the mist couldn't touch me.

I finally saw clearly: the mess of destruction in my wake, the Carbonek candlelight at the entrance to the hall, the roaring ring of fire before me, Loc and his frantically blinking crystal, and the room beyond the ring. A dark chamber full of an even bluer light.

"Enoch—" Loc protested, but I was already gone.

I jumped through the ring of fire into the chamber. After settling my stomach back down, I turned about it. It was made entirely out of black brick, and at the tail end, black columns stair-stepped from the ground to a lone platform. A miniature mound, like the surface of Archengard had broken through the black tile to form a thin plateau.

And hovering four feet off the ground, at its peak, was a hand-sized obsidian crucifix. Etched into its face was a black skull whose eyes cast pale blue light about the chamber.

"Enoch!"

I spun on Loc. "This isn't the Bastion."

He stopped dead.

"There isn't another Bastion." I felt my hands slowly clench back into fists. The taut feeling of the bandages creasing against my fingers bled life back into me, reminding me who I was, what I was doing here . . . and what I lived by.

No one controlled me and got away with it.

"And that artifact right there"—I pointed back at the crucifix without stripping my gaze from Loc—"is a Talisman. The Karnocolix. Now, if I wasn't such a stupid, silly swash, I'd probably have figured out what was happening long before you led me down here. But since I am, I think I can clearly say now that we've broken into a Carbonek vault. Aye?"

Loc's expression of disbelief turned enraged. He didn't look the same when he was mad. He'd been so bloody attractive when we'd met. So warm and witty. This couldn't be the same Nav.

Because it isn't. This is . . . someone else.

"Bravo," the someone who was and wasn't Loc said. "I should've known fire would shatter a spell cast on a Serapharian child. My mistake." He began to walk toward me, and I saw the same darkness that had coursed through his Ignis coursing through the crystal's core. "It won't happen again, I assure you."

Though I still shook from the flames and the realization that Loc had been controlling me—probably controlling me since we ran the Bastion—I lifted my fists.

Call it a bad habit.

"I dunno what's wrong with that crystal or what it's done to you, Loc, but it sure as shite won't be anywhere near as painful as the beating I'm about to give you."

Loc tilted his head but didn't slow. "We'll see. Even the strongest Navigators crack after realizing they fight for a cause not worth winning. Tell me, what will happen to the Karnocolix if it stays in Carbonek?"

"Dunno. Don't care."

"Then you're a fool."

"Always will be. But sorry, bruv. The Talisman stays in Carbonek."

"As will your carcass."

"That's a little dark, but all right." I pumped myself up by shadowboxing, then moved to meet him in the middle. "We always said we wanted to fight one on one—"

A black shadow fell from the rafters of the room, landing directly behind Loc. Though his back was to it, Loc's blue-pink eyes ignited with concern when he felt its presence, then turned.

In the darkness beyond him, I saw a pair of glowing golden eyes.

"I'll try not to enjoy this," they said, before kicking Loc across the room.

CHAPTER 32

Murta

Loc had always been good to me. At least, prior to the time I lost control of the Other and almost killed Maddox. Since I returned, he had eyed me like everyone else: with instant resentment. And despite being squadmates three years ago, he never said a word to me, just glared.

So to say that I didn't enjoy kicking the caca out of him would've been a lie.

Loc sailed a few feet, failed to right himself, then tumbled a few more feet. I threw myself after him, ignoring the gawk of astonishment Enoch threw at me. Ignoring the way my heart leapt when I saw the Karnocolix.

I was certain now. Loc was being controlled by someone who had known that the Karnocolix was located at Carbonek. The information to find it was located in Barco's quarters, and someone like Loc wasn't capable of getting through the Karnocolix's defenses without help from someone like Enoch. Someone with immense power . . . and even more immense drive.

Well, whoever that was, they'd gone after the wrong trainee.

I sped toward Loc with legs on fire. We exchanged one or two blows, Loc's arrows missing their mark every time and my claws skimming his face by inches. Our failed clashes left stinging gashes of Ignis in the air that faded into afterimages as we slammed through them. Our blasts of Ignis strangled the air, threading light through the darkness.

Startlingly, Loc blocked every one of my kicks. That was impossible. Every time he and I had trained with one another, he'd never known how to deal with the lower-body-based Shadarian fighting style. He was an archer, not a martial artist. And here he was defending my body shots with eastern-style elbow blocks. Loc currently fought with an expertise that Biassis would've been surprised by. The fighting style he wielded was ancient. Violent. He tried a number of gut and groin punches.

Fine. You wanna play that way?

When he moved to swing his Ignis-created bow into my forehead, I ducked quickly, and after twisting myself through the air twice, threw a roundhouse kick that knocked him all the way back into the black mound.

But Loc used agility that defied that of a grounded Sharpshooter and sprinted his way up it to the Karnocolix.

I leapt after him in a panic, but it was already too late. Trying to sprint up the disjointed columns was impossible, and armed with his crystal's mysterious power, Loc reached the top in no time. He sneered down at me before snatching the Karnocolix out of the air.

Blue light threw itself everywhere. It shot out of the Karnocolix's eyes, spun about the chamber twice, then separated into fifty separate columns of smoke. Within the smoke, murky forms began to take shape. One of the columns fell right next to me and began to materialize from the ground up.

I saw white bone and black armor. Curdling blue flames and talons like crows.

"You seem to have a death wish, Shadarian," Loc said as the Karnocolix shook in his hands, and I swore that I'd heard his tone of voice in one of my shattered, stolen memories. "Always dancing with the dead even as you live. Perhaps you'd find it more appealing to fight them?"

The smoke from the column fled up to the ceiling, revealing the Karnocolix-conjured creature that hunched before me: a snarling skeleton stitched together with blue fire and black shards of god armor.

Before the creature could chew a chunk out of my shoulder with its cavernous jaws, my Ignis-engulfed foot connected with its rib cage, sending its fragments scattering. The blue fire that had breathed life into it was snuffed out the moment my Ignis passed through it, but as soon as I turned toward the next skeleton, the one I'd disassembled had already reassembled.

Caught in the process of taking a startled step backward, my shoulders bumped into something. I whirled, planning to plant my claws into the remaining forty-eight skeletons—

"Didn't think I'd sit this one out, did ya?" Enoch said.

I ducked around fists thrown by three skeletons. Each of their knuckles sped over my head, stirring my mohawk with fiery hisses. "Shut up and fight."

"I know, I know." Enoch threw Green Fire Fist into a skeleton's chest but timed it perfectly so that the skeleton crossing directly behind it was hit with the fragments of the blast. "I was a bloody idiot . . . or whatever the bollocks you call me. But I'm better now. I think."

"I'm completely reassured."

Enoch laughed, hitting another skeleton with one of the mightiest left crosses I'd ever seen. The fact that he'd hit it while moving backward was crazy, too. What a counterpunch. He put so much of his body into it that the skeleton basically exploded on impact.

Of course, five seconds later, it stood again, dusting wisps of green flame from its rib cage.

"Back to back," I said, but Enoch was already there. Feeling his back against my own again hit me with an immediate wave of comfort, and for a moment, I basked in it. Fighting alongside him felt . . . right. Natural. Was this the Charger-Shield relationship Kaleo and Mathias had once epitomized?

I shook my head. "You know what this thing is, right?"

"Course I do." Flashes of green appeared over my shoulder, followed by tiny hisses of strain from between Enoch's teeth. "The Karnocolix, right?"

"Sí. One of the dark Ignis users that Talen Vento fought put a whole skeleton army in it. We could be at this for decades."

"I'm willing to fight that long if you are."

The scary thing is I actually believe that. "We've gotta find an opening, then go for Loc. The only way to stop these things is to call them back into the Karnocolix."

"Sounds simple enough."

"You'd think so. Whatever's got Loc will keep making wave after wave until we're drowning in bones. He'll tire us to death before we can touch that mound. With two people, that feat is damn near impossible."

"And what about with four?"

A wave of aqua Ignis wrapped itself around the twenty skeletons circling us and reduced them all to flecks of blue fire and dust.

Never was I so happy that my orders for someone to stay behind and go find a High Navigator hadn't been listened to.

Jezna stepped into the corridor, flinging glowing spheres of Ignis every which way, and when I moved to take down the skeletons that were still standing, a spray of neon-pink Aestus slid over my shoulder, pelting one into a pile of smoking bones. My eyebrows furrowed. *Junior.*

I tackled the last two skeletons to the floor so that the Aestus flew over their heads, then stomped their skulls into powder. I stood, scuffing blue flames from my shoes.

"Ya know, a 'thanks, dude' would be nice sometime or another." Prince spun the two pistols that were in his hands. *Weapons for Ordinaries.* "Just a thought. If you have one other than 'brood, brood, brood.'"

"Kiss my culo."

"Does it wear a scarf, too?"

"It's got more Ignis than you."

"Say that again." Prince flipped one of the guns up in the air, caught it, then spun it upside down sideways before pointing it at me. "But to *them.* Voice-modulated pistols. They only respond to me. Wanna see what happens when I say, 'Let's get gnarly?'"

Jezna blasted herself between us, sliding to a stop with her palms thrust outward. "Focus, please? Enoch's struggling."

I jerked my head to the end of the chamber, where the mound Loc stood atop was closely guarded by a pack of ten larger skeletons. The simplest plan should've been to take out the smaller ones on the outside then work our way to the inside . . . At least, that's what someone with a brain would've assumed. And Enoch's job would've been simple—to do his job as Charger and attempt to break through to Loc—except two things had prevented that from happening.

The first was that the smaller skeletons kept regenerating no matter how many we took out. The second had only just come into fruition: Enoch was a Charger through and through in the sense that he was a complete and utter idiota. He'd thrown himself at Loc, hoping for the best.

"Hullo!" Enoch waved over the mountainous shoulder of a bigger skeleton. "I could bloody well use a Shield right about now!" Including the big skeleton, there were at least ten smaller ones surrounding him on all sides.

How does he get himself in these situations?

"I spoke with a Nightguard on the way here," I heard Jezna say as I barreled into the two skeletons preparing to pounce on Enoch. "He has gone to get the Council. They'll be here soon."

"Cheers!" Enoch flashed me double thumbs-ups but gave up his back in the process. I threw myself past his shoulder toward the sprinting skeleton I figured he'd completely forsaken just to see a fist-sized flame of green energy blow its head off.

Enoch spun his arm. "S'got range now."

But even with his newfound range, Enoch struggled to punch through the bigger ones. Prince and Jezna did a good job of taking care of the smaller skeletons, but the creatures' numbers continued to multiply.

Falling back, I watched Enoch. Tendrils of flame pooled off of him as he boxed in the center of an emerald firestorm. It looked so much more natural than the tense lightning from before.

"I'm good, bruv," he said. "Don't worry."

"I wasn't—" I shook myself. "What's taking you so damn long to get to Loc?"

"Their attacks strengthen whenever I make a run for him."

"Have you tried possessing one of them?"

"They keep replenishing."

"You didn't answer my question."

Enoch shook his head as we rolled in opposite directions away from a big skeleton. "I'm not possessing anything right now." As he destroyed the skeleton's jaw with a powerful right hook, I swept my foot underneath and took out its legs. The blue fire sputtered out as the bones collapsed.

We rolled to a halt, side by side. I stood immediately, but the big skeleton stood faster.

Enoch's mouth fell open when its shadow fell across us. "Bollocks."

I had just enough time to cartwheel backwards and watch Enoch slide between the skeleton's massive legs, which looked good as new despite having been severed moments before.

"This is impossible!" Prince said. "Stunning these dudes doesn't work!"

"Bloody difficult, but not impossible." Enoch plunged a fist through the big skeleton's back. The creature paused, looked down at the smoldering green hole in its ribs, then shrugged.

Prince spun his pistols as a skeleton lumbered toward him. "How do you plan on keeping them from regenerating? 'Cause I'm all—"

The fist came out of nowhere, striking him across the face and sending his sunglasses flying. I watched them take flight with joy but groaned when they came to a rest in an enclosed fist. When I looked into the face of who held it, I saw only disappointment reflected back.

"One of our squadmates is in trouble." Enoch's green eyes crackled. "So what do you suppose we do about it?"

"The mission is the Karnocolix," I said. "*Eso es final.*"

"But the Code—"

"I know the Code. That doesn't mean it's right." *It's right.* "That doesn't mean *any* of this is right . . ." *It's right.* "But I suppose Junior's guns will be of use."

Launching myself through the air at the skeleton lumbering over Prince, I moved Ignis up into my knee and drilled it into the creature's skull. The bone crunched satisfyingly, blue fire raining down as I landed in a crouch. The skeleton, now headless, crumbled and began to reorganize itself as Enoch and I formed a protective semicircle around Prince.

"You still alive, Princey-boy?" Enoch called, swinging Ignis-infused fists and gnashing his teeth at the skeletons.

Prince jumped up, pointing at his bruised face. "Look, Noc! We're twins!"

Enoch tossed the sunglasses over his shoulder. "S'a good look. What'd you think, Murta?"

"Hell yeah." Prince snapped the sunglasses back on his face—upside down first, then quickly spinning them right side up. "I'd love to know what the professional bruise giver thinks of another's handiwork."

"Don't tempt me."

"I'll tempt ya all I wa—"

He cut off, eye pressed against the scope of his rifle. He adjusted it methodically. When that seemingly produced similar results, he removed his face from the scope, shook the gun, then stared back through the scope, this time with the other eye.

One of Jezna's tidal waves blasted by him, wiping out two skeletons that had been making a run for him with flaming jaws. Prince merely slid the rifle back into his backpack.

"There's something big-time wrong with that crystal Loc's wearing."

"You'd think so, wouldn't you?" I roared.

Enoch was at my side immediately. "New plan. Destroy that thing around Loc's neck . . ." He glanced around at us. "Just like what we did with the Skrill, right?"

Jezna nodded. "But now, we'll clear a path for you. You won't have to . . . 'connect' with the creatures or anything similar to what you did to the Skrill."

Enoch nodded silently.

"No," I said. "I'll take care of the crystal. Your job *is* something similar to what you did to the Skrill."

The protest from Enoch started within his posture before working its way into his stammering. "But . . ."

"Just shut up and do it." I stabbed a finger at his chest. "Concentrate. Not on destroying the skeletons, but taking them over."

"You can't possibly expect him to possess every single skeleton!" Jezna said.

"Possessing every skeleton would be no different than possessing a Skrill," I said. "Every skeleton here has a singular soul: the Karnocolix. If you think of them as one being, you can possess all of them at once. And this time, you can control them."

"I've never successfully possessed anything before," Enoch said. "Not fully . . ."

"Toughen up. You wanna be the Charger? Then charge for us."

"Being the Charger means going for the crystal first!"

"Wrong," I found myself saying, as though Kaleo had slipped into my thoughts or just being around Enoch somehow brought all of this out. "As Shield, I'm the battering ram. And Mathias always said that the first thing through the castle gates isn't the soldiers: It's the battering ram. The Charger holds the Shield in front. I'm the one that forges the path others walk."

I tapped into Ignis, feeling my legs ignite. "I can get to Loc, but if all these damned things are gonna attack me, my hands might as well be tied. Only you can calm them enough to allow me to get up there." I looked straight into his eyes. "Only you can do this."

Enoch stared back. For a moment, I thought he might crack under the pressure. I thought the orange eyes might shatter into oblivion, but rather than succumb, the depths flickered. Deep in them, I spotted shards of brewing green fire.

If not completely confident, he was at least going to try.

"Wanna make yourself useful, too?" I asked Prince. "If you can't stun these things, why don't you tell your guns to do the opposite of stunning?"

Prince frowned. "Which is . . . ?"

I looked at him.

Though his nose remained wrinkled in his disgust, I saw the ghost of a grin stride across his pale lips. "Guns," he said. "*Kill.*"

I nodded, then turned toward Jezna. "Give me some waves." I faced the rampaging skeletons. Beyond the sound of stomping feet, I heard Loc crying out commands.

Jezna appeared glowing at my side, arms outstretched. "You know, if you asked nicely, people would be more inclined to assist you."

"Who the hell said I needed assistance? The sooner we get rid of these things, the sooner I can go back to sleep."

I stormed back into the mob. Back again in the Jameronjag temple, running from the white creatures. Only this time, I couldn't run. I couldn't leave Lee, Ret, and Nico behind. I fought beside them. I relied on them.

Unsurprisingly, the closer I grew, the harder the skeletons fought. And the more I took down, the more they multiplied. Jezna's Ignis ability soared overhead and drenched my shoes more than once, but after a minute passed and Enoch still hadn't taken over the army, her ability disappeared.

I was being swarmed, I'd lost Loc's direction, and was now completely alone. Even Prince's gunfire sounded distant.

A Shadarian didn't panic. Instead, I gritted my teeth, feeling hot sparks form at the back of my throat. There were so many skeletons that even when tapping into Ignis, my gold vision was consumed with blue. Finding Loc in this mess was a lost cause.

Where's the Council?!

I thought about stopping to get a feel for the ground again, but a moment's hesitation nearly cost me a leg. One of the smaller skeletons took a swipe at me.

"You know," I said as I backflipped about the chamber, "if I wasn't in this damned manor, the Other would've shit out all of you by now."

Beyond the skeletons in front of me, Loc stood on his mound. On the opposite side, Prince was busy pelting more creatures with his machine guns, but steadily being taken over. And behind me, I was still aware of the absence of Jezna's Ignis.

What's he doing? I wanted to scream.

"Enoch?" Jezna's voice rose above the skeletons' screeches. "I don't mean to rush you, but we're in a decent amount of danger—"

"Stop being afraid and start acting like a Navigator!" I boomed. "You think your enemy's going to give you time to rest on a quest? You think you're going to be able to stall, even for a second?"

"That's enough, Murta!" Jezna said.

"You stall and your squadmates will *die*!" The arms that pulled at me transformed my snarl into a scream. The skeletons tackled me. "You hear me, swash? You—"

My voice was stopped by the skull that slammed into my face. The metallic taste of blood instantly formed behind my teeth.

The skeletons had grown to the point that they were unstoppable. I was able to out-combat anyone, but once faced with an unstoppable force—like a Tintagen Talisman—even a Shadarian struggled. The Karnocolix had programmed its army for a single purpose, and in that sense, it had us beat. The skeletons were able to work as a unit. We couldn't.

Thrashing against the bones all around me, I forced Ignis out of me in a miniature explosion. For a split second of uncontrollable chaos, my body became a volcano, and every skeleton in a ten-foot radius turned to dust. But like all of my powerful moves, they couldn't be repeated several times in a row, especially after having been tapping into Ignis for the past fifteen minutes.

Stumbling from forcing Ignis out as opposed to guiding it, I morphed my hands into dragon claws. Less than a fraction of the Other's power, but almost enough to knock me out. My eyesight exploded with spots, which provided the perfect cover for the next wave of skeletons. As soon as I'd gotten free of them, I was once again restrained.

They grew more vicious. Something fueled them with a darker purpose than just blindly following orders. They kicked out in random intervals with their gnarled legs, splitting open the skin around my chest and abdominal muscles. One or two connected with my rib cage, sending shards of pain up through my chest.

Give up, one of the skeletons hissed, its inflamed face and flickering sunken eyes appearing out of the mound of limbs. But it hadn't spoken a word, merely pried open its shriveled jaw in a silent roar. The voice—one of the black ones from my memories—had spoken through it, putting words where there'd been none.

Give up.

"*Vete . . .* a *la mierda . . .*" I rasped through lungs on fire.

Another skeletal face appeared, eyes crafted from blue inferno. *Give up.*

"No . . ."

Give up, the voice crackled, and the flames surrounding me multiplied until there were eleven skeletal faces swimming in the shade. Until their faces became the doglike snouts and grim stares of jackals.

I've . . . failed.

I was surprised by how numb I felt about it. Perhaps it was the surprising faith I still had left in the Council—that I knew they'd never let a trainee die inside Carbonek. Perhaps it was my disappointment in Enoch. My immeasurable disappointment in the Brotherhood.

I closed my eyes tiredly. *So why did I ever care to begin with?*

Give up.

I felt myself begin to relent . . .

A dry snuffle snatched me from the depths of my mind. The squirming sound, whatever it had been, had escaped the skeleton directly across from me, and by the looks of its thrashing face, it was either dying or already dead. Its brethren shuffled in the mound to stare.

The skeleton uttered a soulless cry, shook its tangle of limbs in a frantic dance, then seemed to still itself, head bowed, face cast toward the floor. The blue fire died, replaced with lifeless darkness. Yet something in its swaying movements unstitched a memory sewn somewhere: a fresh one. The cocky way it carried itself felt odd for a mindless soldier.

When it began to lift its head, I thought I'd be greeted by another ghastly grin and blue fire eyes. Maybe they'd all devour me together. Maybe this was all a setup by Loc and the Council. A way to get rid of the Other once and for all.

But instead of coming face-to-face with blue fire, the sockets remained black and dead. It was only after a cold whisper ran through the skeletons that they ignited with emerald flames.

"Taste the connection, ya bony bastards," the skeleton crowed before punching the largest of its brethren in the face.

The swarm broke open, freeing me. I threw a hand up to my neck to reset my scarf and fell to a knee.

Movement only escalated. Skeletons screamed. A storm of limbs blew past.

What?

I rose, preparing to side kick the skeleton to my right across the Grand Sea, but paused. The screams had all been silenced, and the skeleton next to me was occupied at the moment: fully engrossed in a brutal fist fight with four of its brethren. All five of them didn't have a lick of blue in their wicked eyes or along their bodies. In fact, each burned a bright green and frequently threw wild punches that anyone with any sense would've associated with boxing.

I looked around the rest of the room.

Every skeleton, short and massive, was overtaken by the green flames and fought one another. Skulls exploded, limbs engulfed in green Ignis soared through the air, and fists made from bone boxed every empty space.

Across the battlefield, Prince thrust his arms sky high and cackled.

I surveyed the scene with still-adjusting eyes.

He did it. He actually did it . . .

Feeling Ignis outline my body, I swiveled my golden glare to the black mound across the way and the boy that stood gaping atop it.

I began to walk toward Loc.

He started screaming with rage, shaking the Karnocolix frantically. The chaos fought all around but never touched me. The skeletons spread out before me, their blows avoiding me completely. All I had to do was walk up to the first of the disjointed steps and begin to climb.

Loc started throwing Ignis arrows, but with one hand holding the Karnocolix—now glowing green—he couldn't summon the whole bow. Instead, he just flung them with one hand.

His aim was brutal without his bow. Every arrow hit somewhere around me, but never its target. I didn't even need to dodge. That just made Loc angrier.

"The Karnocolix shouldn't stay here! You know it shouldn't!"

He put his whole body into his next throw, and this time, the arrow spun directly toward me. I swung my claws in a dark arc, cutting straight through the Ignis then breaking into a sprint up the rest of the mound. A task in itself, trying to scurry upward, all the while dodging shafts of Ignis, but things were different now. I had others at my back, and the voices had all gone quiet.

I had a cause.

When I reached the top, Loc dropped the Karnocolix and formed the largest bow I'd ever seen. Before he could form an arrow alongside it, my foot cracked across his chin, sending him stumbling. *This is for Enoch.* But before he could fall off the side, I grabbed his crystal.

Whatever was in Loc looked at me with wide, wild eyes, and I saw myself reflected back in them—two golden eyes in a sea of darkness. The eyes of an awoken dragon.

And this is for me.

My claws snapped together.

The crystal shattered, blue remains spilling out through my scales, sprinkling across my dress shoes and the Karnocolix. All the dark energy flew out of Loc's chest in a thrashing black void before turning to smoke, and with nowhere left to go, it drifted lazily up toward the ceiling.

But Loc fell hard. I caught his lifeless body, setting him down as carefully as I could, then quickly scooped the Karnocolix up into my claws . . .

And there it was. The first Tintagen Talisman I'd ever held. An artifact capable of resurrecting an army of the undead. All of that power in *my* hands.

And it wasn't just power; it was *control*. The wielder of the Karnocolix didn't have to fear being taken over by it. Not a crystal necklace, nor a golden necklace used to keep a shadedrake secured. It was just a simple item, and whoever wielded it wielded the skeleton army. Whoever wielded it could create *change*.

Lords, I wanted it so badly. Needed it. If the Jackals were after it, I couldn't let them have it. Artifacts of darkness could be used for good. For light.

Just like me. I can use my darkness for light. For change. I don't have to abide by the Brotherhood or the Jackals' rules. I make my own change.

And with or without the Other, I'd be able to with the Karnocolix.

My fingers traced the Talisman's skeletal pattern, taking it all in. I moved to touch its eyes . . . but it still glowed green. And the skeletons all around me still fought.

I raised the Karnocolix. "I've got it! You can get out now! Stop the skeletons, swash!"

The skeletons didn't stop.

"I've got the Talisman! Banish these creatures!"

Again, nothing.

I lowered my arm in disquieted fury. Enoch was still lodged inside, but that didn't necessarily mean he could stop the skeletons. In fact, it dawned on me that I had no idea how to stop them. What if we couldn't? What if Loc's crystal had infected them, too? What if they wouldn't stop attacking us until . . . until we had to *destroy* the Karnocolix?

No. It wouldn't come to that. I'd come too far just to watch—

"Can't . . . *keep . . . holding . . . !*" the skeletons said in unison. The Karnocolix burned in my claws. If I'd been holding it with human hands, I would've had burns for the rest of my life.

Damn you! I wanted to howl down at the hissing crystal fragments, but instead shouted, "Then get out of the Karnocolix!"

The skeletons, still determined to fight one another, began to stagger. Some fuzzed in and out of reality altogether. Others shriveled into dust, then took to reanimating.

"*Not . . . an option—*"

"Just get out, idiota!" I shook the Karnocolix violently, then watched every skeleton collapse in unison.

Green Ignis from all across the room rocketed back into the Karnocolix, forcing me to drop it and watch the matter turn itself inside out, ricochet back out into the chamber where it formed into a puddle of green fire, then build itself up into a silhouette. Two seconds later, the silhouette solidified into Enoch—tan face flushed, blond hair matted.

I gaped. Enoch looked as though he'd merely been for a jog around the valley, whereas I felt exhausted and uneasy.

He even ignited a tired Green Fire Fist that somehow still looked powerful, and leered over the Karnocolix. "If those skeletons are coming back, then we—"

NO! I dove in front of the Talisman.

Enoch yanked his fist back to avoid hitting me but was tackled by a skeleton in the process. I looked back down at the Karnocolix with surprise. Its eyes had returned to their normal blue, and the skeletons were rising all around us.

The initial turmoil turned into carnage. Enoch's yells disappeared, Prince's gunshots became shouts of fear, and Jezna's distant waves crashed with a firmer intensity than I'd ever heard them. Just as soon as we'd started winning, we'd gone right back to losing.

Because of me.

CHAPTER 33

Jezna

As soon as the skeletons turned back from green to blue, at least a third of them turned their smoldering eyes on me. Fists shattered, jaws hanging loosely from their skulls, and limbs askew every which way, the green flames that had pitted them against one another was dispersed, overcome by the cruel blue flame that had trapped them in the Talisman.

I can never get any rest. Still recovering from their last onslaught, I swayed tiredly against the stone floor, conjuring my waterblade back into my palms and raising my helm. *But perhaps I'll rest when I'm dead.*

I met the wave of bones before it could crash over me. I struck left and right, above and below, letting my waterblade fly free from my hand more than once and go spinning about the circle of skeletons. Ten were decapitated and crumbled. Ten more took their place.

Begone!

Blade returned to my hand, I used my humongous armored shoulders to shove a cluster to the side, then gutted them with a single devastating side stroke. Dust and blue powder cascaded from the flaming skeletons' rib cages, briefly stalling them but barely more than a couple seconds. When their ruined hands began to grasp for my arms—a few smaller ones even making for my legs—muscle memory kicked in, recalling ancient footwork I'd learned in glades and valleys: much fiercer terrain than the smooth stone I waltzed upon.

Yes. That's all this was. A dance of water through flame.

My sword bit every skeleton, dousing the fire that burned about them, emptying their lives onto the black stone beneath. And though they rose again, my water defiled them once more. Again and again. Smoother and swifter. I became a one-woman tsunami, carving open the armies of bone and fire. My confidence swelled, my armor lighter than ever before.

Then the second wave broke through, and I was knocked off my feet.

Some thirty skeletons piled themselves on top of me, latching around my chest, my arms, my hands and feet. Until I could see none of myself, none of the glistening god armor I wore to protect myself, and could feel the skeletons coiling like snakes, squeezing the armor bit by bit. Their flames flew up and down me, threatening to seep into my visor, and no matter how hard I tugged at Ignis, it sputtered feebly. For my ability wasn't fire—it was water. Water should've easily been capable of dousing the flames, like Macín had always said it would.

Yet just like that flaming battlefield, where I'd met Daria and sealed my fate, my water had been useless. The flames roared on—this time, all over me—and putting them out was hopeless.

At least I'll finally get that rest.

My thoughts were shockingly indifferent, as though finally accepting that this had been a terrible idea from the beginning. That I never should've come to Carbonek and had been better off trying to hold back the dam with my Brothers. *I shouldn't die here. I should've died with them.* And then, *But what about—?*

And as the last skeleton moved to cover my visor—flaming so brightly that no amount of water could extinguish it—a rocket of magenta Aestus blew into me, tearing through the limbs and sending them all shattering around me.

I slid back a few paces, hands covering my visor and cursing. Yet when I peeled them back, I wasn't being swarmed, but saved.

My water lay puddled all around me, glowing and slowly seeping back into me—quivering from the power it had wielded just to have it all doused in a moment of fleeting stupidity—and in the center of the madness stood a boy without any Ignis at all. He fought fire with fire, and they weren't even his own flames to begin with.

"Buzz off, all of you!" Prince bellowed, wielding two humongous Aestus cannons on both shoulders that were practically the size of him. The ion blasts hurtled across the room, eating skeletons away to nothing and sending their tattered limbs skyrocketing. And though Prince jittered everywhere from the explosive knockback of both weapons, his sunglasses never slipped from his eyes, his voice still finding a way to carry over everything. "Don't you ever freaking think you can touch my best friend ever again!"

He's talking about me*?*

More skeletons began to turn their attention to the treasure hunter, but each was met with another blast of Aestus. Prince refused to allow a single skeleton so much as twenty feet from me, and for a time, it appeared that I was protected by a wall made of raging Aestus, smoking metal, and a lot of angry cursing.

It wasn't at all who I'd expected to come to my aid one day and stand between an army and me. I hadn't thought it even possible for a rogue to save my life a second time. But here he was.

When the legions had died off enough and Prince was given enough time to drop his guns and let them recharge, he twisted toward me. "Here I am!"

"Yes." I joined him. "Here you are."

Prince barely seemed to take notice of the fact that I'd placed a hand upon the shoulder of his leather jacket. He was too busy rewiring one of the cannons, then switching it out for a rifle he removed from his backpack. "You wanna see something really cool?"

Aware of the skeletons beginning to materialize around us, I conjured my waterblade and kneeled. "Indeed I do."

The boy poured several strange-looking Aestus cartridges into the rifle, spun the rotating barrel until it glowed a brilliant pink—

He was swept up by a dozen other skeletons. They'd seemingly come from nowhere, as though the Karnocolix had given birth to hundreds more of the warriors at once. It was hopeless.

Far off, I heard Prince screaming, followed by the roar of his weapons. Across the room, I saw Enoch swallowed whole by the dark horde. And Murta stood atop the mound, staring down at the Karnocolix in horror. He'd failed.

We'd failed.

Skeletons dove at me from every direction. It was remarkable how fast and fluid they moved. Out of all the armies I'd watched clash over the years, none were as unified as this one. None attacked with the reckless abandon of this one. It was impressive. Astounding.

But more than anything, I was irate. Irate with the Council for failing to come to our aid, with the Brotherhood for failing to see that Carbonek was under siege, with Enoch and Murta for failing to keep control of the Karnocolix, and most importantly, with myself.

I'd dug my grave. I'd chosen a side.

Now I'd lie in it. I'd die for it.

No. Prince's screams forced me to my feet. *I must not give in.*

Throwing Ignis into my arms, I crossed them in front of my helmet and threw myself in the direction of the mound. I slammed blindly through phalanx after phalanx of skeletons, crushing bone beneath my boots, feeling skulls and shoulder pads bounce off of my armor.

"Murta!" I shouted, but he didn't hear. Through the blue macabre curling around me, I saw Murta's immovable posture. The indecision painting his eyes.

He claimed to be this statue of composure, but here he was, dropped to his knees just like the rest of us. Here he was, as foolish and pathetic and . . .

Stop, I scolded myself. *Stop throwing others under the horse.*

Observe. Listen. Save.

But how could I save everyone when I didn't even know where they were at? How could I fight back against a horde that my water was useless against? How could I fight fire with . . .

My eyes flicked down toward the Talisman.

Maybe I didn't have to know where everyone was at to save them. Maybe I didn't have to fight the entire horde to defeat them.

And maybe . . .

Maybe . . .

"Macín," I'd asked one day, trampling through the grove as fast as my legs—my *real* legs—had been able to carry me, tears dripping from my eyes.

"I met someone calling themself a Navigator. They said . . . they said the Orders will never come back. That . . . some 'brotherhood' has replaced them. How? Why? What did the knights do? Why did they all—?!"

"Hush, dear Sister," Macín had said, standing and striding toward me, his armor dead silent. Where everyone clanked, Macín barely stirred the grass around him. "The Navigator is right. The Orders will never return. But that doesn't mean that the ideals they built are no longer present. I've seen these Navigators. They are fools. But they are good fools. They may not look to the Chivalric Code, but they look to a code. And that code was founded by three of our fellow Archengardians: one of which was a knight."

"Talen Vento," I'd whispered.

"Aye. The Traitor, the Orders once called him. But I prefer to call him by a different name: the Resurrector. For although the Orders have all begun to dissolve—and, in time, we Tolkkis will dissolve, too—chivalry, dear Sister, is not yet dead. It slumbers."

And in a gesture I'd never forget, he'd formed his metal hands into a triangle and pressed them against my heart: the Navigator's Vow. "You must find the balance."

And suddenly, it was no longer water that collected around me, but a hybrid between it. No more did my Ignis rush and lap, swim and stream . . . but *burn.*

The world changed, Macín, I found myself thinking as fire and water collided together around me, all aqua and blazing, *and I will change with it.*

I have to.

I flew out of the mob of skeletons like a comet, landing atop the mound and forming my hands into a knife edge. For a split second, I felt something form there, like the beginnings of a blade, then I threw every speck of Ignis I'd been given into my hands and sent them smashing into the Talisman.

I couldn't return Ignis to me fast enough. The Talisman exploding shocked my very soul, slicing through my spirit and sinking deep into me so that I felt every volt.

It's . . . done . . .

My spirit felt on fire. Dark blue lightning raced up and down my burned armor.

I placed a hand to my knee to calm the tempest in me and used the other hand to clutch my chest. I felt around for the last trickles of lightning, trying to extract them physically, but came across the jagged edges of a cavernous hole in my breastplate.

No.

I felt myself sliding between my fingers—cold and formless. I felt myself pour from my armor where I'd soak into the black rock and be trapped forever. I felt myself pulled toward Archengard's core, the circle of fire and iron where all things ended up after death. Where I'd be reunited with the lost departed knights and be able to tell their crippled souls and empty armor of my failed quest.

Of the time I almost, but not quite, became a Navigator.

CHAPTER 34

Murta

I stared down at the Karnocolix.

Destroying it was like destroying myself. The Talisman and I were the same.

I won't destroy it! my mind screamed. *Not when I can use it! Not when Archengard needs it!* But my body didn't listen.

I squeezed my eyes shut and felt my claws instinctively unfurl. Though my mind remained rooted, my body darted toward the space where the Karnocolix was . . .

It exploded.

My whole body clenched up as pieces of blue fire flew up into my face. I rolled backward, eyes throbbing with pain, and looked up at the shattered remains of the smoking Talisman.

Jezna stood over me, but something was wrong. Where trickles of water-like Ignis had spun around her arms, the aqua aura that usually surrounded her seeming to evaporate off of her shoulders, now, there was nothing water-like at all. *Flames* seeped off her armor, and even more alarming: There was a cavernous hole in her breastplate. A hole that revealed . . .

Nothing.

When Jezna saw that I was staring at her, the flames faded in a heartbeat. Her Ignis went out, leaving only traces of faint smoke, and her hands flew to the hole, shielding herself while scurrying to gather something. Something escaping through the hole.

I was still partially blind from the explosion, but it looked like a glowing . . . liquid of some sort.

"Jezna!" I heard Prince shout, then saw the knight tense and stumble down the mound away from me, from all of us, all the while covering her chest. "What the hell happened?! Are you okay?"

"She's hurt," another voice erupted out of the silence. A familiar gruff one. "Lords, Daria . . . Get her to the healing branch. Quickly. We'll see what we can do . . ."

I looked up and saw Kaleo standing in the chamber entryway, watching Daria help Jezna walk back down the debris-ridden hall—the ruinous aftermath of Enoch's charge. He turned, Barco and Hektor moving to flank him, and behind them, rushing past Jezna, were Biassis, Larry, Maddox, and Cowlin. I watched the four Navigators barrel around Barco, then scurry up the mound toward their stirring squadmate.

I rose to my feet, shaking with rage. I didn't care about them. Or Jezna. Because now there were only four Tintagen Talismans.

The Karnocolix could've done the fighting for the Brotherhood. So that Navigator lives wouldn't have to be thrown away.

And now it's gone. Kaleo let Jezna destroy it.

Those skeletons could've been used to win the War. They could've aided the Brotherhood if the Noda ever came calling. If the Jackals themselves ever showed up at Carbonek's doorstep.

But they already have. I stared at my hands, human once more. Flecks of crystal still clung to them. *I thought they were just in Khronera, but it's even clearer now: They're here in Carbonek.*

A soft presence emerged at my side, and I glared over to see Enoch, face fallen. He wasn't even looking at me, but up at Loc, who was being helped into a sitting position by Biassis.

Loc looked pale and feeble, as though the crystal had sucked something out of him.

Enoch glanced back at Kaleo. "Will Jezna be all right?" He didn't sound worried. There was more anger there than grief.

"In time, young'un," the old man answered. "She just destroyed a Talisman. That would take a toll on anybody."

Without another spoken word, Prince shot after her, leaping between Kaleo and Hektor. Barco turned swiftly to stop him, but Kaleo put a hand to his Shadow's shoulder and shook his head. I watched all this happen, still seeing the Karnocolix exploding followed by Jezna's gaping, hollow chest any time I blinked.

Enoch began to climb the mound, moving slowly until he stood before Loc. When his shadow fell over him, Loc looked up, fear coating his hazel eyes before lowering his head in shame.

But then Enoch kneeled at Loc's side and held out a hand. "A bout well fought, bruv. Let's do it again sometime. Only without any bloody crystals, yeah?"

Loc seemed stunned into silence until his bottom lip began to quiver, and he lifted a shaky hand to clasp Enoch's.

"Whatever I did," he whispered. "Whatever that damned thing made me do, I'm sorry. I'm so bloody sorry . . . And I'll accept whatever punishment the Council has for me." He shut his eyes. "Even if it includes banishment."

"There'll be no banishment." Kaleo strode toward the mound. "And there'll certainly be no punishment. You've received enough already."

He took the stones just as meticulously as Enoch but arrived at the top faster than anyone before him. It was terrifying.

"But you do know what that crystal was, aye?"

Some heads nodded solemnly: Biassis's and Larry's. Some shook: Maddox's, Cowlin's, and Enoch's. One head just hung like a noose: Loc's.

"It once belonged to a particular group of interest," Kaleo said. "A group Archengard speaks of only in whispers. Some of those whispers are false, though a great many of those are also true. They do hold standing in the Noda, and they do possess a vendetta against the Code. They take what is ours—what once worked long ago—and corrupt it. They hate, manipulate, and debilitate Archengard around them . . .

"And it appears that they've now found a way to slip into Carbonek."

Loc began to sniffle. "I . . . I found the crystal in Kanbrik. In the same place as the imprisonment box. It was in one of the regular-looking boxes, I don't bloody know . . . All I did was put it round my neck, 'cause it looked wicked." He shuddered. "But then it started messing with me and *offering* me things. And I stupidly agreed."

When he looked up, his eyes swirled with fury, but the edges glittered with half-formed tears. His gaze flew to Enoch instead of Kaleo. "I'm sorry, Noc. I'm so sorry. And tell Jezna and Prince that I—"

"Not your fault," Enoch said. "You were being controlled. You didn't do anything wrong." He chewed his lip. "But what did, you know, the crystal offer you?"

Loc pointed a shaking finger at me. And every set of eyes in the room followed grimly.

"It promised . . ." Loc gasped between stutters. "It promised that I'd never see my squad on their knees again. That I'd never see Mads or anyone else ever wounded by Ignis again." His hand hit the ground hard, but it took an eternity for it to fall for me. "It promised power."

CHAPTER 35

Kaleo

Attack. Parry. Lunge. Parry again. Attack. Attack again. ATTACK—

The Sword flew from my hands, spinning across the tile. Bits of white fire snarled and spat when the flaming blade touched the floor, but several seconds after it left my hands, the blade disappeared, leaving the Sword nothing but a mundane crystal hilt.

I cursed and gripped my right hand, trying to massage feeling back into it. For a moment, I glared at the hilt and just thought about leaving it there. About turning right around, sliding back through the marble columns, and going to sleep.

But my feet moved toward the Sword, and I picked it up. I stared at it in my scarred hands for a moment, then closed my eyes, tapping into Ignis and seeing the white spark ignite within me.

"Light up the night," Mathias used to tell me when I needed help accessing Ignis.

The moment the spark was struck, the Sword made a mighty *shwoom!* that sent fire spurting up to the high ceiling, and the blade flamed once more.

I gritted my teeth and slid back into practice. I spun, and the world—images and memories—spun around me.

Block. Parry. Feint. Attack—

"Strength in numbers," I heard Janne say. "Aye. But what will you be doing off on your lonesome?"

"Kal . . ." I heard Champ say in another scene, on a blackened plateau under an ashen sky. "I don't know if I want to do this anymore. Did you hear what they called us? Killers? We're Navigators. I'm not a killer . . . am I?"

Parry. Block. Defend. Defend. Defend.

"The Noda might've gotten a hold of a Talisman," Lucian yelled, "yet we do nothing? Yet we refuse to attack them? And out of what? Honor? Respect? They burn our brothers, then piss on their ashes!"

Block. Lunge. Attack . . .

And then, though I'd tried to keep his voice from coming back to me again, Mathias spoke, his back to me, looking out at the Grand Sea. "Archengard is dying, Kal. But not from the violence of those who seek to kill it."

His next words had been so seething that I'd felt Ignis burning in the air around him. "It dies from the silence of those who protect it."

I spun the Sword faster and faster, swinging through imaginary Ignis hunter after imaginary Ignis hunter, hearing their screams, feeling my power slice through each of them . . .

"Just so you know, you've almost clipped me five times now."

I snapped open my eyes. This time, before the Sword could go spinning, I clamped my hand down around the hilt and stumbled to a standstill.

Wiping sweat from my brow and sheathing the Sword all in one motion, I squinted at the suited figure. Though he always wanted to wear his cloak, the suit looked natural on him. He moved freely in it.

Unlike me. I'll never get used to this damn fabric.

"How'd you know I'd be here?"

"Old habits," Barco said. "Familiar stomping grounds. If you wanted a dueling partner, you could've asked."

I shook my head.

"If you're worried about Eleri—"

"Already been to see her. Good recovery. She's trained the healers to be just as good as she is. We haven't been giving her enough credit."

"She'll be elated to hear you say that. You had a better view than I did. Was anyone else injured?"

"Outside of the High Elder? No. She contained the entire explosion. Can't believe I didn't see that damned crystal sooner—"

"The High Elder's or Loc's?"

I pressed my fingers against my closed eyelids, trying not to fall over where I stood or throw up the acid boiling in my throat. "Lords above. How's Jezna?"

"The less said, the better. Daria's trying. Half of her time's taken up with making sure Prince doesn't get in . . . I don't know how much longer we'll be able to keep Jezna's secret."

"Tell me some good news. Please."

"My spies have whittled things down to three," Barco said grimly. "Harrenous is said to be in the area, Lucian typically does dealings—"

"Don't say their bloody names."

"You forget that they're just as mortal as the rest of us."

"Doesn't always appear that way, does it?"

"No. I suppose not." Barco hesitated. "So I thought you ought to know that both Reggie and I have begun to oversee . . . special training for a number of higher squads. Some up-and-coming rookies, too."

I frowned. "Aye?"

"Nothing like what we were during the War. But if there is one thing that the incident with Kanbrik and Nothomathos showed us—if there's one thing that *their* infiltration of Carbonek proved—it's that we at least need a group of squads ready for action."

"You're recruiting special forces squads?"

"Not as many as you'd think. The only rookie squad we've taken in is 324. Ben Sedes practically begged me to enlist them, even though I refused initially."

"But you bloody agreed in the end!"

"Without backup plans, incidents will continue to happen."

"You might as well just send 'em off with Chancellor Veres when he comes making his monthly round, then!" I yelled. "Have him take them and turn them into more soldiers—"

"This isn't the time before the War anymore."

My words strangled themselves in my throat.

I know. Lords above, I know. None of this would've happened before the War. Even during the beginnings of it, the world was still . . . sane.

What the hell happened? Have we always been this blind to everything?

"Are we on the right side?" I asked. I'd been holding in a question like that for decades. Spent countless sleepless nights tossing and turning over it. And now, after it had finally escaped my lips, it sounded so pathetic.

"Of the War?"

"Of life. We aren't a storage bin. The Brotherhood's never coveted power. Yet . . ."

"We don't covet. We've always protected."

"Yeah. And what about the countries that don't want our protection? What about Kanbrik? I sent a few squads out to be damage control for what's left. There ain't a structure standing."

"Kanbrik chose their side."

"But we're still at fault. We have to deal with the repercussions of not choosing a side."

"We're on a side: the Lords'."

"Bugger the Lords, Barco. They don't give a shit." I stared at the floor. "During the War, I thought the days after it would be so much easier . . . But the truth is, they're so much damn harder."

"They'll be even harder now that we're down a Talisman."

I glared up at him. "Archengard is better off because of it. They got too close. Better for the Talismans to be destroyed than wielded by them."

"And would you say the same for the Sacred Heart?"

I wallowed in my sorrow. "The Heart is gone. I searched every corner of this wretched planet. If it exists, it's no longer on Archengard."

"If the Noda are here," Barco said carefully, "if the Jackals really are here, then they have to be onto something. They wouldn't be in Khronera unless they had a reason for it. I haven't heard anything back from my spies regarding the Heart, but you can't give up yet. It's the only quest you never completed. It's here somewhere—"

"It's gone."

Barco pursed his lips. "Then what would you propose to be the best course of action for your trainees?"

My trainees. Right.

Where once my heart had lay deflated, now it sung and soared. Watching them learn and grow—watching them grow fast—then take on a Jackal-controlled Talisman . . . And not just take it on, but possess and destroy it?

The Council and I had arrived at the secret chamber just after Jezna and Prince had joined the battle, and although Barco had attempted to fly past me into the fray of skeletons, I'd held him back. And thank the Lords I had.

I knew Barco thought that given the circumstances, I'd keep them here, possibly even coddle them more, but Carbonek wasn't what it used to be. They weren't what they'd been when they'd first arrived here a few days ago. I still remembered the rainbow in the sky flashing across my eyes.

And I still remembered how we'd passed the Trials in two weeks. Then how these trainees hadn't even been here a full one yet.

"While Jezna heals," I said, "I'm sending Enoch and Murta on a doubles quest."

Barco strode toward me until we were face-to-face. "That would be the single most foolish decision you've made since being elected Grand High Navigator."

"That's quite a list to sift through."

"I'm serious. Doubles quests are the last thing we should be sending trainees out on right now. How can you even contemplate that decision after—"

"After the Jackals laid siege to Carbonek? After this manor was defiled by their dark technology and poisonous ideals? Nay. The last thing *my* trainees will be doing is staying here. Archengard is out there. And they've proven themselves time and time again to be more than what's on the surface. They've saved Carbonek twice. *Twice.* In less than a week, they've accomplished more than we did in a month. In less than a week—in my book—they've already passed more than half of the Trials."

"Half?"

"Aye. You need twenty-four points to be confirmed. I give 'em three for holding off the Skrill, two for stopping Nothomathos and Kanbrik, four for the teamwork and connections they've built in such a short time, and four for not only fighting a Tintagen Talisman, but saving Carbonek while simultaneously stopping the Jackals. That puts them at thirteen points, and if their Shield and Charger pass this doubles quests, I plan on giving them three more points."

"Have you forgotten that their Charger assaulted a High Elder?" Barco twitched with anger. Those all-knowing eyes of his seemed tormented now. Like I'd scattered his plans all across the map. "That he was used to get the Talisman?"

"And was that not the same Charger you convinced me to take up by deeming him 'the next Leviathan?' I faintly remember punching the king of some crackpot Nodan country square in his jaw at one point or another, too. And I remember you giving me a high-five afterward."

"That was then. Before the Perpetual War. Now, we're faced with far greater matters. They're not ready."

"Neither were we. Champ couldn't navigate his way out of a doorframe."

"We were ready enough." He paused. "We had the greatest Shield that ever lived."

Given the choice between keeping my peace or letting fly whatever rants I'd grow to regret later, I chose the former. I gripped the worn hilt of the Sword and glared at nothing in particular. I was no longer the quick-witted, fast-talking Leviathan of old. I'd learned from my mistakes—in ways that the Leviathan never could.

"As Grand High Navigator, my word is final."

"Then permission to speak freely?"

"Sorely granted."

"I think you're making a grave mistake. I think you're doing this not just out of *guilt*, but because you want to be able to say that you raised a squad without it melting into darkness. I think you're doing this because you want to remove our squad from the books and replace them with a better, purer version. And, Kaleo, I'm sorry, but they're not it."

"I'll see them in my office tomorrow afternoon."

"You're really going to send Murta out on a doubles quest with the Jackals—"

"The quest I've picked is far from here. A place in Khronera that the Jackals have never had any dealings with. Don't forget that Cahis had us on doubles by the first week, too."

Barco took a few steps back and sulked before speaking again.

"These are your trainees. You know them better than I do. You know how much they've grown, and because of that, if you think they're ready, then by the Lords, they're ready. But this is a vastly different Kaleo from the one that wanted nothing to do with them. And as Hektor has proven with Squad 326, attachment is not often for the benefit of the squad."

"Not all of us champion you and Reggie's emotionless method," I said. "A High Nav's gotta know when to slip in and out of it."

Barco nodded, and for a moment, it looked like he was convinced.

"I watched Enoch run the Bastion with Squad 326," he said. "You should know that he went AWOL."

"So? They ain't his squad."

"The Bastion remembered him."

The secret High Hall we stood in was warmly lit by a hundred torches placed along the walls and columns, yet I suddenly felt unbearably cold. I felt the roots of my teeth stabbing into my gums, my brain quaking inside my skull.

"How is that possible?"

Barco just stared at me, gray eyes unblinking.

I turned away so I didn't have to stare at them, thoughts racing through me. What should've crippled me, what would've crippled the man from a week ago, just made me more determined.

"*No.*" I shook my head. "Foolishness. All the more reason to send them out. They'll prove themselves on this quest. They will. 'If a Navigator can't run, they—'"

"'—might as well fly.' I'm the one that gave you that damned book in the first place. Just . . . keep a close eye on them. Kaster has been known to see shadows in the rafters. And frankly, I think I'm starting to see them, too."

CHAPTER 36

Enoch

I'd been staring at the statue of Adam Evenstar for five minutes already before the gray-suited man shuffled between sitting squads to stand by my side. He swiveled to look up at Evenstar, too.

The Father of the Code, he was called. The First Navigator. Some said before he even met the other two founders, Evenstar was already famous for his one-man crusade and ideals.

A one-man crusade that would become the quest of a guild for four generations. Ideals that would become the Code.

And I'd almost just turned my back on both.

"Don't have any regrets," Kaleo finally said, still staring at the statue. "That's the first thing I learned from him."

"Might be a little late for that. You were right."

"Couldn't care less what I was. What I want to know is what you are now."

I thought back to everything that had happened since removing myself from Kaleo's tutelage and came to a simple conclusion. "I'm not the Leviathan: I'm Enoch Amon."

Kaleo's silence implied more. So I sucked in a hardy good breath and delivered.

"But at the same time, I'm not Enoch Amon: I'm the Charger of my squad."

"Really humbles you to say that, doesn't it? I remember feeling like I'd eaten ash after Cahis made me say those words. Nasty taste in me mouth. Nice suit, by the way."

"You were a Charger, too?"

Kaleo hesitated, then headed away from Evenstar. "I'll show ya."

He paused in front of a smaller image that I'd almost strolled by without seeing. The vast paintings of battles were what really caught my attention. If Kaleo should stop at anything, I figured it would be for one of those, not a measly photograph.

But the photograph displayed four boys in their early twenties. One was short, wearing a jack-o-lantern grin under brown-blond hair—Champ Wozneth—while the boy wrapped around his shoulders bore the familiar gray eyes of Barco Reyveth.

The last two boys were even more recognizable: the black suit, dark bandana, blond hair, and determined glint in the orange eyes of Mathias Flint . . . and beside him, white-and-gold bandana drawn under shimmering blond hair, stood the Leviathan. Each of them was covered in a soft layer of ash, seemingly byproducts of whatever burned in the palm trees behind them. At the bottom of the photo, I saw the scrawled words *Fortuna Favet Fortibus*.

Kaleo stared at it long and hard. "Mathias and I frequently flipped positions. Barco was comfortable at Sharpshooter and Champ loved being Driver . . . but Mathias preferred Shield, even though we had a higher chance of success if he was Charger."

"So why'd he make you be it?" I asked.

Kaleo looked me dead in the eyes. "Because being Charger ain't just about leading the squad. You become the literal 'charger' of the squad. Not 'charger' in the sense of storming into battle. You become the Aestus fuel that keeps your squad running."

"And you think I'm that battery?"

"Well, it sure isn't Kaster. He's a natural Shield. Just like Mathias was. We swashes have got Charger instincts in our blood. We keep things lively. Keep our friends laughing and our enemies on their toes. We find ways out of anything because our brains don't work the way most Navs' do. That's what you did against the Karnocolix, ain't it?"

"Didn't really think about it."

Kaleo tilted his head. "What did you think about?"

"How when I ran the Bastion with Squad 326, we failed because I wasn't a good enough Charger. And then, when we all occupied our positions—when we finally worked together . . ." I shook my head in astonishment. "We kicked arse."

"Indeed. Being a Charger ain't just about charging in. Just like how being a Shield ain't just about shielding. All have to work together. As individual Navs, you're individual streams, but together, a winding river."

When Kaleo stared back up at the picture, I felt gooseflesh rise across my body.

"Ignis, in a way, is a river in its own right," he said sorrowfully. "It runs only when there's no obstacles to block it. When those channeling it do so for the right reasons. A river runs together, not in separate currents. Or else they run the risk of becoming rapids."

In just those few words, I was completely broadsided by everything that Kaleo had been through. It was clear that the Brotherhood's near destruction at the beginning of the Perpetual War, Champ's death, and Mathias's death had all taken a toll on him.

He was frightened for the future of the Brotherhood. That was why he'd turned us all away initially. We'd had zero connection with one another. I probably would've turned my sorry arse away, too.

"Squads are no longer valued," Kaleo said. "Connection is no longer valued. That's why your Ignis ability's so important to us, lad. The individual destroys this world. You saw it in the dining abbey between Kanbrik and Nothomathos. Archengard dies a slow and steady death. And you see that lack of connection in those damaged by the Perpetual War. Them souls like Kaster."

I stared at my fists. "There's more to him than he says, isn't there?"

"He's a black hole. Only the strongest among us dare approach it. And like the black hole, it reveals nothing from its infinite abyss."

"That why you keep him in the basement?"

Kaleo frowned.

"He showed me," I said truthfully.

"And you're not mad?"

"I didn't realize he was so dangerous."

"He needs someone to light the way for him. Someone willing enough to face the black depths and possibly even come out the other side."

Kaleo really thinks I'm the one to do that? "I'm . . . trying. But I'm never prodding him again. If I'd actually possessed him—"

"You were merely ignorant of his power. As were you of your own at the time."

"So why didn't you tell me? Why risk putting Navigators' lives in danger?"

"'Cause you wouldn't have brought out the Other, just like Kaster wouldn't have let you. Stubborn as he is, he's a crafty fellow."

I made sure to phrase my next words as carefully as possible. "Then I have a proposal, if you're willing to hear it."

"Hm?"

"If Murta has as much control as you say he does, then why doesn't he try to spend the next couple of nights up in the tower?"

Kaleo's eyes widened. "What?"

"There's another bed in my room for a reason. He needs to spend more time with us, under the same roof."

"He's under the same bloody roof!"

"In a stone prison. Buried beneath Carbonek."

"Apologies, lad. That's out of the question."

I didn't give in so easily. "If we're going to be a squad, how do you expect that to happen if he spends every night locked away in that thing?"

"Having him spend the night not locked in the containment device is too risky. Although he's got more control, there's no telling what the Other chooses to do when the suns go down. Kaster is most vulnerable when he sleeps. The answer's nay. Spend the day together, but at night, he's to be stored below." Kaleo's face stretched thinly. "I'm sorry, young'un. Carbonek ain't ready to make that big of a leap yet."

I lowered my eyes from the aged photograph—away from the four boys' frozen-in-time roars of laughter. Whereas Squad 327 was together, mine was, well, not. One bloke was locked away in the basement, one was Ignis-less, and the other was out of action for the time being.

"I understand," I said. "Thanks again." And more forcefully, "Kaleo."

He ruffled my hair. "That's a good lad. Now go fetch some breakfast. I'll see you in my office by twelve. And don't worry: I got a surprise for you."

CHAPTER 37

Enoch

I found Prince sulking about the entrance to the healing branch, his guns spread out around him on the floor.

"Oi, Princey-boy."

He didn't seem to have heard me. When I gently kicked his shoe, he flinched so hard that his sunglasses almost flew off his face, then glared up at me.

"Oh," he said emotionlessly. "What's up, Noc?"

"The sky." I winced. "She that bad?"

Prince went back to cleaning his sniper rifle and pointed over his shoulder at the Nightguard standing beside him.

"Jezna is fine," the Nightguard said, maintaining his position of attention. "High Navigators Daria Deckara and Eleri Emeres are overseeing her treatment."

Prince mouthed it all in perfect tandem before scoffing. "That's the answer I've gotten for the past five hours. I barely slept last night—too many dreams about break-dancing skeletons—so I came down here hoping to check on Jezna. But the Council won't let anyone in or out."

My heart twinged. Though Jezna and I hadn't exactly been the closest, she was still a kind soul. She'd saved us all in the Talisman chamber. *And she's still my Driver.*

I attempted to peek my head past the Nightguards positioned at the entrance but couldn't make out anything through the maze of tapestries. I glanced back up at the Nightguard who had spoken. "If it's taking this long, can't we at least see her? We're worried."

"Jezna is fine. High Navigators Daria Deckara and Eleri Emeres are overseeing—"

"Bollocks on your overseeing. I wanna see my Driver."

"Jezna is fine. High Navigators Daria—"

I tapped into Ignis. "And if I don't care?"

Both Nightguards had their silver spears to my chin and Ignis curdling around their silhouettes in less than a second. I threw my hands up and stomped off. "Bloody brilliant. KALEO?! Where's that barmy bastard when you need him?"

When I arrived at the dining abbey—hoping to catch Kaleo on his way back up to his office, then snag some scrambled eggs—I saw that what had been a social gathering had become akin to a funeral. Navigators murmured and whispered. Singing and stomping feet had been throttled. Stories and jokes didn't seem to hold their initial prowess anymore. No one wanted to talk, much less connect.

So when a shadow fell across the entire manor, turning the morning light streaming in through the windows into night, fear spread immediately. The few that had come down to breakfast flew from their tables, running out of the abbey. Glasses and plates crashed against the floor as they were swept aside.

They seemed afraid, yet also familiar with the dark spot. Their fear didn't seem like a fear of the unknown so much as a tiredness.

Quickly stepping out of the archway so as not to be trampled, I took one look at the spot in the sky, then followed.

Outside in the courtyard, the darkness was even more prevalent. It descended slowly, hovering over the entirety of Carbonek like an ominous storm cloud. The vibrations in the air were thick, becoming steely sound and replacing the cold silence with a metallic whine. And when mechanical white lights flickered on around the length of the massive spot, illuminating a grizzled war-cruiser, I shuddered.

"Is it the Noda?" I asked a random Navigator.

I barely heard her response. The cruiser fell from the sky at a rapid speed, moving back toward the west so that it didn't crush the manor on its way down. For as humongous as Peniel Valley was, it barely fit.

"Not a Nodan cruiser," a husky voice said. "Governmental."

I whipped my head around to see Maddox, looking twice as tall with a nervous Cowlin perched up on his shoulders to see better.

"C'mon, Brother," the freckled lad said. "Let's get a closer look." They took off through the crowd toward the golden gates at the edge of the courtyard, where Navigators were lining up against in preparation. I followed quickly.

The cruiser was touching down, lowering itself to the grass until it hung just a foot away. Lights flashed again—yellow this time—to form a doorway in the mess of brown machinery. Smoke hissed off of the lights and rushed outward in white smoke as the door gently slid open.

A man stepped out into the valley. He was tall and wore a business suit made of granite-colored fabric. Unlike the colorful, clean, and sleek Navigational clothing, his suit was plain and almost too clean. Although he stalked to the center of the landing area with confidence, his clenched posture made it look like there were spikes inside his suit.

Navigators murmuring around me, I sifted through the crowd, cautiously stepping over dress shoes until I was back at Maddox's side.

"Who the hell's that?" I asked. "What's—"

"Look," Cowlin breathed.

I followed his gaze back toward Carbonek, where another man in a dark gray suit was making his way through the crowd. Navigators parted around him at an incredible speed.

Excited whispers ran through the crowd.

"Kaleo?" I asked. "What's he . . . ?"

But Maddox and Cowlin were on the move again, getting even closer to the opening in the gates where Kaleo would eventually meet whoever this bloke was. I followed, even more quickly than before, and ran directly into Biassis Ondenecro again.

He turned, blue eyes still smiling, but his face was locked with intensity. To his right, glaring just beyond his muscular shoulder, was that damned albino muskrat.

"Watch where you're walking, eunuch," he said.

"Close your mouth, Larry," Biassis said, some of the intensity fleeing when he saw it was me. "We really need to stop meeting like this, though."

"Agreed," I grumbled. "Now can someone tell me what the bloody hell's going on?"

Biassis pointed at the cruiser. "The Government's intruding on our sky."

"Er, no offense, mate, but no one can own a part of the sky."

"True. But in a time of war, there are boundaries. And this is neutral ground. Neither the Government nor the Noda may come here, unless seeking peace."

"And if this time they seek the opposite?" Cowlin said nervously.

I pounded my fists. "Fine by me. If the Gov wants to throw down—"

"The Government isn't here to attack Carbonek," Larry said. "That man is High Chancellor Veres. If they wanted to attack us, they wouldn't send the leader of the whole bloody thing. Honestly, dimwit, one would think you'd been born yesterday."

I was astonished. *That* was Chancellor Veres? After years of hearing about the man but never actually seeing him, I'd come to theorize that he wasn't real at all. Merely a fictitious role concocted by the Archengardian Senate.

And seeing him in person, I felt anger boil inside me. This was the man who ordered people to their deaths every day. The man who refused to make peace with the Noda and refused to accept anything other than victory for the Government. He put the Government before everything—even its people—because he *was* the Government.

"Mayhaps I was," I snapped back. "But tomorrow I will have been born two days ago, whereas you will remain a saucy wank-faced pantaloon."

Then Chancellor Veres began to speak, putting an instant end to Larry's rebuttal.

"I'd like to speak with you," Veres told Kaleo in a voice that reminded me of the stone-faced Governmental generals I'd avoided in my escapades about the Light Isles. "Alone."

"You never informed the Council that you'd be coming," Kaleo said. "So you'll say what you want to be saying right here."

"Then I'll be blunt. I'm here to make an arrest."

The courtyard began to whisper.

"On whose charges?" Kaleo asked.

"Mine."

"The Government has no say here."

"Does Carbonek rest within the continent of Khronera?"

"Aye."

"Then it's under Government control."

"Not in the slightest. The Shrouded Men's pyramids in the west rest within Khronera, but the Government hasn't once dealt with them."

"The pyramids rest on the outskirts. And the Shrouded are . . . uncivilized folk."

"As does Carbonek. As are *we*."

"Not nearly uncivilized enough to neglect the usage of Aestus technology, it seems. The Government helped the Brotherhood implement Aestus communicative devices around the time that the War began. Therefore, the Government is kept *carefully* informed of all happenings in and around Carbonek." Veres's lips tightened. "Where is Locken Aldradeas?"

So that was why Biassis was so tense. The Navigator's bulging biceps looked on the cusp of bursting. Even a black shadow had fallen over Larry's sneering face, hiding his eyes under the brim of his sports cap.

News traveled fast around Archengard, but it was remarkable how quickly the Government had learned of what had transpired only a few hours ago. Fuck technology.

"Locken Aldradeas is none of your concern," Kaleo said. "The situation has been dealt with. He isn't at fault. He's a fine Nav."

"The Nothomathos Princes informed my men of everything that occurred. They also tell me that Locken was in possession of the Karnocolix for a period of time. That he used it to manipulate others. And that, because of this, the Karnocolix has since been destroyed." His eyes flashed with fury.

"Loc didn't manipulate anyone. *He* was manipulated."

"Into manipulating others."

"You're talking in circles."

"And here I thought I spoke to a fellow soul of strength. It turns out they're right about everything they say about High Navigators: Every last one of you is as willing to bend the Code to your own purposes as the next. Even if it means the destruction of those around you."

"If you're inciting a challenge, Chancellor, we both know how that'll go."

"And if we wanted to," Veres suddenly snarled, "we could *obliterate* Carbonek. We could have the methodology of the Noda. 'Either you're with us, or against us, and even if you're against us, you'll be with us in the end because we'll enslave every last one of you.'"

He unbuttoned his suit jacket, prompting numerous Navigators to step forward, but he merely withdrew a folded piece of black fabric. "But we're not the Noda." He tossed the item to the grass where it lay at Kaleo's feet.

Kaleo stared before straightening it out with the toe of his boot. When the fabric fell open, it revealed a grim insignia: a black jackal's head with orange eyes wrapped in a gold collar.

My whole body locked. Those who saw the flag fell still, eyes wide and unblinking. Those unable to see it pushed forward. Shivers and murmurs spread at a breakneck pace.

I glanced over at Biassis and the others, but they wore similar faces.

So the message was received by all. The Jackals were back in the War. They really had come to Khronera.

"Three battles in three days," Veres said. "Over a thousand soldiers dead. All on our side . . . How many of them do you think were in possession of Ignis?"

Kaleo's eyes traced the jackal like he was hypnotized.

"Five."

"Navigators aren't soldiers," Kaleo said, but he sounded meek. "Combat is merely a single step on the Navigator's road."

"Really?" Veres pulled a cluster of items from his interior breast pocket—photographs. "Because I was told you brought back an old merc of ours named Murta Kaster." He held one out for Kaleo. "And this kid."

From my angle, I could clearly make out a shirtless blond boy—knuckles taped, green bandana wound around his forehead—uppercutting a man in a mud pit. His fists glowed with familiar emerald symbols.

Cowlin opened his mouth wide. "Hey—"

Maddox smothered him with a hand.

"The Nothomathos Princes told me he punched a High Elder," Veres said amusingly. "Sounds more like soldier behavior than the 'protecting and preserving' your kind preaches about. He'd fit among the Armed Forces ranks perfectly."

I became aware of a few Navigators beginning to throw cautious, surprised looks at me, but my gaze never deviated from Kaleo.

"Pitch all those photos," Kaleo said. "They're on their way to becoming fantastic Navigators."

I felt my chest swell with triumph, but Veres wasn't done yet. "Like you. Like Barco. Like Mathias—"

"Not every Ignis user has an ability that pertains to fighting. If it's fighters you want, go sniff around the underworld. They're sure to have a few Ignis-using mercs."

"The Noda would merely outbid us to get them, and they lack the training that Carbonek grants Navigators. They're loose cannons. Dogs with only one trick. Whereas your boys . . ."

"Not every Ignis user has an ability that pertains to fighting," Kaleo repeated sternly. "Not everyone here is an Ignis user."

"But they can still be of use. My soldiers need everything they can get. Elementalists for fires at night, trenches and barricades in the ground, water to drink and clean them, air to control the weather. They need Practicals to cook, to clean, to heal their wounds."

"Navigators *aren't* slaves."

"But they're granted Ignis for a reason."

"We use our Ignis abilities for things that matter."

Veres looked down at the flag. "Apparently not." He spun slowly so that his gaze curdled across the entire courtyard. "And if this doesn't prove my point, then I don't know what does. A bunch of half-drunk hooligans. Fallen adventurers searching for pointless purpose. The very last in line."

I took a thunderous foot forward, but Biassis grabbed my shoulder.

Astonishingly, Kaleo only nodded. "Aye. Never anything else."

Among the crowd, fear and anger were replaced with pride. I felt it immediately, like a rush of sudden, untapped adrenaline. Chests puffed out, heads tilted up toward the sky in defiance, and the stillness of the group turned into a shifting mass. Some Navigators cracked their necks, others stretched limbs to get their blood pumping. A few even threw middle fingers up at the cruiser. The flag that had caused so much anxiety lay grimly forgotten. I felt all of it in my bones, churning through me like molten flame.

Veres broke his stare-down with Kaleo with a disappointed shake of his head. "A pity. When you could be so much more."

"Law One of the Code states—"

"You think I give a damn about the Code?" Spit flew from Veres's mouth. "What I care about is making sure the human race survives the Perpetual War. Not *just* Navigators. Not *just* Ignis users: all of Archengard."

Veres slowed his breathing back down. When he turned back toward the cruiser, his voice echoed across the courtyard in a hair-raising drawl. "So, Leviathan: will it?"

He stepped back through the doorway, the way hissing shut behind him. The battle cruiser rumbled, then began to float back up into the sky. The Navigators watched it leave with disdain, some spitting in an attempt to get it to cling to the metal, others crying curses. I merely stood motionlessly as the cruiser rocketed off in the direction of the capital city.

"Bastard," Biassis said under his breath, then raised his head above the crowd. "All right, everyone! Back to the dining abbey! Drinks on me in the Kavern tonight!"

A few cheers rang out, mostly lighthearted mumbles. Larry had already turned back to the manor, but I still faced Kaleo and the flag.

Kaleo hadn't moved either. In fact, his eyes had yet to leave the flag.

I took a small step toward him, but Biassis touched my shoulder again.

"Leave him be. He has enough to think on. As do you."

Unshakably tense at first, I slowly relented with a nod. When I gazed back up at Carbonek, alight beneath the twin suns, a shiver ran through me. Carbonek looked electrified in the sunlight, like it was glowing.

"Biassis," I said.

"Yea, bro?"

"You're a Charger, right?"

"Until the day I die."

"How do you do it? 'Charge' a squad?"

"Truthfully? You realize that everything Veres just said was nonsense. First in line, last in line . . . it makes no difference." He clapped me on the back before moving back toward the glowing manor. "We're all in line. So start shaking hands with those in front and behind you. You might not know them, but one day, you'll need 'em."

CHAPTER 38

Murta

I shuddered through gritted teeth, sweat-drenched arms pumping downward just to thrust my body up over and over again. Ignis pounded through me, spreading across my body in bright splatter-patterns. I estimated I'd been at it for thirty minutes, but I'd lost track of the number of pushups. Shadarians were taught to never count.

"Don't stop for the pain," my brother had said. "Don't stop when the pain turns to numbness. Stop only when the numbness becomes fear of death: *El Momento del Crepúsculo*. The Twilight Moment. And dare to delve beyond it."

I hated my brother. My family. My whole clan. I pretended that they didn't exist. But there were things they'd taught me that couldn't be so easily ignored. There were things *I* couldn't ignore.

Like if I opened my eyes, I would've seen smoke trickling up from my mouth. A cruel reminder of the creature residing within me. And though I hated my brother, he'd taught me about the Twilight Moment—something that had helped me learn to control the Other.

The numb stage approached. The pain would become so unbearable that not even Ignis would be able to quell it. Everything would clear, like dark clouds parting, but it would signal the calm before the storm. Pushing up would become so much harder, and just when I thought I'd mastered the numbness, the pain would shock me into unconsciousness.

My muscles felt inflamed. Waves of crackling smoke simmered off of my naked, burning shoulders. I felt hot all over, though when the necklace stroked my collarbone as it swung back and forth, it brought with it a piercing cold. And with the cold, came the voices.

You waste yourself, one said. *You seek release, yet you stay here.*

You should've seized the Karnocolix yourself. The only way to stop the army was to take them on yourself. You could've used them to destroy Carbonek. Paths to peace are always paved with devastation.

Carbonek deserves to burn. Unleash it.

"Go to hell," I spat out, along with scattered gold sparks.

Yes, one of them answered. *I've conquered mine. When will you?*

Alarmed I'd actually been replied to, I stupidly opened my eyes and was hit with a hundred different senses. I hit the tile with a grunt and lay gasping, pressing closed eyes against the floor. Ignis hid back inside me.

I am Breaking, I realized.

I never Broke. I'd lasted two hours in the past before hitting the Twilight Moment, even with the voices calling all around me.

Ow. I peeled my eyelids back, sitting up with annoyance. *What's happening to me?*

Since destroying the crystal and watching the Karnocolix be destroyed, I'd felt . . . damaged. Maybe lost was a better word.

I'd beaten Loc. I'd stopped the Jackals . . . but it hadn't just been me. I hadn't beaten them on my own. We had.

And although we'd lost the Karnocolix because of it, although Archengard was down one less Talisman, beating the Jackals beside other people had felt good.

At least, in the moment.

I'd tried to block Loc's reasoning for why he'd done what he did from my mind, but it never left. It pounded around my head as I lay locked in the containment device. It still forced me away from everyone. Every time I so much as dragged myself out of the basement and walked the halls around the dining abbey, all bright and lively, I immediately decided that I could go another day without eating.

I could go another day without connection.

"Hola."

I sprang to my feet, glaring at the shadow of the column closest to me.

Kaleo surprisingly stepped into the light.

He looked the same since the Talisman chamber, only his eyebrows were more furrowed. Most Navigators wouldn't have been able to spot it, but I could.

"I didn't realize anyone would want to be training this early in the morning," he said.

I walked to where I'd set my shirt, vest, tie, scarf, and jacket, rinsing sweat from my hair. "I just finished." I wasn't in the mood to deal with him, not after the Karnocolix. He had to know that I'd been looking for it, too.

"Sure you were."

"Meaning?"

Kaleo's eyebrows lifted. "You didn't see it in the sky?"

"I was asleep. In the basement. You should remind yourself it exists once in a while."

"Veres stopped by."

I slid my arms through the sleeves of my shirt. "To arrest Loc?"

"Aye."

"I assume you had harsh words in response."

"You know me too well."

"And after that, Veres asked me to join the Army again?"

"Amon as well."

"They're getting desperate."

"Nay." Kaleo removed his hands from behind his back to show that he held something—a piece of black fabric. "The other side is."

He tossed it. I caught it with one hand and pried through its contents until I arrived at the sigil etched into it.

The flag slipped through my fingers, bunching together on the floor, where the symbol continued to stare up at me long after I was no longer looking at it.

Because it never left my eyes. Long ago, it had been seared into my mind. It had made a nest there, then started rearranging things. Removing memories.

"I'll give Veres the benefit of the doubt," Kaleo said. "Our conversation was in front of quite a few Navs, including your Charger, and he kept a lot of things to himself."

Perhaps the inclusion of "Charger" was what finally pushed me over the edge.

It was probably due to a lot of things, like how the Council had tested me with the Karnocolix, Breaking a few moments ago, everything Loc said, and now, the flag.

I might've kept the Karnocolix out of their hands and kept them from controlling Enoch, but they were still out there. They were still alive.

"Veres's message was clear," Kaleo said. "The deaths of Government soldiers and civilians are on our shoulders: The escalation of violence between Kanbrik and Nothomathos is our fault."

"They are."

Kaleo retreated into the shadows of the column. It was something Barco was prone to doing, not the mighty Leviathan.

"I know."

I blinked.

"And believe it or not," he continued, "I came here to apologize. For everything."

I swayed silently. "Everything that happened last time was my fault."

"Nay." Kaleo's eyes glistened with emotion. "You've proven that it was always our fault. We neglected you. All your growth, all your training has been done on your own . . . Just like Mathias."

Mathias.

Kaleo's squadmate and the only other Navigator capable of competing with the legend of the Leviathan. The brooding, dark soul that had been hailed as the Dauntless One was the only Navigator I'd ever found any comfort in. He and I had a lot in common.

Both of us came from pain. Both of us dreamed of clear skies that carried on forever, islands out at sea where we didn't have to be afraid to spread our wings and roar . . .

But in the end, Mathias had left his island and marched into the suns. In the end, as all the stories said, Mathias had found what he was looking for all around him at Carbonek.

"If I may be blunt," Kaleo said, "like him, you've exercised phenomenal control, skill—"

"I think I liked the angry Kaleo better."

"Heh. I'm saying this because I'm planning on sending you out on your first quest."

My heart pounded. I had to work hard to keep it from slipping into my voice. "I thought the first quest was always a doubles."

"It is. You'll be going with Amon. That way Caelius can heal."

"Estupendo."

"You don't sound very worried for your squadmate."

"I'm not. If she stole Ignis, she deserves what she gets."

Kaleo's brow furrowed. "You feel the same way about your other squadmates?"

Stop calling them my squadmates. "Enoch has his own issues. He's too—"

"Positive?"

"I was going to say ignorant."

"So help him."

A dark, unintelligible whisper twittered in my mind. I looked down at the jackal head. Kaleo's gaze followed, tight-lipped.

"What do you plan on having us do?" I asked.

"A simple 'get to the location and snoop around.' You can handle that, right?"

But there was something he wasn't telling me. There was more to Jezna's injury, just as there was more to Enoch and me being sent out already. We hadn't even been here a full week.

"Why this early?"

Kaleo gripped his hands. "Because if the Jackals are back in the War, then I'm not going to have the time to train you much longer. We High Navs will be back out in the field in no time. Hektor's already out looking for the Rénan Rings."

My eyes widened, not at the mention of another one of the Talismans, but at realizing what the Jackals being here meant. Realizing why Kaleo would take an interest in getting outside of Carbonek and going after the Tintagen Talismans. One in particular.

"The Sacred Heart's resurfaced, hasn't it?"

"You aren't supposed to be worrying about Talismans. Especially that damned thing."

"I became a merc since last I was here. Try me."

Kaleo paused. "There's a few countries down south it might be hiding in. That's all Barco's spies know."

"I thought you abandoned it."

"I don't abandon quests." Kaleo paced angrily. "Just shelve 'em. And besides, these are new countries that the evidence is leading us to. If it was the same old lands, I'd hand it off to Daria or someone else. Someone younger."

"And the Jackals?"

"The Noda appears to be just as much in the dark about the Heart's location as we are. That doesn't, however, mean that their leaders aren't sniffing 'round the trail."

"I could find it."

"Out of the question."

"You know I could. I was onto the Karnocolix right before Loc found it, and I spent the past year and a half tracking down the Kardem Ka. I found the map before anyone."

"Don't ask again."

"If I found it—"

"The Heart is twenty times stronger than the Karnocolix. If the Jackals were to seize it from you, it'd mean the death of millions. You got that?"

"Not like that hasn't already happened under your watch."

Kaleo was a foot away from me in seconds. "You might know a thing or two more than most, but you're still a trainee. Focus on your squad! Not demons that'll drag you in the darkest depths of hell!"

Buttoning his jacket so that the ends didn't fly backward, Kaleo fled the hall. I watched him do so, lip curled in disgust, but before stepping through the massive archway, he shocked me by slowing. And when he spoke, it was in a somber rasp.

"I don't need to lose another one."

I stared after him. From the floor, the jackal head cackled up at me.

"Don't worry." I scuffed a foot across the symbol, grinding until it left a dirty scar. Until I felt the fabric tear beneath me. "You won't."

CHAPTER 39

Enoch

When pacing before the doors grew repetitive, I tried to make the Nightguards flanking them laugh, especially once neither so much as made eye contact with me. How could someone look directly at and see right through you at the same time? Jezna was a time-and-a-half compared to them.

I instinctually glanced in the direction of the distant healing branch, but found comfort in knowing Prince would be right there waiting for her. I'd passed the bloke on my way to Kaleo's office to clue him in on Veres's arrival. He'd still seemed out of it, and when I'd asked the Nightguard again how Jezna was doing, I'd gotten the same answer as before.

No time to worry about them. Daria and Eleri will help Jezna. Kaleo would tell me if things were looking bad.

Cracking my knuckles as I resumed pacing, I glanced at the grandfather clock up against the wall. I prepared to heave a hefty sigh but stopped short when a figure strode by.

Dark brown mohawk fluffed from having just stepped out of the shower, Murta looked the cleanest I'd ever seen him. His scarf was low, revealing every inch of his face and putting his handsome features on full display. Even the dark circles under his eyes had let up a little, brightening his caramel eyes.

When he cleaned up, I could easily admit that Murta would've been my favorite Navigator if he'd been one before I joined the Brotherhood. He exuded badarsery.

When he came to an uncomfortable stop next to me and didn't say anything, I nudged him. "You know you can always shout 'Oi, wanker' or something, aye?"

"Oi, wanker."

I gawked.

Murta hunched his shoulders awkwardly, dropping my Light Isles accent. "I didn't mean—"

"Don't apologize, bruv!" I beamed. "That was brilliant! You should say things like that more often. It reminds everyone that you're not just an emotionless bag of sand."

Murta didn't seem overly enthused about the comparison. "I saw you had some scars from the skeletons. How're those healing?"

"Great. Still a little sore, but nothing to complain about. Not after everything with Jezna. You tried to get in the healing branch to see her yet?"

Murta chose not to answer. "What about your spirit?"

I shrugged. "Still intact, right? I don't suppose possessing all those skeletons separated it into five hundred halves. I just did what you and Kaleo told me to do and found the spirit of the Karnocolix. I feel bloody brilliant."

Murta gestured at the bandages decorating my face. "And those?"

"Spic-and-span in no time. Bruises are bruises, cuts are cuts. Oi, how's your back? I saw some skeletons messing with it, and after you lifted the mast—"

"Strained—"

"I'll bet."

"From carrying this squad."

I blinked twice, then howled with laughter, to the point that I was rolling around on the floor in front of the Nightguards. It felt good to laugh like that again, like I was back in the Light Isles shooting the breeze at a seaside bar.

Of course, at that exact moment, the Nightguards decided to open the doors to Kaleo's office. In response, Murta lifted his scarf over his face, and I quickly leapt to my feet.

I hadn't expected the office to be so huge. It certainly didn't soar up to the sky like the dining abbey, but what it lacked in space, it made up for in what filled the space.

Bookshelves conjoined with shelves that held artifacts, gold-gilded boxes, silver globes, and glowing prisms. Against the opposite wall stood pedestals with globes. This wall served as the host for maps, star charts, and a massive screen. The back wall was completely taken up by an arched window that looked down on the desk fixed in front of it—and the man leaning against it.

When the Nightguards closed the doors behind us, Kaleo's expression twitched with amusement. I was happy to see such after his conversation with Veres. *And that bloody flag.*

"Another day in the Trials, lads," he said. "And some crazy Trials you've had. But each hour you've spent here just makes me think that you're not just ready to move on to the next stage: You're ready to step back outside Carbonek. That means that your next Trial will be a doubles quest."

Kaleo turned toward the massive screen against the opposite wall. When he removed a silver remote from his interior breast pocket, the screen blinked on, displaying an image of a chiseled mountain of ice against a star-studded sky.

"Squads, as you've probably figured out by now," Kaleo continued, "aren't just about teamwork, but what each individual brings to it. What the parts contribute to the whole. The Council has never taught trainees the squad positions at the beginning of the Trials, as we've found that it's better for the squad to figure it out on their own. And part of the point of a doubles quest is that you're suddenly robbed of two of those positions. You and your chosen squadmate are suddenly forced to occupy all the positions, in case you and your squad ever get separated out in the field. And so, you begin to realize just how important your squad truly is in order to become a strong Navigator.

"But don't worry too much. I'm not sending you into anything wild enough that it can't be solved by two bright trainees. You should know that High Navs receive queries, job opportunities, and distress calls long before the high-ranking squads ever receive them. We take the big ones that need to be taken care of immediately, though the majority are distributed to the squads. The quest I'm having you embark on has been on my waiting list for a while now. In fact, I submitted it for a squad to pick up, but no one did! So it falls to you."

I nodded urgently. "Hit us with it."

Kaleo pointed at the mountain. "Aren's Steeple. A remote mountain a little east of the Frozen Peaks of the Frozen North. It looks like nothing, but a man I met in White Town on a supplies trip was pretty adamant that there was something right well suspicious going on up there. An abandoned temple or something. You'll have to climb it on your own. We'll send a crab cruiser to pick you up after you've done your investigating. Or fighting." He shrugged.

"So we're being sent to sniff around?" Murta sounded bored.

"I never said this would be fun," Kaleo said. "And the less fun, the better the training it'll be. Not every quest is going after the Galagazen loot, young'un."

"Or the Race Across Debáse," I said.

"So-so. You wouldn't believe how bloody consistent the scenery stayed half of the time. Champ's singing got me through that shitshow, I'll tell ya . . . Though any time the Gobogor Ghost Riders caught up to us, it became a quest for the ages."

Kaleo switched off the screen, and after rummaging through piles of paper, finally found what he was looking for: two black devices that fit squarely in the palms of his hands. When I got mine, I examined it with awe. Murta just pocketed his.

"These be talkers," Kaleo said. "Aestus tech. Try not to get too excited, as you'll be handing them back afterward. It's only after getting confirmed that they officially become yours. These are the only things that I'll be able to communicate with you through."

I messed with my talker to no avail and had to have Murta show me the on and off switch on the side. After locating it, the screen flickered on, displayed the symbol of the Brotherhood, then turned into a mess of buttons and square images. At the very bottom, a talker symbol was accompanied by the bolded word kaleo.

"Brilliant," I said. "Still got no idea how to work it."

"You'll get used to it," Kaleo said. "Keep 'em safe . . . Ah, and here's one more thing."

He handed me a small silver disc just a few inches bigger than the coins.

"A portable starglass fire. It'll burn however long you need. Navs use them all the time for signals, but I believe you'll definitely need it up on that mountain. There's a button on the side. After clicking it, you got five seconds to throw it down before it sets you on fire. No cries, no lies, no alibis."

"Thanks for all of this, Kaleo," I said.

He sat at his desk. "I expect a call to say you've completed your quest three days after the cruiser drops you off. However, if you need anything, call anyway. Your cruiser's waiting in the hangar.

"So go get 'em, young'uns. You wanted to be Navigators? Now's your chance. This is a simple quest I'm giving you. You pass it, and your squad will be swearing on the Code in no time."

CHAPTER 40

Prince

Father used to sing me songs. Little ones. Nothing too grandiose. Those were saved for the colder nights, when the Narthesian winter swirled out of the neighboring forests, blanketing the world around our lone cottage in ice and snow.

My favorite of his longer songs—what he'd called "epics"—had been "Evenstar's Ascendance," but I'd forgotten the verses. He used to play the guitar with it, strumming through a thousand chord changes, layering melodies like a madman. It'd been too much for my little brain to handle.

But short song-wise, I'd never forgotten "The Bat Never Looks Back."

Not after it actually happened.

As I fiddled with my pistols, modifying their systems to answer to the phrase "Piss on 'em," I hummed to myself, hearing the song resonate throughout the abyss:

Jackals climb in from the night
Obsidian caverns assemble to fight
A white bat defends his young one
Bloody wings at midnight: all is said and done

Bonfires blazing brightly
Echoes through the youth's head
He chases the jackals back into the black
When the suns crack the sky, the bat never looks back

By the end of it, I'd accidentally coded one of my pistols to "blazing brightly" so that the core malfunctioned, spitting a plume of smoke up into my face. I dropped it with an enraged cough, then wrapped my arms around my legs, listening to the distant voices beyond the Nightguards, searching for Jezna's.

It's like he knew, I thought weakly. *Like he was just getting me ready. He knew it was a suicide mission. That one of these days, they'd finally get him.*

"Bloody wings at midnight . . ."

I coughed again, just to keep the tears far away from my eyes.

But why leave me *behind? Why make me live with this . . . ?*

A streak of purple hurried out of the archway, briskly followed by a streak of red. They moved so urgently that I didn't realize who they were until they were ten feet away from me. I jumped up, but Eleri—looking completely healed, like blocking an explosion had merely been a slight inconvenience—stabbed a finger back at the Nightguards.

"No one is to enter. I'm off to find Kaleo." I saw her eyes slip toward me, as though gauging my level of anxiety, before turning back around. "Things haven't let up."

I felt my stomach drop out of its orbit. Eleri was the most famous Navigational healer of all time. If she hadn't yet found a way to heal Jezna . . .

What's wrong with her?! I wanted to scream. *None of us saw what happened! She can't be . . . dead . . . ?*

I spun back toward the archway. The Nightguards must've seen the desperation in my face, because their postures tightened and they shuffled closer together.

That just made me want to shoot something.

"You're really gonna keep a trainee from seeing their fellow squadmate?" I asked, moving to stand before the two asshats. "That's pretty freaking un-Navigational of you. Then again, not that you're real Navigators anyway . . ."

I squinted to see if I could glimpse a reaction out of either of them, but they didn't move. Thankfully, they didn't repeat their sing-song story again either.

"What the hell's going on here?" I was getting more livid by the second. *Okay, so maybe I liked it better when they actually talked to me. Even if it was just on repeat.* "What're you trying to keep secret? If Jezna's . . ." I swallowed, unable to say it. "I mean, if she's, you know, I'd really freaking like to know that. And I'd like to see her. Now."

I must've been looking pretty sad because I thought I saw the Nightguards exchange quick glances.

Please, I silently pleaded with them. *I can't have someone else close to me die. Not again.*

I can't be left alone again.

Then the Nightguard on the right wet his lips. "Jezna is fine. High Navigators Daria Deckara and Eleri Emeres are—"

I ducked low and dove through his legs.

The Nightguard shouted, attempting to smash the sides of his shin guards together and trap me, but he underestimated just how short I was. Before he could spin around and the other Nightguard could throw himself in my direction, I was already weaving through the healing branch, trying to lose myself in the tapestries and pinned linens.

Once or twice, I accidentally ran in on a couple of healers in the process of nursing a Navigator back to health, and had to see myself out with swift words and even more swift bows.

Then I saw a flash of aqua out of the corner of my eye and immediately backtracked. This area of the branch was covered in the most tapestries, completely walled off by the bright colors and designs. Yet through the empty space where two met, I saw a color that wasn't hanging from the ceiling, but lying motionlessly atop a bed.

"Jezna!" I pulled the blankets down completely . . .

Jezna looked all right, except there was a gaping hole in her breastplate. Like one of the caves in the obsidian caverns Father had sung about.

And when I rushed up to her, feet shuffling nervously before tripping themselves to a halt, I could see directly through the hole into her armor. I blinked in confusion.

There was no body. No skin. Bone. Blood. Veins. Not even tissue.

Just water. An aqua-colored, silky liquid.

No.

My stomach flew up into my throat. I stumbled away with a scream, slamming my eyes shut. It was so much easier to plunge back into the abyss than face what had come out of it. What had returned.

It can't be. She can't be one of . . . It isn't—!

But it was. All of it was the same as that winter night. I was back outside Father's cottage, gazing in on the scene that I kept buried at the bottom of the abyss. The scene of . . .

NO. I won't remember! I won't!

I was no longer stumbling about blindly now. I was on my knees, shoulders quaking, lips quivering. I didn't think. I didn't feel. Nothing but the pain of the last ten years, spreading up into my brain, rising straight out of the abyss and suffocating me. I felt myself choking on my fear, felt the fear force open my eyes to look at Jezna: the glowing water trapped inside the still armor. The water from the memory I refused to remember.

But even through all the fear and against the overwhelming size of the abyss, a small flicker of light rose up out of it to settle at the forefront of my brain. A single thought with repercussions more powerful than any memory: *She's dead.*

And though pieces of the memory finally slithered their way out of the abyss and began to race through me—Father's broken bleeding corpse, the inhuman beings standing over him—my hands began to move on their own, separate from my mind. My eyes stared glassily forward, locked on the water-like substance inside the armor that had haunted me for a decade, but my fingers started sifting through my backpack.

I felt them pick apart and tear the strands and shells off of my guns, fixing and forging away. I felt my hands move back toward my lap, felt myself sit and start working. I felt tools take the pieces' places: wrenches, hammers, my good pliers. I saw sparks fly, puffs of Aestus and hisses of steam. I felt and saw my goggles go on my face as I seemingly welded two pieces together. Yet even through the goggles—through the sparks—I stared at the water.

I stared at the water even as I felt my hands put all my tools away, then hold up my creation: an Aestus core. Not for a turner or machine but for a human. Like a little metal heart.

I felt myself stand, felt myself walk over to Jezna's lifeless armor slowly, no longer stumbling but sure of every footfall. There, I gazed into the abyss of her armor. Straight into the glowing substance, where I saw Father's blank, blood-covered face looking back at me.

When the suns crack the sky . . .

Feeling tears slip from my eyes, I dropped the core straight into the water, all the pink and purple cords trailing off of it, helping it swim to the bottom. Then, when it finally hit the inside of Jezna's backplate, a spurt of electricity spun through the cords as they snapped against the armor and stuck. The heart was in its place.

Through the water, through tears, I watched the heart declare its first beat—a quick pulse followed by a long silence. Then a second beat. A third beat.

Lifting the core's cover—a see-through piece of metal that I'd stripped from my mirror gun and welded perfectly to fit the hole in Jezna's armor—I slammed it down into place, almost praying for the fourth beat to never come. But as the metal cover locked into place with a tiny hiss, the fourth beat echoed out in tandem.

. . . the bat never looks back.

I staggered back and emerged out of the abyss.

CHAPTER 41

Enoch

Snow fell from the charcoal-gray sky, an inverted portrait of the fire-stained skies of Serapharus. Where once I'd sought an escape from the smoldering heat—the burns and oily welts clinging to my fingers—I now searched for a way out of the bitter cold, cracked skin, and numb limbs.

Of course, there was a way out and off the mountain. There was an immediate solution to relieving myself of the pain. The small device in my left pocket, the flick of a switch, and a simple call of just two syllables: *"I quit—"*

I punched myself in the face.

It wasn't Ignis-infused, just meant to knock me awake.

There was no bloody quitting at this stage. Quitting shouldn't even have been a concept.

"Did you just hit yourself?"

I blinked the haze from my eyes. It was like being trapped in Loc's mist again, only this one was of my own making. The mountain still stretched up into the dark sky; one of the single largest landmasses I'd ever laid eyes upon. The last time I'd looked up at it to see how far we'd gone had been four hours ago. The top hadn't gotten any closer. Had we moved at all?

My eyes finally settled on the figure that had spoken to me. Murta stood shirtless in the snow, covered in a layer of white flakes, gold Shadarian bracelets glittering down his arms. Besides his dress pants and shoes, he wore nothing but the scarf wound around his neck, hiding his necklace. I was wearing everything else.

The cold seemed a mere insignificance to him. He was moving as fast as he'd started, eyes glowing and a spiral of fire escaping where his heart was.

"Swash, care to tell me why your nose is bleeding?"

I blinked several times, clutching the sleeves of his suit jacket with quivering fingers, and lifted a hand to my nose. I felt nothing but piercing numbness, but when I looked down, my fingers were stained with fresh blood. The crimson liquid glistened against the pale backdrop.

"S'fine." My teeth chattered. "It's . . . just the cold."

Murta observed doubtfully.

Need to stop, my mind pleaded. *Use the starglass fire—*

No. Can't stop. Won't stop. Never . . .

Murta's skeptical expression faltered. He took a step forward concerningly. "If you really need to call Kaleo—"

"No! We . . . keep climbing. We have to complete this quest. We're going to."

"You're not in the state to be making decisions." Murta's mood darkened back to Shadarian disdain.

"I'm fine." I resumed the slow trudge up the mountain.

"Do you need my pants, too?" he mocked.

"Don't need any of this."

"Until you learn how to harness Ignis to keep you warm"—he pointed at the gold flames wafting out of his heart—"you'll be in need of more of my clothes."

"I know how to harness Ignis."

"But you have yet to control it."

"You're one to bloody talk."

"Your Ignis is weak. There's a difference."

"I'll be fine without your clothes and without Ignis."

"Not good enough, pretty boy."

I squared up to him. "Don't. Call. Me. That."

"How about stop saying that you're fine first?"

"I *am* fi—"

"You're not. *Pretty. Boy.*"

Bugger the pain. I threw off his jacket and tapped into Ignis, but the moment I felt the emerald energy enter my eyes, a feeling like nails being driven into my sockets knocked me flat on my back. I writhed in the snow, then passed out.

Wet snow trickling down my face woke me.

My head pounded with the thunder of a hangover. No. Worse.

Vision clearing, I settled on the distorted outline of Murta kneeling beside me, removing his scarf and wrapping it around my forehead. His collarbones made broadswords look blunt.

"*Suns,*" I heard him curse. "We need to find shelter immediately. Get some warmth back into you."

I tried uppercutting him, but it came out as a drunken slap. Murta caught my hand. My eyes were still too damned blurry to see his face.

"We . . ." Words formed faster on my tongue than my brain could process them. If only Kaleo could see me now; just a day and a half after saving Carbonek. After breaking the Jackals' coercion spell on me. "Need to keep going . . ."

Murta maneuvered me onto his back. The mountain spun in a demented spiral. I nearly lost consciousness again and tried punching the distant peak with a bloodied, bandaged, and frozen fist.

Heh. Frozen Fire Fist.

"I'm . . ."

"I swear, if you say 'fine.'" The warmth of the Ignis in Murta's heart pulsed against my hands. Though my eyes flickered in and out of darkness, the gold that glowed there filled the black with sparkles of starlight. "Either we stop at the first sign of shelter and use the starglass fire or I'm calling Kaleo."

" . . . Im . . . mortal . . ."

"Shut up, idiota."

CHAPTER 42

Jezna

A spark lit in the depths, and my heart was rekindled. Fire couldn't form underwater. Yet when I inhaled, the spark lived, dancing until it fanned into a cool flame. Or something akin to it.

I . . . used fire. I actually did it. I destroyed the Karnocolix.

This fire was definitely Ignis, but there was an abnormality to it, as if the source had been tainted by some unnatural substance.

How am I alive?

I got my fingers working first and foremost. When those were twitching, I jump-started everything else, eager to regain control of myself. My boots shifted. The sound of the metal plates scratching against one another quickened the spark.

I pressed Ignis into a gallop, the exact technique an Ignis user was told never to do. Ignis should be prodded gently. Ignis should be befriended.

But Ignis wasn't mine to begin with, and we'd never been friends, so I pressed on. Pressed until my body coiled itself into waterspouts—thin vortexes that made my breastplate jitter noisily, like pumping pistons and gears and . . .

That sound. The rush of liquid was always a constant, but this was a newer, brighter resonance. I felt one with the sound, as if I were being networked *through* it.

I rose into a hunched-over sitting position and stared down at my chest.

The hole in my breastplate remained a gaping crater into my soul, but instead of watching my body spill out onto the stone, it remained stuck in place, held back by a see-through wall. Peering in terrified astonishment, I saw that a magenta light emitted from within, giving view to a mechanism that looked like . . . an Aestus core. Glowing tubelike cords raced out of the machine and branched off throughout the interior of my armor.

The core *was* my heart.

I flung myself backward in a wordless yell, trying to somehow get the machine to fly out of me, but it remained inside. A trail of bubbles glugged up out of it.

Mind racing, I stood and began to spin about the ruined room in search of what had done this to me. I settled on a small figure crouched in the shadows of the fallen tapestries, backpack slung over his shoulder.

"This spark," I said ferociously. "This isn't Ignis. It's tainted. With *Aestus*."

The figure didn't reply, but they did stand. Slowly.

It unnerved me to see someone so typically full of energy rise with the solemnity of Murta. Perhaps it was that solemnity that reminded me of the reason why I had the core inside me in the first place.

The anger I'd felt toward being tampered with gave way to bleak consternation.

I hadn't been tampered with: I'd been healed. Patched up and brought back to life . . . but at a cost. At a terrible cost.

"Prince," I whispered. "This isn't—"

"What . . . are you?"

I hadn't realized such three simple words could wound me so gravely. They made me want to hurl myself into the Grand Sea.

I tried again. "This—"

"Answer the freaking question."

First, there'd been a spark. Now, nothing but emptiness. *Ashes.*

I tried to return to my river but found only a ragged boneyard.

Macín was wrong, I thought. *Chivalry* is *dead.*

I killed it.

"You're not a normal person." Prince's squeaky voice was taut with emotion. "You're . . . you're not even human."

I bowed my helm. It was so much easier than facing him like a knight.

Who am I kidding? I'm not a knight. Knights don't lie.

And I'd lied to Prince from the beginning. It pained me to the point of shaking that he was afraid of me, yet had still created and planted the device in me to keep my water running.

Prince was the reason I was still alive. And he was *terrified* of me.

"Lords . . ." he said. "You're the . . ."

"I am the water," I said. "Yes. And I'm *so* sorry for not telling you sooner. This is why I don't eat. This is why I never take off my armor. This isn't just normal knight armor; it's god armor, designed to mold around the wearer's form . . . which in my case, is water."

"How?"

He deserves to know. I must *tell him.*

"All my Brothers had Ignis. All except me. And every last one of them died saving a village full of Ignis-less people from a dam that had been broken during the War. While my Brothers tried to hold back the water, they had me get everyone to safety, because I didn't have Ignis like they did. None of the villagers perished that day. My Brothers saved *everyone* . . .

"But they died. And there was no one left to blame but myself.

"So I traveled to the Water Temple of Kakoin in the Light Isles. Where it's said Adam Evenstar once spoke directly to the Lords and took on all of their powers to defeat the Tempest King. And there I found an artifact. A small rodlike thing made of gold and silver, with twin dragon figures twisting around it. It was beautiful. Luminous. I could see Ignis practically exploding out of it.

"And when I held it in my hands, I spoke to it. I told the artifact that if I'd had Ignis, I would've been able to save my Brothers. That the Orders wouldn't have completely died out, leaving me their last Sister . . .

"I forced the Ignis resting within the artifact to fix itself to me, but at a price. No Ignis-less person can access Ignis without first going through the Burning: evolving one's ability to harness Ignis. And I learned that the hard way. I was just lucky that I was already wearing god armor when I entered that temple. If not, I would've been stuck as a puddle forever."

I looked down at my hands—lifeless metal gloves.

"I wanted to be able to fight the water that had drowned my Brothers, so I became water. And if it all ever escapes this armor, I'll be formless, caught in shapeless limbo." I forced myself to a knee. "I am forever in your debt, Prince Larocque. This Aestus you've placed in me . . . This will keep me alive. You've saved my—"

"You're not even a human being."

I lifted my head. "Prince . . ."

"You spoke to me of honor while lying this entire time."

"I did. I broke the Chivalric Code. And for that, I—"

"The Dragon Lords cursed you." Prince stepped into the light, sunglasses clenched in his right fist so that all the hurt in his soft green eyes was visible. They were shattered stained-glass windows, broken beyond mending. "And you talked to me about honor." His lip trembled in agony for two devastating seconds, then he sprinted out of the healing branch.

"Prince!" I shouted, and flew after him.

CHAPTER 43

Enoch

The wind snapped at my eyebrows. I'd grown so accustomed to the cold that not even an icicle dripping onto my forehead startled me awake. It was the warmth in the wind that woke me.

I opened my eyes, peering upside down at the source of light. It was a dancing starglass fire, large enough to warm the cave but small enough not to melt anything. It burned a galactic white, its interior blazing a rainbow of colors. It gave me a headache to look at it for too long, though when I looked past the flames at the shirtless figure sitting in the shadows, I saw that he stared at it unblinkingly.

I rose out of the bundle of clothes I was wrapped in. I lay at the jagged entrance of an ice cave embedded into the side of the mountain. From our height, the wind was a visible skeletal white, blowing itself in spirals. Beyond the entrance and the blizzard's breath was nothing but the black star-scattered sky, remnants of auroras snaking their way among the stars.

The wind howled through the cave, raising frozen hair on the back of my neck and turning me toward the starglass for comfort. I scooted closer, using arms and elbows. When the floor tugged at them, I looked down. My arms, along with my chest and legs, were bandaged just as much as my fists were. My whole body was wrapped in white tape.

Murta looked up from the fire. "Don't—"

I ripped off the bandages wound around my face, beginning to make my way down my body.

"—do that."

I worked silently, stuffing the tape into my dress pants and pretending that the ice against my skin wasn't enough to make me consider jumping straight into the fire.

"Hey."

Rather than reply, I tugged at the tape wrapped around my nose. Dried blood peeled off with them, scattering across the ice.

"What're you moping about now?"

"You wasted all my tape."

"If I hadn't, you would've gotten frostbite. So, *de nada*."

"Tape's for boxing, not bandages."

"Which you really wouldn't have been able to do after your hands fell off."

I continued unwinding my arms but left my hands wrapped.

"And try to not punch yourself in the face anymore. The last thing you need is to be bleeding again."

"I'm fine."

When Murta stood, the shadow he cast cloaked the whole back wall. Though his bracelets glittered in the white firelight, his shadow barely looked human. Humans didn't have wings like that.

"If you keep saying that, I'm going to rip out your tongue. Your body wasn't ready for a journey like this. That's why Kaleo paired you with me."

"It's called a doubles quest for a reason," I said. "It's meant to test us both."

When Murta sat back down, the ghastly shadow disappeared. "And Kaleo told me that we'd be going on one. Don't try to play the favorites' game. You're not his golden boy yet."

"Never said I was."

"Then why always act like him? Why keep this up if not to impress him?"

I took to watching the flames dance. Where most might've seen beauty in their pirouettes, I saw only demons contorting themselves. The sparkles of color that shimmered within the starglass did provide some comfort, but fire was still fire. And any flame that wasn't crafted from Ignis, from my own soul, felt as if it might leap out and crawl across me.

"You're never going to give me a straightforward answer, are you?"

When I didn't answer, Murta frowned.

"Lords, do you even know what you're doing?"

"Course I bloody do," I said, wrapping his jacket around my shoulders. After realizing what I'd done, I threw it across the fire. His vest followed. "Which is why I'm fine. I'm going to be a Navigator. All that matters now."

"No. I refuse to accept that answer. You didn't just wake up one morning and decide to join the Brotherhood. No one does that, not even the best Ignis users. Tell me the truth. How is it that you . . . How do you—"

It was unnerving watching Murta struggle to find the words he wanted to say.

"How do you keep going? What drives you to refuse . . . *rationality*?"

"Belief," I said.

Murta leaned back, falling into the cave's darkness. "That might work. For you. What about those that have never had anything to believe in?"

"That's . . . terrible."

"Is it?"

"Of course it bloody is. If you don't have anything to believe in, what's there to even live for?"

Murta said nothing.

"Well, if we're getting honest with one another all of a sudden," I said, "then why're you doing this? What keeps you going if not for what I have?"

"You mean blind determination?"

Never. "I wouldn't say blind."

"Oh?"

The flames threatened to suffocate me, but talking to Murta, talking about the Brotherhood, somehow heaved the fire off of my chest just enough for me to catch my breath. It was the perfect amount of delusional tiredness and emotional baggage for me to decide to throw the weights slapped across my shoulders off the mountainside.

Better them than me.

"Before I became a swashbuckler," I said, looking off into the night rather than at the fire, "I lived in Serapharus."

Murta looked surprised. "The Factory City? Used to be a big power plant before it was abandoned by the Government. I've heard of it."

"Then you've probably heard about its street gangs. Each of them is run by a demented hierarchy, like a pack of wolves. The older boys always got the most, while the younger lads starved. I was a Younger. We were fed scraps—bones and mold. And the Olders made us fight for them. Kill for bits of barely digestible food.

"But I never killed. I'd rather go hungry than kill another Younger. But some days? I had to break a few bones. I had to make it *look* like I'd killed them or . . ."

The starglass fire crackled, making me flinch. Murta's scarf danced in the howling wind.

"One day, I just got tired of it all. Tired of going hungry, vomiting after every 'meal,' being forced to work twenty-eight hour shifts on the machines until I could barely walk. Tired of watching lads kill each other for crumbs. So I stole from one of the Olders. But another Younger ratted me out."

"I assume your punishment was quite severe," Murta said.

Frantically blinking away the sound of whirring gears and searing flesh, I hummed the tune of an old swashbuckling shanty to still my racing heart.

"When a Younger does wrong once, the punishment is no food for four days. Twice, he spends an hour in the furnaces. After that, the time limit just keeps adding up. Some Olders will throw you in the compressors if they think you really deserve it . . . Most Youngers never do wrong more than once before they turn into obedient dogs. So naturally, I was expecting no food for a few days. What I didn't know was that the punishment for stealing from an Older was *so* much worse.

"They . . . took me down to the Black Factories. Where the Bone Grinders and Axe Men live. And they held me under the blade of a rotating fire beam."

I peered back into the flames, just to prove that I could still face them. I'd expected to see the sneering, tattooed faces of the Olders in them, but what I hadn't expected to see was that beyond the fire, Murta's billowing scarf had fallen completely still. He gripped it in a fist, white-knuckled.

"I just lay there on my stomach," I said, "praying for Ignis to finally manifest in me, and watched as one of them put a gun to my forehead. He said, 'If you move before I say you can, *pretty boy*, I'll blast your brains out.'"

I untucked my dress shirt, turned slowly so Murta could see, and unveiled my back and its huge burn scar.

"So they switched on the beam and I stayed. And stayed." I paused. "And stayed."

After stuffing my shirt back in my pants, I glared into the white flames. They popped angrily, but this time, I didn't flinch.

"But do you know what? I survived. I told myself that I wasn't going to die and that when it was all over, I'd rise up from the ashes like a phoenix. Nothing could kill me after that: not fire, not ice, not Skrill, not dragons.

"I swore that I'd never be held down again. Not by gangs, not by the limitations of my Ignis, not by the whole bloody world.

"In Serapharus, no one gives a bollocks about you. You're a machine. A dog. You might hate the Brotherhood, but at least in Carbonek I feel like I'm working toward something that's worth working toward. At least I feel alive. And I'm not alone."

I stared down at my lap. "What about you?"

It took Murta awhile to register that it was his turn to talk. His hand unclenched from around his scarf, dropping it into his lap. He remained leaning backward so that his face stayed submerged in the darkness, but the way his upper body twitched hinted at a significant amount of tension.

"Kaleo said you were involved in the War somehow," I tried.

"He did?"

"Veres said something about you, too."

"I became a merc after the Brotherhood . . . banished me," Murta began. "I'd been thinking about leaving long before they did, though. I felt like I was wasting my Ignis ability—like we were wasting our abilities—so I joined up with a local mercenary band." His eyes seemed to grow dim and distant. "We had a good leader. Anders was his name. There were some thirty of us. The Government bought us and we served them. I even flew crab cruisers for a bit."

Then his eyes brightened, threads of gold flame filling them. He shook his head.

"But instead of asking me to do too little, like the Brotherhood, the generals that paid me asked me to do too much. They expected me to remove my necklace completely. They didn't care about ending the violence; they only sought to continue it. That was when I realized that both sides profit off of the War.

"So I left that, too. I despise the War, but I despise the methodology that the Brotherhood has taken up regarding it, too. The Council hasn't done enough with what they've been given. We have the ability to end the War. To truly end it." He shook his head. "But the Council refuses to do so because it would mean crossing the line in the sand."

"It would mean becoming just like mercs," I said. "Soldiers. It would mean becoming what Navigators have sworn never to become."

"Sí. It would go against the Code. But it would also mean Navigators would be able to tap into the full potential of their Ignis. They'd finally be able to fight back."

"Who says we should ever need to use the full potential of Ignis?"

Murta adjusted his scarf so it hid his necklace again. "The Shrouded Men of the Western Sands say that before the Brotherhood, the Dragon Lords went to war over what to do with humanity. The bodies of those that died supposedly disintegrated, the dust settling into the atmosphere around Archengard. That dust became the air we breathe, but only those chosen by the dead Lords' spirits manifested their powers. Only those chosen by them were able to directly manifest their own spirits.

"The most skilled of Ignis users are said to possess one-tenth of a Dragon Lord's power. That makes their power comparable to a grain of sand. Now imagine being born a volcano of that power." He turned his hands into their scaly counterparts and began picking at the claws.

"There will come a time where I'll erupt," he said. "And if I don't, I'll destroy myself in the process. This Ignis, no matter how hard I try to keep it closed off from the rest of Archengard, exists only to fight. It craves carnage. And there'll come a day where it'll once again get what it wants."

I eyed the claws but cast fear to the wind. "You always talk about your Ignis ability like it's another entity inside you. Is it not a manifestation of your spirit, just like you said?"

Murta seemed slow to answer, which surprised me. I figured the question was by the far the simplest one that either of us had asked each other.

"I don't know."

I frowned. "You dunno?"

"Didn't you hear me the first time?"

"How? It's your Ignis ability. You manifested it! The Dragon Lords granted you Ignis, just like—"

"I don't know how I got it!" Murta rubbed the gold bracelets on his wrists like they stung. "You remember your Burning, yes?"

I nodded silently. Every Ignis user did. The Burning was the moment one first accessed Ignis. Mine hadn't come until years after Serapharus, when I was in the Light Isles fighting a particularly tough bloke in the ring.

"Well, I don't," Murta said. "In fact, I have no recollection of my childhood whatsoever. The earliest memory I have of my life is waking up outside my Sanctum at fourteen years old, having no idea who, what, or where I was. I figured Ignis out the rest of the way but never figured out how I'd manifested it."

"You *what*?"

"Keep your damned voice down." Murta snatched a glance at the entrance.

I held my tongue but couldn't stop the words from spilling out. "No one just forgets an entire portion of their life."

"But you can have it wiped from you."

"Murta, this is ranging into some conspiracy-level rubbish. What're you on about?"

Murta stood to pick up his thrown clothes. I watched the gold rings disappear as he drew his muscular arms through the sleeves of his dress shirt.

"But . . . who would do that?" I continued. "And for what purpose?"

Murta turned away from the fire. "Do you recall the flag Veres brought with him?"

Part of me wanted to laugh—to get a much-needed chuckle out and say, "Good one." The other part just stared at Murta's chiseled backside in disbelief.

"The symbol that flag bore is the only thing I remember from my youth," he said. "The only thing I remember clearly. That, and their voices."

I wet my lips. "You think that the Jackals somehow *stole* your memories?"

"I know they did."

The certainty in Murta's voice made me swallow. His argument wasn't very convincing, but the way he threw his emotions into it was almost enough for me to completely believe him.

"What do you think Loc's crystal was for?" he asked. "Who do you think was controlling Loc? Using him to use you to get the Karnocolix?"

I clenched my fists. "I know Kaleo said something about it. But you're certain that it really was the Jackals?"

"Sometimes I think there isn't half a brain between the treasure hunter and you. Who else could infiltrate Carbonek in that way? Suns above . . . everything was them. I bet they were controlling Loc from the beginning. They *made* him drop the imprisonment box. They probably meant for the Skrill to be released in Carbonek all along."

"I dunno much about them," I said cautiously. "Besides that everyone thinks they run the Noda. But I thought the Brotherhood wiped them out at the beginning of the War."

"They'd want you to think that."

"Kaleo's fought them before."

"But he's never beaten them. No one's ever killed a Jackal in combat. Injuring them is supposed to be the equivalent of spotting a shadedrake in daylight: impossible, or, immediately after spotting one, it'll eat you."

Murta swept bits of ice from his jacket. "If there's a reason why Navigators should begin moving more toward warriors instead of protectors, it's the Jackals' infiltration of Carbonek. Kaleo and the Council have shown that we're the only ones on Archengard that can fight them . . . And if there's one thing I proved against Loc, it's that *I* can fight them."

I shuddered. "Why the bloody hell would they mess with you and me, though? Why waste their time on trainees? What do you think they, er, did to you?"

A flicker of night fire crossed Murta's face, whispering of a greater, deeper desire.

That whisper died before it left his lips. The light crossed over and returned to night.

"Get some sleep, swash," he said. "We start again in four hours."

Sometimes all a bloke could do was file the fire away and move on. I respected that.

CHAPTER 44

Prince

The healing branch raced by. I ran straight through the still-searching Nightguards, both of whom appeared incredibly confused as to why I was now making a beeline for the exit. I heard one shout, but I was already rounding the archway and ducking down another hall.

Barco had said Father had been a coward. Not the noble warrior he'd always made himself out to be every night in our cottage, but the rogue that he really was. A deserter.

Yet, even through it all, he'd somehow found bravery in the end. Though he'd fled the Brotherhood, he'd still upheld the Code.

Barco had said the Fearless Forger was a façade—the greatest of all Father's frauds—yet still, Dante Larocque had defied all the odds. He might've been afraid when he was young, but as an old man, facing down all of the Corbin Criminal Underworld, he'd been the bravest man I'd ever known. He'd looked death in the face every night and laughed.

And what was I doing? Fleeing, like a coward. Like a thief.

Father was wrong, though. Standing and fighting's what got him killed. The one time he should've been a coward . . . Not for himself, but for me.

He left me *all alone.*

Though I was short, I almost knocked over a six-foot Navigator walking by with his squad. I heard him curse as we went down but didn't turn to apologize. I couldn't. Not when I heard those stomping feet pursuing me.

I don't care if history remembers me as a coward anymore. As long as I get as far away from the knight as possible . . .

No. Not a knight. Knight's weren't made of . . . *that.*

I squeezed my eyes shut, attempting to enter the abyss, but my bad luck just made me trip over my own feet.

I fell chest first. My backpack went spinning down the hall, slamming against the walls and sending sparks of Aestus bouncing everywhere. I scurried back to my feet and lugged the bag back onto my shoulder.

Behind me, the knight was shouting, fear and franticness lacing her voice.

I ran.

Not them. Please, not them . . .

My bad luck attacked me again. This time, a torch holder snagged the latch of my backpack. I jerked on it ferociously, pulling and yanking with all my weight, but the silver-blue armor emerging from the other end of the hall sent me scrambling. I left my guns where they were.

Anyone but them. Please.

Everything in the healing branch had been the same as that horrific night: the dimly lit room, the assassins in the dark . . . and the water.

"Prince!"

"Stay away!" I dove down a perpendicular hall, sprinting for my life, like I had the night I feared above all other nights. But it seemed that the faster I sprinted, the closer the night came until I'd returned to it.

The night I'd come home late from pickpocketing and seen the silky figures standing over Father, water-like daggers brandished in hand. Father's blood had soaked them from tip to hilt, glistening in the abyssal light reflecting off of his killers' inhuman bodies.

Bodies that had looked identical to Jezna—made of some glowing, unnatural gelatin. A hybrid between water and energy.

Between alive and dead.

It was a memory I'd fought hard to keep buried in the abyss. I'd built the abyss around it to keep it hidden.

But after I'd rushed into the healing branch, the demonic creatures and their weapons standing over Father's pale carcass had reemerged from the dark prison I kept them locked in.

Because Jezna was one of them: a Dragon Lords–cursed soul.

But my body had defied my fear anyway.

I'd built. Created.

And then Jezna had lived.

How? What's wrong with me?

I pulled another memory out of the abyss: one where Father had still been alive and all that I needed. I'd been working in the forge, just welding some twisted pieces of metal together to make a toy bat—the one from Father's song—when my creation had come to life. One moment I'd been holding a lifeless ball of metal fitted with metal wings and a demonic metal head; the next, it started flapping and squeaking in my hands.

I'd been so scared that I threw it straight into the fire, then ran back to our cottage wailing. There, Father had scooped me up, set me down on his lap, and whispered:

"The rest of the world likes to think we Ignis-less folk don't have little bits of fire in us, but never forget, little prince: Ignis ain't the only spark. And the Lords ain't the only gods." Then he'd winked.

And though I'd prodded for years what he'd meant by that, he'd never given me a straightforward answer. Nothing but more winks and spookier sentences. "It means someone's out there in the big ole universe watchin' out for ya."

"Prince!"

"Stay away," I croaked. My voice was dead. Father's leather jacket weighed a ton. I could barely run in a straight line. "Please. Let me go—"

I ran into a wall. Stars engulfed my eyes as I slid to the floor, and through the stars, I saw the wall trickle away into glowing brown specks that flew back inside someone.

Ignis, I thought automatically, then, *Fuck*, when I recognized who the brown Ignis had come from. As well as three of the other Navigators that stood behind him.

"The deserter's boy," said the brown-suited Navigator, whose feet I'd set on fire. Now that he was right in front of me, I could finally see just how humongous his arms were. "Damon, was it? Darren? Daniel?"

"Dante," I spat, trying desperately to blink the stars away faster and somehow replace them with the guns I'd stupidly left two corridors back. "Dante Larocque."

"Ah. 'The Fearless Forger,' right? What a joke. My old man was a Nav, too. Trained alongside your father. You wanna know what he said about him?"

I tried to rise to my feet but only succeeded in falling back on my ass. I smelled blood, felt it beginning to drip from my nose. The same metallic scent that'd wafted from our cottage that night.

Shove off, bad luck, I thought. *Not now. This is the worst possible—*

"He said that during the War, his squad and Dante's were fighting alongside one another. Said that things got particularly bad. The Noda started closing in from all sides. Mathias wasn't in sight. The Leviathan was missing. Navs were dying left and right . . ." The Navigator's eyes simmered with disgust. "And you know what your father did? When his squad needed him most?"

No.

I shook my head until the stars started multiplying. Until I was slammed right back into dizziness. I could no longer tell if the panic racing through me was from the fact that I was injured with no weapons against a group of Ignis users . . . or that what the Navigator was about to tell me was what I thought it was.

Barco said Father's whole squad died and that Father left because of it . . . He didn't—

"He left them where they stood. Found a way out of the mass and just took off. *Killing* his squad." The Navigator's fists shook at his sides, Ignis rushing up and down his upper body. "And almost killing my father with them. If it hadn't been for the fact that my father's squad worked together, they would've never made it out."

"Your father wasn't fearless," the green Navigator at his side said. "He was an Ignis-less turncoat—"

"*SHUT UP!*" I threw myself at them, not even aiming for one person as much as the entire mass, and ran into the Ignis-conjured wall again. Only this time, it was a five-foot-long Ignis-conjured sword held in the hand of the head Navigator. When I staggered back, seeing red stars now, I noticed that the blunt side was tipped with blood.

"And judging by the fact that you've yet to use your Ignis on us," the brown Navigator added. "I'm assuming you are, too." He took a striking step forward.

Legs shaking, I watched the sword speed toward me, like the tip of the daggers that the water creatures had drilled into Father. Shoulders quivering, I watched and remembered.

They'd been assassins. The water creatures were a branch of the Nine Assassin Orders—known as the Ajakaji to their friends, and the Cursed Ones to their enemies. They were called out only for the most secretive of jobs, and they'd been at our quiet cottage in the middle of the Narthesian night for a reason: to keep Father from ever sniffing around again.

Why couldn't he have just dropped the quest for the Obsidian Obelisk? Why couldn't he have stopped obsessing over a Talisman and stopped poking his nose into things that had only gotten him more involved with the Jackals?

Why couldn't he have realized that his Navigational days were better left in the past? That he couldn't just say "fuck you" to fear before riding off into the sunset?

I felt a hole widen in my chest, even before the sword sank into me.

Because he was trying to redeem himself. For everything. Abandoning his squad, abandoning the Brotherhood . . .

Abandoning me.

I was an idiot. Father was everything everyone said he was.

A fool. A traitor. A turncoat. A thief. *Afraid.*

And I was so obsessed with being like him that it was making me be those things. I was becoming him, when I should've been becoming better than him.

That was what he'd always wanted, right? For his only son to find his way to Carbonek in the end and redeem him? For his only son to be the one to flick off bad luck and fear, find the Obsidian Obelisk, and never betray his squad?

All three of which I've failed to do.

So, instead of trying to roll out of the way of the sword, I just closed my eyes.

But the sword never came.

Instead, flecks of aqua energy exploded in front of me.

I leapt back with a terrified yell in response, thinking the Cursed Ones had come back to take me, too, that they were the physical manifestation of my bad luck and not whatever god Father had said was up there looking out for me.

Then the brown Navigator said, "YOU?!"

I opened my eyes.

Jezna stood there, a glistening barricade between the Navigators and me, both hands clutching the hilt of a freaking broadsword made of Ignis.

"Me," she said, flicking particles of the Navigator's brown Ignis from her blade.

CHAPTER 45

Enoch

After having my feet dangle in the open air for hours, I discovered one could grow accustomed to it. The abyss looking up at me wasn't fear-inducing as much as it was comforting. I knew that if I were to let my grip go, I'd fall off the mountain silent as a stone. Then the impact. *Then* I could sleep. Maybe the snow would even cushion my fall . . .

If my fingers hadn't been so tightly interlocked around Murta's neck, my left arm secured under his armpit, I would've punched myself again.

Every time I drifted off, my mind gravitated toward death. It was pathetic. If I instinctively thought that, then maybe I did deserve death. Maybe letting go was exactly—

"Shut your bloody hole," I said.

Murta removed his right claws from the mountainside and inserted his left ones all in a single motion. Flecks of Ignis and ice shot up into his face, stirring the trails of smoke sizzling up from his mouth.

"Why don't you try climbing with someone on your back, then?"

"I . . . didn't mean you."

"Talking to yourself again?"

"How much longer do we have?"

Tufts of Murta's hair brushed my forehead when he glanced up. "Just don't look up."

I took his advice.

After analyzing the current trek we'd been on, coupled with my decreasing pace, Murta had decided that climbing vertically was the only way to get us to the peak by the end of the day. I'd protested but hadn't had enough energy to defy him. I'd awoken from a lackluster sleep even colder and more drained than before. The only reasonable option, as much as it pained me, had been for Murta to scale the rest of the mountain with me on his back.

As the wind blew shriller, I swam in and out of consciousness. In my mind, I was back in the ice cave, recounting my time in Serapharus and listening to Murta explain his own past. In my mind, I prodded Murta for more, got real answers out of him, maybe even asked about his time at a Shadarian Sanctum, but no matter how many false assumptions my imagination conjured, the story involving the Jackals stayed the same.

Stolen memories. Voices. Loc's crystal. The flag.

No one just made those things up, and Murta wasn't the joking type. That left only one disturbing answer.

He was telling the truth.

"We're here."

My eyelids flickered. A surface now lay under me. I was no longer clinging to Murta's back. Archengard had stopped moving. Finally. It was still cold—perhaps colder than before—but at least it wasn't moving.

"Swash."

I peeled open my eyes, trying to sit up. I failed.

"You're in terrible condition."

"S'fine." I dug my fingers into the ice, peering into the cloudy distance. Rectangular silhouettes jutted out of the blizzard, revealing angular roofs and gray brick walls. "The bloody Lords is that?"

"Looks like a village. There'll be warmth. *Vamos.*"

After a few minutes of slow trudging, the entry to the village loomed ahead: a frost-covered arch made of the same gray bricks as the buildings behind it. There were no guards, no gates, no doors. Not even a wall around the perimeter. Just an empty arch and the village beyond.

"Guess they don't get many visitors," I said.

Silhouettes began to move, shifting in and out of the haze. They shuffled between the houses, intersected, and sometimes conjoined.

Murta shoved me down a narrow alleyway. "This way."

I stumbled into the darkness. "What about—"

"We're not sauntering down the street." Murta peered around the corner with Ignis-infused eyes. "We don't know who these people are. Or what they're doing up here . . . Kaleo never said there'd be people."

I tapped into my own Ignis slowly, igniting both of my fists. The green flames did little to heat my frozen nerves, but any fragment of warmth was welcome.

"Mayhaps we go ask them."

"Spoken like a true Charger. That's also foolish. They could hold animosity toward . . ." Murta noticed the green glow illuminating the alley and spun.

"What're you doing, idiota?!" He swatted my hands, making me disperse Ignis in shock. "Are you stupid?!"

"I thought—"

"I doubt it! These people have likely rarely ever seen Ignis, nor do they probably admire those who wield it, and you're over here making bonfires?!"

"I can't feel my hands."

A cluster of silhouettes strode by. With nowhere to hide and nothing to do, Murta and I watched them pass in frozen silence. There were three in total, all wearing huge overcoats made of white fur. Beneath their fleecy hoods, I spotted muscular noses and beady dark eyes.

And around each of their necks, they wore a thin black wire with a singular piece of violet crystal threaded through.

My heart dropped out of my chest, and as we stared at one another, I became increasingly aware of the clothing Murta and I wore. Our brightly colored tailored suits contrasted terribly with the bleak background. We were clearly outsiders. And they clearly weren't happy.

The figures considered us, took a few steps forward, then seemed to think better of it and returned the way they'd come. Murta and I remained rooted to our spots several seconds after they'd left, breathing raggedly in the silence.

"Then they seem like jolly enough blokes," I said.

Murta glared at me.

"So." I shivered. "What do we do now? Look around for Kaleo's sake?"

"Not here." Murta pointed up the street.

I followed his finger. As it turned out, we still hadn't reached the mountain's peak. It resided a good mile away, past the village and up a rocky slope. When I saw something standing atop it, I rubbed my eyes and squinted. It was another building, only this one loomed gothic and uneven as opposed to the village's square homes. Instead of being made of gray stone, it was made of obsidian.

"Kaleo said there was a temple at the peak. Well, there it is."

I raised myself to full height. At least, I tried. "Let's be off."

"No. I'll find you an inn. You need rest."

"I'm coming with you."

"I'm just going up to investigate. If I find anything, I'll bring you back up. But only after you've at least warmed up. We still have time."

"Running out, actually."

"Then I'll go alone. It'll be faster that way."

I ground my teeth, ready to die on the hill I stood on, but it was painfully obvious that Murta was right. He'd be able to cover ground far faster without me staggering behind. If we wanted to complete our quest on time, for the time being, I'd have to take one for the team.

Even as Murta led me down the street, sticking close to the houses with my head bowed so as not to attract attention, I simmered, thinking of the photo Kaleo had shown me. Letting his and Biassis's words roll through me.

A Charger wasn't supposed to become the weight for the rest of the squad to bear. A Charger needed to be the one who carried the weight. By the end of my Navigational career, I needed to be able to carry Murta, Prince, and Jezna up the mountain. What good was a Charger who could barely climb a mountain on their own?

A Charger wasn't supposed to sulk about in the shadows and try to appear less noticeable; they broke down the front doors and announced their squad's presence to the world.

I sucked in a breath of piercing air and quickened my pace to reach Murta's side. I opened my mouth wide, but when I saw his expression, I hesitated.

With half his face covered, Murta looked as emotionless as ever, but I'd gotten to know him better than most. I'd gotten to the point where I could read his eyes—could snatch hints of what he was thinking about.

At the moment, he was gravely agitated.

"What is it?"

Scarier still was his silence. Instead of replying, he glanced up the street with a mix of familiarity, astonishment, and maybe even misplaced apprehension.

Before I could repeat my question, he tore down a perpendicular alley. I followed at a shuffle and immediately ran into his back.

He stood in front of a stone building. Warm candlelight danced in every window and a sign hanging above the wooden door read: AREN'S INN.

I gaped. "How did you—"

"I don't know," he said quietly. "It just feels familiar."

"The whole village or just the inn?"

"Everything. I guess. Since we started climbing, I've felt . . ." He ran a hand through his mohawk like it itched.

I swallowed. "Do you think it has to do with, you know?"

Murta cast his head in the direction of the temple. "Just stay here. Go inside and warm up."

"I'm not leaving you—"

"Look, swash. If this place has something to do with my past . . . something to do with *them*, then I need to face it alone. I have to. And you need food, water, warmth, and sleep."

"But Navs don't—"

"This isn't about being a Navigator anymore." He hesitated before turning away. "If I'm being honest, it's probably nothing. Probably me looking too much into their crystals, but I just need to be sure. And after that, we'll call Kaleo and say we made it to the top. Try not to beat yourself up anymore."

He left me swaying in the snowdrift.

CHAPTER 46

Jezna

A brief pause occurred as the brown-suited Navigator and his squad stared at the hole in my breastplate and seemed to put two and two together.

"What the hell's going on?" the head Navigator whispered, the glowing sword in his hand shrinking with uncertainty. "What . . . are—"

"You call yourself Navigators?" I asked, surveying the four of them.

"You . . ." The Navigator finally flicked his eyes back up to my helmet, a nervous smile tugging at his lips. "You call yourself a human?"

"You were about to kill an unarmed boy." I ignored him. "One without any means of fighting back. Yet you call yourself a Navigator."

His face purpled, his sword growing back to its normal length in response. It was humongous. How could he hold such a thing?

"And you think the Ignis-less treasure-hunting son of a Navigational deserter and a knight made of water *are* Navigators?" he asked. "The Dragon Lords cursed both of you at birth, yet you think you have a right to be confirmed? You're nobody!"

Some of the Ignis churning through my blade lost its warmth. That made me freeze and glance at it.

Fire. But it wasn't. In the Karnocolix chamber, I'd definitely made fire with my Ignis, but it hadn't been *only* fire. The brief blade I'd summoned to destroy the Karnocolix had been as much water as fire. And the same blade boiling in my hands—a blade I'd forced into existence with my spirit—now wasn't only fire either. It was still water.

I still haven't found the balance. I'm still lost . . . What more do I need to do, Macín? What more must I learn?

"I . . ." I found myself stammering, watching the brown blade burn in the Navigator's hands. It was closer to fire than mine, and it was bigger.

But though the foe I faced was a Navigator, I was a knight.

"I am Jezna Caelius, Knight of the River, Guardian of Anamana, inducted into the Tolkkyan Order by Sir Macín of Menesbrökmen. If you have quarrel with any of Archengard's children, if you continue to seek vengeance and propagate violence, then you will face a knight." I raised my sword, pouring all of my spirit into it—until I felt the warmth begin to return. "And we shall duel."

The Navigator tilted his head. "A duel without first making peace? You've betrayed the Chivalric Code already, pretender."

"I most certainly have." I dropped my sword from high guard to point at his chest. "But not toward you."

Words seemingly spent, the Navigator bellowed and charged, the three Navigators of his squad right behind him.

I gripped my waterblade. "Run, Prince! Get out of—"

I glanced briefly over my shoulder.

He ran off, I realized, dumbfoundedly jerking back toward the squad, who had begun to spread out before me. *He still hasn't forgiven me—*

The tip of the brown sword missed my new Aestus heart by inches, almost killing me all over again. Latching onto Ignis and channeling it down into my boots, I used it to enhance my speed, allowing my body to slide out of the way of the figures all around me. I lunged—left foot forward, arms extended like Macín had shown me—preparing to knock the head Navigator off his feet, but stumbled when I realized that I no longer held the waterblade. In pouring Ignis down into my boots, I'd lost the sword. In recalling my chivalric teachings, I'd forsaken Ignis.

Fool, I cursed, narrowly avoiding one of the other Navigators' rocklike Ignis abilities.

What had just occurred was the exact reason I'd been so reluctant to make the blade to begin with. Sustaining a sword made of hardened water—and traces of fire—took every ounce of energy and concentration I had. Using the sword, I realized that it meant I could no longer use Ignis for anything else. All my focus had to go into keeping it alive.

And though his other squadmates weren't, the head Navigator was fast for his size. He raced around me, dodging every one of my strikes, deflecting the strongest of my blows with his far bigger, far stronger sword. He wasn't as skilled in footwork, but he made up for it with power and precision.

He put his whole body into his thrusts and swipes, so much so that his sword left great gashes in the tile where my head and shoulders had been mere moments before.

Defending grew tiresome and attacking just sapped more and more of my strength. More than once, I had to duck and dodge around his squadmates' Ignis abilities, but the head Navigator grew so furious with his failure that he finally swiped his sword back at them and screamed, "GET BACK!"

Out of the corner of my eye slit, I saw the green-suited Navigator stumble and fall back. He didn't look angry toward his squadmate's actions. Just . . . sad.

"Marq—" he began agitatedly.

"She's mine!" the Navigator Marq said, charging after me. "If any Nightguards come, take care of them! Stay out of my way!"

And his squad did. I was now able to focus on one instead of four. But with no one getting in his way, Marq's power only increased. More than once, I felt his massive blade slam so hard against my waterblade that it almost went through it. I defended and deflected as fast as I could, but every attack thrown was followed up with another even fiercer than the last.

I was the weakest I'd been in a long time. Keeping a hold of Ignis was a burden unto itself. I couldn't fight Marq while fighting my own Ignis.

I've no other alternative. Either I take him down or . . . My new heart pulsed with fear. *He'll* kill *me and go after Prince.*

I latched onto that thought, using it to strengthen Ignis. My blade burned brighter.

I swiped and rolled, searching for ways to take down Marq, recalling Macín's parries, Junia's swings, and Bebel's violent stabs.

"Flow like water," I used to hear Macín whispering to me after I'd undergone my transformation—after he was already dead. "You think your new form has weakened you, but it has only made you stronger. You have become water, Sister."

But the more I evaded Marq, the faster he became. Until his sword was a single streak of churning energy—so fast that I felt my shins nicked by the blade.

I swung for the streak but felt the sword catch me again, this time scraping the back of my breastplate.

No! I won't die again! I—

A second cut appeared. Nicked again. Marq was all around me, one with his Ignis sword.

Everything sloshing inside, I recklessly swung my waterblade in a blind circle, hoping to at least catch some part of him, but I failed to make contact. Instead, he slammed into my back.

Miraculously, the tip missed and the sword's flat side made contact instead, but it was enough to throw me across the hall. I tumbled helmet first into the stone and toppled over with a murmur.

Prince . . .

There was nothing left for me to give. Ignis fled me, my water spinning itself through the Aestus chamber and all throughout my armor. Marq was simply too fast, his sword simply too powerful.

Even now, with Ignis—the one thing I'd thought then would've kept Macín and the rest of my Order alive—I'd lost.

What more could I have done? I lifted my helmet off of the stone, watching Marq stride forward. *What more do I need to do for Ignis to finally accept me? I thought I found the spark, but I still haven't. That was the spark of life, not the spark of fire.*

I still haven't found balance.

"You fought better than I expected," Marq said. "But like the rest of your kin, you should've eroded away with your castles."

He charged at me for the last time.

CHAPTER 47

Murta

Something was wrong the first step I took back out onto the cobblestone street. The sense of familiarity only grew—vines spreading to the corners of my mind, tickling the empty spaces where there should've been memories. It turned especially overpowering when I looked up at the temple's obsidian towers.

Another cluster of coated villagers passed me on my way down the street, only this time, their gloved hands reached up to caress the crystals they wore. Their eyes followed me until I passed; their hands remained on the crystals after.

Faces appeared in the windows around me. Crystals hung around all their necks. Even the children. But whereas Loc's eyes had spun with mist, these people's eyes looked lifeless. Or terrified.

This doesn't make sense. What connection would I have to this place? Did Kaleo know about it?

But the very last thing Kaleo would've done was send me after anything that had a whiff to do with the Jackals.

A ghostly wind whistled down from the temple, rushing down into the street. I lifted my scarf higher up onto my face, transforming my walk into a jog. Snow trampled beneath my dress shoes, slowing me. Shadarians trained in every kind of weather imaginable, but it had never snowed in the cornfields surrounding my Sanctum.

Then why does everything feel as familiar as the Sanctum?

At the end of the street, an arch identical to the entrance appeared out of the fog, but before I could walk through, I was flanked by hooded villagers in seconds.

When the group of ten men sprang out of the alleyways, I almost didn't register what had happened. I'd been so engrossed in uncovering the mountain's connection to me that I'd completely forsaken Shadarian instincts. I'd let my guard down again.

I watched the men close in. Each kept their hoods up, revealing few features save chiseled chins and beards. Most clutched their crystals, but the braver ones held knives made of serrated ice.

I prepared to throw myself at them but felt my body hesitate.

A Shadarian made sure to attack first so that the enemy never stood a fragment of a chance. But a Navigator waited to be attacked. According to the Code, I was unable to confront them until the first attack was thrown. According to the Code, I was supposed to attempt to make peace first.

Fuck that. As the first few men grew close, I tapped into Ignis and turned my smoldering eyes on them. The Code never said anything about intimidation.

"Fighting me would be an incredible lapse in judgment, *caballeros.*"

One man dropped his knife, fingers flying back to his crystal for comfort. The largest of them spat something in High Northerner, then picked up the knife.

"You're not welcome here," he said in a thick accent.

"I don't care. I'm going up to the temple, then we'll be right on our way. I have no quarrel with your village."

He tilted his head. "We?"

I turned my hands into claws.

The man barked something close to "Kill him" and charged. Instilled with newfound determination, the remaining villagers followed.

Damn the Code.

Surrounded on all sides and losing patience by the second, I prepared to roundhouse kick the first few. Then I saw the crystals all around me.

I fell to my knees.

The way the crude glowing rocks swarmed me, hanging beneath hoods, returned me to dark chambers. Not where the Karnocolix had been stored in Carbonek, but another black citadel. Just like the one at the mountain's peak before me.

In my broken memory, the landscape outside the purple stained-glass windows was an endless plain of barren pale rock instead of snow and stars. The gargoyles that watched from the rafters of the chapel weren't gargoyles at all, but the demented white creatures from Jameronjag Jungle.

And the men standing around me were all clothed in midnight robes with pointed hoods, crystals around their necks.

I tensed my muscles to rise up off of the floor, but I was strapped into a horizontal iron crucifix, a bar of cold metal stuffed between my teeth. I felt piercingly warm, like the fire inside me was trying to claw its way out of my body.

Forcing the stifling fear to the back of my mind, I looked away from the leering figures. Enormous scrapes and claw marks engulfed the tattered skin of my naked chest. From the inside.

I heard the cloaked figures laugh, watched their crystals pulse with energy, then saw the largest of the scars expand until it consumed all the other scars, breaking my chest open. Snapping teeth and dragon fire exploded outward with a monstrous roar as my jaw came unglued in an agonizing scream.

The mountainside returned, and I was back out in the cold, surrounded. Out of the corner of my eye, I saw dark energy dripping up to the sky from my claws. I felt the shadow expand inside me, threatening to consume and transform me into something else. I felt the necklace go cold against my neck, felt the Other stir . . .

The villagers' ice blades should've been cutting deep into my abdomen by now, but instead, they were scurrying away.

I looked up, thinking they'd seen the darkness peeling off of me, but they were too busy dodging fists surrounded in green flame.

"Back off, ya ugly bastards!" The flaming fists forced the head villager to dance backward. Rather than charge again, he stood his ground, sword fixed in front of him.

"You are Navigators," he said darkly. "No use denying it with clothes like that."

Enoch loosened his tie. "You're damn right."

Idiota! I wanted to holler, but the man was laughing.

"You take pride in such a sin?" he asked. "You take pride in stealing energy from Archengard? Bleeding the world at its core, then claiming you keep the peace?"

"That's mental!" Enoch said. "How's the Brotherhood doing that?"

"You covet Ignis users. Steal artifacts. You claim protection, yet come to our village seeking the opposite. You claim preservation yet deplete everything in your wake. You're just a group of lost boys messing with places that would rather be left alone. None of you are the protectors you claim to be." He tossed the blade between his hands. "None of you can fight, either."

Mierda.

Enoch lifted his fists, symbols springing up along them. "You sure about that?"

Some of the villagers stepped back.

"What your crystals probably failed to inform you numpties," Enoch said, "is that I've been begging for a brawl for quite some time now."

The head villager leapt forward, ice blade held over his head, but Enoch dodged his first three sword strokes with ease.

It seemed even the cold couldn't rob a boxer of his footwork.

Right as the fourth attack swooped in from the left, Enoch countered it with a devastating right cross, punched the hilt out of the man's hands with a quick jab, then surged forward to uppercut him. The villager roared as he hit the ground, but before Green Fire Fist sent him flying, Enoch stopped his burning knuckles inches beneath his chin—poised directly at his crystal.

"Navigators might be protectors first, fighters second," he said. "But never try to outfight one, bruv. You'll end up on your arse every time."

In seconds, the clearing had cleared of every villager, and after a moment of cursing, the head villager scooped up his fallen blade and chased after them.

Enoch offered me a hand. I rose on my own, ignoring the phlegm and fire I felt rising in my throat, trying to pacify the Other.

"You didn't listen to me."

"Course not," Enoch said. "Chargers stay with their Shields. The Leviathan stayed with Mathias, so I'm staying with you."

"Whatever." I glared up at the temple. "Those putos will be back. And angrier. Though I don't imagine they'll follow us up here."

"I'm coming this time."

"Just don't get in the way."

The trudge was a simple walk next to the climb up the mountainside. The slope grew steeper toward the end, but we moved briskly until we emerged into a dark courtyard.

In the shadows of the towers, the jagged area seemed to shift with the snow flurries. And now that I stood in the middle of it, I knew for certain.

The snow-covered gargoyles looking down from their perches had gazed on me before. The statue of the carnivorous ice demon in the corner and I had crossed paths.

"Bloody hell," Enoch said, following me toward the front entrance. His eyes stayed fixed on the statue. "Anything coming back?"

"Barely . . ." A similar steeple had stood outside just beyond the pits and blood-soaked cornfields of my Shadarian Sanctum, up on Witchfire Mound. We'd never been allowed up there, but I'd seen my father ascend it more than once. "Definitely used to be a temple. To the ice demon, Tharthes."

"And it isn't now?"

"There are other citadels like this scattered across Archengard. There was one not too far from my Sanctum. Some Shadarians say they were built by demons. Some say they're even from before the Before. When Archengard had two moons, not just one."

Enoch looked as though he was about to storm back into another confused rant, but just chewed his lip in silence.

Inside, the foyer was flanked by spiral staircases and dead torches. Several suits of armor lined the walls alongside pinned weapons from all over Archengard and shields with strange coat-of-arms. I eyed them, trying to recall if I'd seen them before. I hadn't.

Whoever dwelled here had an affinity for history, it seemed. For . . . design. Everything bore an unyielding level of high craftsmanship to it. From the architecture itself to the things decorating the walls.

"It looks lived in," Enoch said.

I felt myself drawn toward the staircase on the far left. Wind whistled down from it, stirring my scarf. For a moment, when I blinked, I saw red lines wrapped around my wrists, pulling me toward the stairs.

You seek healing, I heard a voice say.

I flinched.

"What is it?" Enoch asked.

You seek control.

I began to climb the stairs. Enoch hurried over to follow.

It was dark on the staircase. I lit a flame in my claws and pushed the pace. Enoch lit his own flame around his fist.

"What do you think the crystals mean?" he asked. "You think they're controlling the villagers, too? And why? Do you think it's . . . them?"

You seek an end to Archengard's suffering. Your *suffering. But you won't find it here. Run back to the manor of false hope.*

I brightened my flame, as if to banish back the voice, then stepped into the room at the top of the tower.

It was lit by purple candles that sat on the many desks that filled it. Leather-bound books lay clumped in piles on every surface, some even scattered across the floor. The desk at the end of the room was covered by the most. A board hung on the wall directly above it, where notes, drawings, and manuals had been pinned. The wall adjacent had four desks littered with strange machines.

Enoch's mouth hung open in suspended disbelief.

Don't say I didn't warn you, the voice whispered, then was gone.

I headed for the desk immediately.

Yes. This was exactly it. It made perfect sense. Of course this was here. Of course it looked like a flipped redesign of Kaleo's office.

"Murta, what's going on?" Enoch demanded. "Why's all this rubbish here? And why's it look like—"

My mind splintered. The bubbling of the chemicals in the corner grew to the sound of an earthquake. Just the rustling of paper was enough to make my head spin. I stuck out a hand and slouched up against a chair, trying to gather myself while digging deeper into the pain. Deeper until I entered the Twilight Moment and was able to master it.

You're not getting away from me this time, I swore at the memories, diving into my mind as I did. They scattered like fish, but I finally seized one.

I'd been brought here before. Only last time, there'd been someone sitting at the desk. Someone writing, his back turned to me. I hadn't seen his face at all. There'd been a hooded figure standing next to him, clutching one of the leather books, a pink crystal on his chest.

"Shall we head for the pyramids and seize the Shrouded Men?" the hooded figure said in the voice from the stairs—one of the many resting with me. "Jehal could find ways to make them talk. They'll give up its location in time."

Then the man at the desk spoke. And as soon as he did, I *never* wanted to hear that voice again. No emotion known to man could ever hope to encapsulate it.

"Time does not matter," he said, his pen never leaving the paper. The back of his hair, visible just above the priestly hem of his black robes, was blond. "The Shrouded will not speak. Not now. I have seen it."

The hooded figure stroked his pink crystal, uncomfortable. "I know that you have, brother, but the others grow . . . tired of that answer. There has to be more we can do. The Sacred Heart will not be found on its own—"

"The Sacred Heart, Lucian, will emerge when it chooses to. And how it goes about doing that resides out of my control."

"I don't understand."

"To put things simply, we'll wait for 'fate' to run its course." Then the pen fell and the man finally turned to look at me. Only his face wasn't a face—just a distorted blur. A missing piece of an already misplaced memory. "Then follow the rainbow it bleeds from the thousand wounds I've already punctured in it."

My mind finally cleared. I got my balance back and righted myself as the present returned to me in a vortex.

Enoch's hands were clamped down around my shoulders, his eyes wide with concern.

I shoved him off. "I'm fine."

He scowled. "So you can say that but I can't? What just happened to you?"

"Just help me look around." I turned toward the table of chemicals. "Tell me if you see anything suspicious."

"Shouldn't be very difficult," Enoch said, sifting through the papers on the desk. "And tell me before you start to go crazy again. Aye?"

I looked over the test tubes and their multicolored liquids. Something crackled in my memory again, but nothing emerged. The sliver took shape but shattered just as quickly.

This had been lived in recently. I wasn't sure if test tubes had been here last time. Or some of the bookshelves. Back then, the room had been more naked. *They* were still in the process of figuring everything out. The War was still young.

"Wait . . ." Enoch suddenly said.

I turned. "Find anything?"

"Dunno . . . But it looks like some kind of map. Bloody confusing one at that. It's not written in Archengardian, I don't think—" His eyes widened as he cut off abruptly.

"Qué es?" I prodded impatiently.

"This is a map . . . of a kingdom." Enoch's voice wavered as he turned the paper over with a sharp inhale. "And from the look of things, this kingdom seems to be in possession of *this*." On the other side of the map was a page of scribbled notes side by side with a sketch of a glowing heart-shaped rock.

I snatched the page out of his hands.

It was written in the Dark Tongue.

My eyes raced through the notes, translating every other sentence at a breakneck pace before flipping over to the map.

Sure enough, it was a map of a kingdom. The desert city of Ryjen, to be exact. Only a day and a half's flight away from Carbonek . . .

Suns above.

In my search for the Kardem Ka, the Shrouded Men hadn't told me their prophecies, but I was aware of the rumors. I was aware that they'd rather die than give up the location they thought the strongest of the Talismans might reside in . . .

But if someone were to threaten them, to threaten them like no one had ever threatened them before . . . With blood and torture and mind control . . .

My eyes settled back down onto the map, the section of Ryjen, just east of the Serrated Keep—Ryjen's royal palace—where a red circle had been drawn.

Heart hammering war beats against my rib cage, I switched back to the notes, stared at the sketch, then gaped down at the map.

The Sacred Heart wasn't just in Ryjen: so were the Jackals.

"Get outside." I shakily stuffed the page inside my jacket before shoveling several other pages of notes in with it.

Enoch's shoulders shook. "Murta, that's—"

"Get outside." My hands flew across the desk, searching for anything else that might help. "And call Kaleo *now*."

Run, little Shadarian, one of the voices said. *Run back to your manor and hide.*

A spark crackled in the back of my mind, but I smothered it. It became harder to see. The same static that had blurred out the man from my memory's face spread over my eyes until the pages I thrust into my pockets became white blurs. I squinted up at the board. After discovering I couldn't read anything, I pulled the whole thing down, stuffing every note somewhere in my jacket. On my way out of the archway, I kicked over the desks with the test tubes and weapons.

You cannot fight fate, Kaster. It always comes hunting.

Have to get to Kaleo, my mind thundered as I stumbled down the dark stairs after Enoch. Everything was dark around me. Couldn't see.

When I tried to summon Ignis, I felt the Other rear and sink its jaws into my lungs. That sent me stumbling faster.

Kaleo will know what to do, I thought. *He'll help me fight them . . .*

"CALL KALEO!" My voice rang off the walls, turning my hot breathing into the whirring sound of machinery. I rushed down the stairs, trying to beat the noise from my head while dashing through the foyer. The metallic sound only grew louder. I found Enoch standing in the entrance, arms limp at his sides.

I rushed up to him. "Did you—"

My vision suddenly unblurred, perhaps from the ferocious gusts of wind. The whirring belonged to the crab cruiser that had just touched down in the center of the courtyard. Its dragon-like wings folded mechanically as its four legs jabbed into the ground and held it.

I felt a hefty weight lift from atop my shoulders. Kaleo was already here.

When the side doors began to slide open, I tiredly stepped out from under the archway to greet them but felt my spine lock in place.

Two men dressed in silver suits of armor leapt out onto the courtyard. Each wore a helmet that masked their faces except for their mouths and chins, and the area around their eyes consisted of a single orange slit. In their armored claw-like hands, they wielded the largest firearms I'd ever seen; metal cannons fixed with three different scopes, four barrels, and several tendril-like cords that were plugged into their armored backs.

The dreaded Ignis hunters of the Noda. Malicious soldiers tasked with capturing or killing Ignis users.

And striding between them was a black-cloaked figure with a pointed hood and a pink crystal around their neck.

CHAPTER 48

Prince

Yeah, so after Jezna saved me, I'd fled for my life. Again. The flickering sword she'd carried was just too similar to those wielded by the Cursed Ones. The water weapon saving my ass hadn't conjured happiness or relief, but memories embroiled in pain. And at the emergence of pain, I'd plunged back into the abyss, letting my body act on its own.

But on my way down the hall, I paused.

By some ill twist of fate—by remarkable, freaking *luck*—I'd ended up in the same place that I'd left off. My backpack of firearms lay in a metallic pile of holsters and barrels at my feet, having fallen from the torch.

"Shoo," I said to the backpack.

But the backpack didn't move.

C'mon, bad luck, I pleaded. *Or whatever god Father thought was watching over me. Make my guns . . . disappear!*

When that didn't work, I closed my eyes and tried to conjure them away myself but instead just slipped deeper into the abyss. Deeper, until I found the box of memories I'd buried there. And within their contents, the cold winter's night replayed over and over until I could recall every fragment in full detail.

The frozen mud beneath my bare feet. The warm scent of the bundle of bread I carried. The blisters I bore on each hand from another long day at the forge. Familiar things.

Then came the eerie parts—the stuff of nightmares.

The ominous crescent of the blue moon in the Narthesian sky. Father's detailed notes on the Obsidian Obelisk torn to shreds, scattered across the kitchen floor beside his ripped entrails. The way that the water assassins had folded into the shadows of the open doorway, daggers drawn like little blue flames.

And when I'd looked up into their faces, away from Father's tattered body, I'd seen spinning whirlpools.

"The Son," one had rasped. "He knows."

Before they could lunge after me, I'd run.

I'd run as fast as I'd originally run from Jezna. As fast as I'd just run from Jezna, even after she saved my life.

But after I tore myself out of the abyss, the backpack was still there, its contents waiting patiently. They *wanted* to be used. They were ready, but only if I was willing to forsake running.

I'd run so much of my life. From coast to coast, continent to continent, every time I failed to pay off an employer or was too afraid to continue living in one place or wanted to get away from the Perpetual War. My whole life had consisted of running, and even though I was an ionsmith, I'd always prioritized fleeing before fighting. Even after the Big Kahuna killed Bret, I'd fled rather than fight him.

The Navigator's shouts carried down the ruined hall. He sounded triumphant.

I stared at my weapons—years of thievery, but also dedication—and felt like tearing my hair out. I'd deserted my squadmate just like Father had, but she deserved it for lying to me. I'd run from a creature like the ones that had killed Father, but she was clearly not one of the ones who had infiltrated our house that night. I'd called her a thief and a coward, but had I not fled? Had I not forged these weapons from the pieces of scavenged guns?

The Navigator's voice grew louder. The excitement in his voice took me back to warmer nights in the Narthesian house. Those nights had been full of stories and laughter, excitement and wonder. Honest and good laughter. The soft laughter of stars and midsummer eves.

Those nights, Father had reminisced about his time in the black-and-gold manor. His days in a squad, their first few quests, the time he fought side by side with Mathias Flint, and of course, the time he met the Leviathan, to whom he claimed he owed his life several times over.

Those nights had kept me shielded from the burning world around me. They'd kept my father young and forgetful of the life he'd forsaken at Carbonek, the life he'd still clung to. That was why he'd been so determined to find the Obelisk, even after his employers forbade him from continuing his search.

The Navigator in Dante Larocque had refused to give up. Refused to give in to fear.

I exasperatedly threw my hands in the air and began to restuff the firearms into my backpack.

A minute later, I was casting the bag back down, removing my favorite pistols and screaming, "GUNS: STUN."

Arrows of pink Aestus began to explode from the barrels, pummeling the brown Ignis-wielding Navigator's body. He went flying back into a column where he sank to the tile, his Ignis sputtering out with him. The sword he held faded into smoke, leaving him looking . . . pathetic. I almost felt bad about the way I'd shot him when I saw his hands clench at his sides in an attempt to fight incapacitation.

"Not done . . ."

"You are too," I said, keeping my pistols tracked on his hung head. "I got both my eyes on you, buddy boy, and nothing's gonna . . ." I drifted off at the sight of movement out of the corner of my eye.

The other Navigators of his squad were being restrained by four Nightguards, though they didn't seem to be rushing to their leader's aid at all. They merely stood behind the Nightguards, swaying with agitation. The green Navigator's face was wrenched with emotion.

"Marq, please," he said. "We've done enough harm already. Murphy's . . . He's not coming back. I'm sorry."

That only made matters worse. When Marq finally jerked his head up, I saw that his eyes were wet with tears. "You think I don't know that, Col? You think I—"

"Let's go, son," one of the Nightguards stated, sounding oddly similar to the one that'd stood guard outside the healing branch, the one who'd tried to squish me between his legs. "Barco wants to have a word with you."

"I'm sure he does," Marq shouted. "And what'll he do? Exile us? He and Kaleo give that drunken prize fighter, a cursed knight, the son of a deserting thief, and that . . . *monster* special treatment, yet we get the short end of the stick? Yet we're the ones not given a second chance?"

"Hey," I started, but Col stepping forward silenced me.

"If Murph were still here, he wouldn't want us to be given a second chance," he said. "Not after everything we—"

"IF MURPH WAS STILL HERE, I'D BE HAPPY!" Marq said, then sank to his knees, sniffling uncontrollably. As soon as he did, two Nightguards walked over and gently hoisted him to his feet, keeping their hands on his biceps.

I watched the whole thing happen with discomfort until Col turned toward me.

"Sorry." He looked at the ground. "For everything. I don't expect forgiveness in return . . . None of us do. We've broken the Code, and for that, our fate rests in the Council's hands."

I prepared to say something possibly a little edgy, not one to forget almost being *killed*, but Jezna beat me.

"I understand." She sounded as though she'd forced the words out. "But who is this Murphy you speak of?"

I didn't think Col's face could've fallen any more than it already had. I'd never seen a dude look that devastated before.

"Our squadmate," he said. "Little lad about yea big." He held his hand up to exactly my height. "His old man was friends with Marq's old man, too. He died."

"*Hecton*?" Jezna whispered.

Col nodded sadly. "We were just supposed to look around for an artifact in the area with a few other level-two squads, but things headed south when the Government arrived. Shortly after, the Noda was there, and suddenly we found ourselves smack dab in the middle of the Perpetual War. First real quest we ever went out on, too. Damn."

"I apologize. If I'd been there sooner, I would've—"

"No. Not your fault, um, miss . . ." He looked over at Marq sadly. "It was my Charger's."

Marq didn't respond. He barely moved his feet as the Nightguards led him and his squad in the opposite direction. The Nightguard positioned behind Col just waited patiently.

"Your Charger's?" Jezna repeated.

"Aye. But I can't blame him. When a Charger's forced to watch their squad burn and bleed around them . . ." His voice broke. "I'm just the Sharpshooter, and I can't stand to see it. You wanna do something, anything. But you can't. Not when you're in the center of the storm, Aestus and Ignis blazing all around you.

"So you do the only thing you can do: You abandon your post for a better one. Lose yourself to the rage and the emotion. Forget about the ties that bind you."

"You forget about your squad," I thought, but it came out of my mouth.

Col nodded. "In that moment, none of it matters. Nothing but the mission and the need to cause as much violence to those wreaking violence upon you as fast and fiercely as possible . . . An eye for an eye, and so forth. Foolishness. Whoever came up with such a principle wasn't a human being."

The Nightguard's hand fell upon Col's shoulder. Col looked at it like it was a dead man's hand—possibly Murphy's—then followed. "Keep your squad together, mates," he said over his shoulder. "Don't make the same mistake we did."

When he was gone, I noticed that the Nightguard whose legs I'd snuck through stood behind us. I eyed him.

"What do you want?"

His eyes glinted within the darkness of his helmet. "Daria will want to speak with you two, as well. Come."

"But we didn't do anything!"

"Come."

I stuck my tongue out at his backside but found myself following when a metal arm brushed my shoulder, gently prodding me after the Nightguard. I bit my lip and followed with annoyance. I might've slightly made up with Jezna, but the wounds were still healing. She and I still had our demons, our fears and hates. I'd saved her, a knight, for the *second* time, but it'd also been in unknightly combat. I'd used guns. Hardly the stuff of chivalric legend.

After a moment of silence broken only by our footfalls through the halls and the thumping of her Aestus heart, she leaned low to whisper into my ear.

"Disgraceful hunk of tin," she growled, stabbing a metal finger in the direction of the Nightguard a good ten paces away from us. "He should've rushed to our aid long before he arrived. With the amount of time it took him, we could've defeated thirty of those Navigators. It would've been a tale for the ages." She looked directly at me, though I'd busied myself with lifting my jaw up off of the ground. "He might bear armor similar to that of a knight, but he is not one. I may call him whatever insults I may please."

A warm and fuzzy feeling overtook me. I fixed Father's sunglasses, recalling the stained-glass window dedicated to Talen Vento, a knight that had turned his back on the Chivalric Code to become one of the founders of the Brotherhood. Though he'd been made of flesh, he'd refused to ever take off his armor, too.

And if I remembered Father's stories correctly, he'd saved Adam Evenstar's ass on more than one occasion.

"I . . ." Today wasn't my day with words. "Wow. Didn't expect that."

Jezna bent her helmet even lower to make sure I knew she was looking at me. "I apologize that I didn't tell you about my condition. I didn't realize you'd take it so to heart."

I shook my head embarrassingly. "You're, uh, fine. Sorry I ran off like that. It was dishonorable. Stupid and childish."

"Fear often feels as such, but it's only a natural emotion, I think. Those around us help us get through it." She tapped the glass chamber in her chest. "And keep us alive."

I looked up at her in shock. *Father always said that Adam Evenstar and Talen Vento never got along when they first met. One was a treasure hunter and the other was a knight . . .*

Heh. Look at that. And they ended up founding the Brotherhood together.

"Well, I mean," I sputtered. "If you're the Driver, there's always gotta be a guardian dragon out there watching over you, right? Gotta keep those eyes on the road." I tossed my pistols between my hands, considering. "An Ignis-less thief and a bucket of knightly water."

"Is there anything wrong with that?" Jezna said.

"Not at all. On the contrary, Jezy, I think this friendship might actually work out."

CHAPTER 49

Enoch

A Jackal and two Ignis hunters. It was impossible to focus on anything else. All thoughts of calling Kaleo and getting back to Carbonek were sidelined. All the world stopped.

These were no longer the legends I'd heard from old peddlers and rumor lads on street corners. No longer the myths. These were *real*, and that meant the myths held truth to them. And that terrified me.

But it also made me quite uncontrollably furious.

For every instinct that there was to make for the village as fast as I could all the while trying to call Kaleo, there was also the instinct to stroll up to the three buggers and give them a taste of Green Fire Fist.

But these were Ignis hunters. Professional slaughterers. They specialized in killing Navigators. And walking beside them was a real, live, in-the-flesh Jackal.

No way. It's just someone dressed like one. They're just trying to spook us.

"How kind of fate," the Jackal suddenly said, "that as I'm making my rounds, I chance to stumble upon two Navigational trainees." They halted twenty feet away from us.

"But not just trainees," the Jackal continued. "No. These two are different. They carry with them a certain familiarity. Like Mathias Flint and the Leviathan themselves stepped out of their time and into this one."

I tensed already taut muscles, eyeing Murta through my peripherals. His expression was unreadable, though he hadn't moved since the cruiser doors opened.

"Well?" The Jackal waved us over. "We have much to discuss. I'm quite interested in . . ." They glanced around the open courtyard with annoyance, then turned toward the Ignis hunters. "Fetch a table and three chairs. Put a spring in your step."

I was so astonished to hear the Jackal speaking normally, ordering Ignis hunters around, that it took me several seconds to realize that they'd drawn back their hood.

Removing it freed curly black hair and fair olive skin. He was a young man, a little under Kaleo's age, and handsome.

But the ominous gleam of the pink crystal reflected back in his pale green eyes was anything but. I'd expected a monster, not a man, but those eyes spoke of something in between.

The Ignis hunters returned carrying three wrought-iron chairs and a round table that looked better suited for a garden party. All four pieces of furniture were immaculately designed with a flowery, almost draconic-level craftsmanship, and after the Ignis hunters set everything up, they looked up at us with sneers.

The Jackal relaxed into his chair with ease, long fingers tracing the tabletop proudly. "Sit, gentlemen. I made this set myself, you know. Indulge me."

Neither Murta nor I moved. I flicked my eyes back toward the leering Ignis hunters. The Jackal followed my gaze.

"Take a good twenty steps backward," he ordered them. "And wipe those looks from your faces." He shivered. "I could really do without them. I'm an Ignis user myself, actually. But alas, we must all abide by rules and orders . . . and codes we oftentimes loathe." He nodded at Murta. "Time to spread our wings. Right, Shadarian?"

Murta moved slowly toward the table and drew out a chair. He even took the time to remove his suit jacket and set it around the frame before sinking into it.

I couldn't fathom what was happening.

"Murta—"

"Sit down," Murta told me.

The Jackal smiled, a look that unsettled me beyond words.

"You've always had an incredible wit about you, Shadarian," he said. "A truly remarkable work ethic, too. I've always respected that. Your amigo, however, often leaves the thinking to his fists. And I already removed my hood to make things more comfortable." He turned his pale eyes on me. Within their green, I saw the pink of his crystal glowing there. "Here, I'll even offer up my name if it comforts you. I'm Lucian."

"I don't care," I said, sucker-punching the pink mist that began to converge on my mind the longer I stared into those eyes of his. "Murta, get your arse out of that chair."

Lucian threw up his hands. "Lords, I come in peace! I'm not here to cause havoc—just sit and chat. If I wanted you dead, your ashes would already be scattered across the Grand Sea."

I shook off the fear that slunk down my spine, turning back toward Murta. "We can take him. I know we can. We can kick his arse if we—"

"We can't," Murta said emotionlessly.

A hole widened in my chest. "We . . . can't?"

"No."

"But you—"

"You don't understand." Murta finally looked at me. "This is a *Jackal*. You'd have a better chance of beating Kaleo. I'm sorry, but this isn't a fight you can win with belief alone."

Threads of fear laced his pupils, and it was enough to cripple my spirit completely. It was either that or punch the Jackal. Either succumb or surely be killed.

I depressingly chose the former. My mind lingered on taking Green Fire Fist to Lucian's smug face, but my body moved to pull out the chair. I sat and stared at the tabletop before realizing what I'd done.

Lucian clapped his hands. "Much appreciated, Shadarian. But I must admit that although I'm a fan of you, I'm quite possibly an even bigger fan of your squadmate. Enoch, right?"

"Bugger off," I said.

"I most certainly will after I speak my peace. Serapharus really does weld its men like its machinery."

"What do you want with us?"

Lucian leaned forward, his locked gaze taking on a more sinister hue. "What the Jackals need: more Ignis users. Particularly those with promising Conflicted–Transformative abilities. Such as your own."

"You're *recruiting* us?"

"You scoff?"

"You think two Navs will ever join the likes of you? After what you did to Loc? After everything you do in the War? *Bugger off.*"

"A rational point. But about the War, we're doing quite a bit more than the group you operate under are doing. Just ask Nothomathos and Kanbrik . . . And I think you'd be surprised what the prospects of freedom and forging change does to some Navigators, whether it be a growing disenchantment toward those they serve or glorious aspirations of doing . . ." Lucian considered for a moment. "More."

Murta remained eerily quiet.

No.

I threw myself out of the chair, seizing Murta by the shoulders. "You can't possibly think that's right! After all we've done, after everything Kaleo—"

"We?" Murta's eyes spun with rage and mist: the same mist that had spun throughout Loc's eyes. "*I'm* the one that's been dragged through the dirt. I'm the one that's tested night and day by the Council. They see you as Kaleo's copy, but I'm nothing to them."

"That's absolute bollocks. You carried me up a mountain!"

"Because if I came back without you, they'd lock me in the containment device and never take me out!"

"So this is your way out, then?" I rebelled against those spiraling eyes, trying desperately to somehow unspiral them. "Joining the Jackals?"

Murta looked away. "I never expected you to understand."

I wanted to punch him, but it wasn't him I should've been mad at. The only reason he was even considering joining was so he could learn about his past. All the emotions and doubt and manipulation that he'd ever felt were their fault.

I locked eyes with Lucian.

THEIR fault.

I shattered the table with Green Fire Fist. "WHAT'VE YOU DONE TO HIM?!"

The Ignis hunters had their massive cannons resting against my head in seconds, but Lucian merely waved them off, eyebrows raised tiredly at the smoking remains of the table.

"Stand down," he said. The Ignis hunters listened. "Let go of Ignis and calm yourself, boy. Murta makes this decision on his own. He doesn't want answers as much as he wants freedom."

I brightened the fire swarming around my fist until it cast half of the night in an emerald glow. "Freedom from what? He has freedom."

"He unfortunately doesn't. Though he is aware of the lie he's being fed. You're still asleep. Wrapped in mist. They've completely clouded your mind."

He's talking about the Brotherhood. "The Council didn't cloud anything," I said. "You're the ones that manipulate others. You're the ones hiding behind mist. You use Ignis for evil. We use ours for good."

"I thought a Serapharus street rat would've grown past such black-and-white views on the world. I suppose breaking my table was 'good'? Fighting those villagers was 'good'? Seizing artifacts from numerous kingdoms—artifacts that were never yours to seize—is 'good'? Murdering thousands in the War is 'good'?"

I felt my Ignis fade. "I haven't . . ." I drifted off to look at Murta.

His time as a mercenary . . . How many people has he actually *killed?*

"Ignorance," Lucian said. "That's what the Brotherhood has given you. They claim peace and protection are the way of Ignis users, then hide their own acts of violence. They claim to be instilling peace upon the world, but all they've ever done is fail Archengard by continuing to follow their ridiculous Code."

"The Code isn't ridiculous."

"And how would you know, boy? You haven't even sworn to it yet."

"How would you know?! The Jackals, just like the rest of Archengard, only despise the Brotherhood because they don't understand them. They're afraid!"

Lucian frowned. He opened his mouth once, closed it, then, after studying my expression, serious and set, swiveled to look at Murta. "You didn't tell him?"

My stomach turned inside out. "Tell me what?"

Murta closed his eyes.

"This is *fantastic*," Lucian said.

I whirled on Murta. "What didn't you tell me?!"

"You think a group of Ignis-using thieves and warlords just dropped out of kingdom come at the beginning of the Perpetual War?" Lucian leaned back in his seat. "You think that after the Brotherhood was used as the Government's own private army for half a century that no one would leave? Would see the Code and the 'protection and preservation of Archengard' for the folly it is?"

Dread climbed into my spirit. I shook my head several times in an attempt to pry the truth loose. Nothing came to the forefront. There was no way. It couldn't be.

But the more I shook, the more obvious it became.

"Say it with me, Enoch," Lucian said. "The Jackals are rogue Navigators."

Every negative action that the Council had taken was out of guilt. It was why Chancellor Veres had used the Jackals' flag to get a reaction out of Kaleo. It was why Kaleo had seemed legitimately afraid to train us, afraid to even let more trainees inside Carbonek.

And now that I thought about it, the designs on the table I'd shattered looked incredibly close to those of the Draconic Arches that Loc had shown me. All while he was being spoken through by a dark, familiar voice.

And if memory served correctly, the Arches had been finished by a Navigator named . . .

Lucian spread his hands. "Cat got your tongue?"

"You . . ." I whispered. "You're the one. *All this bloody time—*"

"Getting Kanbrik to join the Nodan cause was actually the easiest part, if you can believe it. Getting your friend to drop the imprisonment box, sneak into Barco's office and obtain information on both the Karnocolix and the Sacred Heart, then use him to use you was a trial in itself. Strong will, that Loc has got. In another age, he'd have made a splendid Jackal."

"You bloodsucking, barmy bastard—"

"Save your curses for the men that molded us. They're guiltier, I assure you."

I fell to my knees; my legs just gave out. Kneeling in the snow-covered courtyard, I clutched the pieces of the broken table between bandaged fingers, sifting through them as though I could find the truth there, somewhere scattered among their fragments.

"You're lying," I repeated, resorting back to my days in Serapharus. Crippled by fear. Knelt by weakness. I hadn't been forged there, like Lucian said. I'd been destroyed. My spirit had practically been stolen from me.

"I wish I was," Lucian said. "But Archengard killed that dream long ago. I don't dwell on the beginnings of the War like most of my brethren, but I do acknowledge that that was the moment it all went wrong. The moment the Code fell apart, and the Brotherhood with it.

"That was when Harrenous introduced us to the crystals, and the rewriting we could do with them. The ones we Jackals wear are perfect: windows that enable us to move the more mundane crystals around us. The mundane crystals themselves—the one your friend found in Kanbrik and those worn by the villagers—are mere experiments. They sway the wearer's spirit, but their mist can be fought off. The Sacred Heart, however, cannot. It is the master controller."

I felt Lucian's boots scuff to a stop before me. He could've kicked me in the face.

"It's true that we're after the strongest of the Tintagen Talismans," he said. "But you can control others, too, Enoch Amon. You may not be a complete controller like the Sacred Heart, but given time and proper training . . . no one would be capable of standing against you. You might even be capable of controlling the Other."

Never, I thought, but it came out, meekly, as, "You're lying . . ."

Lucian tapped his foot. "It appears I was mistaken, Shadarian. How you've fallen: hiding the truth from him to preserve his purity. Joining a squad. Forsaking your quest to find us, your quest for answers dropped in place of returning to Carbonek. Agreeing to be trained by that pathetic old man."

That made me drop the bits of broken table and look up.

"His name," I said, "is the Leviathan."

"And I fought beside him every day," Lucian said. "Don't try to act like you know him. I was once a Navigator. You've never been."

"Don't care if you were a Navigator. Don't care if all the Jackals were Navigators. I still have faith in the Code. I didn't betray the man that trained me. Memories or not, answers or not, Murta's coming back with me to Carbonek."

"Do you know how many times that beast sitting next to you has broken the Code? If I were to tell you the things he did as a merc or at his Shadarian Sanctum, you'd kill yourself in horror. He's closer to us than he is to you."

The light from the crystal made Lucian's eyes spin. "That's why he seeks us. He hears us in the dead of night . . . *Always calling*."

Murta flinched, his face contorting with pain.

"*Always whispering*," Lucian said, watching Murta writhe. "*Always lingering* somewhere in the scars of his mind . . ."

Green markings engulfed my body instantly. I ignited both fists with a bellow and threw myself at Lucian, but a triangle of pink Ignis spurted to life behind him, widening until it resembled a demented portal into endless black. I was so focused on the black that when a twenty-foot long tentacle made of pale skin, suckers, and spikes flew out of it, I didn't have enough time to dodge.

The monstrous tendril sped toward me but was blocked and held by two black claws.

Murta stood in the ruins of the table, claws locked around the tentacle, body humming with light. A grunt of pain escaped him as the demonic limb pressed down, sinking one of its grueling spikes into his shoulder blade.

He looked the same as when he'd caught the falling mast—triumphant, dauntless—but this time, trickles of darkness flew off of him, mingling with the golden aura of his Ignis to create something a shade darker. Like ripples of midnight.

I leapt to my feet with a wordless cry.

Murta looked over his shoulder—gold eyes cracking with black threads, veins popping out of his skin—and jerked his head down toward the chair. I pulled myself away from him, following his fixed gaze.

His suit jacket was still draped over the back, its interior pockets stuffed with the Jackals' notes . . . and the map to the Sacred Heart.

I looked back at him, eyes wide. His own, no longer spinning with the crystal's pink darkness, turned the brightest gold I'd ever seen before his pupils thinned to serpentine slits.

"*Run*," he whispered, then finally fell to a knee. He thrust his shoulder into the spike, lowering a bloodstained black claw to his neck. "RUN."

The scarf fell away from his shoulders, something gold and metallic sparkling within its folds.

A bolt of black lightning sped down from the night, casting the stars under a jagged shadow, and slammed into Murta, arching his back as it threw him to the ground. Lucian withdrew his tentacle immediately, throwing aside his chair.

The cold winds that galloped across the courtyard sent me spiraling in the opposite direction. Murta jerked violently in the center, clothes ripping as his muscles bulged: doubling, tripling, *quadrupling* in size. I grabbed his jacket and slid my arms through the sleeves, feeling around to make sure the papers were still there, then watched him convulse.

Murta was gone.

In his place, a reptilian creature spasmed, its limbs growing. Its claws grew to be at least five feet, two more dark legs sprouted out from its chest, a long spiked tail slid out, and dark wings unfurled from the mountain of spikes that ran up its back. Thick obsidian scales replaced fleshy skin, and when its face took shape—a monstrous head that dwarfed the crab cruiser—it was the single most wicked being I'd ever seen. Set within, just above serrated rows of mountainous teeth, demonic dragon eyes glowed burnt gold.

The shadedrake took a single step toward Lucian, heavy enough to shake the mountain, and breathed a torrent of golden flames across the courtyard.

I sprinted out of the area before the fire could touch me, tumbling through the thick snow. The dragon's screams and stomping of Ignis hunters in my wake sent me tumbling faster, willing my body to keep on rolling, but I could barely wade through the snow.

I couldn't see through eyes blurred with tears.

CHAPTER 50

Enoch

"You can't run forever, Nav! You're never getting off this mountain!"

"We've gotten a hold of every Ignis user we've ever snatched the scent of!"

My fighting spirit had been stomped into powder. Turning around to take on two Ignis hunters was out of the question, so I sprinted down through the village streets, hands frantically working to turn on the talker. When a blast of orange Aestus slammed into the stone five feet away from me, I bolted down an alley, trying to lose myself in the pathways.

"You can't hide from an Ignis hunter, Navvy! Sooner or later, you'll fall directly into our hands! And once you do . . ."

A cackle rang out of the night.

Taking an abrupt right and finding myself in front of the inn once more, I sprang to a stop in the shadows, hiding myself behind a stack of barrels.

"Come on . . ." I flicked the talker on how Murta had shown me, shaking it in an attempt to load it faster.

"Keep on running, Nav!"

I dove back the way I'd come, still trying to work the talker. When the home screen appeared, I smashed the kaleo tab until the screen turned white, save the mountain-rainbow-sun in the middle. The talker emitted a soft beep before speaking in Kaleo's voice.

"Amon? Are you done with—"

"Kaleo!" I shoved the device up to my ear. "You need to come to Aren's Steeple right now! The Jackals are here and two Ignis hunters are chasing me and—" I choked. "Murta's turned into—"

The barrel of a cannon slammed into my face. I saw red, felt the pain all throughout my face immediately, and hit the ground. The talker sailed off into the darkness.

Devastatingly powerful hands seized me by the jacket and lifted my hands over my head. I struggled in the Ignis hunter's grip, hurling as many curses as I could before the sting became unbearable.

Another punch silenced me.

I spat blood, felt it drizzling down my nose, and slumped forward. I heard the Ignis hunter snort and the sound of a large weapon being holstered, probably the cannon that had been used to nearly cave my face in.

In the cannon's place, the hunter withdrew disclike silver manacles from its belt and slapped them around my wrists. The metal dug into my flesh, drawing blood.

"Damon!" it shouted up the street. "I've got him!"

The other hunter came running.

Murta . . .

I lifted my throbbing head to gaze back up the mountain. Gold fire torched the night, soaring upward and turning the area surrounding the peak into a bonfire. Deafening roars accompanied the blazing scenery, and when I squinted, I saw black wings emerge from the flames. They dwarfed the sails on a galleon.

Damon finally arrived, his cannon already humming with orange light.

"Let's kill him!"

"Absolutely not," the hunter holding me by the handcuffs said. "Lucian gave us strict orders not to harm the blond one. His Ignis's rarer than the Shadarian's."

"Let's see him use it."

"He can't, numb-nuts. Not with Ignis cuffs on."

Damon squirmed. "So he can't do anything? He's just useless here?" He licked his lips. "Eh, who cares if we slip, Jaken! Just a bite . . ."

"Not a chance."

"They won't know that we purposefully killed him! We'll say he attacked us. He found a way out of the cuffs."

"If you touch him, we'll both be turned into one of Jehal's experiments by morning. If it's killing you want, go help Lucian. He said we could kill the Shad—"

"No!" I writhed in the cuffs. "Murta isn't—"

The cannon cracked across my face. Jaken let go, and I fell face-first in the snow, blood gurgling out of my nose and mouth.

"You say one more word"—he placed the cannon against my skull—"and I *will* consider putting you out of your misery."

"Pull the trigger," Damon beckoned. "Let loose for once!"

Snuffling blood and hacking when it flew into the back of my throat, I turned my head to the side. Through blurred vision, I saw the Ignis hunters standing over me, Damon's armor quivering with anticipation, Jaken's face considerate . . .

A daunting silence echoed down the street, devoid of draconic roars. I didn't even notice it until Jaken pulled his weapon back in toward him. Damon tensed, too, cocking his head to the sky. A visible shudder ran through them, then a shadow fell across the village.

At first, I thought Jaken had pulled the trigger and I was dying. Then I heard the hunters' howls followed by the firing of their Aestus weapons.

They had no effect on the darkness. It fell, smashed two houses into dust, then charged at them. Claws bigger than their bodies sliced them down the middle, straight through their armor. As if that wasn't enough, the shadow then pinned each of their remnants to the stone and breathed columns of flame down onto their split-open bodies.

The minute Jaken died, the Ignis cuffs sprang open.

"Get control!" I bellowed at the creature, staggering blindly down the street. "Fight it off!" I was almost at the end of the village now, the entry arch looming ahead. If I could just make it to the edge, then maybe I could get back down to the ice cave and hide until Kaleo arrived . . .

A black-cloaked leg stuck its foot out and tripped me.

"I really didn't want it to come to this, Enoch."

Lucian pulled me up off of the road by the throat, wrapping me in a choke-hold. I struggled lethargically. His elbow and arm were as strong as a steel beam, and he kept my left hand pinned behind my back. I was so afraid that I couldn't have called upon Ignis if I tried. I couldn't find the spark with so much darkness around me.

"But honestly," he said. "Why not? I'm not the butcher, just the cook."

I focused on the looming shadow in front of me. The creature paused, its wings flaring lightly. I clung to the moment of peace, pleading silently with its mind just to have it smothered, when the golden eyes narrowed. The shadedrake began to pace toward us, its feet creating massive cracks up and down the village.

"He has the strongest Ignis ability on Archengard." Lucian's words tickled the inside of my ear. "That's why the Brotherhood keeps him. He is, in a way, their most coveted artifact. A living Talisman unto himself."

"He's not an artifact!"

"Then why do they treat him as one? Why did they treat us as simple means to an end? Pawns of the Government during the Perpetual War and pawns of the people of Archengard? Why should the Brotherhood protect those that would rather see them hung? The Brotherhood cares nothing for you, Enoch. All they care about is that their Code is upheld, an impossible ideal no man can ever hope to achieve.

"They kept us locked in a cage, locked in Carbonek. We were living comfortably in those halls. Told we were using our Ignis, our skills, for just purposes. When in reality, we wasted them. The Brotherhood had convinced us we were saving the world by doing nothing. In a world howling for blood, Navigators continue to turn a blind eye. Continue to make futile attempts at peace.

"Think, boy. What purpose is there in connection when the whole world is at war? What purpose is there in connection when Archengard itself cries out for the blood of Ignis users?"

"Because . . . that's not the way of the Brotherhood."

Tendrils of smoke wafted up out of the shadedrake's nostrils. Its jaws parted, wings folding back into its sides. With every step, the mountain shook. With every inch it crept closer, its jaws resembled the yawning entrances of the Black Factories more and more.

"Then what is the way of the Brotherhood?" Lucian bellowed. "Extinction? Men are islands. The Code has failed in *every* age. Adam Evenstar failed to end the conflict between the Thunder Lords and Star Knights, Dresden Roberts failed to stop the cracks from spreading between Khronera and Narthes, and Kaleo Ashai's failures led to the Perpetual War."

Lucian gestured at the dragon. "Your friend understands that having Ignis isn't about hiding power, but seizing it. Because he feels no connection, he has no weakness. The perfect peacemaker."

I looked back into the shadedrake's face, praying that Lucian would be wrong, that there was still some flicker of Murta's humanity left, but found nothing. The black pupils were empty. The golden rage in the creature's irises were the eyes from my nightmares.

Lucian's grip slackened, sensing my defeat. "Yes."

I dropped my arms to my sides. I'd be torn to bits just like in my dreams, my ribs pried open, intestines scorched before being eaten. I'd die by the Other's claws . . .

Unless I broke my promise.

Immortal.

I looked the shadedrake straight in the senile eyes, deep into the raging darkness. This time, I surprisingly felt no fear. Only a disturbed sadness regarding what I was about to do.

"I'm sorry, Murta," I said, latching onto Ignis with my last fragment of strength and possessing the shadedrake.

Whereas possessing the Skrill had been like fighting back a hurricane, possessing the Other was like trying to reason with a black hole. I felt myself sucked in and out of existence several times, heard the distorted roars of the Other, and felt the darkness drag me down into the depths where I was almost swallowed whole by its gaping maw.

But down there, I also felt another presence. Against the black hole that was the Other's otherworldly spirit, I was a speck of dust compared to a supergiant star.

But I wasn't alone.

Another spirit fought beside me. In fact, I didn't think that it had ever stopped fighting. It felt like it'd fight the Other until its dying day.

But now that I was here, I'd help it. We could defeat the Other together. We could—

GET OUT! it said.

My spirit was suddenly pushed to the forefront instead of the deepest pits, and teetered on the edge. I was slipping, the mind-contorting wrath of the Other coupled with the fighting spirit throwing me around unconscious purgatory. I almost fell off the edge back into the jaws of the Other, but the fighting spirit gave me a final enraged push, and I solidified back outside—clothes and all—a good twenty feet away from the stunned Lucian.

In an act of panic, the shadedrake tossed its head, spewing flames across the village in an attempt to scorch me, but in the process of turning, its tail slammed full force into my chest.

Even Ignis couldn't stop the brute strength of a dragon. I had no choice but to absorb as much of the impact as possible and succumb to flying off the mountain, the icy cliffs waiting darkly some thousand feet beneath me.

No . . .

The cold wind ate at me, but it was nothing compared to the sadness I felt.

My depression only deepened when another crab cruiser soared out of the night—this one with the mountain-rainbow-sun symbol painted onto its side—and began the process of catching me.

CHAPTER 51

Murta

Burn. Destroy. Feed. Kill.

The world was nothing but a cage. The sky looked small. The stars were pellets of dust. I wanted to burn them, too. The stars deserved destruction most of all.

My tail swung around the corner, leaving long gashes in houses. Out of spite, I burned them. I'd melt the whole mountain until all that remained was a black scorch mark. I'd do it all because I could.

Burn.

My serpentine tongue flicked in and out of my cavernous mouth, tasting the cold air and remembering how it felt to burn the Ignis hunters.

A faint poke in my hide—the nip of a mosquito—tore away my concentration. I swiveled my great neck, hunkering down to gaze at my underside. A villager had attempted to stick a scimitar into me, but the blade had shattered against my scales.

As the cretin stood paralyzed, I felt the flames roil deep in my chest before I opened my jaws pleasingly. It became ash.

Destroy.

My stride toppled structures. If I wanted to knock down a house or breathe fire, I did so. There were no repercussions like there were in my limited form. A shadedrake never tired. My fire never gave out because my fire was meant to be free. That damned necklace had kept me restrained, just like the device in the Carbonek tunnels. But now that I was free, I'd never be put back in it again.

I flared my wings to feel the wind, no longer shackled by the mundane Shadarian's fear of it. I controlled the wind now. Archengard was mine to conquer. No Council, Government, Noda, or Jackals could shackle me when I was free. Not when I felt so alive.

Feed.

Sniffing the air, I relocated the scent I loathed: the tentacles. The Jackal.

Stomping through collapsed houses, seeing screaming figures rushing out of the way, I emerged onto the main road and spotted the cloaked figure standing at the end . . . holding a boy out in front of him.

I charged. The Jackal mocked me. A hostage? That would do him no good. I cared little for bystanders. They were all in the way. If they died, that was their fate. If the Lords really cared, then why didn't they stop me? If they died, then the Lords meant for them to die.

Kill.

I slunk toward the two figures, stomach burning with the whispers of flame.

Then the boy that the Jackal held was gone in a shower of green sparks and suddenly—

NO.

What was I doing?! I'd almost just killed Eno—

I bellowed at the imposter, digging through the shadows, lunging out at every speck of green. I needed to suppress the green, the new voice in me that had somehow penetrated the obsidian walls I'd thrown up—

I tried to fight—

There was no one else in me. No Shadarian. No green. I was the Other. I'd find the spirit that had infiltrated me and burn—

GET OUT! I said, slamming my spirit into the Other's like a battering ram and propelling the green spirit that had possessed me outward. I'd allow the Other to keep hold of me in exchange for the survival of—

That fool!

Feeling the green escape, I sprang out of the shade in an attempt to take one last bite out of it but felt the spirit that I rested within—the spirit I shared—clamp down around me. I bellowed in a rage, turning to slaughter the foolish Shadarian, to drag his spirit down into the true shade, where he'd go insane from the pain and feel his own consciousness deteriorate into flecks of broken galaxies . . .

Then everything calmed. I blinked, shaking myself.

No Shadarian. No green. Only peace.

BURN.

I turned the village into a pyre, heaving until every last drop of fire had escaped my chest. I roared up at the sky, cursing the stars for shackling me to this weak planet, and swung about the village in search of the green. I felt my tail collide with something but paid no mind to it. I collided with many things but never found the Jackal or the green.

Both had seemingly disappeared from the mountain.

Burn . . .

A metal roar echoed out of the night.

I cast my head back to the south, eyes slanted with irritation, and searched the frosted mountain peaks. The roar had been familiar. Not the roar of my brethren, but the grinding screech of an engine.

I took a violent step forward in preparation to leap into the sky when a gray-suited figure jumped up over the ledge of the mountain, soaring high among the stars.

Trickery! I trailed the figure, preparing to burn it. But the figure fell faster than I could've imagined—cold eyes glowing white in the darkness—and for the first time since I'd been initially imprisoned in the Shadarian, I felt . . . afraid.

The figure emerged under me so fast that I stumbled. I regained myself quickly, folding my wings in preparation to exchange places, then felt the figure already upon me.

How? No mortal man could move so—

A crack of white light made me scream. A shaft of white lightning dug into my heart, piercing the obsidian scales I'd grown to value more than my fire, and felt myself wither away.

I reared my head up to the cold stars to give a final wounded roar, to curse the green and the white and the foolish Shadarian . . .

Shivering in the snow, I curled up my naked body. My head pounded. My limbs ached. I felt twisted. Scars decorated me: long bloody things. Flecks of dirt, metal, and bits of charred tentacle stuck to my skin, squelching with every shift.

And it hurt just to breathe. My ribs felt broken. If only I had some of Enoch's bandages . . .

Enoch.

Regardless of nudity and the pain that threatened to incapacitate me all over again, I lurched to my feet, spitting globs of phlegm.

The last bits of fire had faded into embers, but where there'd once been a village, there was now a smoldering wasteland.

Every house had fallen. Every street was cracked. Every stone had been overturned, cracked down the middle, or charred . . .

And the villagers.

Some peered at me in horror from behind piles of debris, others ran screaming, and some even lay still. A few were burned beyond recognition.

I staggered away, pleading to wake up in the containment device back in Carbonek's underbelly. I tried to run but succeeded only in falling to my knees.

This isn't . . . I didn't . . .

A shadow fell over me.

I leapt upward, ready to strangle the Jackal with my bare hands until his misty eyes squelched out of their sockets like insects from eggs, until every last bone in his body burst open . . . and came face-to-face with Kaleo.

His upper body was hidden by the night, but his eyes burned a pure, untampered white.

Behind him, a crab cruiser rested in the snow, its side door open to reveal a group of four or five Navigational squadrons. Three of the Navigators frantically applied their healing-oriented Ignis abilities to a limp blond boy wearing a bandana and my jacket.

I felt my stomach drop off the side of the mountain.

Look at you, I thought as I hung my head. *Didn't even last a full week this time.*

CHAPTER 52

Enoch

"We're here," a gruff voice said.

I stirred. "Kaleo . . . ?"

The walls of the cruiser rippled noisily. My eyes tried to open but failed when the pain crept in. Dress shoes shuffled by. Voices swam overhead and around. One voice in particular, a soothing but scared tenor, cascaded from above, all the while applying warm pressure to my body.

Ignis. Purple light tickled my closed eyelids, turning the black a lighter shade. I was being healed, my wounds closed. More bandages had been applied to my body. I felt them on my skin, under my arms, blanketing my face.

"Don't worry," the healer said. "Relax."

The cruiser shuddered as it landed. My eyes snapped open.

Three Navigators—two women and one man—stood over me. The man was kneeling at my side, glowing purple. The two women who watched above wore expressions of worry.

"He's awake," one said.

"He shouldn't be." The man put his hand back on my chest to continue healing, but I pushed it away.

"Where are we?" I asked, but what I'd meant to be a demand escaped my throat in a skeletal rasp.

Everyone had begun to leave the crab cruiser through the open side doors. I'd already missed half of them.

The man looked at the women. "Help me with him. He isn't ready—"

I leapt to my feet. The Navigators protested extensively, but I ignored them and sprang toward the side doors.

We'd landed in the hangar, its launch pads covered in crab cruisers. We were already back in Carbonek.

The Navigators who had come to my rescue had exited and were swiftly making their way down the path toward the manor's interior halls. They moved agitatedly, keeping a good amount of distance between themselves and the two figures moving at the helm. One wore a black vest over a red dress shirt, his hands secured behind him by Ignis cuffs similar to the Ignis hunters'.

And leading him was a blond man in a steel-gray suit who walked with a slight hunch.

I flew out of the cruiser doors.

Feeling in my legs still hadn't returned. My sides and arms still hurt from being smacked by a shadedrake. My face and hands felt numb, to the point that tapping into Ignis would've probably knocked me out, but still I sprinted.

Something flew from my mouth: a howl I hadn't meant to utter. The crowd of Navigators turned. The black-vested boy tried to, but the gray-suited man forced him forward.

I said something again, preparing to bolt directly through the crowd, but the Navigators stopped me, securing my arms in their own. Two even had me by the legs.

The gray-suited man still didn't turn. He held Murta by the head, pushing him forward.

I fought against the group, the ringing in my ears from the dragon's roars sending me into a frustrated spiral. I didn't hear the Navigators' protests, just the ringing. Just remnants of draconic pain.

Murta hadn't enjoyed it. He hadn't wanted to become the Other.

He'd hated it and had been in pain every damn second, but he'd done it to protect me.

I fell to the floor. The hands followed me down, but their grips loosened.

In my sadness and exhaustion, that Serapharian grit, that swashbuckling fury, reignited. I seized my opening, throwing myself back into a maddened sprint.

The gray-suited man stood in front of the doors to the throne room and gestured for the Nightguards to open them. Even as I tore toward them, Murta's body went limp and obedient as the two stepped into the room and the Nightguards slammed the doors shut behind them. I dove as they closed and ate marble.

Instead of rolling around with laughter in front of the doors, as I'd done a few days prior, I became a puddle. Sleep knocked on my doorstep, beckoning me into a much-needed rest. Pain tried to pull me toward the healing branch to receive more healing. I refused both. I . . .

The gentle *swish-swish* of a leather jacket zipper and the clanking of armor made me stir and look up. Two figures approached steadily, coming from down the staircase that led up to the towers, moving with reluctance.

"Hullo, Jezna." I sniffled, dabbing at the holes that had been poked in the bandage around my nose. "Hullo, Prince."

"Enoch." Jezna looked between my mummified face and the doors to the throne room. "Tell us everything. Now."

I stood slowly, turning my back to them and placing my fist where the two blocks of marble met. I stood on shaking legs, but in that moment, my spirit seemed unshakeable.

No matter what . . .

I faced my squadmates.

I'm still a Charger.

CHAPTER 53

Murta

Once alone, Enoch's cries of protest painfully cut off by the doors, Kaleo removed my Ignis cuffs. After that, he'd just had to stare.

I climbed obediently into the containment device positioned in front of the throne, careful not to snag my recently remade suit on the manacles. The second that I was inside, clasps clamped down around me, the hand and foot restraints locked, and a sharp sedative was injected into my neck.

I blinked at the sudden stab of pain, then took to staring at the marble floor as opposed to the man standing on it.

"You'll find that the new necklace Barco made works better than the old one," Kaleo said, his back to me. "No cutting corners this time."

There were so many things I wanted to say to Kaleo, so many things I needed to say but could never bring myself to. So I'd reap the consequences of my silence.

"You shouldn't have tried to fight them . . . Lords, why'd you try to fight them?"

"What would you have rather had me do?" I asked quietly.

He spun. "Not what you did! Turn and run—not try and go toe to toe with a Jackal 'cause you think you'll get information about something you don't even know is real! Not lose control and destroy a whole village!"

"The life that was stolen from me is real," I protested, trying to blink away images of burned ruins. "They made me like this. They've tampered with my spirit somehow . . . With the whole world. When I close my eyes, I see red strings everywhere. They're all always leading back to their symbol . . . And there was nowhere else to go. He would've followed us."

"But you could've kept running until we got there."

"Navigators don't run."

"They do when necessary."

"Clearly." If Kaleo wanted to put all of the blame on me, then he was lying to himself. He'd scrubbed all the blood and ash off me before we set foot in Carbonek for a reason. "Because *you* keep running from the Brotherhood's responsibilities. How many times do the Jackals have to get ahead? How many times do the Shrouded Men have to speak another prophecy or another Talisman have to reemerge? How many more villages, kingdoms, and countries have to either announce their allegiance to or live in fear of a group founded from inside the Brotherhood? When are we going to stop running and start—"

"Because we can't fight!" Kaleo roared. He fell silent, dropping his voice to a murmur. "It would be against the Code. More violence won't create peace, just end more lives. And you just proved it."

I listened to the sound of the Other picking around the back of my brain, still whispering about the "green" that had infiltrated it.

"You took seven lives," Kaleo stated. "And nearly took Amon's."

I hung my head.

"And for a while, I honestly thought you did. And that you might've died with him." Kaleo's whole body shook. "I thought that I'd lost two pupils on their first quest."

I had one hope. One way to make this right. "Kaleo. What Enoch and I found in that temple . . . The Jackals were using it as a base. And the notes we recovered . . . They've found it! They've—"

"Doesn't matter. I threw you back out into the field too early. I'm speaking with the Council tomorrow morning. Either all of you go back to square one immediately or every one of you fails the Trials."

"What?!"

"You heard me."

"But Jezna and Junior—"

"Need more training. And Amon was too reckless with his own life. Putting both of you in the same squad was a mistake."

I strained against my bonds. "We were just starting to—"

"To what? Connect?! You call throwing someone off a mountain connection? You deliberately brought out the Other knowing full well that Amon was there. You just proved to me that his life means nothing to you!"

I sank back into the device, waiting out the onslaught as misery roundhouse-kicked me.

"You've learned nothing from me," Kaleo said. "Every Trial was pointless. And all it took was one bloody run-in with the Jackals to derail you all over again. Just like last time." He jabbed a finger up at me. "And don't even think about telling me that the first thing you did was fight a Jackal. You tried to bargain. I don't need a talker to know that."

"But if you'd just—"

"I gave you the chance to make amends for all the things you've done and you threw it away! You have since day one! This manor is no longer your—"

A loud scuffling erupted from the end of the hall, followed by the sound of an anvil slamming into a brick wall.

Or an Ignis-infused fist slamming into marble.

Kaleo stopped dead, whirling to look at the Nightguards, whose surprised expressions could be seen even through their enclosed helmets. The guards turned toward the doors, glowing with Ignis, spears barred.

Silence.

Then the strike came again, and this time, a fist-sized indentation appeared in the marble.

The Nightguards shuffled back a few inches. Kaleo stood in astonishment. And just when the second silence went on for too long, the third blow burst the doors open.

Chunks of rock sailed across the room, falling to a rest around Kaleo, and the Nightguards flew back into the walls, their spears scattering.

Silhouetted in the open doorway were three figures, and the one in front lifted his bleeding, bandaged left fist, now blanketed in marble dust, and locked teeming green eyes with Kaleo.

"Start talking."

CHAPTER 54

Enoch

I looked into the eyes of the man I'd once worshipped—the man I'd proudly been mistaken as more than once on my crusades through the Light Isles—and felt nothing but agony.

And shame.

"There's nothing to talk about," Kaleo said. "Except that door you'll be replacing with your bare hands."

I walked the length of the hall. "I'll rephrase," I said once I was in front of him. Jezna and Prince moved to flank me uneasily. "The Jackals used to be Navigators. *Start. Talking.*"

Kaleo turned toward Murta.

"Don't look at him." My hands curled back into fists at the sight of him strapped into the machine. "He kept your secret. Lucian told me."

Kaleo flinched at the name.

"I saw what was in that temple," I continued. "I saw their office. They're doing everything that we're doing, aren't they? They're not just the secret leaders of the Noda; they're an anti-Brotherhood." I whipped the map out of Murta's jacket and threw it. "And they've found the Sacred Heart."

Kaleo caught the roll of paper with reflexes that briefly startled me, but he didn't linger on the feat. Eyes wide, he ripped it open.

"How'd you—" he stammered.

"Murta snuck it out."

Kaleo ferociously scanned the document until his eyes settled on the map. His brow shot upward, flattening out his wrinkles, restoring him for a moment to his once-youthful legend.

"Ryjen," he said. "I searched the sands of that city for weeks but found nothing. I gave up too early . . . Of course. The Shrouded Men once spoke of a temple washed away by the sand when Archengard's second moon fell . . . A temple trapped in shadow: the Lost Temple of Jâhic.

"Long ago, the Shrouded Men told Magnar Stromsson, the Navigational Chronicler at the time, that if the Heart could ever be found, he'd find it 'where the sand meets the sun, under stars.' Ryjen is located in a spot where only Tanten is visible in the sky, yet it's also eternally night there. Suns and stars . . . And the spot the Jackals circled is Star Plateau! The tallest landmass in Ryjen, 'where the sand meets the sun!'"

"You've been looking for it your entire life," I said. "It's the only quest you've never completed. Well, there it is."

Kaleo's breaths came out ragged. He was back to being twenty-four. Watching him uncover all of this swept away my shame, replacing it with excitement and emotion. *This* was the legend I'd been inspired by.

"I thought it was in the Desert of Tile," Kaleo said. "Buried miles under the dune mountains. I didn't even think they were close to finding it . . ."

"Of course they were," Murta said from above. "*You* taught them. They know how much power lies in the Talismans. And now, they're weeks away from winning the War."

"They weren't taught by me." Kaleo's eyes remained glued to the map. The pain twisting across his face looked as though it were tearing him in two. "We were trainees. They looked up to me. Viewed me as a sort of older brother. To a select few, I might've even been their equal."

"How did they become, you know . . . ?" I asked.

"That's simple, really." Kaleo pointed a crooked finger up at Murta. "Power and immediacy. They saw the Brotherhood's purpose as lost and assumed that because they were in possession of Ignis while others weren't, they shouldn't just keep the peace: they should dictate right from wrong, too. They should take action without hesitation. Without remorse.

"They saw what the Government did to the Brotherhood during the War and swore never to allow it to happen again. But instead of assisting the Brotherhood, they did that by usurping the Noda—the ashes of the very government they'd fought against—believing the only way to establish true peace on Archengard to be the annihilation of everything, so that from the dust and destruction, they would rebuild it. Better."

"And what did you do?" I asked.

"I . . ." Kaleo trembled. "I never said a damned word. Just let them defile the Code and walk out the door. Only after they'd left and the War began did I vow never to let another Nav slip through my grip. I'd never let another Nav lose control and turn the Code into something beyond mending."

"Then let us show you that we can stay under control and follow the Code," I said. "Let us help you find the Sacred Heart."

Kaleo's eyes burned white. "Didn't you listen to a word I said?! You're suspended from active duty until the Council can decide what to do with you!"

"But Jezna and Prince didn't do any—"

"Take a good look at Caelius's armor!"

I turned and noticed the new plate on Jezna's chest for the first time. I couldn't believe that I hadn't already. It was see-through and took me a moment to realize that within it, an Aestus heart sat in a tank of water. It took me even longer to realize that it was showing *into* Jezna's armor.

Where her body should've been, there was only water.

"I'm sorry, Enoch," Jezna said. "I should've told you. All of you."

"Your time in this manor was supposed to bring you closer together. Instead, you drifted further apart. There were flickers of hope. Flickers I foolishly fanned into flames . . ." Kaleo closed his eyes. "But as with all the flames I create, I was blinded by their initial beauty."

I stared at Kaleo. Made of water or not, Jezna was still my squadmate, and I, her Charger. It didn't matter to me what somebody was made of: only what they projected out onto the world. Murta had shown me that even the darkest of souls had traces of light in them.

"Is this the Leviathan I'm speaking to or a senile old bugger?"

"I warned you when we met. I'm not the Leviathan."

"And I'm not an idiot." I pointed at the map. "I've heard legends about the Talismans since I was a child. Lords, the Heart has the ability to heal any injury! It can make water and trees and plants grow from ice! It can grow arms and limbs back! If the Brotherhood were in possession of such a thing, we could create real change! Good change—"

"Did you also hear that in the hands of a Jackal, it can enslave whole countries?"

"Immortal, I think—"

"You're not immortal, Amon!"

The image of the Leviathan grew distorted. Where once there'd been a monument in my mind, there was now nothing. Only the cold remnants of the man who had once been called the greatest Navigator to walk Archengard. Now, there was only a scared fool.

A mortal.

"What?"

Kaleo's face divided itself between anger and remorse. He turned away, as if seeking solace in the vacant corner between those he scolded and the contraption that held Murta. He turned away from his problems, pretending they didn't exist.

"No one is," he finished.

When I looked up at Murta, the boy's eyes were closed. The dark sarcasm and relentless defiance I'd grown to adore had been snuffed out. He'd given up.

No. I panicked. *I'm immortal. Immortal . . .*

I squeezed my eyes shut. The fire beam drilled into me. The Olders shoved me down into the Red Cell where I ate punches from the other Youngers and learned how to dodge. Where I learned how to beat someone to the point that it looked like I'd killed.

Where I learned just how mortal we all are.

Immortal. I'm—

“Return to your quarters,” Kaleo said meekly, storing the map away in his jacket. “And stay in the Rookies Tower. Food will be brought up.”

Immortal—

Jezna’s hand fell upon my right shoulder. Prince clasped my left.

I shoved them both away. “You’re at least going to take Murta out of that thing, right? You’re at least gonna go after the Heart?”

Kaleo refused to turn. Jezna wrapped another hand under my arm. I could hear the low pulsing of her new heart through the turquoise metal. Or maybe that was the thunder of my own.

I threw myself forward but was held back. “RIGHT?!”

They began to drag me down the hall, Jezna pleading in my ear, Prince cursing softly through clouded eyes.

“RIGHT?!” My voice slammed off of the stained glass. “WHERE’S THE MAN THAT FOUGHT TWO HUNDRED THOUSAND ON HIS OWN?! WHERE’S THE MAN THAT NEVER GAVE UP ON THE CODE?! WHERE’S THE LIGHT IN THE DARKNESS?!”

“Dead,” Kaleo whispered.

“I JOINED THE BROTHERHOOD BECAUSE OF YOU!”

CHAPTER 55

Jezna

Flanked by five Nightguards, we were escorted back to the tower and told not to leave our quarters except for designated bathroom breaks. Food was already set down on the table in the common room, but upon arrival, Enoch threw everything into the fireplace. Prince protested madly before collapsing on the carpet, twittering sadly.

In the strained silence that followed, I watched him do snow angels from my seat in the armchair next to the hearth. When that grew unamusing, I turned my attention to Enoch.

He paced the back of the common room, shuffling through the strange notes he'd removed from Murta's jacket. Now and then, he'd mutter to himself, sometimes offering me a page to attempt to configure. This was never to any avail from either of us.

Everything was written in the Dark Tongue. No one on Archengard willingly spoke it. Only the demonic creatures that were said to have roamed the world before the Dragon Lords created humans spoke the Tongue, and all of those creatures were said to have been hunted to death. So what good was there in knowing a black-as-night dead language?

Bebel used to know traces of it, I thought, trying desperately to recall the fiery, foreign rasps the big knight had often hurled Macín's way in an attempt to get under his skin.

Shuffling through the pockets of Murta's jacket, Enoch withdrew another paper and set it down on the table between us. His eyes flicked toward my new Aestus chamber every so often, but never lingered for longer than a second. He barely seemed bothered by it or the fact that I'd lied to him.

Perhaps that's why he leads and I follow.

"Look at this," he said grimly.

I did. The paper wasn't written in the Dark Tongue, but instead bore a detailed sketch of a cloaked figure standing on a hill, holding a gleaming green-and-black rock in their outstretched arm. All around the hill were white-clothed people, and the bolts of mist and lightning that shot out of the rock seemed to either be blowing them back, crippling them, or forcing them to their knees.

A shiver ran through me. "I'm beginning to see why the Jackals are so . . . infatuated with this object. It's like their crystals, but . . ."

"Bigger?" Enoch said. "Badder? Impossible to fight off?" He flipped the page over. "And check this out."

Scrawled in Common Archengardian was a small signature.

"Barco Reyveth," I read at a whisper. "You don't think—"

"That Lucian made Loc steal Barco's notes, too? He said he did. These *are* the Talismans we're talking about. World shapers we know nothing about."

"Jezy blew one up," Prince offered from the floor.

More like split in two. At the expense of my life. "Have you found any more of Barco's notes, though?" I asked Enoch. "They'll be in Common Archengardian."

Enoch shook his head. "Murta mostly only grabbed the Jackals' notes . . . Which we can't bloody read."

"This doesn't appear to be working."

"Don't remind me. Murta's the only one that can read these and fly a crab cruiser." Enoch sank into the armchair next to Prince. "We need him."

"I know that Kaleo's making many questionable decisions," I said, "but he's also right. We aren't quest ready. Enoch, you have to know that finding the Sacred Heart, even without taking on the Jackals, is an insurmountable task. We couldn't even dream of doing it."

"But the Jackals already know where the Heart is," Enoch protested. "And if Kaleo doesn't go after them, who will? And it's not like we have to throw down with them. All we need to do is grab the Heart and bring it back to Carbonek."

"You say that like it's easier said than done. It's the only quest Kaleo ever failed to complete."

"Kaleo . . . isn't the Leviathan anymore." Enoch stared into the fireplace unblinkingly. It looked as though he were forcing himself to maintain a stare-down with the flames, and after a while, he said, "He might not have completed it. But mayhaps *we* can."

Rationality warned me that we veered toward increasingly dangerous territory. I needed to end these thoughts as soon as possible.

"We're trainees," I said. "How are we supposed to finish a quest that Kaleo deemed impossible?"

"Because we have three things he didn't have: the Jackals' notes, my inextinguishable resilience, and Murta."

"Murta's under house arrest! *We're* under house arrest!"

"So let's break out."

Prince sat up. "You mean like, *rebel* against the Brotherhood?"

Enoch began to remove the bandages from his face and reapply them to his fists. "Aye."

I couldn't believe what I was hearing. I also couldn't believe I cared. Had I not yet lost faith in the Brotherhood after being attacked twice? Had I ever even had it to begin with?

Who was I kidding? I couldn't be a Navigator. I was pretending, attempting for Prince and Enoch's sake. Maybe even for Murta's. They were too similar to my Brothers.

And as I swiveled to look between the two boys who couldn't have been any more different from me—and I from them—I heard Col's final words to us:

Keep your squad together, mates. Don't make the same mistake we did.

"We—" I sputtered. "We'd be exiled!"

"Instantly," Prince said.

"Most definitely." Enoch stuffed the papers back into Murta's jacket before pulling it back over his shoulders. "In fact, the minute we're flying south, they'll probably send a search party out after us . . ." This time, he didn't need to stare into the fireplace for his eyes to light up. "But imagine if we managed to do it! If we actually found the Sacred Heart and managed to return it to Carbonek—"

"The Council would have to confirm us," I realized. "And they'd have the Heart secured within Carbonek. Noc, this is both extraordinary genius and absolute insanity."

"Those two traits have come to define me, I think." Enoch lifted a finger. "But we have to break Murta out. He can get us to Ryjen."

I stared at him. I needed to know he was at least aware of what he was doing. That he knew better men than him had made decisions like this and failed. Men I'd seen perish with my own eyes.

"You are sure about all this?"

Enoch returned my stare with one of adamantine determination. It took me aback. There wasn't a hint of prejudice, fear, or loathing in his gaze. He was the only person in recent memory—the only non-knight—who had ever looked at me as an equal.

I saw Macín in that gaze of his.

"Sure as the sea," Enoch said.

"And what about Kaleo?"

His face darkened but retained its directiveness. "Doesn't matter. Our squad does."

"I don't know how much of this is your 'immortal' philosophy and how much is factually true."

"Does it matter?"

I sighed. "I suppose not. For you, at least. But indulge me on this. Say one thing goes wrong. Say we fail to rescue Murta or we don't find any usable cruisers in the hangar. Say it turns out Murta can't fly a cruiser. Say we find out that the Heart isn't in Ryjen but instead in Narthes. Say we're intercepted by the Brotherhood.

"Say that somehow, we do find the Heart and we do succeed in seizing it, there are still a thousand other things that could go wrong. That wrong being the Jackals themselves. We'll have both the Government and the Noda after us. We'll have angered the Brotherhood and the Jackals.

"And if any of those things does decide to go quite horrendously wrong, we'd be landless. Returning to Carbonek would be a fool's errand. There'd be nowhere else to go."

Enoch nodded. "Thought that was obvious, mate."

I froze. Prince stood.

"I mean, come on," Enoch said. "The Brotherhood isn't made up of somebodies. We're outcasts. Outliers. Swashbucklers and scallywags. Knights and jesters. Pirates and bandit princes. Mercs and treasure hunters. Adventurers and wanderers."

He stuffed his arms through the sleeves of Murta's jacket, looking between Prince and I. "We don't need a map, nor a set destination. We don't need logic. We're Navigators."

It wasn't the Navigator's spark yet, but something did ignite within me at that moment.

Enoch's speech moved me. It shaped and created, built up and molded. It was foolish and illogical and not even remotely rational or any bit sane, but it didn't have to be. It was enough.

Our Charger had a remarkable way with words.

"Bollocks on all the bloody things that could go wrong," he said. "The Code says that a Navigator places their connections before everything. *Everything.* And that's exactly what we're doing. We're connecting up a storm over here."

Prince and I eyed one another in astonishment.

"I know I sound barking mad, but what's the worst that could happen? We gotta fight the Jackals? Fine by me. We've already fought 'em twice in the last week, and if we broke one of their crystals, we can break their faces, too."

CHAPTER 56

Enoch

The fact that there were zero Nightguards outside our door pissed me off. Did Kaleo really think that little of us? That I'd just lay down and take it?

"At the bottom of the stairs, take a right," Jezna said, moving as silently as her armor allowed her to.

I did as instructed, glancing up the side hall before listening sharply. We tiptoed past the entrance to the hangar, open and humming with yellow security lights. No Nightguards stood outside, but a few did pace its distant interior.

"They'll attempt to stop us from leaving," Jezna said as we progressed back toward the throne room.

I pretended not to hear her and glanced back at Prince. "We're close to the throne room. Cover me if anything goes wrong. Stun only."

"You don't have to tell me twice," Prince said, hands already creeping down to his pistols. "Just pray I don't have to use 'em on Scarfy."

"You won't."

"If he starts changing—"

"You won't."

We came to the passage adjacent to the throne room and immediately dove into the shadow of two pillars. The debris had been swept up, but the bottom of the doors was still a gaping hole from where I'd Green Fire Fisted it. I couldn't see beyond the hole from the angle we were at but more than made out the two Nightguards posed in front of it.

"Shit!" Prince hissed. "What do we—"

I held a finger to my lips, eyes locked on the guards.

"Find the spirit of all things."

Feeling through the dark of my mind, I fanned the spark into a flame, then traced the pathways. I felt and saw Jezna's and Prince's spirits behind me—an aqua flame and a much dimmer but angrier magenta flame—but blocked them out to focus on the Nightguards, particularly the one closest to us. His spirit, a silky yellow, was much weaker than his partner's jagged maroon. He was more tired.

More susceptible.

Clearing my mind before choosing the path that led directly to the Nightguard, I seized his spirit, possessing him.

His partner jerked his head to the side when he saw the green markings pop up all over his comrade's armor and body, but by then, it was too late. I, as the Nightguard, took advantage of their famous physical strength and struck the other guard across the jaw with a single Ignis-enhanced punch. The man's helmet flew off as he dropped, unconscious. After punching myself in the face, I escaped the Nightguard's body before he hit the ground next to his brethren.

When my body solidified back behind the column, I rinsed a hand through my hair, shaking the chills away. The spirit I'd traversed into had been worn and experienced, but it hadn't expected what I'd done to it. The element of surprise had allowed me to easily turn his yellow flame green and take control. I doubted I'd ever be able to possess him again. I didn't *want* to possess him ever again. Messing with blokes just didn't sit well with me.

Prince clapped me on the back with a quiet whoop before flanking the doorway alongside Jezna. Stuffing my doubt back below, I rushed past the fallen Nightguards, then dove into the throne room.

My heart caught in my throat.

Suspended over the hall was the containment device, and locked within was Murta.

His eyes were closed, chest rising and falling. One of the Navigators on the cruiser had remade his clothes, save the suit jacket I still wore, but his scarf was still missing. A gleam of gold along the back of his neck hinted that he'd been given a new necklace as well.

I crossed the throne room with increasing speed. "Oi. Murta?"

His eyelids twitched, beginning to open around the edges. I sped the last few strides until I was standing so close to him that I felt his breathing. A spark of gold beneath his eyes almost sent me scrambling away, but when they opened fully, they were warm brown.

"Enoch? Why're you—"

"Less questions, more action," I said. "How do I get you down?"

"But you're—"

"Betraying the Brotherhood. Ironic, innit? But am I really if it's to lend a squadmate a much-needed hand? Er, claw?"

Murta's eyebrows furrowed with annoyance, but the rest of his face softened. "All right, idiota. So you've conjured up a plan. Am I allowed to know it?"

"We go after the Sacred Heart."

"It's the only option."

"Brilliant. Glad we're ridin' the same wave." I failed to bottle my excitement. "Do you, er—"

"Recall how to fly a crab cruiser?"

"Yep."

"Go around back. I'll walk you through the control panel. But be quiet."

Heart soaring, I sped behind the containment device. Just as Murta had said, there was a large control panel full of levers. Some of them looked like they'd have incredibly disturbing side-effects. Luckily, he was able to walk me through exactly which ones to press in what order. When the process was done, the core of the machine emitted a low hiss, and the manacles suspending Murta snapped open.

The moment he dropped to the floor, a siren began to blare out across the throne room.

"That supposed to happen?" I shouted over the noise as we fled the hall.

"No." Murta shook his head angrily. "But I should've assumed it was at least rigged."

I gritted my teeth as opposed to calling Kaleo a name that would've made Light Isles bar crawlers cringe. We met Jezna and Prince in the shattered doorway, the latter bouncing up and down.

Prince started. "Well, that was freaking—"

Murta blew past him.

"Run before bickering, shall we?" I popped Prince's sunglasses down over his eyes.

And run, we did. Where once the four of us had walked nervous, separate paths through Carbonek, now we sprinted out of it together. Alarm bells screamed around us, calling the manor out of its slumber and sending Nightguards streaming down the halls. I might've laughed with the rumbling joy of a thunderdrake if I hadn't been trying to escape Carbonek.

Three guards came at us from the opposite direction, flinging Ignis abilities, but Murta slid between and spin-kicked them. When another crept up from behind, Prince stunned him into the next room.

"Please don't kill me when we get back," he shouted after them.

We moved in tandem down the hall. It was just another Trial, another attempt by the Jackals to derail us. The thought of death or failure barely crossed my mind when we were moving as a unit, and from the look of my squadmates, they felt the same way. Though we fled Carbonek, running under stained glass and launching ourselves over marble statues, I felt all the great Navigational eras pass us by in that bloody good moment.

Kaleo might've abandoned the Code, I swore, patting the statue of Adam Evenstar on the foot as I leapt across it, *but I haven't. Not yet. We'll be back. And we'll be better.*

Upon entering the docking bay, the five Nightguards who were stationed around the perimeter began to do everything in their power to stop us. In response, Prince stepped forward and launched round after round of Aestus in their direction, swinging his stun gun back and forth. The thunder of rapid fire was interrupted only by him screeching "Nighty-night!"

Murta pointed at the nearest crab cruiser. "Vamos!"

I sprinted for its open side doors, Jezna scooping me up on the way there.

"Hey, now—" I said when I felt my feet lift off the ground, but Jezna had already thrown me into the hull.

"Let's go, Prince!" she called.

Jittering all over the place from the blasts of compacted Aestus escaping his cannon, Prince barely heard her. Murta, who was already halfway toward the cruiser, backpedaled and snagged him by the collar. Prince continued to fire at the pile of cargo that the Nightguards had taken cover behind as he was dragged.

Once inside, Murta dove into the cockpit and began smashing buttons. I stumbled over to the open doorway and watched through the windows as the Nightguards gathered themselves.

"You think they'll fire on their own ship?"

"Probably." Murta threw down a lever that closed the side doors.

His hands flew across the panel frantically at first, starting and stopping, then began to move strategically, familiarizing themselves. After a series of crazed combinations that made my head spin, a high-pitched rumbling emitted from the floor and increased in pressure until I felt my ears pop. Right hand resting on the throttle lever, left hand secured around the control wheel, Murta pulled back on the throttle, and the cruiser began to steadily rise into the air.

A blast of Ignis slammed into the side, rocking the whole machine and sending Prince flying around the hull. Murta smashed a button on the steering wheel. The four legs that had kept the cruiser grounded folded inward and snapped shut.

This time, when a second Ignis ability approached, Murta jerked the wheel to the right. The cruiser spun in that direction, now facing the triangular arch that led out onto the grass of the sky island.

A third blast of Ignis smashed into the cruiser's rear but succeeded only in shoving us toward our destination.

Murta shook his head. "Idiotas." He threw back the throttle.

Fire exploding from its thrusters, the crab cruiser surged forward. I grabbed the sides of the cockpit doorway to keep from being whipped back, and Murta put both hands on the wheel, swiftly steering us through the hangar opening into the night. When we emerged out of the manor, he angled the cruiser upward so it rode just beneath the cloud level, then righted it with a grunt of triumph.

We sailed for minutes as fast as the cruiser could carry us, then I felt Murta let up a little.

There was a moment of disquiet. I watched mountains replace the valley through the window. Mountains I'd sailed over not but two weeks ago on an airship.

It felt coldly disturbing. The weight of what we'd just done seemed to fall on everyone, silencing us to stares and gapes. Prince crawled his way across the iron floor to look out the cockpit window, Jezna poked her helmet around the corner, and Murta just stared aimlessly as we flew south.

Perhaps we were waiting for the sound of cruisers in pursuit. But no such sound ever came, and Murta was flying too fast for anyone to catch up that quickly.

Just when the quiet felt as though it'd never end, Murta glanced at me. "I'll take my jacket back now."

I exhaled a long sigh of relief and began to remove it. After setting the pages down on the dashboard for him to see, I placed the jacket over the back of his chair.

Prince leaned against the cockpit doorway. "Well, then. So the dragon's got wings after all. That was some fancy flyin'—"

"I'll claw your nuts off," Murta said, keeping one hand on the wheel and using the other to shuffle through the notes.

I bit my lip to contain a smile, cocking my head at Jezna. "Can you, er, give us a few seconds?"

Jezna ushered Prince to the seats on the sides.

I took a seat in the co-pilot's chair and watched Murta work. "Still in Ryjen?"

"Definitely. The rest of Lucian's notes all point to it. There's direct quotes from the Shrouded Men scattered everywhere, except Lucian doesn't seem to be a hundred percent sure that Jâhic's under Star Plateau. There's something they're missing. Something the Shrouded Men managed to keep hidden from them. See?"

He pointed at the pages. I leaned down, feeling something in me stir at the feel of his breath warm against my neck, and stared at a paragraph of the Dark Tongue. It looked jumbled and made up of bullet points, like whoever had written the notes had been extremely flustered.

"I don't know what it is that the Shrouded Men hid from the Jackals about the Heart's location," Murta said, "but if there's something Lucian doesn't know, I might stand a chance."

"And no matter what," I said, "we'll be there every step of the way."

Murta said nothing.

"Er, how far is Ryjen?"

"Thirty-two hours Mach speed to the city walls. And if the Jackals are already there, landing anywhere closer won't be an option."

"We'll get comfortable, then." I turned toward the doorway.

"Wait."

I froze, turning back toward the cockpit.

Murta was an ever-changing compass, but in that moment between us, I saw him for who he really was. The compass finally pointed north, and the façade between us slipped completely.

"About me joining the Jackals . . ." He squirmed in his seat. "I—"

"You didn't actually mean it," I said calmly, smiling at his astonished expression. "I know, bruv. Don't worry about it. 'Twas the heat of the moment, as we swashes like to call it."

"Right." Murta exhaled. "The heat of the moment."

I paused, unsure whether to leave or stay.

"Swash?"

Heart pounding against my rib cage, I looked at him.

Say what you want to, not what you think you need to. Just speak your mind. For once . . .

The wind picked up outside the cruiser, howling against the metal sides. A shadow instantly fell across Murta's face, returning him to the window and the task at hand.

"Keep an eye out for other cruisers."

But he didn't grunt or growl.

Aye, Murta. I nodded, stepping back into the hull and staring out at the stars between the slits in the side doors. *I will.*

CHAPTER 57

Kaleo

"Move!" I bellowed, shoving through a squad in an attempt to get inside the hangar. The siren's screams had finally ceased, but Carbonek swam with motion, half-asleep squads scurrying about in an attempt to uncover what had happened. Of course, the experienced Navs I'd taken with me to Aren's Steeple knew—and they watched with astonished, unblinking eyes, some even attempting to calm the clueless squads.

But it was hard to keep things under wraps when the siren's cause had left a trail of victims straight to the hangar. Eleri's healers were already in the process of healing the Nightguards that had taken damage, but the worst, it looked like, had been saved for the hangar.

I finally pushed my way out of the mass and stalked among the damage, stepping through puddles of glistening aqua water.

Caelius.

"What happened?" I asked Aio'ke, captain of the Nightguards, who surveyed the damage that two crab cruisers had taken to their wings from rebounded Aestus blasts.

Larocque.

"They took Cruiser 18," Aio'ke said. "We were originally tracking it south, but then the signal just disappeared. We have no idea how. It's like someone ripped the tracking device straight out of the control panel."

I clenched my fists. *Kaster.* "No need to track them."

Aio'ke blinked. "Sir, one of my men claims that one of them went *inside* him. If they've gone rogue—"

"They haven't. No need to track them because . . ." *Amon.* "I know where they're going."

"Where, sir?"

But I couldn't answer. The hangar floor felt as though it spun beneath me, as it had the innumerable times I'd been dropped off by a crab cruiser and pulled out on a stretcher flanked by healers. It was odd being back here and not seeing Eleri standing over me shaking her fists, all while Ignis burned around her. All while *healing* me.

"You come back here with twenty bullets in your chest one more bloody time," she'd said between sobs, "and I swear to the Lords, I will end you *myself*!"

It hadn't been during the beginning of the Brotherhood's time in the Perpetual War, but during the last days. When I'd fought, although the Brotherhood was beginning to pull out.

Because I'd had to.

Because sitting around doing nothing, sitting behind a desk and greeting trainees wasn't what the Leviathan would do. Because watching the world burn rather than fighting darkness with the blazing white fire of my Sword wasn't what the Leviathan would've done.

Because even after everything that had happened, after all the lives I'd saved, I hadn't saved enough. I hadn't saved the ones that mattered.

I'd failed to save the Jackals from themselves.

I didn't feel Aio'ke's hand on my shoulder. I didn't see the squads waiting outside the hangar as I waded through them. I didn't feel the steps as I climbed them back to my office. I didn't hear the major general as I passed, his roars for me to go after them, to go after the Sacred Heart and the Jackals and the squad I'd trained. The squad I'd championed.

I felt none of those things except the door of my office slamming open as I stood within its stuffy interior. I didn't have to turn to know who it was.

"You're not going after them?"

I stared out the window behind my desk at the swaying sky isles and silent grasslands of Peniel Valley. The stars were bright tonight. Bright and ready to be navigated . . .

"No."

"Then I don't think you understand the insurmountable gravity of the situation," Barco said, the closest he'd come to a snarl. "One of us must go. And if you won't, then I will."

"I forbid you."

"I refuse."

I spun. Barco had returned to his robes. For a moment, I mistook him for the youthful, witty Sharpshooter who had saved my arse on countless occasions, until I saw the disgust etched into his cold features. Young Barco had never felt that hate.

Because the young Leviathan never felt fear.

Barco was deliberately defying my orders. Treason. But the man standing before me didn't seem to care about any of that.

"Fine." I turned my back on him. "But don't come crawling back begging for reinforcements. You'll get none."

"I wouldn't ask for any."

"Good."

Barco exhaled bitterly. "Well, you've made your point clear. If Grand High Navigator is a role you no longer see yourself fit to operate, then I suppose I'll be inheriting it and making the decisions from here on out. Let this be a farewell address, then.

"You've successfully burned two generations of Navigators to the ground, and I'm sorry, Kal, but I won't see another burned, too. The Brotherhood deserves someone strong enough to keep the Code. Not tarnish it beyond mending."

I stared at my shaking hands.

"On the other hand," Barco continued, "you'll be elated to hear me finally speak the words you've so desperately wanted to hear for a decade and a half: I wish you a happy retirement and hope you never train another squad again."

The door slammed behind him.

I stood in the darkness long after, willing my limbs to stop shaking. I finally stumbled my way to my office chair, messily collapsing into the wooden frame.

I stared at the door Barco had left through for even longer, fists clenched, eyes teeming with Ignis.

Then the cold hands of realization wrapped around my heart and my eyes began to peel back the world, revealing pieces of memory . . .

I JOINED THE BROTHERHOOD BECAUSE OF YOU! Enoch said. Then Barco replaced him. *The Brotherhood deserves someone strong enough to keep the Code. Not tarnish it beyond mending.*

Eyes blurring, I looked up from my lap at the papers decorating my desk.

They weren't the business letters, construction manuals, and Navigational rankings that everyone who wandered into my office thought them to be. They weren't papers from today, but ten, twenty, *thirty* years ago.

Maps of places where we'd been ambushed. Battle plans that had resulted in Navigator deaths; deaths that could've been prevented had I been less drunk and more like Mathias. Burial locations of the fallen. Mathias would carry the bodies of every Navigator that died during the War up the tallest mountain in a fifty-mile radius and bury them at the peak. It was safe to say that almost every mountain in Narthes had a Navigator buried at its peak.

And among the maps and battleplans, there were notes, too. On the Talismans, statistics on where they might show up next. A book of the places I'd searched for the Sacred Heart. A list of prophecies from the Shrouded Men and my many meetings with them; all speaking of suns and stars and fallen moons and even gods greater than the Dragon Lords.

But the most painful of them all was a faded photo I knew sat at the bottom of the pile, hidden from the eyes of the world.

Fingers clawing like crooked spiders, shoulders shaking, I crept beneath the mound until I felt the faded, nearly tattered photo. My hand retracted.

The day we were confirmed.

Barco, Mathias, Champ, and I stood arm and arm with Hektor, Eleri, Daria, Reggie, Lance, Tyson, Alexi, Lucian, Harrenous, Erika, Vendren, Dante . . .

And I realized.

A third of them were dead. The other third hated me.

And the final third had become the Jackals.

I hope you never train another squad again.

"Trust me," I said, tears rolling down my face as I completed time's work, tearing the photo in two. "I won't."

CHAPTER 58

Prince

Once we landed in the desert and had to walk two miles to the city, the heat became unbearable. A kind of scalding heat that stuck to the sand and got under your armpits. Coupled with the Navigational uniform Barco had given me back at Carbonek, it was absolutely maddening.

Turning away from the smoking crab cruiser with a groan and popping out the first two buttons of my magenta collar so my black tie could hang loose, I surveyed the yellow land all around us.

I freaking hate deserts.

The sand wasn't the white-gray of the dune mountains of Tile or even the orange-purple slopes that made up the lands surrounding the Night Palace, but a bright gold. It sparkled like diamonds, probably an after-effect of the perpetual intermission the sky above rested in. It was uncanny; only the second sun Tanten was visible while the rest of the sky lay black with stars.

I shrugged. Weather had never been my strong suit. If night and day wanted to combine for a bit, I didn't care. I'd been to places on Archengard where the sky was pink and the water was green. Nothing surprised me anymore.

A few feet away, Murta stared at me, arms crossed. "So?"

"So?" I repeated, imitating his growl, but more nasally. I had no idea what he was on about now. Always something with him.

"You were supposed to check the cruiser over. Did you?"

"Course I did. What's the issue, Your Edginess?"

Murta's face purpled. It was a good look on him. "You're the expert! What do you make of the damage it's taken?"

What I'd intended as a sweet-as-honey reply quickly disintegrated into madness. "Well, damage doesn't really seem to matter anymore, does it, since we're about to go *hunting for the SACRED FREAKING HEART*!"

"Shout at me again and I'll barbecue your legs. In the meantime . . ." He pointed south, shedding light on a glittering citadel in the distance. There were several domed golden towers, too. "Let's get moving."

It was a pretty sight, but knowing what might rest there froze me over.

I still could hardly believe Enoch's story about what had happened to them on Aren's Steeple. The fact that they'd been that close to a Jackal was unbelievable, much less survived.

The anxiety I felt seemed to run rampant through everyone else, because Murta readjusted his scarf, shaking sweat from his hair. "It's not gonna get any closer. Vamos."

We began the long walk. I fumed nervously the entire time, glancing over my shoulder every few seconds to watch the smoking cruiser fade from view. Then my neck started to cramp up and I just decided to stay forward.

As we trudged, Murta taking up the front and Enoch following close behind, I noticed Jezna watching the sky with fascination. Staring at Tanten for too long didn't seem to have much of an effect on her. I guessed that was how it worked when you didn't have eyes.

At least the Aestus heart seems to be working. I'm just glad she doesn't seem bothered by it anymore.

"This is quite beautiful," Jezna said. "I'm ashamed to say I've never been here."

I kicked sand up at Tanten. I'd always liked the green sun more. "So what happened? The Lords just decided to remove Rolarns from the equation and make it half night? What'd Rolarns ever do to them?"

"The Sky Sea," Murta said. "Haven't you heard of it?"

"Course I have," I said, then seized Jezna by the helm. "What the hell is it?" I whispered into her eyehole.

"It's not bad that you don't know," she whispered back. "You don't have Ignis."

I scowled.

Jezna gestured around the sky. "According to many religious texts, after the Dragon Lords passed on, the remnants of their bodies were trapped in the atmosphere above Archengard, where they disintegrated over time. They became particles of dust, which molded into our world's very essence, creating a strange substance in the sky that steadily rained down, imbuing itself onto Archengard. That source became Ignis."

"So you're saying even this freaking desert has an Ignis ability . . . And I don't?!"

"I'm saying that like all places, this desert bears Ignis in it. Think about the sky isles that surround Carbonek—"

At the mention of the manor, everyone's moods darkened even further. Our escape was better left an unsaid thought. For the sake of my squad, I'd focus on the quest. For the sake of *Archengard*, I'd focus on what would happen if the Jackals had already found the Sacred Heart.

But how do we *stop them? What good will guns do to Ignis users Father called literal demons?*

"For your sake, little prince," he'd said, "I hope you never run into them. They've got flames of time and darkness burning in each of them. They've shackled gods, eaten worlds . . ." But then he'd said: "Only the Brotherhood can match 'em blow for blow. I know, because I've seen it. They can be fucked with."

This time, I looked up at the stars.

Help me with this, Father. Help me to be the best Sharpshooter I can be. The Sharpshooter you failed to be for your squad.

The towers of Ryjen began to appear out of the mirage, and the thick sandstone walls followed. But then, so suddenly that I almost staggered, something emerged before them. It wasn't as massive as Ryjen, but it was closer, as though positioned in front of the city.

I became the first one to speak since Jezna mentioned Carbonek. "Tents?"

Murta's determined stalk slowed to a confused shuffle. He put a hand to his brow.

"A campsite," Enoch said. "Almost like—"

"A campaign." Then Murta was walking faster than before.

Both were right. When we arrived at the entrance, the blue-and-white flag of the Government flew from a wooden command tower, barbed wire curled around the whole perimeter, and a mass of dingy tents could be seen through the gates before us.

I've seen Government camps, though. They're always organized to a T. And this looks anything but. They've been hit hard. A lot. And there doesn't seem to be any clear authority. You can see that even from the outside.

To underscore my assumptions, two dark men slunk out of the shadows from behind the gate. Neither one was dressed in the blue-and-black military garb of Governmental soldiers. Instead, both wore black-and-brown combat robes that clung tightly to their muscular bodies. The man on the right had thick black hair and a face covered in black tattoos, while the man on the left's face was wrapped in gray bandages, silver-blond hair poking out over them being his only visible feature. That, and the glistening green eyes set in the mask of bandages.

"Travelers," he said, shouldering the rifle he carried. "Out of the desert. Under the stars."

"I've seen their ilk before," the tattooed man said, cracking his knuckles. "They come from the sky."

"Pardon me, gents," Enoch said, suddenly stepping forward. "We, er, are just passing through, and were wondering . . ." He licked his lip nervously, glancing up at the Governmental flag. "Are you lot here for—"

"The sky clouds minds, it seems," the bandaged man said. "We ask the questions."

"That we do," the tattooed man said. "I'd like to know the secret of the Serpent."

Enoch frowned. "I don't follow."

"'The Sun crosses the sky every day,'" the bandaged man began, "'and every night, delves below to face the Serpent. And every night, the Sun wins. The Sun then sleeps the day away, healing its wounds. But we must not forget . . .'"

"Not forget what?" Enoch looked beyond confused. I felt the same.

Some kind of code? I wondered. *I've no clue.*

"Gentlemen," Jezna said, stepping forward. "If you'd just let us into your camp, I believe we're both after the same thing—"

"'The Sun then sleeps the day away,'" the bandaged man repeated, "'healing its wounds. *But—*'"

Enoch looked back at us helplessly, but then Murta stepped forward. I saw the two gatekeepers lift their heads in surprise, saw the bandaged man stop cracking his knuckles and the tattooed man set down his rifle, then Murta lowered his scarf.

"'But the Serpent never sleeps.'"

The tattooed man moved to raise the gate.

The bandaged man just nodded. "Indeed."

Not Governmental soldiers, I realized. *Mercenaries.*

CHAPTER 59

Murta

One would think that after spending so much time around the War—even fighting in it—that you'd get used to the simple things: an overturned wall, a crooked grave marker, limbs tangled in barbed wire, and the black silence of the living more than the dead.

But you didn't.

As the bandaged merc led us toward the center of camp, I did slow, unsettled circles. Before long, they were all far ahead of me, and I was still stuck in place, spinning as though my body refused to do anything else. The sheer shambles that the camp was in was enough to steal the words from my lips. Enough to steal the heart from my body.

It was all too familiar, a bleak plain trapped in time, between struggling to survive and praying for death. A purgatory realm where change could truly occur.

Peace wasn't made in a room; it was built through battle. War led to peace. Suffering was the only way to eventually gain comfort. And though it was bloody, it still had to be done.

But this . . .

These were pieces of debris being launched at the enemy by stuffy, soulless generals. These were men condemned to die that could all be easily spared if the Brotherhood got involved again and fought alongside them. The arms and legs that decorated the fences would've all been gone. There would've been twenty less grave markers.

It was a thin line to walk, but it was my line. And now that I was here, I'd fight. I'd aid.

"You coming?"

My eyes shifted away from the open flaps of a healing tent swimming with flies to settle on Enoch. He stared at me sympathetically, eyes hinting at a fierce admiration, too.

No. He can't admire me. Not after Aren's Steeple.

I looked away. "Yeah."

The bandaged merc looked at me. "You fought once, too."

"For a time. The Government enlists all us 'pawns' at one point or another. It just depends on what square they move you to."

"We've been on this square for a month now." He gestured up at the sandstone walls looming over the camp. "The Noda has taken Ryjen. And Ryjen, out of desperation, it seems, has aligned themselves with them. Or at least struck up a fragile truce. No Nodan forces are allowed within the Serrated Keep yet, though they've completely taken over the surrounding land. They've strategically placed themselves in the desert hills with Star Plateau as their center point. And any time we make a run for the keep, well, the results haven't ended well. Though still at odds with one another, Ryjen and the Noda seem almost united in their hatred for us."

I saw Enoch look at me out of the corner of my eye. The shock was written on his face.

The Government doesn't know the Heart's here, I realized. *Either that or they're keeping the mercs in the dark. They have no idea what they're fighting for.*

"Or their need to protect something," I added, glaring up at the pale city darkly. "If the Jackals are here, then the Government is keeping things from—"

"The Jackals?" The bandaged merc stopped walking. "Nay. They're not here. Ryjen isn't important enough for them. Why do you say so, though?"

I racked my brain for an answer that wouldn't send the bandaged merc and the other dark-clothed, scarred figures I saw beginning to emerge from tents into turmoil. Mercenaries were a superstitious group by nature, always stabbing one another in the back. They feared the Jackals just as much as the Brotherhood; in fact, they'd fought them on the field more than the Brotherhood ever had.

"And on top of that, dark son," the bandaged merc said curiously. "What's a mercenary doing dressed like a Navigator?"

So if there was one group that mercs despised even more than the Jackals—the men responsible for their misery—it was the group that failed to sedate it.

I opened my mouth, having no idea what to say, but Enoch was already up in the bandaged merc's face, fists glowing. "You got a problem with Navigators?"

We were surrounded in moments. Ignis abilities, Aestus weapons, and unquenched rage forging a blazing ring of fire. The mercenaries surged in on us, and I felt my back bump into Jezna's as I tapped into Ignis, preparing to launch myself at the bandaged merc . . .

"Knock it off," a gravelly voice called outside of the ring. "Let go of Ignis and get the hell back. That means you, Dero. Beat it."

Heads turning all around us, the ring broke steadily. Weapons lowered, Ignis faded, and a few even cleared a path for a short boy that looked a little older than me with half-black, half-blond hair and bright-blue eyes. Silver tattoos covered his face in long jagged markings, making him look more demon than man. One I recognized.

Anders walked slowly through the crowd, ruffled the bandaged merc's hair in passing, then came to a rest in front of me. I let go of Ignis.

"Stand down, fools," he called. "I know this idiota . . . From our Rolling Chaos days."

I scowled around the circle. "Are they all this eager to die for the Government?"

"For the Government?" Anders said, face falling. "No. To die? Don't ask."

"They're feeding you to the beast."

"We're all beasts here. You know better than anyone." Anders ran a hand through his tangled hair, sizing me up and down with depressed awe. "The rumors were true. You've gone back to Carbonek."

I flinched. Recent events had probably snuck it out of me. "It's . . . not what you think. Don't ask either."

"Well, once a Nav, always a Nav, they say. And that means you're here for a reason. Something me and my motley men probably don't know regarding why we're being flung against these sandstone walls." Anders cocked his head. "Spill."

I looked around. "Find somewhere quiet first."

CHAPTER 60

Enoch

Murta stepped forward, the single flickering candle sending shadows sprinting across his face. It was almost enough to make my whole body clam up, to return me to Aren's Steeple and the creature that had almost devoured me. Fire and darkness: those were the things I feared the most. Murta embodied both, yet I couldn't look away from him. Not from someone who would've given Mathias a run for his money.

I guess that makes me Kaleo, then, I thought glumly.

The black-blond merc—who'd identified himself as Anders, to which I'd identified myself as "your worst daymare"—swiveled his gaze from the bandaged merc stepping into the tent to Murta. I opened my mouth to mention how we were supposed to be alone, and that the bandaged bloke's intrusion had brought a swift end to that, but Anders beat me.

"Biorn stays," he told Murta. "I trust him as much as I once trusted you."

"And where'd that lead you?"

"Point taken. But I trust he won't leave me hanging off the edge of a cliff."

Murta surprisingly seemed to falter. "I didn't mean—"

"Of course you didn't." Anders sighed. "We all don't. We all wish we had; we all wish we hadn't. The cycle of a merc. I'm just happy you escaped it when you did. There's so many I still wish it for. Remember Lee? I really hope that kid finds his way to Carbonek soon."

"He's dead."

"Damn."

"But he died for the right reasons."

"And what's *your* reason for coming back?"

Silence boiled throughout the tent before Murta responded. "The Sacred Heart."

Anders's eyes widened. They looked ghostly in the candlelight. "That's . . . *impossible—*"

"It isn't. I have notes straight from the Jackals that say it's located right—"

"What the hell are you doing having notes from the Jackals? And what do you mean, the Sacred Heart? It's here? And the Jackals—"

"I'm not sure. If you'd just calm down and let me—"

But the cool-headed bloke I'd seen get an entire gang of riled-up mercs to calm down was gone. This bloke, who I'd originally viewed as something short of a rival, was more afraid of the Jackals than *I* was.

"*Calm down?*" Anders said. "After years of hearing nothing from you—nothing but rumors that you'd left the War and were back to hunting artifacts—you suddenly turn up on the frontlines telling me that you're looking for a Talisman? And that *the Jackals* are involved?"

"Anders—"

"Lords, Murta. We're mercs! If you brought your Navigational business all this way, you might as well turn right around. And if it involves *them*, then I want nothing to do—"

"*Anders.* Listen. Please."

Anders closed his mouth but kept glaring.

"I'm not the man you think I am," Murta said. "I'm not this 'born again' soul that decided to cast aside violence and embrace the Code. There's things about me . . . things that'd make you want to shove a sword straight through my heart.

"But none of that matters. Mercenaries and Navigators don't matter. This is about the fate of Archengard. So please, just hear me out."

Anders hesitated, then nodded.

"Gracias. The Heart's located under Star Plateau." Murta turned to look at the bandaged merc. "Biorn said the Noda's set up camp with the plateau as its center. That means no one here has even gotten close to the plateau. You have no idea what's going on up there, right?"

Anders was too busy gnawing through his lip, so Biorn answered for him. "Aye. We've seen nothing of its top."

"That's because they're digging," Murta said. "The Jackals or the Noda. They're digging for the Lost Temple of Jâhic. They spoke with the Shrouded Men—probably tortured it out of them. They know that the Sacred Heart is—"

Anders looked shocked beyond comprehension, but it wasn't him that made Murta stop abruptly. Biorn had keeled over and begun to cough. He hacked so violently that I thought he might throw up a lung, but then pale blue Ignis began to swim around him and he straightened. A cold wind blew through the hot tent, stirring Biorn's robes and bandages, and when he looked up at us, his whole eyes burned with Ignis, a fire that seeped out from the corners of his eyes in a river.

Prince yelped as we all watched Biorn sweep a godlike gaze about the tent, then settle on Murta.

"*You,*" Biorn said, but he sounded like a thousand Biorns, not one. Something spoke through him, but it wasn't like how Lucian had spoken through Loc. This was Biorn . . . speaking through Biorn. The other voices were all his own.

"What the hell?" Anders crept closer. "Biorn?"

"No," Jezna gasped. "A Shrouded Man."

My nervousness bled into awe. *A Shrouded Man? Here?!*

I looked over at Murta, but his confused gaze was locked with Biorn's, squinting against the blue light pooling from the Shrouded Man's eyes.

"*You*," Biorn repeated, seemingly still at Murta. "*El Cazador de Sombra.* You've come."

"Now that I think about it," Anders said, sounding oddly proud, "Biorn always said he was from the Western Sands. You know how it goes, Murta. A merc never asks questions. Biorn might not be full Shrouded, but clearly there's a bit of Shrouded in him."

Murta licked his lips. "Then tell me, Biorn. Is the Heart really under Star Plateau? Have the Jackals already found it?"

Biorn seemed to consider slowly. "I am forbidden to reveal such information. For generations, we have kept the silence. But you are not just a Navigator. You do not seek what lies in the sand for your manor, but for the world. So the Shrouded shall speak."

The Ignis seeping from his eyes began to dance about the tent's interior. I immediately felt myself tap into Ignis, thinking it to be the workings of another crystal, but Biorn's mist wasn't controlling. Quite the opposite: it seemed to make the air clearer. It was *revealing.*

"Once, a Shrouded spoke to a Navigational Chronicler. Once, the truth was revealed. And so this Shrouded shall say again: 'For hearts on fire, and the truth they seek, venture to the west where the sun and sand meet. Under the stars in a dying land, where one is none, but all must be one.'"

"Yeah, but we already know all that," Prince said. "'Under the stars' means the Star Plateau, right?"

But Biorn wasn't finished. "Once, a Shrouded spoke to a Navigational Chronicler and said thus. But time has changed. A serpent rises, preparing to devour both Tanten and Rolarns. Aldrisno shivers in the night. Archengard cries out for comfort, so this Shrouded must speak the final verse."

He bowed his head.

"Ground to powder by the gears of time, sleeping in the sands, yet stairs must be climbed. Ash-black arrows fixed toward their enemy, there Archengard's Heart shall lie in Navigational memory."

Biorn shook all over, then the mist began to dwindle, slithering back into his eyes and fading. The Shrouded Man returned to the strange bandaged merc we'd met at the entrance, though blue Ignis still continued to swirl in his irises.

Anders broke the silence ringing through the tent. "Arrows. That can't possibly mean—"

"Suns above," Murta breathed, shoulders shaking. "It is. It all adds up . . ."

"What does?" Prince asked. "What adds up?"

"The Arrows of Eclipse," Anders said. "They're black spears tipped with arrow points—weapons once wielded by a dark army—and they ring the domes and sides of the Serrated Keep."

"'Stairs must be climbed,'" Murta said. "The front steps of the keep."

"And if there's one thing Ryjenians hate more than the Government," Anders said, "it's the suns; the thing that's drained their land for centuries. That's why they positioned the Arrows around the keep. That's why they're 'fixed toward their enemy.' The suns. Or, er, *sun*. It seems that like the demons once did to Archengard's second moon, the Ryjenians want to strike Archengard's second sun out of the sky."

I flipped through my brain, watching Murta with wide eyes. "But if the Heart's in the keep . . . then that means—"

"The Jackals are digging two miles away," Murta said.

And for the first time ever, I saw a smile creep across his lips. It didn't fully form, but the fact that it was at least trying to . . . It felt like being back in the training hall punching the Rock of Sages beside him again. Though I wasn't tapping into Ignis, I felt the flame of my soul brighten. Maybe even strengthen.

"That explains why the Ryjenians are so protective of the keep," Anders added. "And adds some spice to their relationship with the Jackals. It's like they're keeping the Heart's location hidden from them. Some partnership."

"Or," Murta said, "the Ryjenians don't even know where it is. Or if they do know, they still can't get to it. Whatever guards the Heart is doing its job." He looked at Biorn. "Why are you telling me this? Why have other Shrouded Men kept this information secret from me—secret from the Brotherhood and the Jackals—but you tell *me*?"

I looked at Biorn. Throughout history, the Shrouded Men had never chosen sides, but they did seem to hold a great deal of respect for the Brotherhood. A Shrouded Man had helped Dresden Roberts cross the Fireroot Trenches.

But there was something greater than admiration in the eyes of Biorn when he looked at Murta, then slowly swiveled to look at me. There was awe.

"The Ember of the world lies cold and dead, El Cazador de Sombra." Biorn turned to leave. "But this Shrouded has seen the spark. The star of two colors." He parted back the tent flaps, sprinkling the sun and stars in briefly, and spoke again before leaving. "For now, I've completed my purpose."

Anders waved after him. Murta stared, but Anders just shrugged weakly. "You think you know someone."

"You had a Shrouded Man in your camp all this time?"

"I wasn't talking about Biorn."

Murta shook his head angrily. "Whatever he thinks I am, I'm not." He paused. "But we have to get inside the Serrated Keep."

Anders seemed to deflate. "That's . . . a lot easier said than done. My boys fought their arses off just to get inside the city walls. Let alone reach the Great Steps of the keep . . ." He set his jaw firmly. "But if the fate of Archengard lies somewhere in this bleeding desert . . . so much so that the Jackals rest a mere mile away from us . . . then it will be done."

Murta nodded. "We'll charge our way through Ryjenian bodies if we have to."

"No," I said.

Every head spun to look at me. Prince looked confused, Jezna looked uneasy, Anders astonished, and Murta? Enraged.

"No?" he repeated.

I stood my ground. "We won't. These aren't Nodan soldiers; they're innocent people protecting their land. The Heart has been in Ryjen for centuries. That makes it theirs." Lucian's words rolled through me. "If we're going to do this, then we're going to do this right. Navigators wouldn't fight first. Not if they could find a way around it."

Murta stepped out of the shadows. "A swashbuckling boxer proposes talking before fighting. I've seen it all."

"Not a boxer. Not a swash. A *Navigator*."

"Not even a Navigator apparently: a sunburnt idiota. The Code means nothing anymore. Even the High Navigators defile it. Why the hell should we follow a dead document?"

"If we don't follow the Code, what else do we have?"

The looks I'd received turned toward the ground. Murta seemed suddenly contemplative—maybe even remorseful—but the rage returned.

"I have my pride."

"Like I said: What do we have?"

Though thoughts of Kaleo pained me, he was just Kaleo now. He'd been right the day we met him: The Leviathan was dead. But it was the Leviathan that'd lit my dark nights, not the old man who had tried to keep us locked away.

They keep us locked in a cage, I remembered Lucian saying. *In a world howling for blood, Navigators continue to turn a blind eye . . .*

"We won't turn away from the Heart," I said. "But we won't directly seize it from Ryjen either. I say we try to avoid injuring as many Ryjenians as possible, and if we can, bring them back to the side of good. Of Archengard." I looked at Anders. "You said they hate the sun, right? It's depleting their water, spoiling their food . . . This is a dying land. So we use the Heart to heal it. We stabilize the climate. Maybe even build a bond between them and the Brotherhood—"

"Have you lost your mind?" Murta asked. "You think people that side with the Jackals will listen to us? You think Ignis-less people coveting a Talisman will listen to us?"

"If we promise to help them, then yeah, I think they will. And Anders said they don't work with the Noda, right? They're working as separate entities."

Murta continued to protest, but when I looked at Anders, expecting the same, I only found the mercenary deep in thought.

"I suppose you expect us to assist in this," he said.

I shrugged. "Only if you're comfortable. Could always do it on our own."

Anders laughed, but his face was dead serious. "And I suppose you've forgotten that we aren't Navs. We're Government-bought mercs. I thought Carbonek didn't choose sides."

"We're not choosing to align ourselves with the Government. We're siding with Archengard." I cocked my head toward the tent flap, where I knew ten or so eyes watched curiously. "Now it's your turn."

"You know that a company of organized mercs haven't aligned themselves with the Brotherhood since the early days of the War, right?"

I nodded. "When Mathias was captured in the Black Cells by the Noda, the Leviathan enlisted mercs to help break him out. 'Twas a time when the majority of the mercs in the world were enlisted by the Noda, too. They only agreed to help the Brotherhood because whereas Mathias was respected by all mercs, the Leviathan was *admired.* He symbolized everything they could *never* be: free, fair . . . and fearless."

The candlelight twinkled in Anders's eyes. "So we're rescuing Mathias?"

"If that's the story you'd rather go with."

"I thought the story was that all the mercs died rescuing him."

I elbowed one of the spying mercs through the fabric of the tent in what I'd assumed had been his shoulder, but it was his skull. He disappeared with a curse.

"If we play our cards right," I said, "no mercs have to die here. In fact, not a single drop of blood needs be shed at all."

Though Anders had begun to nod, Murta slid deeper and deeper into the shadows until it swallowed him whole. Until not even the gold swimming in his eyes was visible.

CHAPTER 61

Enoch

I thrust my face beneath the water. Though the rest of the camp was in disarray, the quarters we'd been granted by Anders were located in a wooden bath house rather than a tent. There were hot springs too, which meant hot water.

In the Light Isles, showers or swims in the Grand Sea had been my rechargers, moments of bliss before departing for another isle to fight a monster or box an opponent. I always made sure to step in some form of water and cleanse myself. It helped me think.

I pressed my head against the wooden wall. Threads of water streamed down through my tangled hair, tracing the white sun carved into my back. I flinched briefly at the memory of fire but felt it extinguished when I heard my squadmates rustling around.

Jezna was always on the move, pacing between the showers and the quarters the mercs had given us. Prince soaked in the bath and every few seconds would sigh hysterically, as though the warmth was too pleasant to be enjoyed in silence. And far off in Murta's room, I heard low thumping followed by patterned grunts of exhaustion. He was working out again.

My relaxed expression tightened, and I began to scrub the remnants of dried blood from my face. Blood from where the Ignis hunters had tried to reconfigure my face. From where Lucian's fingers had dug into my neck.

It was terrifying having to pretend that we were a confirmed squad. If the Brotherhood ever got their hands on us before we got the Heart, we'd likely never set foot in Carbonek again. But that just made finding it all the more important. Finding the Heart was our passage back into the Brotherhood. It was the only way to show Kaleo that we were worthy.

I closed my eyes. Now that there were four of us, it was time to take what I'd learned and apply it. I couldn't cave in like I had against Lucian. I couldn't let myself be outfought, like I had against the Ignis hunters. I'd be solely responsible for whether or not my squad succeeded. That was the duty of a Charger.

And after that, we'd have a choice to make. I still didn't know the details of how the Heart worked or how one used it, but once we had it, we'd have all the eyes of Archengard on us. There'd be no time to dawdle with choices.

It needed to go back to Carbonek—that was a given—but Anders had told me of the state that the city was in. A country with no technology, no resources, and no hope. How could the Brotherhood turn away from something like this? The Government at least seemed to take Carbonek's opinion into account; that much was clear from Veres's meeting with Kaleo. If the Government was set on stripping Ryjen's resources—forcing mercenaries to fight for them—then the Brotherhood had to intervene.

You know, those decisions would actually apply to you, I reminded myself, stepping out of the shower and beginning to dry off with a linen cloth. *If you were a real Navigator.*

I dozed off as I redressed. After popping the collar of my green dress shirt and throwing the tie over it, I stepped out of the showers in search of a mirror and ran into Murta.

He wore only dress pants; the rest of him was flushed a fierce crimson. He'd worked out so hard that when his breathing hissed out, it was short and rapid, and his necklace dripped sweat down the planes of his chest. When he saw me, something in his face flinched.

I scrambled to escape the moment. "Er, I can't find a bloody mirror. You mind helping me tie my tie?"

I felt my eyes widen. *Talk about digging myself deeper . . .* Murta appeared just as shocked.

"I—I . . ." I stammered.

"You need someone else to tie it?" He sounded disgusted.

"Sometimes Jezna or Prince help," I muttered.

But then: "You never asked me?"

"I'm asking now."

Murta stepped close, making my heart flip. As his hands fell upon the ends of the tie and measured them out to equal lengths, he began to work. I watched quietly as he wound it into a perfect double knot, and when he moved to adjust my collar, I bowed my head to make it easier for him—and to avoid his eyes.

"Lift your chin."

Murta's voice was so close it almost made me jump, and when I obeyed, our eyes locked.

He's gorgeous.

I lost track of how long we remained there.

I couldn't pull myself away, couldn't blink. I felt completely magnetized. Like when I'd looked at Loc's crystal, only so much more natural. I felt myself drawn in, felt something shoving me one way instead of another, but it was a good kind of shoving. This time, I wanted to be drawn in. I *wanted—*

His hands paused, almost touching my neck, face inches from mine. Then he flattened my collar around the tie and took a rapid step backward, darkness flooding his face in tides.

Before I could fish the words out to thank him, he'd already disappeared into the showers, leaving me in breathless purgatory.

CHAPTER 62

Murta

The walls of Ryjen grew until they were on top of us. Enoch had wanted us to walk spread out, slowly, so they knew we meant no harm, but I walked as fast as possible.

This was all foolishness. Approaching the city in full view and knocking on the front door? The Jackals were inside, and Enoch thought sauntering up to the entrance asking to be let in would work?

I'd asked—ordered—Anders to have his mercs hidden in the trenches outside their camp with Governmental cannons on standby in case what I suspected would happen happened. Enoch had seen me getting them in position and scowled. I'd scowled back.

"That's not the Navigator way."

"Fuck the Navigator way."

"You don't remember how we saved Carbonek from Lucian?"

"I remember the Karnocolix going up in smoke. I remember one of the Talismans being lost forever. If you think I'll see that happen to the Sacred Heart, then you're out of your *maldito* mind."

"You don't trust me?"

"Trust is for the weak. Ask Kaleo about it."

"You trust Anders. You trusted that Biorn bloke. Why not me?"

I thought about that as we came to a stop in the sand, as I saw orange-armored Ryjenians holding Nodan Aestus weapons emerge from the gate, the open sandstone windows etched into the sides and the top of the walls. I repeated the question ten times over as I tapped into Ignis, heard the shouts of the Ryjenians, and lifted a black claw to the sky to give the signal for Anders to launch the attack . . .

Enoch stepped forward so that he was between us, arms outstretched in a near identical pose to the one he'd taken against Nothomathos and Kanbrik.

"STOP!"

Enoch's command rang across the desert. I felt it ring through my body, as though the words had become a fist that'd slammed into my chest. I felt them ignite something in me—a warmth I'd never felt before—and I calmed. And all around me, from Jezna and Prince to the poised Ryjenians, it looked like everyone felt a similar way, too.

"We aren't here to fight," Enoch said, facing the wall. "We aren't with the Government. We aren't with the Noda either." He paused. "You know by our clothes and powers who we are. We haven't come to take anything from you, only give. We're the Navigational Brotherhood."

Voices ran amok over the wall. There were at least a hundred armed Ryjenians in total, all glaring at us through the barrels of their Nodan weapons, all looking as angry as the last.

Then the weapons began to lower. Snarls became whispers. Glares became confused, even emotional glances. And I felt myself release my hold on Ignis.

Out of the group of Ryjenians located behind the gates I saw one step forward, sifting through the group to stand before us. He had the same caramel skin and dark eyes of everyone behind him, but his hair, rather than deep black, was a scalding orange. It looked dyed, and the thin armor he wore was the only armor fixed with a black cape. A hush fell across the wall.

"Navigators," the man said. Unlike the soldiers around him, he didn't carry a weapon. Maybe it was just from Enoch's spell, but maybe it was just him, too. "We've prayed for your arrival many a moonless morning. And now, you are here. But you are too late. The enemy is within, and they promise us healing."

"They won't give you it," Enoch said. "I guarantee you."

"Perhaps. The Government has sought to seize this city since the Shaded Days. But where have you been?"

I saw Enoch clench his fists and felt those same fists clench around my soul. "Holding back the shadow," he said. "Aiding as many people as we can. And I'm sorry that we're late. But we're here now." Enoch paused. "We're here to find the Sacred Heart."

Many Ryjenians tried to play it off like they didn't know what he was talking about, but the shock was written across all their faces.

The weaponless man sighed. "You don't know what guards it. We don't even know. Many have gone after it, delving deep into the Serrated Keep's heart, but none have returned. You think our land would be in this state if we had it? Used by the Government and seized by the Noda?"

"We'll succeed where everyone else failed," Enoch swore. "We'll get the Heart, then after that, the Brotherhood will use it to heal Ryjen. Because we're Navigators you can trust."

With those words, Enoch's spell broke around me. I tapped into Ignis, struggling against the lines of green energy that bound me—bound *all* of us surrounding him—and finally pried myself free. I saw Enoch visibly falter, but he maintained hold of everyone else. They were too focused on him and the green Ignis spiraling through his eyes and body.

I saw what he was doing and I despised it. He thought forcefully connecting with these people would get them to connect with him, but it wouldn't. No matter how much he swayed their spirits, they were still their own.

He's no better than the Jackals. Playing with fire and people.

"I am the sultan of Ryjen," the weaponless man finally said. "The Serrated Keep has been my home since birth, passed down to me by my father. I've seen the entrance to Jâhic. I've heard the stories. I've sent men into the abyss myself and heard their screams."

He opened his eyes, but I noticed that they didn't spin with the mist of the Jackals' crystal. They didn't spin at all. Just . . . gleamed. Enoch's green flame burned in all of their eyes, but it wasn't forced into them; it was reflected.

"If you can indeed succeed where Ryjenians have failed," the sultan said, "then you will forever have our city's allegiance."

"We will," Enoch said. "But on the agreement of two things."

"I'm listening."

"First: you end all alliances with the Noda and the Jackals."

More whispers. "There are no Jackals here," the sultan said. "That I can assure you." *He's lying.* "We would never side with such dark forces. And the second?"

I saw Enoch wet his lips, felt the green strings of energy tighten, and saw him glance back at the camp. "We're not here alone. And though I trust you and your people, I want guaranteed protection for me and my squad. And I also want the two of you to know that you're fighting for the same things. You're all on the same side." He gestured for the mercs to step out of the trenches.

I spun, watching heads pop up. Anders became the first one to stand, brushing sand from his black-blond hair and shyly gesturing for his men to follow. At first, none of the heads moved. Some even hid away again. Then the tattooed merc that had stood guard at the camp entrance stood, cracking his knuckles and spitting. Heads all around gawked up at him, then a few shook their heads in disbelief and followed.

They followed Anders toward us, toward Ryjen. A city that had spilled their blood. *Unbelievable.*

I looked back toward the sandstone. Similar reactions were written throughout the Ryjenians. There was definitely discontent—the sultan in particular looked unnerved—but then the iron gates began to shift, the boundary between merc and Ryjenian opening steadily until it was wide open.

My lips parted as Anders passed, but no words came out. I watched him walk past Enoch, then toward the sultan, that same bravado I'd once admired about him shining through.

"Howdy." He extended a hand, smiling sadly. "I'm Anders. Sorry about the mess on your front lawn . . . Always been a dream of mine to meet royalty, actually."

The sultan, though startled at first by Anders's uprightness, looked down at his hand before slowly accepting it with his own. "It's a pleasure, Anders. And I'm sorry our people have shed so much of your blood."

"I—" Anders choked. "I'm sorry, too."

CHAPTER 63

Murta

The Arrows of Eclipse hummed as we passed them, our host surrounded by Ryjenians so as not to attract the attention of the possibly watching Noda. That was nonsense. I'd already searched this area seventeen different times. Ryjen was a city carved completely out of sandstone, to the point that everything was built from the same whole; everything except the Serrated Keep. Its black-and-orange metal rose out of the sand like the Arrows adorning it, and the steps we had to take to reach it revealed all the city around us.

I suspected the Ryjenians meant to flank us like prisoners, because the Noda were anywhere but here. From our spot on the stairs, I could see Nodan war machines decorating a camp positioned just a little outside the main body of the city. A camp that surrounded a golden plateau that now resembled a crater. Drilling machines had been installed all around it and were hard at work, their long necks reaching into the darkness.

I squinted for any sign of Ignis, maybe a pink tentacle or flash of black crystal, but returned empty-handed. And the Ryjenians behind me were muttering disgustedly about my constant stopping and starting.

"Sháedardín," I heard them say. It flew all around me. They were more wary around me than around the men who'd attacked them for months.

I watched Anders exchange friendly words with the sultan at the head of the group, overseen by Enoch in the center, and felt fury build in me. And when I felt the Other stir in response, I did nothing to calm it. I let it writhe.

I was tired of the War and mercenaries dying for nothing, but this was an entirely new field. This involved the Jackals and the Talismans. Blood had to be shed. If there was ever a time to fight, that time was now. And Enoch was trying to heal wounds that would never close.

Didn't he learn from Nothomathos and Kanbrik? Didn't he learn from Aren's Steeple?

The front gates of the keep opened for us, revealing an orange-and-black-tiled interior. I saw traces of metal etched into the sandstone columns—traces that reminded me of the jungle temple I'd entered with four other mercs seeking a map. Only, if the Shrouded Man I'd met could be believed, far greater than a mere map awaited us here.

On our way out of the camp, I'd met Biorn again, the bandaged merc staring up at the sky rather than the city we were about to attempt to infiltrate. I'd asked if he planned to join us. Biorn had answered in that voice of a thousand voices once more.

"You have your flames, Shadarian. And that is all you need."

We passed arch after arch, open to rooms full of thin, sickly looking people. They looked starved. Hopeless. In need of a savior.

"But you must choose a side."

"No one ever lets me choose," I'd replied. "That's the thing. Everyone's always trying to manipulate me."

I saw Enoch watching the Ryjenians, looking more and more like Kaleo with each passing hour. Straying further and further from the reckless abandonment and forever-fighting spirit I'd grown to . . . respect about him. This Enoch was manipulative. This Enoch thought peace was the only option.

"True," Biorn had said, and in front of my eyes, immovable double doors made of orange brick appeared, their center carved into a black heart among a patch of tangled vines. "But the chains are only chains because you think they are. Your flames can shatter them."

"How? What do you see in me?"

The sultan brought us to a halt before the doors, then, with a simple glance, stepped back so ten of his armored men could step forward. They began to push.

"Archengard's Heart. It sleeps within, sealed away in the keep, then fought over until all lay dead. Their servants inherited the land. The descendants of their servants became the Ryjenians, and for centuries, they have kept it safe.

"But there was another. An Ignis user turned his back on the shade, right when the light needed him most . . . Don't you see? Jâhic can be reached. And the Heart is not just the dark controller all make it out to be: it can also craft life."

A crack appeared in the doors. The Ryjenians hissed with exhaustion, veins bulging. The sultan remained motionless, hands clenched behind his back. Enoch swayed next to him as the crack widened, revealing orange-gold light—torches fixed to the walls of a circular chamber.

"You seek Archengard's Heart, El Cazador de Sombra?"

The Ryjenians pushed the doors until they were wide open, until the farthest on each side removed their spears and slid them into small holes in the floor.

"Then Night and Day must find a way."

The soldiers immediately formed single-file lines to the entrance as the doors swung back toward the set spears and stayed there. But I was too busy gazing beyond the doors at what awaited us, hearing Biorn's final words before starting his journey across the desert. "And I swear, I'll see you at the rainbow's end, Navigator."

A gaping hole lay in the center of the chamber, at least twenty feet across. I entered even before the sultan and slowly stalked to the edge. When I looked down, I felt my eyes narrow. There was no bottom in sight.

The sultan, Prince, Jezna, and Enoch crept to the edge as well, though Enoch kept sneaking glances over at me, as if to get my attention. I ignored him.

Prince stared at the hole long and hard. "Oh."

Jezna looked up at the sultan. "How are we supposed to get down there?"

"Excellent question." The sultan tore away from the hole with a shiver and gestured at the sides of the doors. Several giant rolls of chain had been set into the walls and were connected to a number of leather harnesses that lay on the floor.

"These are chain-based descenders," he said. "They've been measured out perfectly to get you to the bottom. After that, you'll slip out of them and be on your own. Easier said than done."

"And when we're ready to return?"

"You shall reel yourselves up."

Prince headed for the doors. "I'm out. Peace." But Jezna blocked him.

I'd already picked up a harness and began to slip it on. Annoyingly, Enoch moved over and began to put on the harness next to mine.

Jezna dragged Prince over to the other side and held up her harness for the Ryjenians to see. It looked incredibly small compared to her. "Do you perhaps have an extra large?"

"I ain't going!" Prince said, arms swinging about. "Put me down, ya metal mucus!"

The Ryjenians hurried off into a side chamber to find Jezna another harness, leaving us all to get situated. Enoch struggled with the complicated buckling of the harness and turned toward me. I pretended I was still messing with my own.

Good, a dark voice squeezed out from between the wet crevices of my brain, then Anders was in front of me.

I knew I'd failed to keep the surprise from my face.

"Good, er, luck," he said. "I guess. If Navigators even need it."

"I told you. I'm not—"

"You might not think so, but I highly doubt anyone other than one could find the Sacred Heart. If it, you know, exists."

"It does."

Anders nodded. "Then find it. We'll be here. In case anything goes down."

I couldn't shake away my rage that easily. "How?" I hissed under my breath. "How can you just forget everything? The War, all the mercs that died—"

"They were my men. But that's exactly why I'm so in favor of peace. That blond bloke's right. We're both being used. We've both got a lot more in common than I thought." He hesitated. "And sometimes, Murta, you gotta just let things go."

My head spun. Anders's words collided with Biorn's, Enoch's, Kaleo's, and the dark voices until I was falling down the pit into the black. Until memories packed on top of memories hurtled so fast around me that the only way to disperse them was to grip Anders by the shoulder and say, "*Never.*"

I spun back toward the pit, fidgeting with the trigger system attached to the front of the harness. Then I headed for the edge.

"Wait!" Prince said. "How do you work these things?!"

Enoch held the trigger on his vest so his chains slackened and walked over to Prince to show him how it operated. His roll unwound noisily, loosening more chain as he crossed the chamber.

"How far down is it?" I asked.

"A mile and a half exactly," the sultan said. "The length of the passages, on the other hand, I don't know."

"Let's find out."

Before I could jump, Enoch materialized at my side, eyes swimming with determination, bruised face etched with nervousness. And rejection.

You have your Flames, Shadarian.

Biorn was right. Peace had only ever lied to me. Light had only ever burned me. I was a shadedrake. Dragons didn't burn; they did the burning.

"*Ra'lenv Ro'drac*," the sultan said as I took the first step over the edge and fixed my footing so I teetered backwards, so I saw Anders and the mercenaries behind him watching me with hollow, disappointed expressions.

Enoch followed, fingers shaking around his trigger and letting too much chain go. He quickly reversed the trigger, activating the descender's pulling technique before he could plunge into the abyss and righting himself with a nervous frown.

Shaking my head, I kicked off the sandstone, the Serrated Keep disappearing as I dove into the darkness. That was where I thrived anyway.

CHAPTER 64

Enoch

Daring to take the first step was the hardest part. But once we were scaling the rock face backwards, things grew less stressful. I got the hang of the harness's descending mechanism and perfected my backwards glide in minutes. Though Prince flew all over the place and Jezna's chains were constantly creaking, the experience was nowhere near as bad as I'd expected. It helped not to look up or down.

I did both anyway.

Above, the light from the keep steadily disappeared, widening the gap between us and safety, but below, the abyss was a black hole. Murta raced into it faster and deeper than everyone. In fact, he frequently pushed off the wall completely, riding the descender down.

What does he think he needs to prove? I thought, watching his chain speed downward at a quickening pace. *We all know how fearless he is.*

"Stars . . ." Jezna swore, glancing upward. I reluctantly followed her gaze and felt my stomach drop out. The opening had become a pinprick.

Keeping my right hand secured on the trigger, I lit my left fist with Ignis. Emerald light flooded the darkness, though now Murta was completely out of view, lost in the darkness below. And his chain kept on sprinting.

"Thanks." Jezna shuddered.

I nodded silently and pressed the pace. We needed to catch up to Murta. The Shield shouldn't be that far from the Charger.

But now that I pondered it, that was probably what Murta wanted. Was he really that mad that I'd found a way to forge peace between the mercs and Ryjenians? I figured that after all that had happened to him during the War, he'd be overjoyed. I'd forged peace for him.

Just when I'd thought we'd started to get closer . . .

Prince moaned with frustration when I began clicking my trigger faster.

"Getting closer, Prince," I promised.

"Don't lie to me, Noc," he said through clenched teeth. "We just freaking started . . . And what's Scarfy doing?"

"Yes, I'd very much like to know that, too," Jezna said.

"He's just scouting ahead," I assured them. "Being a right good Shield. Making sure we're extra safe."

Murta's chain noisily increased in speed.

"*Definitely*," Prince said.

Jezna turned toward me. "Now isn't the time for recklessness. I don't know what happened between you two, but you need to resolve it."

"I dunno what I even did!" I said. "How do you ever know with him, honestly?"

"I'm not blaming you, necessarily. Though you did do some things with Ignis that may have upset him."

I thought back to our arrival at Ryjen and my big speech. I hadn't felt myself tap into Ignis. I'd just started talking, desperately willing for their spirits to connect . . . and before I knew it, that dream had become a reality. I hadn't possessed anyone—I was certain of that—just tugged on the right strings here and there. I'd brushed aside their hate and revealed an alternative . . .

But that was exactly what Murta was afraid of. And after Aren's Steeple?

I wanted to beat myself up. *I'm such a stupid bugger.*

I stared at my flaming fist, looked over at Murta's sliding chain, then down into the darkness. "Can you keep Ignis up here?"

Jezna extended her free hand and created a sphere of aqua light.

When I pressed and held the trigger, my chain went limp. I flew down after Murta, sparks of Ignis escaping off of my fist and racing upward. Jezna's aqua Ignis began to dim the deeper I dove in pursuit.

There was a moment of cold silence in the pit where I thought I was catching up to him, then his chain stopped.

"Murta!"

Black rock sprang into view so suddenly that I almost thought it was a trick of the darkness. But when the darkness remained and the rock continued to race upward, I yelped and released my hold on the trigger. The chain went taut, jerking me to a halt two feet from the ground. Ignis went out as I dangled, eyes searching the shadows. Murta already stood up against the wall, harness discarded and eyes glowing gold.

I saluted uneasily, then listened as the sound of Jezna's and Prince's chains echoed above.

"Hold on!" I shouted up at them. "Watch out for—"

Prince screeched just before the two of them let go of their triggers and stopped four feet above me. After swatting Prince's shoe away, I tapped the trigger twice. My feet touched solid, uneven ground.

"'Twas a pleasant arrival," I said, dusting myself off.

Murta lit a flame between his claws without so much as a glance in my direction and gazed out over the area with Ignis-infused eyes. I stripped off my harness solemnly and did the same, igniting both fists to create more light. I should limit the jokes.

We'd arrived in Jâhic.

Alight with green and gold Ignis, we were in a wide cave about the same size as the one Murta and I had stayed in on Aren's Steeple. The only difference was that the ceiling was taller. And smoother compared to the disjointed floor. Almost too smooth.

"We're trapped," Prince panicked. "The sultan tricked us. He's gonna cut the chains and trap us down here for all—"

"*Cállate*," Murta said. He looked as though he were straining his ears. Even with Ignis coursing through me, I barely heard or saw a thing.

"What is it?"

Murta began to walk toward the center of the cave. I followed closely. Whatever animosity he felt toward me could be put on hold until we had the Heart. If it was shame and self-loathing he felt toward everything that had happened on Aren's Steeple, I'd show him that that was in the past. And that he could go wank itself.

The first step I took following him planted me in a puddle. I winced when the water soaked through my shoe in seconds, but Murta stepped in one directly after, expanding its reach. When a faint red aura began to emit from it, we paused.

The strange illumination revealed that the puddle was more of a small pond. It only went down a foot in depth, but it took up the entire back side of the cave and continued to brighten until the murky blackness looked more like glowing blood.

"Ignis?" Prince asked.

Murta waded deeper. And when the strange crimson energy reached its full brightness, it illuminated the far corners of the cave.

Cavernous holes had been drilled into the walls like great gaping wounds, forming a labyrinth of black tunnels that disappeared around curved corners and bends.

I slowly lifted my fists out in front of me, throwing green light into the red. The holes in the rock were passages all right. They ran *deep*.

"A maze," I said.

Murta pointed at the hole directly in front of us. "But there's one main path."

Unlike the other jagged holes, the one he'd pointed out was far smoother. Its archway looked vaguely similar to those within the Serrated Keep. Whereas the other holes looked dug, the main hole looked designed.

Prince voiced my thoughts. "So what are all the others for?"

A shiver ran through us even before Jezna spoke up. "Not passageways." She stepped into the glowing water and turned about the cavern. "Burrows."

Among the cold churning of water we waded through, a deeper sound came rattling out of one cave, then carried off into another until it was all around us. What started out as a hum turned sour near the end, converting into an animalistic rumble.

I felt my bones freeze in my body then jitter in the silence that followed.

Silence that was only broken when Prince emitted a noise that sounded something like, "Eeep."

"Back to back," Murta said.

Jezna was the first one to listen. I followed dizzily, putting my back to her and Murta. Prince attached himself to Jezna's side, the Aestus cannon humming in his hands.

We waited in the darkness, Ignis and Aestus burning around us. My emerald collided with Murta's gold, Jezna's aqua, Prince's magenta, and the puddle's red to construct a hazy rainbow. It sent ripples of energy shimmering across the burrows, making the darkened crevices shift about like thick curtains.

The rumble came again, closer. A sickening rattle echoed after it before disappearing off into the distance. Murta began to slowly turn our circle, taking in each of the burrows one by one while brightening his flames. I brightened mine and began to turn, too. Prince dug in his heels but was nudged by Jezna.

"Can someone *please* tell me what that is?" he asked.

"Something big," I said. "Something close."

"No *shit*, Noc!"

"Judging by the size of the sound and burrows," Jezna said, nurturing her ball of aqua fire so that it grew to be twice its size, "I can narrow it down to at least fifty different species. Noc, you're a professional when it comes to fighting . . . monsters. Perhaps you can identify—"

"It's a vortexurn," Murta said.

Jezna sucked in a terrified breath.

My toes curled. "Bollocks."

"A vorte-what?" Prince asked.

"Giant carnivorous worms that are only native to Narthes," Jezna said. "It's impossible for one to be here right now." She glanced over her shoulder at Murta. "Are you absolutely certain?"

Murta's silence implied he was.

Prince jerked his head back toward me. "You've fought one, right? Ripped it in half and beat it over the head with its ass? During your swashbuckling days?"

"There weren't many places for them to burrow in the Light Isles. And I . . . er, kind of avoided them if I saw them listed in a job description."

The rattling started up again, sweeping through the hole closest to Jezna, then carrying over into those closest to me before fading again.

"Can we use the Other?!" Prince asked.

"He'd bring the whole keep down on top of us," I said. "We'd be crushed."

"It would kill you before the rocks could," Murta growled.

I closed my eyes and began trying to pinpoint the spirit that belonged to the sound. The darkness of the burrows was endless and the vortexurn—if indeed it was—never stopped moving. I had to scrunch my face to keep up. The presence was there, but its spirit looked more like a pitch-black flame.

That didn't stop me.

"Should I try possessing it?"

Murta whirled, finally looking at me for once. "The Other?"

"No! The, er, vortexurn."

Murta spun back to the burrows. "Their brains are built like granite. Like a dragon, their minds are impenetrable."

"But—"

"No."

I ground my teeth. "All right. We have a plan B, perhaps?"

"I assumed you had one," Murta said.

"I assumed you did."

"You're the Charger, aren't you? Charge us out of here."

I felt my face heat up. "I'm trying. Maybe if I received some actual cooperation from my Shield, I'd be able to."

"No more 'immortal' nonsense?"

I turned completely around rather than continue to speak over my shoulder. "It's not nonsense. It's what saved me up on Aren's Steeple. It's what helped us rescue you. It's what almost helped me possess the Other and finally get through to—"

"You did *nothing*. All you did was put yourself in greater danger. Just like now. Not everything can be solved by making peace. You can't connect with everything."

The rattling was on top of us now. Jagged shifting—skin sliding against stone—blared against my ears. I ignored it.

"I never said I could," I shouted, images of Olders cackling, Kanbrik Elders shouting, and Loc crying converging around me. "Sometimes you have to fight. I've spent my entire life fighting. But . . . if there's a possibility of making peace, why wouldn't I take it? That's what a Navigator would—"

"We're *not* Navigators."

"YES, WE ARE!"

"Halt this nonsense, both of you!" Jezna said, her aqua sphere growing into a broadsword made of water.

"Then show me!" Murta said. "Get us out of here!"

I licked my lips, eyes flicking about the cave. Part of Murta was right. The last two times I'd possessed a monster hadn't gone well. And the rattling had risen to a ferocious metallic clanking.

Prince gripped his cannon in both hands, sweat glistening from them. Jezna's sword pierced the air, throwing particles of water down into the red puddle. Murta's gold fire raged between his claws, the black ice of his pupils reminding me of the draconic eyes that had almost feasted upon me—

I focused on the fire in my fists, poured them into my spirit, then closed my eyes again.

Where there had once been absolute darkness there was now a snarling black fire spirit the size of a boulder hurtling toward us. There wasn't enough time to reach out and find the pathways. Using Green Fire Fist was out of the question. We barely had time to duck.

"DOWN!" I threw my shoulders into Murta's stomach, wrapping one arm around Prince's neck and using the other to clothesline Jezna.

The tree-trunk-sized body barreled over our heads, charging out of the topmost burrow then escaping through one of the bottom ones across from it. The vortexurn's body was steel gray and made up of overlapping metallic plates, like armor. Its top and bottom portions sat on two different swivels—a perk of its incredibly rare bone-structure—which enabled it to spin in two different directions as it charged. If I hadn't forced everyone down when I did, its jaws would've decapitated us.

The worm thundered overhead for what felt like forever, its scales getting caught along the burrow entryways and creating explosive crackling sounds. I counted how many seconds it took before its end finally emerged to get a feel for how large it was. Ducking extra low and flattening myself to the water so it soaked through my vest and shirt, I watched the spiked tail hurtle out of the burrow then disappear down the opposite one. The rattling faded.

Fifteen seconds.

I leapt to my feet, but Murta beat me. He looked unhinged.

"What're we standing around for?!" Prince scrambled to his feet. "Let's take the main path and get the hell outta here!"

"The burrows run through the main path," Murta said. "If the vortexurn wanted to, it could just follow us. Or bring down the ceiling. We have to fight it."

I clenched my fists. "Let me try to get through to it."

"Shut up."

"How're we supposed to kill that thing?" Prince asked.

"We don't," Murta said. "Only deep incapacitation."

I looked at him, shock turning into fondness. "Aye. The Code."

"I'm not doing it because of the Code," he snarled. "We're not Navigators. Never were. We have to incapacitate it because—"

"Vortexurn plates prevent them from being killed," Jezna finished, the glowing water trickling off her shoulders as she rose to her feet. "Their bodies are like dragon scales. We'd be chipping at them for years."

"Then how do we incapacitate it?!" Prince asked. "My guns could barely tickle it!"

"Distraction," Murta said. "It's like a crimson bull from the Bone Meadows just east of Vaief Fields. They charge at the first thing they see. Once the vortexurn spots something, it dives in an attempt to either swallow its prey whole or decapitate it with its spiked jaw."

"Bulls don't do *that*!"

"Can't say I know how to knock one out either." I felt around the darkness of my mind for the vortexurn's spirit again. It was far off, racing around the maze of burrows it had created but could reroute toward us at a moment's notice. It was toying with us.

"Correct me if I'm wrong, Jezna," Murta suddenly said, like asking for a second opinion caused him physical harm, "but they're attracted to Ignis."

"They are," Jezna said.

"Then someone has to be matador. Looks like you lucked out, Junior. Whoever's the matador will stand in front of the tunnel the vortexurn is coming out of, then jump out of the way at the last moment. Everyone else: Start launching as much Ignis—or Aestus—at it as possible."

I nodded. "I can get a feel for which tunnel it'll come from if I concentrate."

Murta ignored me. "I'll take the left side. Jezna, you take middle back . . . Swash, you take right. Junior, stand up against the wall and get ready to shoot."

"Name's not Junior," Prince said under his breath, wading through the water to the side of the cave least covered in burrows.

"Should I try to flood the passages?" Jezna asked.

"Water won't affect them," Murta said. "Only fire. So I'll be doing most of the work."

Jezna bowed her head, conjuring her sword once more.

The vortexurn's rumble came so suddenly Prince almost dropped his cannon.

We quieted. I tapped into Ignis, letting the energy turn my outline green. I uneasily stepped up to my designated burrow and peered down the menacing hole. I nervously retightened my bandana and began to wring water from it, never tearing my glowing eyes away from the passage.

Rattling echoed far off, but I located the vortexurn's spirit just in case.

Twenty feet away from me.

I threw myself out of the way with a yell as the worm knifed out of the burrow.

The cave erupted in a fireworks display. Murta threw balls of fire at the twisting armored body, Prince emptied his cannon, and Jezna swung her sword in upward arcs. The madness went on for ten seconds before halting with the worm's disappearance down the opposite burrow. In the aftermath, a pained scream reverberated off the cave walls.

"Bueno," Murta said. "Just like that."

I sprang to my feet. It was refreshing to hear Murta compliment us. Despite the direness of the situation, the mood of the cave lightened noticeably.

"You okay, Noc?" Prince asked.

"Aye." I reloaded my fists and faced my burrow. "Right as rain. Also just as wet."

Ten seconds passed before I found the vortexurn again. Though it moved so fast that I almost missed it, I had just enough time to shout, "It's coming to you, Jezna!"

Jezna flung herself away from her hole as Murta and Prince resumed the barrage.

I picked up a jagged rock and locked onto the vortexurn's spirit while pushing pieces of my own spirit down into my fist. Just like how I'd punched the cannonball, I Green Fire Fisted the rock so it became a blazing comet and connected with the vortexurn's drilling underside. The beast cried again before escaping back beneath the surface.

Prince whooped. "You know, I could really get the hang of—"

My spirit flared. "JEZNA, WATCH—"

Jezna had been in the process of standing when the vortexurn blasted back through the same hole. Thankfully, her Ignis was faster. The aqua energy wrapped around her legs and boots in slippery cocoons and moved her out of the way. Jezna scarily slammed chest first into the opposite wall, but at least the creature had missed her.

Prince panicked when the vortexurn dove into the hole closest to him, and fumbled with his weapon. He didn't get a single shot off. Murta threw as many fireballs as he could, but when I went to punch another rock, I missed. The emerald comet streaked past Prince and stuck to the wall directly behind him.

"Watch it!" he said, matting his hair for green sparks.

I cursed. "Apologies! Y'all right, Jezna?"

Jezna clutched her chest like she was out of breath but had Ignis surrounding her. "I shall be fine. Where did it go?"

Murta turned about the cave in cautious circles. "Down the burrow to the right of Junior. Keep Ignis flowing and don't—"

The black fire tugged on my spirit again. I fearfully whipped my head around to look at Prince: fidgeting with his cannon and silhouetted directly in front of the same burrow the vortexurn had disappeared down. My eyes widened.

It was impossible, yet it was happening.

"DODGE, PRINCE!"

Throwing himself to the side, Prince's backpack was nicked only slightly by the vortexurn, but it was enough to send him spiraling out of control. He crashed face-first into the puddle.

Not only had the worm come back out of the same burrow and managed to almost get a hold of one of us, it had also gone after the only Ignis-less member of our squad. It was adapting remarkably fast, using trial and error . . .

Like a Navigator.

I didn't know why that was the first thing that popped into my head, but Murta was ready for it. This time, instead of just throwing fireballs, he jumped up into the air and raked his claws, aiming for the skin between the plates. Despite her initial tiredness, Jezna swung her water-sword at its head, but the vortexurn was still too fast. I picked up two stones this time, latched onto the worm's spirit and launched both items behind the force of one of my finest uppercuts. But it was gone again in a shorter time than before and my flaming stones almost took Murta's head off.

"Are you trying to do the damned thing's job for it?" he yelled.

The vortexurn erupted out of random burrows two more times. On the first trek, it almost ripped off Jezna's breastplate. On the second, Murta overshot completely. My flaming stones missed every time.

"Bloody hell!" I dug sweat out of my bandana with frustration. My patience had reached its boiling point.

"New plan!" Murta rose from the water, golden flames collecting around his shoulders.

"None have worked so far!" Prince said.

A scream introduced the vortexurn's next charge, this time from out of my tunnel. I didn't have enough time to dodge. Just flattened myself to the ground and held my breath under the water.

The beast tore through the air where I'd been, causing ferocious gusts of wind to nip at the back of my vest. When the wind disappeared and the air above me no longer rumbled, I emerged, turning toward Murta with green eyes. "That's it! I'm possessing—"

"Don't!" Murta's own Ignis flared with anger.

Ignoring him and boxing back the darkness, I seized the vortexurn's spirit between my fists and tracked it.

Its deranged path led directly toward Murta's tunnel.

I sprinted across the cave, throwing myself in front of him. If I could possess a Talisman, a rock, a Nightguard, and the Other for ten seconds, then I could possess a twisty worm. I had to. It was that or watch my squad die. This wasn't Serapharus anymore. I actually possessed the power to save lives.

"Immortal, I think," I said, glaring down the black fire spirit charging toward me. "Immortal, I—"

Gold energy slammed me into the puddle.

It was the same gold that had been there in the tidal wave of darkness that was the Other's mind. The same gold that had forcefully expelled me. The gold that refused my help.

I sat up in the water and stared.

Murta stood before the burrow at the center of a seething bonfire. Dark suit stained with dirt, face etched with stubborn defiance, he looked almost identical to Mathias Flint—the man who all of Archengard had once referred to as the Dauntless One.

Gazing down at me, body and soul ablaze, Murta was far from the boy who claimed to loathe the Brotherhood. Far from the Navigator he claimed he wasn't. In fact, this whole time, including now, he'd been . . .

Shielding me.

"Idiota," Murta said before being taken in the chest by the vortexurn. The creature and the Shadarian secured at its front dove back into the burrows and were gone in a blur of black.

CHAPTER 65

Murta

Jagged points and uneven bumps in the tunnels tore at me from every angle. The vortexurn's spiked jawline had me hooked by the pants, driving me along for its infernal ride. I had to latch my claws onto the top of its mouth to keep from being forcefully tossed into its throat.

In the pitch darkness of the burrows, it was impossible to see where we were going, what hit me, which way thc tunnels veered, or how close the vortexurn's jaws were from my face. But from the rank smell of decay and the snapping that skimmed my nose, I estimated pretty damn close.

A turn in the path slammed my skull against a jut in the ceiling. My brain spun. A wave of nausea flashed down my spine. With the urge to vomit came delusion. And with delusion came Shadarian rage.

As I was being scraped and scratched and attempted to be digested at a quickening rate in complete darkness, I was given remarkable time to think.

What had happened to me was obvious. A real Shadarian would've picked up on it eons ago. The vortexurn smashing me through its burrows while I clung helplessly for dear life was symbolic. I'd done this to myself.

The vortexurn roared in my face. Acidic mucus and goo shot out of its mouth, coating my upper body. It burned my skin, beginning to eat away at the fabric of my suit.

I closed my eyes to avoid the spray, but within, my mind was the calmest it had ever been. Even as I was thrown around the tunnels, my stomach fighting for superiority over the rest of my organs, a smile tugged at my lips.

My problems were so easily fixed. I was a fool for not seeing it sooner.

Not a fool. Just blinded.

I needed to stop thinking like a Navigator, stop trying to conform to a mold that others propagated, and start doing things how I did them.

Others weren't my equals; they were baggage. They were the reason I was being thrown through the tunnels.

So, a voice in the dark chided. *Figured it out, have you?*

This changes nothing, I told it. *I'll still kill all of you one day.*

One may speak words but never act on them . . . But do you understand now how much strength you've wasted?

Yes.

Then show me.

The vortexurn tried to pry its mouth wider. A full-grown one possessed twenty times the strength of a human in their jaw alone, but when I sank my claws in, it was unable to move.

Stunned, the worm almost halted its momentum, and when I felt it pause, I opened my eyes, opening Ignis.

Biorn said I have my flames, I thought. *And he's right. I do have my flames. They're all I've ever needed.*

My body became fire, brightening the passage and revealing the vortexurn's horrific eyeless face. The multiple layers of teeth that ringed the inside and out tried to snap together, but I pried them farther apart. So far apart that I heard skin tearing, tendons snapping. The tissue began to burn where my claws dug into its jaws.

I'm not a Navigator. I'm a merc. A Shadarian. A killer.

Right before the vortexurn forcefully pried its mouth open further to scream in agony, I welcomed the teeth, the pain, and the chasmic darkness.

The mouth was just like the Shadarian Pits, the snakes and spiders that escaped the slots in the walls. The force of the vortexurn was like the demonic creatures I'd waged war against out in the fields with nothing but Ignis and myself. And like every Shadarian before me, I'd conquered all . . .

Alone.

I dove inward and was swallowed whole.

Everything pressed down and burned at once, but a Shadarian didn't panic. I held on to Ignis, increasing its intensity until it burned the vortexurn's insides around me. I built up Ignis until fire sizzled out of every cell in my body, until the necklace turned ice cold. Until my shoulders were steaming, my throat crackling with sparks and my eyes threatening to splinter. I held and held, sucking Ignis in in tidal waves until there was nothing left.

But I held for more.

I don't need the Brotherhood.

And when I was beyond building up, beyond channeling Ignis and stranded in the Twilight Moment . . .

I don't need a squad. I don't need Enoch.

Only then did I let go.

I don't need anyone.

The vortexurn's body exploded around me. Bones, intestines, moldy flesh, and blackened iron plates flew outward, reduced to charred remnants. The bones shattered against the stone of the burrows. The intestines and flesh melted. The iron plates scattered.

And I landed on the floor of the burrow, smoke and pieces of gold fire wafting off of me.

My entire body felt damp. I was soaked through; my face had earned a number of scabs and light scars. My jacket had been dissolved completely, one of the sleeves of my dress shirt torn off. I was on the cusp of losing the other sleeve, and my eyes burned. Every tendon pounded in pain.

But it was a price I'd willingly paid. I'd conquered the obstacle. *Obliterated* it.

Wiping the filth from the gold bracelets along my right arm now on display for everyone, I controlled the pain with faint trickles of Ignis, just enough to keep me steady and begin the healing process. Glowing gold, I left the graveyard of gore behind.

It took me ten minutes to find my way back out of the burrows and into the cave. The vortexurn hadn't bothered taking me deeper into the tunnels, which looked like they went on forever below the keep. Instead, strangely, it had kept me close to the cave.

I frowned. From a strategy standpoint, it made no sense. It was as though it had been testing me, measuring my skills . . .

"Murta!"

I stepped out of the tunnel into the puddle. The red light was gone. Everything sat in its initial darkness, save the green and turquoise light emitting from the two Ignis users. Enoch immediately tramped toward me, and Jezna—suns, even Junior—looked relieved.

How could they be so content at a time like this? How could they feel such emotions when I was racing against the clock, against the Jackals?

Remove them from the equation. Go after the Heart yourself.

When Enoch finally saw my expression, he stopped. Ignis faded from his eyes in time with the smile that vanished from his lips.

I waded through the rest of the puddle in the direction of the main pathway, brushing away the wisps of flame that still clung to my shoulders. "You're welcome."

CHAPTER 66

Prince

Murta moved fast. Too fast for a short treasure hunter carrying a backpack that weighed over fifty pounds. He fled deeper down the hall until I lost sight of him completely.

But Enoch continued to rush after him. Calling his name and pleading. Even though it was clear as day that the Shadarian wanted nothing more to do with us, *still* Enoch pursued him.

Honestly, I would've rather just continued on without Murta and figured that our squad was far better off without him, but Enoch wouldn't let him outpace us.

"It makes no sense!" I told Jezna as we pounded down the passage. An aqua sphere glowed in her palm, providing much-needed light. The temple passages were getting dark, creepily so. "When's Noc gonna learn that we don't need this kook?"

"As much as I hate to admit it," Jezna said, "we do need him. A squad must have a Shield, and when Murta puts his mind to being a Shield, he's perfect. You've seen him and Noc work together. They're like Kaleo and Mathias. Back when Kaleo was the Leviathan."

"That's a little much, don't you think?" I cocked my head in the direction of our current situation. "I really doubt Mathias-freaking-Flint ever deserted his squad."

Jezna was silent for a moment. "If everything Enoch told us about what happened on Aren's Steeple is true, then Murta is an extremely tortured individual. His mind and spirit are battlefields. And we're just cannon fodder."

"That's refreshing. So we'll be torn to bits if he keeps this up?"

"Not if the battle is won."

"And how's that gonna happen?"

Jezna looked up ahead—at Enoch. "As long as he stays with us. And as long as we follow him and find the Heart."

I said nothing. I had zero aspirations to go up against another vortexurn, but it wasn't like I had much of a choice. As the only Ignis-less dude, I was kind of forced to follow. There was nothing wrong with that. Sure, I'd gotten good at seeing in the dark and using the light of my guns, but it was nothing like the light of Ignis. Following was in my genetic code. It was like Father had always said—

Jezna's flame disappeared. I stumbled around in the sudden darkness, pocketing my sunglasses and beginning to spin around the tunnel.

"Jezy? You hiding?"

No answer.

"Jezna? Enoch?"

It was like I'd been transported to another area entirely. And from the way my voice echoed off the walls, I seemingly had. The tight tunnel was now a wide-open courtyard. When I squinted to the point that my eyes were almost closed, I could see the pointed gothic markings in the stone.

I whipped out my cannon. "If something spooky like another one of those ugly worms is waiting somewhere in here, I swear to the Lords, I'm gonna blast your ass in half so fast. That's some rhyme for ya." I paused. "Hello?"

A yellow orb hovered out from behind a column, swaying faintly in the air.

I jumped back. Pointing my cannon at it, I fired up the core so that the weapon emitted a violent growl, but the orb only hovered silently.

I lowered the gun to forty degrees, frowning. "So, you're the next trial, are ya? A freaking cotton ball. What'd you do with my squad? I mean, go ahead and keep Scarfy, but give me back Noc and Jezy . . . I'll poke ya, I swear."

The orb brightened. I put a hand to my brow. "Turn that light down! What're you . . . ?"

"Damn," a familiar gruffness suddenly called out of the light. "Forgotten your old man, already?"

I felt the cannon slip between my fingers. Metal met stone, and as the light died, the orb growing to form a man then folding in on itself. I lowered my empty hands.

The voice stirred up memories of late nights, tales of great Navigators, stories of ancient treasure. It was the very last voice I'd ever expected to hear down here.

The man swept dust from his leather jacket—the same one I wore—and cracked his neck before spreading his hands. "How do I look?"

I threw myself into Dante Larocque's arms with a barely contained sob.

As we held each other for what felt like hours, him stroking my hair and me weeping into his shoulder, I sucked in his scent through sudden gulps of air. It wasn't exactly as it had been—the scent of beer wasn't anywhere to be found—but I supposed coming back from the dead did that. What was still the same was his tenderness.

Father held me tightly, patting me on the back and letting me cry years' worth of tears while whispering, "It's all right, little prince. I'm here."

I finally looked up at him, sniffling. "Father . . . how's this possible? You can't be here. Can you?"

"Of course I can!" Father said. "How could I miss this? The moment my little prince finds the Sacred Heart and becomes a real Navigator?"

I chuckled, rubbing my eyes. Just being with him again was enough for me to ignore the strangeness of the situation . . . and the soft mist that swam around my eyes. "You really think we'll find it?"

"Why not?" A brief flicker of static shot across Father's face. I squinted when I saw it, but I was too happy. "No one better has tried! You've already come this far, right?"

"I mean, I've had loads of help. Tons. Without the dudes I've met, I'd be toast by now . . ." My face lit up in realization. "Hey! Why don't you come meet 'em? The third might not care, but I know you'll get along with the other two great!" My heart soared thinking of how Enoch would react. "One's like Talen Vento and the other'll lose his mind! I bet you that!"

Surprisingly, Father shrugged. "That's all right, kid. I appreciate the thought, but I wanna spend more time with you."

I felt my smile disintegrate. The abyss widened.

Back when we were traveling from village to village in search of the Obsidian Obelisk, I hadn't had any friends. It'd gotten so bad that Father had followed me to lessons one day, stood on the playground in a cloak to disguise himself, and forced kids to befriend me—even handing out money to get them to play with me. That, of course, had backfired brutally, but it'd shown how much Father cared about me making friends. Even as I'd seen him spending every waking minute simmering over maps, charting courses, and studying notes written in a foreign language surrounded by sketches of a striking arrow-shaped building, he'd still taken time away from his quest to stand on a playground for me. He'd still wanted me to attend lessons so I could make friends.

Now that I had a legitimate Navigational squadron—or one in training—I'd expected him to want to meet them immediately, not brush them off.

The static came again, more noticeable this time. I took a slow step back.

Father's eyebrows furrowed. "What's wrong, little prince? Aren't you happy to see your old man?"

Father's right. I should be happy to see him . . . So why aren't I? Why do I feel so freaking . . . alone?

"Little prince, what's the matter?"

I took another step back to where my Aestus cannon lay on the courtyard floor, eyeing the figure of Father warily, blinking away the mist every time it tried to converge around me.

"Nothing's the matter, Father . . . I just have one question for you." I swallowed hard, wetting my lips as I did. "One of my squadmates . . . he's a stubborn bastard. I really hate him sometimes—all right, all the time—but he's part of the team whether I like it or not. Should I convince my friends to boot him out or keep him?"

"That's easy," Father said. "You do whatever you think is right, kid."

No.

My abyss flipped itself inside out, turning into a mountain. Light flew everywhere, and with the light came fear.

Everything going on around me was a lie.

NO!

I reached for my pistols, but Father was faster. Inhumanly so.

"Wait!" His face flashed between ten different people before revealing a twisted skull face beneath all the others. "Prince, it's your father! Can't you see that?"

I shoved him as hard as I could with my elbows and removed my pistols. When the cores hummed to life, I fought through stinging eyes and pointed the weapons at his chest, the same chest I'd curled up around on stormy nights. The chest I'd watched blood dribble from, surrounded by the blue creatures and their churning waterblades.

Though it hurt more than a million Aestus blasts, it was the brutal truth.

Father was dead.

"I see it just fine," I said. "I see that it's you, Father . . . But you're not who I need right now." I fought back the tears. "Don't you see? I *have* to get over your death. I can't keep stumbling my way through life, thinking the abyss is the only thing I can find comfort in. You taught me better than that. You wanted nothing more than for me to have a squad. Well, now I have one. Now I can make you proud. I can be *better*."

I looked Father dead in the eyes, into pitiless black holes that had never belonged anywhere near his face.

"Guns," I whispered. "Kill."

Father opened his mouth to roar, face sloughing off completely, but before he could throw himself at me, the fireball of magenta energy fried his intestines from the inside out. As opposed to burning up like a human usually did when hit by an Aestus cannon, Father sizzled, becoming something dark and skeletal before fading into smoke. The only sign that he'd ever been there was the scent of sulfur and old attics.

Now that whatever the hell it had been—not Father—was gone and I was no longer blubbering like a baby, I could both think and see perfectly clear again.

Forget what just happened, I heard my mind saying in Father's voice—his real spirit. *Forget what you just saw, little prince. It wasn't real. Get to the bottom of it. Work out the kinks and bends. Fix the machine.*

Navigate the abyss.

The courtyard was dark but illuminated around the edges by dozens of yellow floating spheres, and situated at each of the opposing points were Jezna, Enoch, and Murta. Each of them stood talking with a thin black skeleton seemingly made of sinister smoke. Each of them looked both distraught and completely unaware of their fates.

Darkwisps, I recalled from Father's songs and bedtime stories. Creatures of the night that lingered in caverns and preyed on travelers, transforming into those they cared about the most.

"Luckily, I'm worse," I said, throwing my cannon over my shoulder then spinning one of my pistols back into its holster. All I needed was one.

Whatever the other three were seeing, they'd have to deal with watching it be killed. It pained me to fire on each of the darkwisps, knowing my squadmates were speaking with someone they loved, but we were trapped.

Only this time, I was going to save them. Without Ignis and without fear.

Striding over to the creature standing over Jezna, I lifted the pistol to the darkwisp's skeletal face and blew its brain out.

Just like the creature that had posed as Father, the darkwisp's "body" ignited before evaporating into smoke. Jezna stood in shock, the slit in her helm glowing with aqua Ignis. At first, there was fury in her posture. She loomed over me, shoulder plates quivering. Then, as the smoke that was now the darkwisp drifted into the air, she calmed.

"Prince," she said. "You killed—"

"A darkwisp. Not whoever you were seeing. I know it seemed real. One pretended to be Father. But Father's dead." I pointed the end of my pistol over at Enoch and Murta, who were still snared in the darkwisp's facades. "Take a look for yourself."

Jezna did. "Stars above."

"Not for the darkwisps." I cocked and pointed the pistol again.

When I shot the one hovering over Enoch, his reaction was far more heartbreaking.

"NO!" Enoch roared, eyes a green tornado as he tackled me to the floor.

I cried out in fear, but then Jezna was on top of Enoch, restraining him in a heartbeat. He bucked under her weight and surprisingly—*terrifyingly*—managed to throw her off of him. All two hundred fifty pounds of armor.

He charged at me again, Green Fire Fists raised. I clambered back.

Then just like Jezna, he paused. Ignis fled him, returning his eyes to their normal orange. When he looked down at me for the first time since seeing whoever he'd seen die, his face split between grief and astonishment.

I fixed my face and pointed at Murta. Enoch spun, but when he saw the darkwisp controlling the Shadarian, he seemed more relieved than horrified. What should've made him irate, like it had Jezna, calmed him. I immediately wondered who it was that Enoch had seen me kill.

"Darkwisp," Enoch said. He winced when he saw Jezna crumpled on the ground and took a knee to help her up. "Damned darkwisp . . . Deepest apologies, gents. I didn't mean any—"

"Don't bother." I shakily placed Father's sunglasses back on my face. "If I'd seen you kill Father, I would've reacted the same way."

Enoch chewed his lip. "Just . . . help Murta. I'll try to restrain him as best as I can. There's no telling who he's seeing."

I cocked the pistol. "Who did you see?"

His silence revealed little. But where his eyes looked—to the wide-eyed Shadarian—spoke volumes.

I walked the last few feet across the courtyard, Enoch and Jezna following close behind.

Let's hope to the Lords for Noc's sake that I don't end up cooking us shadedrake for dinner.

CHAPTER 67

Enoch

I'd gotten good at hiding it—Serapharus had made me an expert—but inside, I was shaking.

The darkwisp trap was ingenious, a true Navigator's trial. It only added further fuel to my theory that the temple was strangely testing us. The darkwisps had been meant to test us emotionally, whereas the vortexurn before had been about physicality. Everything so far was like the Trials.

I just hadn't expected mine to turn into Murta.

It had been so devastatingly cruel. Murta had approached me with earnest sincerity, then *apologized* for his actions.

It'd been wonderful. He and I had been having an honest moment, actually connecting, bodies moving closer and closer . . .

Then Prince had shot him.

The moment afterward was all a blur now. All I remembered was feeling a massive upheaval of relief when I discovered the real Murta was alive. But my heart had also sank in tandem. That meant he still hated me, and that moment had just been a cruel concoction.

Now all I wanted was to see that the last of the darkwisps got what they bloody deserved.

But was that as simple as we thought? Murta looked . . . calm. I couldn't hear what he and the darkwisps were talking about, but from the sadness in his eyes, I estimated that when Prince finally did pull the trigger, all of our lives would be up in the air until his mind cleared of the mist.

I looked at Prince. He raised his pistol to his sunglasses, giving me an affirmative nod. I returned it, already tapping into Ignis in preparation.

Whatever happens, Murta: I'm sorry. We'll find the Sacred Heart and make all this right. I promise—

Prince pulled the trigger.

Jezna swept around Murta's backside to restrain him while I emerged from the front, but both proved folly. He exploded with Ignis.

Fiery golden energy slammed into the three of us, surging out from Murta's spirit. It threw Jezna and Prince into the wall and I across the courtyard. If it hadn't been for my physical conditioning, I wouldn't have made it back to him in time.

Murta's hands crept up to his neck, eyes seething serpentine. Dark energy began to trickle up from his shoulders alongside the smoke that escaped his nostrils. Jezna cried out in horror and Prince cowered, hands searching for his pistol, but I tackled Murta before he could reach his necklace.

"Enoch!" Prince said, but I ignored him.

There's only one way to keep the Other from taking over. One way that doesn't involve me possessing him again.

After securing my legs around Murta's torso and wrapping one arm around his neck and right arm, I wrapped my hands around the necklace, squeezing my eyes shut.

Murta roiled beneath me, contorting his body as he continued to burn, but that wasn't the worst part. The necklace was colder than ice. I could feel the burns piling up on my palms, withering away scar tissue from years spent beating at blokes with my fists, to the point where I tasted blood. Murta's free hand pulled against my own, fighting to steal the necklace away from my hands.

I just sucked in a jagged breath and tightened my grip.

"Wake up," I pleaded. "We can't be a squad without a Shield. And I know you'll never admit this, but we can't be us without you." *I can't be me without you.*

Remarkably, Murta began to still. His roars strangled somewhere in his throat. His taut muscles against mine twitched and relaxed, and his veins folded back beneath his skin, no longer coursing with Ignis. The dark energy fizzled out of existence.

Ignis fled his eyes, then swirled back into his spirit and was gone.

Murta shuddered, eyes human instead of reptilian, and looked right at me.

CHAPTER 68

Murta

"*We can't be us without you.*"

The words fished me out of the oceans on a line made of green energy. And I awoke to hands curled around my necklace.

I pried the fingers loose, watching the cold smoke waft off them and the gold metal alike. The burns they'd sustained were gruesome but could be healed with Ignis. In the moment, though, the pain would've been mind-numbing. Any rational-minded person would've withdrawn. What idiota had thought to do such a stupid . . .

I pulled myself out of the tangle of limbs and looked down at Enoch.

My eyes spun. I tried to sit down, to nurse the nausea and confusion away, but it only made me stumble. I refused to fall down, to lie on my back or fall face-first. A Shadarian didn't fall.

But when I opened my eyes, there was Enoch again—the real one, rising up off of the courtyard floor and putting his burnt, bruised hands on my shoulders. There he was again, sacrificing his body for my sake, selflessly protecting me even when I berated him for it. Protecting me even when I told him not to.

But I'd watched Prince kill him.

"Murta?"

Enoch is dead.

"Murta, can you hear me?"

Enoch is . . . alive?

"Murta?!"

He's . . . !

"MUR—"

"I hear you." I hacked the remaining smoke from my lungs, burping up a spark or two. "Stop shouting." I looked up into his face. The childlike hope that erupted there filled my heart with the same emotion, no matter how hard I tried to suppress it. It was . . .

It was peaceful.

Enoch let out a thunderous sigh, removing his hands from my shoulders. "Thank the Lords. Thought you'd gone deaf or blind. Or both. How're you . . . ?" He drifted off when I lifted his hands to my eyes.

They were wastelands, layers of skin, tissue, bandage, and dried blood all meshed into blistering scabs. When I gently worked my fingers around them, Enoch whimpered.

"Bloody hell." His face soured. "Pretend I didn't just make that sound."

I tapped into Ignis. It'd been so long since I'd had to heal anyone other than myself. I didn't know if I could still do it. The last time had been when I was still in the War. Still in the fight . . .

No.

Aren's Steeple had still happened. My life was still what it was. I couldn't erase it.

I dropped Enoch's hands, turning toward the end of the courtyard and the chamber beyond. "The Heart is near." I straightened my necklace, reminding myself who I was, what I had trapped inside me.

But when I removed my hands from the golden chain, flakes of bandage stuck between my fingers. They fell from my hands, reminding me of the blizzard I'd weathered on Aren's Steeple, in which I'd carried someone up cliffs, glaciers, and crags. For miles.

The blizzard where I'd been alone, trudging through winter's eternal night in silence, save for a boy's slow breaths in my ear. Save the gentle beats of his heart against my back, more warming than a thousand dragon fires . . .

I left the thought unfinished.

CHAPTER 69

Enoch

I made bloody certain not to fall behind this time, racing after Murta as noisily as possible.

My hands howled with pain any time the muscles twitched the battered veins, but that didn't stop me from grabbing his shoulder in an attempt to pull him back around.

"Oi, hold on." But Murta slapped me away. I ground my teeth at the spasm of pain that arched up my arm. "We're not done talking. We're gonna figure this out whether or not you—"

A churning sound echoed down the tunnel. I paused and tapped into Ignis, but it didn't sound like another vortexurn. It had more of a rhythmic pattern than a natural one. Like turning machinery, moving parts and gears. It sort of sounded like . . .

My mouth fell open.

It can't be . . .

Before Prince could ask why I looked so surprised, I shot off into the final chamber, the churning sound in my ears.

It was the largest room out of them all, a true cavern that dwarfed every room before it. The first half was a simple cobblestone platform running from wall to wall horizontally. The second half, however, hung suspended over a dark chasm, twisting itself in a squirming ball of walkways, platforms, and boulders. Each moved in accordance to the others but at a chaotic, jumbled pace.

At the center of the mess sat an unmoving platform. And hovering two feet over it, casting a dark-green glow across the entire cavern, was the Sacred Heart.

We watched the walls revolve around the Talisman in astonished silence.

"It's here." I looked over at Murta, whose shoulders had begun to shake. "The Heart's exactly where you said it would be."

"But . . . how do we get to it?" Prince asked.

Murta's eyes flicked around the iron mess, spinning patterns and pathways until I grew sick just from watching him. "Got it." He made for the edge.

My spirit flared. "Wait!" I grabbed him by the arm again, keeping him from jumping into the mix of grinding stone. He looked back at me with golden eyes, but I wasn't afraid anymore. Not when I knew.

"It's impossible to get through on your own," I said. "You'd be stupid to try."

Murta snatched his arm back. "No more immortality? I thought you'd be jumping at the chance to get the Heart."

I shook my head, painfully recalling the way my foolishness had almost gotten Murta killed by the vortexurn, recalling Prince's gun emptying out the fake Murta's brains.

I wouldn't see him dead again.

"This has nothing to do with immortality." I gestured at the spinning formation. "Because that isn't something out of the ordinary . . . It's the Bastion."

Prince tilted his head completely to one side. "Here?! How?"

But Jezna had begun to put the pieces together. "If this is the Bastion, then that means—"

"Whatever dark Ignis user built Jâhic wasn't dark at all," I finished. "They were a Navigator. I know they were. I can feel their spirit . . . It's why the vortexurn tried to pick us off. It's why the darkwisp tested our emotions by trying to pull us away from one another. They tried to forcefully separate us. These aren't guardians of the Heart: They're the Trials.

"And I think that's exactly why so many Ryjenians have failed. If they were all competing for the Heart, they would've never gotten past the vortexurn. They would've left those that came with them to be devoured by the darkwisp."

I inhaled. "And then they would've failed the Bastion instantly. Because it can only be beaten if a squad works together."

"That's nonsense," Murta said. "Mathias Flint beat the Bastion on his own. Dresden Roberts beat it on his own. And now I'm about to."

"What're you trying to prove?"

"What are you trying to say?"

"That you're trying to prove something."

"I'm not trying to prove anything."

"Bollocks. You almost returned to normal after I stopped you from turning into the Other."

"Which was immensely estúpido of you."

I put both hands on Murta's shoulders, only to have them slapped away for the hundredth time. When I sternly moved to place them back up again, he took a step back.

It demolished me.

"Why?"

Murta clearly hadn't expected that. "Qué?"

"You came to Carbonek for a reason," I said. "We all did. You didn't join the Brotherhood out of hate. No one joins thinking that . . . You once told me that you never had anything to believe in, but that's rubbish. You had to believe in something."

Murta shook his head with frustration. "What does this have to do—"

"Everything." I took that last step forward, softly placing my hands on his taut, tense shoulders. This time, he stayed. "Because I know that whatever that hope was, it's been snuffed out. You don't have to tell me what it was. You don't have to tell me how it was snuffed, but you do least have to let me try to replace it."

I looked down at the sigil in the middle of the platform, the same one that was in the starting circle of Carbonek's Bastion. It was dusty and decrepit, but if I squinted hard enough, there was the mountain-rainbow-sun looking up at me. *Reminding* me.

Letting go of Murta, I stepped up to the sigil and looked out over the familiar sight, now turned on its head, flipped inward, and thrice as ginormous. The margin of error was completely eliminated from the equation. Going on my own wasn't even an option.

So I closed my eyes.

"W-what are you doing?" Murta asked.

The temple was dark and rigid around me, without a spirit, without life, but the Bastion was the same as it was. Instead of Jesper's orange spirit, there was a beautiful yellow one in my mind, and instead of the bonfire of Carbonek's Bastion, it was a supervolcano erupting outward. Taking control of such a thing, making sense of it all, was an impossible task. But I'd always prided myself on doing the impossible.

"Helping you," I said.

"How many times do I have to tell you?! I don't need your—"

"It's not about if you need it!"

I sifted through the thousands of strands floating around me in my mind and seized hold of the two hundred or so that made up the Bastion. I grabbed them all, then tied them off with a stray one so that they all filtered back to me—back into my spirit.

"I don't feel obligated to help you, bruv. I never have." I opened my eyes, a feat I hadn't known I was capable of when latching onto the spirit of something, especially the size of the Bastion. "I *want* to help you. So let me."

The Bastion gave a twisted shudder, forcing my eyes closed, but I snapped them open, letting go of the strand briefly to pat Murta on the shoulder. "From a Charger to a Shield." The strand began to unknot at the speed of a hurricane. "Bollocks." I delved back into the darkness and spun it—a green spider spinning a red web—then grasped them tightly in my spirit's hands.

I winced. "Let's carpe—"

My spirit flew into the Bastion, growing to the size of its massive structure, flowing into every cog and piece. I lost count of how many working parts there were, letting my mind shuffle between them. If I focused too hard, I'd get lost and never find my way back. It was better to keep one hand secured on the strand that was my body and the other sifting through the Bastion.

The whole ordeal was maddening. My spirit was thrown around the Bastion's crimson spirit. I nearly lost my way ten times over, but never did my hand leave the strand that led me back to the platform. Never did I forget who I was and what I was doing.

Murta, I remembered. Or more like the Bastion remembered . . .

I—er, the Bastion—didn't feel anyone running along myself. There was no extra weight. No golden spirit within. No Murta beside me.

I panicked. Had my speech failed? Had Murta even been listening? Had something happened? Was there another vortexurn? Another darkwisp? Had Murta been a darkwisp? Had he fallen off the ledge already or been squashed by one of the rotating walls? Had we failed after coming this close to getting the Heart?

The dreaded absence of gold echoing out of the Bastion confirmed any one of those possibilities. Holding on to the thread of the Bastion and keeping myself lodged in it became increasingly difficult. What had been a spirit to inhabit became something darker, a machine I was locked in. As bright as its spirit burned, the Bastion became something resembling the furnaces, and I, though I could escape at any time I wanted, was trapped inside.

My mind splintered into two halves in a fight for survival. One half screamed to let go, to abandon hope and realize that Murta had abandoned me. The other half, the stubborn idiotic half that constantly got me into trouble, told me to persevere, that Murta hadn't forsaken me and was on his way.

But if my second half was to be believed, what was taking him so bloody—

I lost my grip. The emerald line that bound me to my dematerialized body snapped out of my hand, spinning off into the darkness.

I threw myself after it, but the Bastion didn't have a body. I got tangled in the machine's turnings, the never-ending pursuit of motion, until I began to think like it.

I began to lighten up to my newfound purpose, grinding gears and chugging out new patterns for all eternity. I began to think in numbers and turns, not words and emotions. I began to feel my spirit molding to the structure of the Bastion, replacing its soul with my own and my soul with its. I began to think only of the turns and tunnels I had, not the people I'd met. I began to think like a machine. Twist, turn, twist, turn, twist—

I'M STILL A CHARGER!

I emerged from the bundle of crimson strands burying me with a roar, shattering the spiderweb and lunging toward the shining strand that would grant me passage back to my body.

And right when my fingers curled around the spiritual substance and coursed back into me, gold stepped onto the Bastion.

Glowing green and under my control, the Bastion parted back the difficult paths and formed naturally easier ones, and Murta ran through them, dodging obstacles and walls. We might not have thought as one, but we moved as one.

Minutes passed in seconds. The joy I felt was further accented by the gold blur racing back through me down the way it had come, and when it left, leaving the Bastion to turn silently, I missed its presence.

In my excitement, I threw myself out of the machine, re-forming back on the sigil. I felt wobbly and the pain in my hands gnawed at me, but I was alive.

Only Murta wasn't yet out of the Bastion.

He sprinted down the main path, flipping over a wall and clutching the item secured in his left hand against his chest.

He wasn't going to make it.

Realizing my mistake in horror, I threw myself toward him just as he erupted out of the Bastion. He reached out with his right hand, and I clasped it in mine without a moment's hesitation. His eyebrows lifted in shock.

Others might've abandoned you, but I won't.

We fell together, sailing into the dark pit below, but still I kept my tattered hand locked around Murta's. I felt his hand tighten, his spirit, his fire, lifting as we fell, the world speeding past us in a million multicolored comets . . .

Then another hand, one smaller than both of ours, wrapped around my ankle. He fell with us—far louder than either Murta or I—but before we could fall back into the black, everything jerked to a halt.

I peeled open my eyes, fighting off the pain in my hands.

Murta swung beneath me, his hand still intertwined with mine. Above, Prince held on to my ankle, face purple and hissing with strain, and holding on to his ankle with one hand wrapped around the ledge of the platform was Jezna.

I saluted up at them. "Hey there, lads. Hangin' in there, I see."

"ENOCH!" Prince yelled as Jezna dragged us up. "YOU FREAKING MORON!"

When Prince and Jezna were safely back up on the platform, their combined might lifted me up. When my knees were under solid ground, I put my entire body into helping Murta.

"Appreciate the help you're granting us," I said between breaths.

Murta's eyes flicked between my blistered hand and my pain-engulfed face. He didn't utter a word as we lifted him.

When my hands finally felt as though their very bones were burning, Murta's knees met ground, and we all collapsed onto the cobblestones, listening to the sound of the Bastion churning.

"That's it," Prince said, chest heaving up and down. "I'm done. No more navigating for Prince. I'm stopping the turner right here and now."

"The dining abbey cooks will be delighted," Jezna said.

I lifted my head tiredly, looking toward Murta.

There was a second of disquieted urgency, perhaps laced with some panic at the possibility that we really had failed.

Then Murta's annoyed expression slowly transformed into one of tired contentment. He lifted his left hand from behind his back, revealing the Sacred Heart.

Prince fainted, causing Jezna to fly into a frenzy and begin dousing his forehead with her Ignis. This woke Prince immediately, who began to roar.

Rinsing sweat from my face, I looked down at the Heart.

Murta set it between us and stared. "We . . . did it."

"You're right." I looked up at him. "*We* did."

When I stood, I offered Murta a hand.

It didn't take my spirit flaring for me to know that he'd finally accept it.

CHAPTER 70

Prince

Lemme get this straight," I said as we stepped back into the vortexurn cave. "We took down a giant unbeatable worm . . ."

"Yep," Enoch said.

"I did," Murta corrected.

I waved my hands lazily. "Then we were manipulated by darkwisps and sent them back whence they came."

"You sent them back whence they came," Enoch said.

"And then you possessed the entire Bastion while Scarfy ran through it, got the Sacred Heart, then almost fell off the ledge, thus making us *all* almost fall off the ledge . . ."

"Please don't remind me," Jezna said.

"And now, we have to find a way back to Carbonek, then get down on our hands and knees in front of the Council, and plead until our hair falls out for them not to banish us."

"Not a bad first quest, aye?" Enoch picked up his harness. "Long way to the keep, though."

"Even longer to Carbonek." Murta helped Enoch adjust his buckles before slipping on his own harness. "If Kaleo isn't in Ryjen by now."

"How do you think he'll react?" Enoch asked.

Murta gathered the loose chain between his hands. "Hopefully not how I predict."

To my absolute terror, we now had to climb. I couldn't wait to breathe open air again, but the moment we flipped the triggers the opposite way and the chains began pulling us up, I didn't care much anymore.

Whereas everyone else climbed, I hung suspended in the air, chest horizontal to the steadily disappearing rock beneath us, arms spread-eagle. Enoch saw me and laughed.

"I feel like a spider," I said.

"I feel like a million brown dollars." He shook his head in disbelief, glancing over at Murta. "You still got it?"

"Yes. For the hundredth time."

"Let me see it."

Murta scowled but removed the Talisman from his pants pocket once more. The majority of it was a glistening emerald with black scale stone etched up its sides, and where the black parts did creep in toward the emerald center, they formed webbed patterns. Enoch stared at the Heart in awe, blinking after Murta returned it to his pocket.

I craned my neck. "I didn't see it. Whip it out again."

"Buzz off."

"I would if I was a jaguar hornet, but since I'm not *flying out of this pit right now*—"

"Maybe you just had your wings removed."

"Maybe you just had your brain emptied."

"Maybe—"

"You still got it?" Enoch asked.

"Yes! I still have it!"

I gritted my teeth before slowing down my chain to get closer to them. "I think the real question that we're all kinda avoiding right now is: What do we do with it?"

Silence.

Oops.

Not even Murta spoke. Enoch seemed detached. It was impossible to see his face from several feet below, but I knew he was going back through both his promise to the sultan and our need to get back to Carbonek as soon as possible. Duty or not, the Sacred Heart was the strongest of the Tintagen Talismans. Father had always said so. The moment we got to the keep, everyone would be after us. I just hoped that the Ryjenians and mercenaries remembered the peace Enoch had instilled in them. And if both Anders and the sultan were wrong about the Jackals not being here . . .

"I made a promise," Enoch said determinedly. "For better or for worse. I swore that the Brotherhood would aid Ryjen, and the Brotherhood will." He looked at Murta carefully. "We'll use our powers to help them in whatever ways we can, then we'll take it to Carbonek."

Murta was slow to return to the wall he climbed. "They could be planning to betray us."

"But we saw down in Jâhic that not all the masters were bad. Good runs deeper than darkness. And besides: we're Navigators. Or at least they think we are. Betraying us would be . . ."

I swallowed. Betraying us to the Jackals . . . I didn't even want to think about what that entailed. I figured the dark organization of apparently ex-Navigators was better left in stories than in front of us. Any time Father had ever spoken of them, it had always been with a stern, shadowed face. Jackals—as in the animal—had been the ones to invade the obsidian caverns and kill the white bat in "The Bat Never Looks Back."

I stilled my rioting nerves by reciting the second-to-last verse:

"*He chases the jackals back into the black . . .*"

"It would be unthinkable," Jezna said, bringing a grateful end to the silence.

Enoch exhaled. "Right-o. The Heart belongs in Carbonek, but Ryjen and the mercs need us first."

"I have no problem with using the Heart," Murta said. "But right now, we're in no position to be making promises on the Brotherhood or the Code. Especially to a nation that once aligned with the Jackals. I know the sultan says otherwise, but I have a hard time believing that he hasn't at least been approached by them . . . And besides, we're not Navigators yet."

"But we're about to be."

"We'll see."

The light from the keep grew increasingly brighter. We were moving fast now. I could almost make out the keep's columns through Enoch's and Murta's silhouettes. They were ahead of me now, practically sprinting up the rock face.

Enoch slapped Murta's arm playfully. "Lighten up! We're the first blokes in history to bring the Heart back to the surface! We've completed the quest that not even Kaleo was able to complete!"

"When you put it like that . . ."

"Prince!" Enoch shouted down at me.

"Wha-what?" I asked.

"Gimme a victory song!"

"Wh-why?"

"We're trainees, and we just passed our first quest with flying colors! We got the Sacred bloody Heart!"

The orange light from the Serrated Keep illuminated the pit to the point that Enoch swam in the light, one bandaged hand wrapped around the chain that pulled him up, the other secured on the trigger. Next to him, the Shadarian looked the most content he'd been in a long time, and Jezna displayed movements of happiness even under her faceless armor. It was almost enough to make me forget how high we were off the ground and how fast we were moving.

Is this them, Father? Is this . . . home?

"Well, then." I coughed, stretching my vocal cords. "A song you shall have."

Enoch beamed with anticipation.

I let the nearing keep take my heart where it wanted. "*Four Navs came a-questing in search of sacred hearts,*" I sang. "*But lo and below, they had lots o' false starts.*

"*The Shadarian, in all his edginess, beat the worm open, but it was the swashbuckler who mended the heart already broken.*"

"This song sucks," said Murta.

"*The mighty treasure hunter uncovered the darkwisps' plot. Without his quick acting, the squad's skeletons would rot.*"

"I doubt that."

"Then came the Bastion, which the hunter and knight sat out, while the swash and merc powered through with teamwork that'd make Mathias and Kaleo pout."

Enoch eyed me fondly. The keep was right on top of us now. Murta lifted his free arm and grabbed the edge of the pit.

"So now they head for Carbonek," I concluded, *"where dreams and hopes brew . . ."*

"Anders!" Enoch said, scrambling for the ledge. "We're back! We've . . ."

"Now, the sky's the limit, so I pass it on to—"

I poked my head up over the side of the pit, the last to do so, and felt my song go up in flames.

The sultan stood in the shadow of a column, back hunched with discomfort. His armored guards lined the walls en masse, those with spears and swords holding them at the throats of bloodied, bruised mercenaries. Anders himself was panting, a thick line of blood making its way down his forehead.

But the stuff of nightmares were the five Ignis hunters who lingered in the doorway and the black-cloaked man crouched over the pit a mere two feet away from us, a pink crystal dangling from his neck.

I clamped my jaw closed in horror.

Enoch looked between the sultan, Anders, and the Jackal. "What've you . . ."

I squeezed my eyes shut. *No. Not like this. Not when we were so close.*

"Young Navigators," the sultan croaked from the shadows. "I'm truly sorry. But my people are of greater importance to me than your Code. I cannot put my trust in your promise to return . . . I must have *guaranteed* peace."

The Jackals were always here. They knew where the Heart was from the very beginning. They knew it was in the Serrated Keep all along. They just needed a Navigational squadron to fish it out of the temple for them.

We were played for fools.

Lucian held a gloved hand up to Murta. "The Heart, if you'd please."

"Go to hell," he whispered.

"It's quite cozy." Lucian snapped his fingers. Eight sparks of pink Ignis materialized behind him, widening to form eight portals. Pale tentacles overgrown with suckers and spikes shot out of each, swarming us en masse, then halted inches from our skin.

"The Heart," Lucian said. "Or every mercenary and Navigator dies before you can get to that necklace."

It sounded like Jezna had forgotten how to breathe. I could hear her Aestus heart pumping so fast that I thought it might explode. My own sounded louder.

"You betrayed us," Enoch said, still talking to the sultan. "You were setting us up the entire time. The Jackals were always here." He stared aimlessly ahead. "You betrayed us."

The sultan retreated farther into the shadows. One of the Ignis hunters shoved him forward, earning cackles from the others.

"Pure spirits are like expensive glass," Lucian said. "Incredibly see-through and always shatter the easiest. I'm still waiting, Shadarian."

Murta looked to Enoch, our Charger, but he was in limbo. His face and posture had gone completely slack. The Enoch who had gotten us through Carbonek and Jâhic was gone. All that was left behind was an empty, *mortal* husk.

Left without his Charger, Murta averted the Jackal's gaze and removed the Heart from his pocket. No tricks, no grunts, no kicks.

He bowed his head and placed the Talisman into the black-gloved hand.

Lucian wrapped his fingers around it and stood abruptly. With another snap of his fingers, the tentacles retreated back into their portals and were gone.

He examined the Sacred Heart giddily, tossing it between his hands, holding it up to the torchlight and running long fingers down its markings and sides. When the green light lit up his face, the deranged greed in his eyes was unmistakable.

In those eyes, I finally realized what Kaleo had been saying. Where there'd been wonder in Enoch's and Murta's eyes, there was corruption in Lucian's. Enoch and Murta had looked at the Heart and seen beyond it; they'd found solace in knowing that it would be either used to protect Ryjen or kept safe in Carbonek.

But when Lucian looked at the Heart, there was only hunger.

"Just like Kal." Lucian stroked the Heart. "Always a step behind even when he thought he sprinted three miles ahead. And to think we could've had the Karnocolix, too." He clicked his tongue. "A shame, really. Little Locken was an easy target. Harrenous wanted to use Biassis, but I suggested a far more malleable spirit. Unfortunately, we underestimated the will of a certain foolish swashbuckler." He looked at Enoch. "I don't underestimate anyone more than once." And with a shrug, he turned toward the Ignis hunters. "Alas, it was fun while it lasted. Cut them loose."

"NO!" Anders and the sultan howled as the metal soldiers sprang on each of our chains, converted the tips of their cannons into serrated blades, and sliced through the rusted metal.

The strain of the chain that kept me afloat suddenly went limp.

Tears stinging my eyes, I grasped for the edge of the pit and Enoch, but he'd already accepted his fate, falling like a dropped stone.

"HASTA LUEGO!" Lucian called.

I screamed as the light of the keep disappeared. Jezna yelled. Murta roared.

But Enoch fell as silently as someone already dead.

CHAPTER 71

Jezna

Could a spark ignite underwater?

Fire couldn't physically find refuge in a place without air. Stones couldn't be struck together in liquid. Sparks couldn't take form in a place that couldn't make them.

My body tumbled downward, the walls etching dents and scrapes into my armor. Everyone flew around me, Murta searching for a ledge, Prince screaming, and Enoch lost in soundlessness. I remained as silent as I could, but within, I was a raging tempest.

Twice, I'd failed a code. Twice, I'd been so focused on what I had to the point that I hadn't thought of what might be. And twice I'd failed to protect my brethren.

Using my hands to press off the walls speeding past us, I righted myself in midair and concentrated. Murta flew beneath me, Prince and Enoch above.

In water, there was peace and calm but also emptiness and loneliness. In water, I was wet and cool. No air, no heat . . .

But I wasn't completely made of water now, was I?

If a knight is out of balance with the world around them, I heard Macín say again, *something must change. The world or the knight.*

I'd been gifted with a heart, a *new* one that operated on Aestus as opposed to life. Aestus . . . which maybe contained enough room for a spark.

Not just the spark of a knight, but a Navigator.

They said fire couldn't start underwater, but in that moment, it did. Within *me*. I felt it course through my heart and all throughout me until my water became one with it. Until I was no longer water, nor a hybrid between the two elements, but pure fire.

All those years ago, I'd watched the dam come crashing down from my spot in the distant forest atop a hill. I'd watched the water roar forth from the cracks, turning the village valley into a lake. And at the end, when the crashing had quieted and all was silent save the whisper of water, I'd seen seven multicolored flames escape from off of the lake's surface where they sailed up into the stars.

If there is something greater than chivalry that your time among us should have taught you, it's that the world is a river. Macín's final words before sending me off to help the villagers out of the valley. *It moves on. What makes humanity so special is that we're given the option to either move with it or stand against it . . . And the honest truth of Archengard, dear sister, is: You cannot save every soul. I've already tried.*

I'd watched my Brothers die once. Then, when the darkwisp had taken on the form of those I cared for most, I'd watched them die again. And now, my new brothers were about to die all around me.

Just this once, you're wrong, Macín, I thought, feeling the words rebound through my flaming soul. *This time, the world doesn't change.* I *change. For good.*

This time, I find the balance.

THIS IS MY SQUAD, AND THIS TIME, I SAVE EVERY SOUL.

Digging my fingers into the rock to slow my momentum, I caught Enoch in my free arm, then flattened myself to allow Prince to latch onto my back. Prince wrapped his arms around my neck, but Enoch felt almost weightless. It was a struggle just to keep his torso from escaping upward under my arm.

"Hold on!" I scrunched into a ball to move faster.

Murta looked up, seeing me hold out my open arm. He expertly spread his limbs outward to slow his descent, allowing me to catch up to him in seconds. When he launched himself at me, my right arm curled around his torso, and squeezed.

We plummeted, my knowledge of distance telling me that we were approaching the bottom fast.

I looked at Murta. "Slow us down!"

Sparks of gold light illuminated the darkness, allowing me to see the sides of the pit and the paleness of Enoch's face. The swashbuckler barely blinked as particles of dirt and rock barreled past us.

Murta raked his claws at the rock but nothing held. It'd been stupid to ask him. Dragon claws were capable of cutting through any material on Archengard, even solid rock. It would be impossible for them to stick or latch onto anything.

Murta took a final slice at the wall, which spat sparks back at us, and looked up with a shake of his head.

"Prince, get to my chest!" I said.

"What?! Why would I—"

"Get to my chest, now!" I snuck a glance below.

"We're running out of time," Murta said. "I can turn into—"

"Now, Prince!"

Cursing with frustration, Prince climbed across my shoulders to cling to my chest. When he was situated, he looked up into my face, eyes wide with fear.

I let my outline shimmer with Ignis. "Prepare for—"

My back slammed into the stone. There was an explosion of sound in my helmet and a fear-inducing pounding hammered through my Aestus heart, but everything else felt normal. I thanked the indestructible strength of god armor and the creatures that had forged it. I thanked the Lords for the first time in my life—

Prince pointed up at the keep. "Look out!"

He was nearly interrupted by the thunder of falling rocks, massive ones that had been dislodged from the top of the pit. It seemed that Lucian and the Ignis hunters didn't just want us dead; they wanted to make certain of it.

Feeling the first few pebbles pattering off of my helmet, I ordered my fire to rush out of my backplate and filter into my legs. I latched onto Ignis to assist in the process so my whole lower body was wrapped in aqua flames. Then, moving the flames up through my chest, I ordered them into my arms. Kneeling beneath me, Prince watched in horror.

"Please don't think ill of me for doing this," I told him. "I know how dishonorable it is to die for something that I barely believed in."

The first few rocks slammed into the stone surrounding us, shocking Prince from his trance. Murta scrambled for shelter under my massive form, but Enoch remained on his knees out in the open.

"Swash!" Murta said as the first pieces of ceiling crashed into me. "Get under here!"

Enoch's lips parted, but he spoke too softly to hear. A chunk of black rock slammed a foot away from him. More followed until he was in the middle of it, somehow never getting hit but too close for me not to worry. Rocks had begun to hammer against my back, creating more dents than I was comfortable with. My soul shook with every blow.

"ENOCH!" Murta finally roared. "Dammit!" He threw himself into the fray, seized the motionless boy by the collar, and dragged him to safety under me.

The stone rain continued steadily, making me believe, for a moment, that there wasn't that much.

Then came the downpour.

I felt it immediately, the weight of several floors, chunks of dug-up rock, and perhaps even pieces of the keep ceiling. I felt it, and I screamed.

Ignis spasmed, sparking around my shoulders and arms as I held the pile of rocks like the Dragon Lord Draconus holding the universe on his back, and I realized that perhaps this was how he felt every second. Perhaps I should sympathize more with him.

My spirit never gave out—not with my newfound spark—but the strain proved too much for me. Even something as indestructible as god armor began to give in. The seams widened, letting trickles of water escape and rain down onto the three boys I hunkered over. Cracks began to snake their way down my arms, past my shoulders, and venture eerily close to my Aestus chamber. The cracks widened, but still I dug in my heels, holding the rocks. Still, I kept the flames burning around my upper body.

This is how Ignis finally accepts me, I realized, watching Ignis blaze around me, the purest it had ever been. Fire for the first time as opposed to water. *Balance . . . That was all I needed. Navigator* and *knight . . .*

Prince was the first to notice the droplets falling into his hair.

"What're you doing?!" His hands shook as they moved to grip my helmet.

"My armor and Ignis will still stand," I said. "It will provide you enough time to dig your way out through an alternative passage."

Silver tears began to leak out from the corners of his eyes. "But you'll . . . you'll die if all of your water gets out!"

"Then I shall die as a Navigator."

I'd meant it as a fact, not something to be recorded in the annals or remembered as my last words, but it seemed to awaken something in Murta. Not the darkness of the Other, but something that made me understand perfectly why a Shrouded Man had taken such an interest in him.

All at once, he jerked his head upward. The dark energy from before was gone, replaced with pure golden Ignis. He stood as best as he could in the tight crevice, turned both of his legs into pillars of flame, and executed an upward kick to the pile of rocks.

The move was so wickedly fast that I almost thought it hadn't occurred, that it was merely a figment of my steadily deteriorating mind. It was only when the growing load disappeared from my shoulders that I looked up faintly.

Murta's kick had done the work of dragon fire, destroying, dispersing, and melting the rock. The whole pile had gone flying up the way it had come, some parts incinerating completely and others becoming so suddenly hot that they stayed stuck to the upper walls of the pit and cooled, becoming bumps in the walls.

It was the single most incredible usage of Ignis I'd ever witnessed.

Murta's knee remained angled toward the sky after he'd cleared the pit, flames of Ignis running down it and seeking haven back in his spirit. He kept it raised for a silent moment, gold eyes glaring up at the pinprick of light from the keep high above, then looked down at us.

There was an eternity of light in that gold of his.

A light I'd only ever seen in Enoch.

"No one dies," Murta suddenly said. "No one gives up."

CHAPTER 72

Murta

"You hear me?" I looked around the circle.

Jezna fell to a knee squeakily, smoke wafting off her damaged armor.

Prince hunched his shoulders and curled in on himself. "Some pep talk, Scarfy . . . It's over." He turned his pain-stricken eyes on Enoch. "The Jackals won. We're finished."

No. We're not. Not even close.

When I'd punched Enoch, he'd refused to stop training. When I'd shown him the containment device, he'd refused to give up on me. When I'd yelled at him in the training hall and in the Karnocolix chamber, he'd found a way to win. When I'd lost myself to the Other, he'd tried to pull me out . . . And when I'd been locked in the containment device for almost killing him, he'd still forgiven me.

When Biorn spoke about my flames, I thought, the Ignis that coursed through my eyes revealing the spirits of fire residing in the three people in front of me, *he didn't mean Ignis at all . . . He meant them.*

Turning my attention to Enoch, kneeling in the shadows of the passage, head bowed and docile, I moved without thinking, before I had time to analyze what I was about to do. For now, rationality could bite its head off.

I lifted Enoch to his feet by the fabric of his dress shirt so I could stare fire into his glassy unmoving eyes and snapped my fist across his jaw. He crumpled.

"What're you doing?!" Prince asked.

Lifting Enoch by the vest, I back-fisted him.

"Have you lost your mind?!" The weight of Jezna's armor fell upon me.

But she was weak and depleted, so I fought her off and threw myself back at Enoch. My heart beat with the blood of a dragon as I threw human fist after fist. In this state, I could've escaped the containment device.

"BE IMMORTAL, DAMMIT!"

Enoch took it in silence. He didn't try to shove me off, just lay motionless in the pile of rocks. His submissiveness inflated my fury.

"*Stand!* Fight . . ." My words faltered, but my blows didn't. "Just when I finally started believing in you, you choose to stop believing in yourself?! FIGHT! BACK!"

A blistered hand caught my next punch. I saw Enoch rise beneath me, his face a bruised mess. His eyes had been restored to their original fire, but there was fear in their once-proud liveliness.

"So now you side with me?" he asked. "What do you want us to bloody do?! The sultan betrayed us, we can't get back up to the surface, the Brotherhood thinks we betrayed them, and the Jackals have the Heart!"

He shook his head. "Kaleo was right. We're not strong enough . . . I'm not strong enough. I've always been the weak link, ever since I got stuck in the Skrill. You were all bloody brilliant, and I failed you. Just like I've always failed you.

"Jezna: You're the smartest, most caring lass I've ever met. Prince, you bastard son of a bugger: You're a genius! No Ignis and you're already twice the lad I'll ever be . . . And Murta?"

His lip trembled. "You're everything I should be."

I made sure that my next punch hurt my hand. "*Shut up!* You don't want to be me! You're not me! You're . . ." I stood over him. "You're Enoch Amon! This is just one setback!"

Enoch sprang to his feet, wiping bleeding lips with the sleeve of his shirt. "If this is a setback, then what do you expect us to do?! Take on all of Ryjen and the Jackals?"

Face-to-face with my squadmates, I finally saw just how much I'd hurt him. My point had gotten across. I calmed myself. I didn't have to keep hurting him.

"Yes," I said. "That's exactly what we're going to do. Because it's what you would do."

Enoch squinted. His cheeks were so swollen that it looked like he was closing his eyes. "You've done nothing but ridicule me for acting like that. Ever since we met, you've named me idiotic, immature, and foolish."

"You're right. I have. Because it's idiotic, immature, and foolish for me to act like that. But it's how you should act. Kaleo said each of us has a part to play, and without your . . . your . . ."

I glared at everyone—especially Prince—before continuing. "Remember on Aren's Steeple when I said that I've never had anything to believe in?"

Enoch's inflated eyelids widened.

"Even after I almost killed you, you never gave up on me." I took a slow step forward before jabbing my finger down at his chest. "So what the hell makes you think you can give up on yourself? You're our Charger, dammit."

"Lucian's a Jackal! You told me that not a single Navigator in history has ever beaten one! How do *we* stand a chance?"

"We have something no other Navigator's had: the Other."

"But you can't control—"

"I know I can't . . . But maybe someone else can."

It wasn't much of an "I'm sorry for punching you more times than I can count," but my words seemed to have the same effect.

He was the only boy I'd ever met who hadn't treated me as a Shadarian, mercenary, or ex-Navigator. When we'd first met in the throne room, I'd just been another face to a plant a fist into. And after Aren's Steeple, I'd seen that he was just another human: another soul shattered by the miserable state of our world. I'd looked across the starglass fire . . . and seen someone equally as stubborn in mind as they were in spirit.

Maybe that's why we worked so well together.

Enoch tapped into Ignis to begin healing his face. In response, I offered him a fist coated in his own blood.

"I know it sounds impossible," I said, "but impossible's all we have right now." I looked around the circle. "Let's find another way out of here and get the Heart back. It's either that or stay stuck in this damned hole." Complementing Enoch's green eyes, I turned mine gold. "And I'm pretty sure neither of us plans on the latter."

Closing his eyes, Enoch returned the fist-bump.

"One or two of those punches should've knocked you out, you know," I grumbled.

He grinned as I helped him up. "Boxer's chin."

CHAPTER 73

Enoch

Pieces of desert rock and temple debris flew all around me as I punched us up into the Serrated Keep. After that, we helped one another climb up out of the mile-long pathway we'd forged from one of the vortexurn's higher burrows, then sprinted through the orange-and-yellow labyrinth. I tapped into Ignis, searching the world around me for a pink flame, a familiar darkness that I'd once seen curdling around Loc's throat.

Though I almost ran into one of the keep's columns more than once, having to be frequently steered by Jezna, I finally found the pink flame opposite a flickering brown-colored candlelight.

"This way." I threw us through an empty open corridor. And as we ran, I closed my eyes, allowing Jezna to steer me, and listened to the flames conversing far off.

"The resources are packed, sir," a voice that didn't belong to a flame said. It looked as though the darkness behind the pink flame had said it. Something inhuman. Without a soul. An Ignis hunter.

The pink flame spoke. "See if you can pry those spears from the guards' hands. The Noda could use weapons like those."

"Yes, sir. Shall we kill the prisoners?"

"You can try, ya ugly bastard," a far-off voice said.

The pink flame never wavered. "No. Let the sultan decide their fate. I'm actually quite fond of mercenaries, you know. And have the pilots tell Harrenous that I'm in possession of something she'll find most . . . illuminating."

"Right away." And the darkness disappeared. I then noticed that the brown candlelight—a spirit barely lit—had begun to dangerously fizzle out of existence. The pink flame brightened in response.

"Something on your mind?"

"The Heart . . . ?" the brown spark asked.

The pink flame snorted. "The Heart will be returned to Ryjen when we no longer have use for it."

"But, you said—"

"I lied. You chose to put your trust in demons? Reap the consequences. Your people will get the Heart, but not immediately. Maybe now's the time to give them a speech about patience."

"Patience? My people have waited two hundred years—"

"And *He* has waited two million." The pink flame flew forward until it was inches from the brown. "Get in line." It settled back into its place, leaving the brown spirit fizzling dangerously. "You're a Nodan nation. I suggest you make this speech good."

The brown spirit just continued to whittle away until I heard quiet sobs. Until it was as though the flame had already bled to black.

First in line, last in line . . . I heard Biassis say as we neared the wall at the end of the corridor; when, with my eyes closed, I could see the pink flame on the other side. *It makes no difference. We're all in line.*

And though my hands were bleeding through their bandages, scars piled on top of scars, I opened my eyes, poured Ignis into my left fist, and threw it at the wall.

The desert rock burst, sending the sun and stars shining through.

We'd made it.

By the skin of our bloody teeth, but we'd still made it.

Lucian looked as though he'd seen a ghost. Or four of them. In fact, I would've taken the time to cement his expression firmly in my brain if we hadn't seemingly arrived at a crucial moment in Ryjenian—maybe Archengardian—history.

Glancing between the astonished Jackal, the whirring crab cruisers situated among the keep's towers, the kneeling mercenaries all in a line, the sobbing sultan, and the confused crowd of Ryjenians spread all around us, I realized exactly what was happening.

Time to Charge.

Grimly moving the sultan aside, I strode up to the balcony. Lords, they were a mass of people, stretched as far as the eye could see before running into the sandstone buildings.

Swallowing, I tapped into Ignis and observed all the strings of light in the darkness. There were hundreds of them, all so fragile and spindly. Looking at the thick strand of my own spirit, I didn't even know if I could offer mine to them.

C'mon, Noc. Just do what you do. Be immortal. Show these people what the Brotherhood's really about. It's not possession . . . It's connection.

The feeling of Murta, Jezna, and Prince stepping beside me gave me all the confidence I needed. I opened my eyes, spiritual hands gathering the Ryjenians' cords, and inhaled.

"I, er, know this looks bad. And I definitely know that you lot have been through too much rubbish to ever even consider taking our word over your sultan's . . . but you're being lied to. The Jackals and the Noda aren't the heroes. And yeah, neither is the Government. But we're not the Government: We're the Brotherhood."

Reactions, mostly negative, flowed through the crowd. I winced, trying to keep hold of their spirits, and plowed forward before they could begin conversing.

"Look, we believe what you believe in! Every nation has a right to be free, to refuse to join a conflict they know is wrong on both sides. Every person has the right to choose their *own* path, regardless if others disapprove. Even their best friend calls them a right-honorable idiot for walking it."

I swept my gaze across the crowd. "The difference between us is a title. You call yourself Ryjenians, we call ourselves Navigators. But we all bleed the same. We're all Archengardians. You might not have Ignis, you might not be like outcasts and outliers like us, but you don't have to bow before these blokes. None of us do.

"You may think you've no other option but to surrender, but that's nonsense. The Brotherhood has never surrendered, even when we're battered from every angle. The Brotherhood has never joined a side, even when we're pressured at every opportunity.

"You might think you have to fall, and you might hate us because we've yet to, but even through the hate, we'll always be there to protect what's most important: the connection all Archengardians will forever hold with one another. I promised your sultan that we'd use the Sacred Heart to heal your city, and I don't break my promises. We *will* assist you."

I pointed at Lucian. "We're Navigators you can trust, and we're not going anywhere without the Sacred Heart."

There was a moment of energized silence where it looked as though my words had done their job. I let go of the spiritual strands in anticipation. I could practically feel my spirit lifting out of my body and flying through the sky to settle into every Ryjenian scattered below . . .

But unfortunately, letting go of the strands snapped every single one.

Instead of cheering, the crowd began to boo noisily and throw wadded clothing.

I tiptoed away from the balcony. "Tough crowd."

Jezna patted me on the back. "It was worth a shot."

"I thought it was fantastic," Prince fumed, sticking his tongue out at the Ryjenians before getting hit in the face with a pair of soiled underwear. "FREAKING HELL—"

"I don't mean to steal the attention of the moment," Murta said, watching Lucian scale the keep wall, "but he's getting away."

I pounded my fists. "Well, we'll just have to prevent that, then, won't we?"

Fire flew up and down Murta's legs. "Thought you'd never ask. You with us, Anders?"

The merc nodded. "To hell and back." He stood beside the rest of his brethren, facing down their captors with smug looks. "We don't need guns to fuck these dudes up."

We stalked toward the Jackal. Lucian slung himself up onto the second balcony and glared down at us.

"You want this?" He removed the Heart from his cloak, ripping off one of his gloves. "You'll have to fight it first!" When the stone connected with his fingers, his body convulsed and turned his eyes a forest green. Shards of dark energy shot out of the Heart and flew across the sky, slamming down into the crowd of Ryjenians in a bolt of lightning.

We all flinched and tapped into Ignis, the Ignis-less mercenaries raising their weapons.

Prince ran to the ledge of the balcony and came back with wide eyes. "Oh."

The eyes of every Ryjenian gathered outside the keep now glowed the same dark green as the Heart, and the veins around their faces, necks, and arms pulsed a sickly black. All of their heads snapped up to leer at us in unison.

Prince leapt back with a screech, and when the possessed people began to scale the walls in an almost demonic fashion, he started changing frequencies.

Lucian's glowing face wore the same demented leer as that plastered onto the Ryjenians. "Here's a speech for you!" His fingers dug into the Heart. "Stop at nothing until the Navigators are dead!"

The first few Ryjenians sprang up over the balcony just as Lucian leapt across the towers. Mercenaries threw themselves forward without a moment's hesitation, already clashing with the Ryjenians.

Though everything seemed to be happening all at once all around us, time slowed for the four of us. In fact, it hit a blessed standstill.

Jezna's waterblade materialized in her hands, Prince's stun gun hummed to life, and Murta's legs crackled with flames. Joining them and turning toward the Ryjenians, I ignited Green Fire Fist.

"Back to back," I said. "And let's carpe diem this shite."

CHAPTER 74

Enoch

Possessed Ryjenians swarmed the balcony. The first few sprinted at us, black veins pulsing, teeth bared, but were met with immediate retaliation.

We smashed through their ranks, Ignis and Aestus twisting around us. Jezna's waves sent them scattering. Murta's kicks threw them backward. Prince's stun gun reduced them to crumpled heaps. I saw Anders and the mercenaries, too, some flinging themselves from the balcony into the courtyard below.

Like the skeleton army created by the Karnocolix, though, the Ryjenians kept coming. Even when I uppercut the Sacred Heart out of them and watched their eyes fade back to normal, the menacing dark-green energy always returned. Their veins always bled back to black.

"Incapacitate, don't kill!" Jezna shouted at a group of mercs that had taken up a position beside us. "They aren't the enemy!"

Murta elbowed me in the back. "This won't stop unless we get the Heart. We *have* to go after it."

I eyed the crab cruisers. The first two had begun the process of taking off—their wings extended outward, legs folded inward—and were steadily heading east along the wall of the city. When I saw that the third had started to follow slowly behind, I cursed.

"I know this is a lot to ask," I asked Jezna and Prince. "But do you think you could lead these bastards on a merry goose chase?"

Prince fired eight rounds of magenta Aestus, ducked to allow Jezna to slam her waterblade into two Ryjenians, then sprang up, sunglasses fixed to his forehead. "Noc, I *am* the merry goose chase."

"Jezna?"

She transformed her waterblade into spinning aqua spheres and flung them around the balcony. "Do what you have to do. Just be safe. I mean it."

"You bet, Mum." If a faceless helm could scowl, hers did.

Anders slid into view, tendrils of brown-orange Ignis exploding from his back. "We'll help 'em as best as we can. Never thought these words would ever be strung together but . . ." He stared straight at Murta. "Go give that Jackal a Navigational ass-kicking."

Murta nodded, then cocked his head toward the line of escaping cruisers. When I saw a black-cloaked figure hovering in the doorway of the first, I clenched my fists.

We ran for the wall, hurling ourselves across rooftops, maneuvering through the skies of the evening city. The wall that wrapped around Ryjen loomed a few yards ahead, nearly level to the roofs we ran on, but the cruisers were gaining ground. If we wanted to catch the last few, we had to move fast.

Sensing our deteriorating window, Murta tapped into Ignis and pushed the pace. I followed, feeling my markings cover my body as I poured Ignis into everything. Murta sped ahead a few paces, but I was proud to say that I kept up with him. We reached the wall at the same time and looked to the sky.

All three cruisers flew in a perfect line, stair-stepping upward with the first cruiser already twenty feet above the wall and the third lingering around five feet.

Sprinting toward the fleeing third cruiser and the rising wall, I kept a hold on Ignis, digging my shoes into the sandstone and gritting my teeth.

The leading two cruisers flew to the point where it was impossible for us to reach them—mechanical dragons against the rays of Tanten. That left only the third.

Whether it was low on gas or sheer luck, it lingered behind, hovering much closer to the ground, and when the end of the wall neared, it merely drifted away from it and remained level.

I sprinted for it, ready to jump off of the edge and onto the sides, but was held back by Murta's arm. He'd already skidded to a stop, breathing heavily.

"What now?"

I gawked. "What do you mean?!"

"The doors! We can't reach them from this angle!"

The cruiser's engine hummed back to life, increasing in volume.

I touched my toe to the end of the wall, gazing down at the desert dunes far below, then took twelve steps back. "So we reach the roof."

"Now's not the time for that swashbuckling mierda! Think rationally here! Once the cruiser starts ascending, it's not coming back down!"

I watched the cruiser move beyond reach, beyond rationality. Murta was right, of course . . .

My eyes focused on the tower at the edge of the city, the guards' tower, and the roof that the cruiser had yet to reach the height of.

I jumped off the wall onto the tower and began to scale it. The hard sandstone bit into my hands, reopening scars I'd healed with Ignis while digging out of Jâhic, but I powered through the pain. I always had.

Murta followed angrily. "We won't make it!"

"We can." I pulled myself up onto the ledge around the golden dome and watched the cruiser fly level to it. It was right there . . .

Murta emerged at my side. "I know you think this'll work, but—"

"It will." I clutched the tip of the dome with one hand and leaned forward with the other, gauging the distance.

I'd stood on the edge of mortality too much lately. It was time to face the fire. No longer would I turn away from it. You didn't greet danger with fear, but with a pair of fists.

Murta grabbed me, face right next to mine. "All right! Pretend I didn't say all that stuff down in Jâhic! We can't—"

My hands were pinned, my strength wasn't. I lifted Murta up onto my shoulders, clenching his body with both arms below his and staring at the cruiser roof. "We can!"

I threw Ignis down into my legs. My body churned with the green symbols, emerald fire flying around me. The white sun scar burned into my back aligned with Tanten in the sky, becoming interlinked rings.

Murta saw what I was going to do, felt me dig my shoe into the roof, and chose the only rational option: holding on for dear life.

"Nononono!"

When my feet left the ground, the top of the tower shattered, the sandstone unable to withstand the pressure. With nowhere left to go, we sailed silently toward the cruiser. The last sparks of Ignis shot back into my heart as Murta and I fell in an arc. The iron top of the cruiser rolled forward, looking as though we'd fall short by inches, then my feet connected with the roof and we tumbled.

So that was why Murta had been so doubtful. Getting on was easy. *Staying* on seemed a wee bit harder.

The cruiser dipped when our weight hit it, but righted itself. Though it stabilized quickly, we didn't, and when Murta was thrown off of my shoulders, he dropped off the edge of the cruiser. I threw myself to the right.

Thank the Lords, his hands had latched onto the ledge just under the wings. His feet dangled for a moment, then found the space beneath the side doors.

I heaved a sigh of relief, but the cruiser gained speed. Murta pried his left hand loose from the ledge, turning it into claws.

"The pilot knows we're here! I'm going in!" He pointed a single claw up at me. "Stay here!"

"I'm coming with you!"

"Stay here! We might be able to get the Heart without the Other!"

"And if that doesn't work?"

"It will! I won't risk any more innocent deaths!" Murta let his eyes turn back to brown, and my heart leapt when I realized that he'd stopped using Ignis so he could look at me normally.

So he could *look* at *me*.

"I will get you out of this alive. And when that's done, we'll go back to Carbonek. Together."

"You bloody promise?"

Though Murta only had one free hand, he formed it into the sixty-degree angle of a triangle and pressed it against his heart. Then he tore open the door with his claws and was gone.

CHAPTER 75

Enoch

When the curses and yells grew too much to bear, I tapped into Ignis and pummeled open the ceiling.

"Heads up, blokes!" The piece I stamped into the cruiser smashed through the helmet of the Ignis hunter standing beneath it.

It's them.

A cold concoction of fear and fury lit within me. Igniting Green Fire Fists, I sprang up, preparing to pound on the downed hunter until it was incapacitated, but Murta leapt out of the shadows, crushing its chest with his burning feet. Blood and black liquid spilled out onto the floor.

I blinked slowly. *Everything's all right. It's . . . dead.*

Though the hunter most certainly was, it took Murta throwing the pilot from his seat and knocking him out with a kick to snap me from my trance.

"Get up here!" He gunned the steering wheel forward.

"Er, yeah! Apologies!" I stumbled my way to the front. "What'd you need?"

"Do you see the buttons attached to the co-pilot wheel?"

"If you're asking me to fiddle with 'em, I'd really rather stay technology-ignorant."

"Just press the damned buttons! I promise you'll like them!"

I swung myself into the chair with a shrug and did as he suggested. A soft click echoed out of the nose of the cruiser, but nothing else happened.

"I . . . love them?"

Murta cursed, plowing the cruiser forward. "They disabled the guns. Fine. We'll do things my way."

Watching the second cruiser approach at a speed even I wasn't comfortable with, I scrambled for the seat belt. "Which means . . . ?"

"Ram 'em 'til you damn 'em.'"

The sudden hoot of laughter in my throat was smothered by Murta ramming our cruiser into the second's rear. The impact shook both machines and took off quite a bit of metal. Fortunately, Murta hit the cruiser at just the right angle to cause enough damage to its engine. The second cruiser began flying sideways, twisting in midair.

Swerving our own cruiser around it, Murta broke formation. But when he prepared to jerk the wheel to send our left side flying into the second cruiser's right side, the side door snapped open, revealing an Ignis hunter.

Murta let go of the lever to stop our cruiser. The opposing cruiser sped by us just as the hunter fired a blast of Aestus. It missed us by a foot. When the pilot snapped up the lever to backtrack toward our own, the hunter stumbled from the sudden stop. Murta took advantage of the moment by slamming down the lever. I was pulled back into my seat as we catapulted at an angle into the second cruiser's right side.

Iron split iron, and the Ignis hunter was crushed somewhere in the tangled madness. I whooped as Murta reversed our cruiser out of the smoking one and watched the burning machine tumble out of the sky.

When Murta set his sights on the final cruiser, a cold chill ran up my spine.

Lucian was somewhere in there with the Sacred Heart. We wouldn't be able to get one without the other, and how exactly we'd go about attacking him still seemed up in the air. I could think immortal all I wanted, but that didn't change the fact that Lucian was still a Jackal. A Jackal with more power in his pinkie than more than half of Carbonek.

I racked my brain for a plan, but Murta stood.

"Take over."

"Flying?!"

"Just hold it steady. It's not as hard as it looks." He moved out of the way, freeing the wheel. Left with no other option, I scrambled into the pilot's seat and seized it. Murta locked the acceleration lever in place to cruise.

"What's your plan now?" I asked, watching him stalk toward the hole in the roof of the hull.

"Do the best I can to hold him off."

"And you do recall what happened last time, right?"

Murta jumped, latching his fingers onto the outside of the hole, and pulled himself back up without a word.

I jerked my gaze between him and the cruiser in front of me. Flying one was terrifying. It felt weird to be in charge of such massive power, able to maneuver an enormous piece of weaponized iron. It unsettled me. Technology had never been my strong suit, nor had my time working the Serapharus machines made me any fonder of it.

Murta's shoes stomped across the front window. I bent my neck at awkward angles to make attempted eye contact, but he ran down the short slope of the nose and leapt off without Ignis. I held my breath and watched him scale the back of the cruiser, spring onto the roof, then messily drill his way inward with his claws.

I hunched forward in anticipation. My palms nearly slipped off the steering wheel from how much they were sweating. I felt hot and enclosed in the cruiser. I felt alone, isolated. It wasn't the furnaces, but it was still torture.

When the silence reached the point that I grew concerned, faint crashes echoed over the combined roar of the two engines. A golden fireball escaped out of the ceiling of the cruiser, followed by a dozen tentacles shooting out from every angle.

The gnarled limbs carved gaping holes in the machine, tearing the walls and wings apart around it. My eyes widened, imagining Murta somewhere in the center, then one of the tentacles lurched outward and struck my cruiser across the nose.

The desert spun around me. I blindly threw my fists at the window, shattering the glass and trying to make sense of the violently tilting world around me. I caught sight of a dark silhouette on the roof of the torn cruiser facing off against another figure and jerked the wheel in an attempt to right it. Remarkably, it worked, but I was still out of line and drifting away. And Murta was losing.

The tentacles overwhelmed him, striking from a hundred different angles. It was impossible to track their movements completely, even for a Shadarian apparently. Murta fought hard—weaving lightning kicks, claw rakes, and fireballs of Ignis into a thunderstorm of power—but as hard as he fought, he was still slapped off the cruiser into the open sky.

And from the lifeless position his body took as it tumbled, he'd been incapacitated on impact.

Charge.

I let my mind go numb. Thinking slowed me down. I just bloody moved, letting Ignis flow into every cell and enhance every muscle.

Eyes tracking both the falling Shadarian and the damaged cruiser with the Jackal on top, I threw myself through the shattered window and rolled up the side of the cruiser, feeling the weight and hardness of it with Ignis. With every step I took, I felt the emerald cord that connected the spirit of the cruiser's core to my own spirit tighten. With every breath, I strengthened my connection to the cruiser until the cord was in my hand, ready to possess.

But as I flipped myself over the smoking rear and began to fall, I twisted myself in midair, separating the strand into two.

As I'd punched the cannonball, I thrust Ignis forward and uppercut the soul out of the cruiser.

Emerald energy twisted out of my fist, cracking against the back of the cruiser. Instead of breaking, the soft filtration of my spirit into the cruiser kept it intact, but my Ignis consumed it until the machine was a roiling fireball.

The Ignis-infused cruiser sped upward, controls and core completely fried but just as deadly. Even from two hundred feet away, I saw the whites of the Jackal's eyes when he turned and saw what soared toward him, but by then, it was already too late. The burning cruiser slammed into the first one and exploded.

I blinked. Everything hurt, but that seemed to be a minor inconvenience at the moment.

Oh. I'm falling.

So refusing rational thought did have its flaws after all. I'd sacrificed myself for a killing blow. Or what I'd *hoped* would be one.

Doesn't matter anymore. I was surprised by how calm I felt. *As long as Lucian's dead. As long as my squad makes it out alive. That's all—*

Something metallic nipped at the back of my neck.

In midair?!

The item slipped off of me, escaping upward where it floated among the burning wreckage of the cruisers. It looked like . . . a gold chain.

Flipping myself over in the air to look down at the desert that sped up to meet me, I discovered only darkness. An ocean of black rose up out of the sand in a demonic tidal wave, yet welcomed me with safety. Unable to fight against it, I was slowly drawn against the warm scales along its chest. Then black wings wrapped themselves around me, enclosing me in midnight tapestries. *Shielding* me.

We fell together.

CHAPTER 76

Enoch

The shadedrake gave a wounded howl as its back slammed into the sand. I felt the wind knocked from my chest as I fell back against its scales, then immediately realized what had happened and scrambled through the creature's wings to escape.

It was still the Other, and once it gathered itself, who knew what would happen? Either it hadn't had enough time to move around in the air to fly . . . or its priority had solely been on saving me. Fragment of hope aside, it had still tried to kill me before.

Upon escaping the tangled shadedrake, I made sure I was a good fifty paces away before looking toward the cruisers that had fallen with us. Green flames and natural fire combined to turn what had once been two machines into a mound of burning rubble. It was an ugly, twisted sight. No one could've survived it. Whatever Ignis hunters were left had surely perished. Whatever Jackals were left—

"Noc!"

I looked back toward the city. Driving across the sand from a good half mile away was a rundown vehicle, the tiny silhouettes of Prince and Jezna sitting in its front seat. I prepared to shout back at them that I was all right, but the shadedrake rumbled through closed eyelids, flopping over onto its belly. My eyes widened.

"Get back!" I shouted, watching the dragon stir, careful not to be struck by its twitching tail again. "Get back in the city! Don't come any—"

The Other's eyes flicked open.

I froze as it slowly brought itself to full height.

The shadow that fell across me might as well have been a mountain. The shadedrake blotted out the sun and half of the stars. Its obsidian scales glittered, the jagged crooks and spikes in its muscular chin the size of twisting crags, and its breath hissed out in volcanic shudders.

I took a step back and tripped. My heart pulsated until I thought I might drop dead. My eyes were unable to move beyond the gold circles of the Other's eyes.

Those eyes. They reduced me to a terrified child, a boy trapped in a flaming city.

But in those eyes, there was also familiarity. The way the creature stood was reminiscent of a familiar fighting stance. The chiseled chin and muscular legs were still there. The mane of dark spikes resembled a short mohawk. The scowling brow was all too familiar, too. The dark claws were larger versions of the smaller ones I knew.

And then the eyes.

Murta was in those eyes. He always was. He always had been.

Rather than continuing to clamber back, I dug my blistered palms into the sand and climbed to my feet. Outside of the dull rumbles echoing out of the shadedrake's chest, the only sound was my bandana whipping about in the hot wind. I moved slowly and silently until I had my hands raised.

"Murta," I said. "Murta, we did it. We won. We can dig the Heart out of the remains and take it back to Carbonek. But I need you to get control."

The cord that connected me to him was both the thickest and thinnest cord of them all. The strongest and the weakest.

"I know you can do this." I refused to filter Ignis into my words. I'd calm the Other, not possess it. I'd sworn on the Code. "Don't let the Other control you. I know you're in there. Just . . . connect." *With me.*

The shadedrake blinked its glowing eyes, then shook its head with a snort. Jezna and Prince pulled the turner into park, then gawked at me from a few yards behind the dragon. I held a finger up to my mouth, silently pleading.

"Connect." I lowered my hands to position them outward. I could see my eyes reflected back in the dragon's. "Shh. It's okay."

And as the beast's breathing stilled, it finally began to calm. Its wings stopped flaring. Its tail no longer slunk back and forth. The scalding fire in its eyes cleared into faint flames as opposed to lava pits, and its chest rose and fell softly.

It's working! It's actually—

The buckled side door of one of the damaged cruisers burst open.

Against the bright green flames, it was impossible to see anything other than a smoking figure stumble out of the burning remains and pull his cloak around him with a raspy cough. When he straightened, wiping blood from the deep wounds now covering his face, pink-tinted slaughter ignited in his eyes, spinning out of his crystal.

"You think you can kill a Jackal?" Lucian's voice was softer than a shout as he walked toward us, Ignis brightening around him with every step. "Navigational trainees think they can kill a Jackal?"

The Other's eyes thinned back to serpentine slits. It opened its jaws and roared—but not at Lucian.

The sound was loud enough for my ears to ring for thirty seconds and still hear it afterward. The coiled hunger in the beast's face was protruding so much that I almost just offered myself up to it. I should've known that there was no stopping the Other. No mortal man could ever hope to bring a dragon—let alone a shadedrake—to its knees.

"Mere children believe they can mess with the Jackals and not pay?" Lucian looked up at the shadedrake fondly. "There are plans on top of plans in motion.

Works behind works. Tapestries to weave, wells to fill, kingdoms to topple. And children think they can prevent a Jackal from getting what He wants, what is rightfully His?"

Though Jezna and Prince sprinted for me, I held my ground, returning to the ring. The Jackal, my squadmates, the city, the desert, the sky, and the sun evaporated.

Gone in an eyeblink.

I was alone in a white ring, the familiar dirty canvas beneath my tattered shoes, the white ropes and black posts gleaming around me, the harsh torchlight glinting in my eyes, and my opponent across the way.

All voices disappeared. I heard nothing but the beating of my heart and the guttural snarls emitting from the colossal shadedrake standing over me.

No mortal man, aye?

Rather than pull on the spiritual strand that connected me to the dragon, forcefully try to possess it, give another big speech, plead with it to get control, or even just say screw it and try to beat the darkness out of it, I chose the simplest path.

The Other lowered its hulking head, eyes burning with malice, jaws crackling with the beginnings of fire. And I just lifted my left fist to its snout.

I offered it a fist-bump.

The shadedrake wavered in bewilderment. Perhaps it hadn't expected to be so willingly offered a free arm to snack on. Seemed like that was the case. The veins in the dragon's throat flared as its jaws parted hungrily.

Prince's screams erupted through my ring, nearly bringing me surging back to clarity. The dragon's eyes burned tunnels through my skin, coiling with glee at the food it was about to feast upon, but I continued to glare into them. I wouldn't look away, not even when my fear was thick enough to strangle me. I refused to blink, even when the tears fell enough to sting.

"The Code is the Brotherhood's greatest flaw, Enoch." Lucian's voice shattered my ring into smoke. The desert returned in a wave of husky yellow and scalding pink. "Creating peace through connection means failure. It forever means death."

The shadedrake scowled. In the tempest of its eyes . . .

My heart skipped a beat.

Did it just . . . ?

The scowl deepened. There was barely a flicker of hunger, bloodthirstiness, or hate in it now. If anything, the gold was tinted with . . . annoyance.

The eyes were saying, *Is this idiota ever going to shut up?*

And before the scowl could deepen back into hate, the shadedrake swung its head downward and pressed its snout to my fist.

Brilliant golden Ignis collided with my spirit, wrapping me in its wings and reminding me of the light inside the Other, the spirit that never stopped trying to fight its way out.

And for a moment, it finally won.

When I'd tried to possess the Other on Aren's Steeple, I'd nearly gotten stuck. Not just because of the rage that had brought the Other out, but because the gold spirit had refused my help. In fact, now I realized that it wasn't the Other that had prevented us from connecting; it was the soul within. Murta's soul.

Keeping my shaking fist flush to the dragon's snout, I reached out into the darkness of my mind and held my hands over the golden flame that suddenly appeared, protecting it from the dark wind that tried to snuff it out.

I made a promise that I'd never possess you again, I told the flame. *And I already broke that promise once. I don't intend to break it again.*

The flame quivered before replying. *A long time ago, I made a promise, too. That I'd never end up like those that have messed with my life, that keep Archengard divided . . . And I broke that promise. Shattered it, actually. I became them in my rage. But now, I've gathered up all the pieces. All this time I thought I was searching for them when they were always right in front of me.*

Then, do you accept my spirit?

My spirit trembled as the flame danced in silence.

I do.

When the spirit of emerald filtered into the shadedrake, the heavens sprung out of its body, shooting across the sky.

Midnight-black scales became cosmic diamond white. Patches and trails of green and gold spread up through the white, circling around the beast's face and splitting it between emerald with black, and gold with white. Gnarled black wings became glistening gold and verdant. Dark serpentine eyes became spiral galaxies; one flamed gold with a green iris, the other flamed green with a gold iris.

And when the transformation was complete, the dragon unfurled its wings, sending stars rocketing around the desert, then began to stalk toward the petrified Jackal, the knight and treasure hunter howling with exhilaration beside it.

Before Lucian could bring himself to snap his quivering fingers, the dragon opened its mouth and belched forth the most stunning green-gold firestorm Archengard had ever witnessed.

CHAPTER 77

Enoch/Murta

It was difficult to imagine how we were doing it, but we did. Rather than one mind gaining superiority over the other, we wielded power equally. We worked as a whole instead of against. We worked as *one* instead of two.

Murta . . . Enoch said as Ignis raced through us in quasars. *This is* . . .

Beautiful, Murta finished, basking in the overflow of power. *You're glowing, swash.*

Enoch laughed. *Might be both of us, bruv.*

Black scales fled over to crystal white with patterns of green-and-gold swirls, and when our wings unfurled, constellations gleamed in them.

Murta, look at us! Enoch said. *This is the wickedest—*

Quick, let's intimidate him before the light wears off.

Like strike a pose?

No! That's a dumb—

We set our right foot forward, positioning our left foot back, and threw back our head in a devastating roar.

"Impossible." Lucian's jaw hung askew. "That cannot . . ."

I'll show you what's impossible, idiota. Murta fed movements up into Enoch's half, and Enoch followed through gladly. We began to march forward, wings batting the air. *Surviving this damned fight!*

Enoch began to build up the fire resting in our chest. We were vaguely aware of Jezna and Prince at our sides, waterblade and Aestus weapons churning.

Better not get in the way, Murta rumbled.

They're here to help, Enoch assured us. *It's four on one now. We stand a chance.*

Then let's make it official.

We stomped across the sand and opened our jaws, Enoch throwing up spiritual middle fingers as we boomed, *TASTE THE CONNECTION, BASTARD!*

Multicolored flames belched forth. Lucian barely had enough time to throw up his sleeves and block the majority using his cloak.

We emptied out our chest until we were left with nothing but smoke, then swung white claws burning with green and gold Ignis at him.

Lords, what's he made of? Enoch asked.

The Sacred Heart's protecting him, Murta said. *That, and his cloak's made of a material stronger than god armor.*

We continued rampaging at Lucian, swinging claws, wings, and our tail in wide arcs. Jezna and Prince danced around us, throwing as much Ignis and Aestus as they could. We made sure to give them room while creating more fire in our chest . . . but it all proved to be disastrous folly.

Lucian's moves were simply inhuman. He ran and reacted just as fast as a dragon, dodging every blow we threw at him. He took the hits—even a devastating clawed kick—and kept going.

Just like a Navigator.

He's fast, Enoch said.

We're faster.

We didn't give the Jackal time to regroup. As long as we kept him dodging, as long as we kept him on his toes—

A tentacle finally flew out of a portal. Enoch's spirit flared with fear, but the spiny skin that dragged along our scales did nothing. We caught the cretinous limb and severed it in two with claws trailing gold sparks and green fire. Lucian snarled, snapping the wounded tentacle back into wherever he pulled them from. He snapped his fingers in a strange pattern, then threw them outward.

This time, twenty pink triangles formed in the air behind him. Tentacles shot out of each, flying toward us. Using draconic speed coupled with being infused with two different Ignis abilities, we sprang in front of Jezna and Prince and began to deflect the limbs back.

It was like trying to hack through a jungle thicket that was constantly replenishing itself. It reminded Enoch of a hydra and Murta of the Field Fiends . . .

That's it! Enoch suddenly emoted.

What's it?! We weren't exactly in the best moment to be discussing things. The tentacles were everywhere, trying to snap off our wings and dig past our scales.

We've both dealt with creatures like this, so we're trying to fight it like how we fought them! We're thinking too hard!

You're saying we shouldn't think at all?!

Exactly!

Murta mentally ground his teeth but did as Enoch suggested. We lost ourselves to the patterns of the tentacles and focused primarily on fighting. Not fighting as a boxing swashbuckler or a Shadarian mercenary, but as a Charger and a Shield.

Our movements grew more coordinated. The tentacles' attacks seemed to slow and become predictable. We saw things in green and gold, not pink, and when two of the demented limbs clamped down around our skull, we spun in a thunderous arc, severing them completely. Lucian continued the barrage, quickening it, but we saw it coming. Right when the limbs shot in toward us from every direction, we curdled the flames inside us, then bellowed outward. The jagged line of green-gold inferno cut through the sickly pink skin, barbecuing them.

Brilliant! Enoch said. *That's—*

LOOK OUT!

The tentacle was at least five times bigger than those that had been attacking us, and unlike its predecessors, it *did* knock us off our feet. And it hurt. The spikes bounced off of our diamond-like scales but left a stinging aftertaste.

Lucian gave us little time to rest. After we'd righted ourselves with a shake of our hulking head, the tentacle was at us again, slashing against our wings.

Our unified cries escaped the dragon in a roar, but the tentacle came *again.*

Does this bloke ever rest?!

I'm getting severely annoyed, Murta said.

How many does he have in his arsenal?!

I don't think it's an arsenal as much as it's a bottomless pit . . . He replenishes them just as fast as we destroy them.

So we have to get faster?

I don't know how much faster we can get.

Enoch had been so encompassed in the flames of hope that he hadn't stopped to consider the possibility that Lucian was still a Jackal. Whereas we had only lived twenty sun cycles, using Ignis for less than a decade of them, Lucian had lived as a high-ranking Navigator and been instrumental to the Brotherhood's time in the War. He had more combat experience than ten swashbucklers and Shadarians.

So this is it, then? Enoch asked. *We fight 'til we can't fight anymore?*

Murta was silent, but with our minds and spirits connected, Enoch felt everything. Murta felt as determined, stubborn, and excited as Enoch did, but within the emotions, there was desperation. That desperation quickly gave way to hesitancy and uncertainty. To fear.

Enoch's heart sank.

I'm sorry. Murta's heart sank deeper when he felt Enoch's dampen. To restore some of our initial momentum, he threw up a façade of confidence, but Enoch read right through it.

Lucian's tentacles arrived, and this time, we were unable to stop them. With a mind being split in two, we lost control of the dragon. Our white scales spasmed back to black. The green and gold disappeared. Enoch felt the Other emerge and begin charging toward him.

Murta, we have to fight this!

The tentacles struck as one and we toppled. The dragon emitted a pained cry as we hit the sand hard. Enoch focused through our left eye and saw Prince and Jezna running toward us. He felt Murta's spirit spasm beside him.

I don't know how much longer I can do this. It's not working.

It'll work, Enoch promised. *It has to. We'll beat him. We can't give up.*

He forced us to one paw, grunting through the dragon, but without the help of another spirit, it was an impossible feat. One paw was all he could get to. Murta refused to cooperate.

C'mon! Enoch shouted, watching the tentacles knock Jezna across the sand and nearly take Prince's head off. *Get up!*

Every time Jezna fell back, she charged forward with her Ignis-created sword, now swirling with fire as much as water. Prince roared as he emptied his cannon, then moved to a machine gun and pistol combination.

Enoch's spirit writhed. *We have to help them! We can still beat him—*

Enoch. Murta's voice cut through the chaos. *I was wrong. We can't beat him. We're never going back to Carbonek. We're . . . done.*

Enoch let go of the strand and tried to throw himself out of the shadedrake's body, but Murta's spirit wrapped around him.

You can't fight him! Don't you realize that?! You're better off in here! His Ignis ability can't pierce dragonscale but if you go out there in flesh and blood—

Enoch fought off the gold flame. The fire from the cruiser wreckage burned in the dragon eye he still held claim over, and in front of the flames, the silhouettes of Jezna and Prince were beaten by a cloaked figure armed with teleporting tentacles. They fought hard, just as hard as Enoch fought against Murta, but in the end—just like Enoch—they failed and fell.

Enoch's leg gave out, slamming us back down into the desert. The tentacles slapped Prince and Jezna thirty feet and sent them tumbling beside us.

"Ridiculous," Lucian said.

The tentacles dispersed back into their portals, leaving the air around Lucian hazy from pink Ignis. He began to walk back toward us, gloved hands clenched behind his back.

"You caused me to lose my control over the Ryjenians with your Charger and Shield's more . . . creative tactics. I'll give you that. But I've watched the light leave the eyes of a thousand squads. What made you think yours would be any different?

"You aren't even confirmed yet! You fight like pieces, not the puzzle! You rely on luck and off-the-cuff moments as opposed to serious thought and skill! You think that connection and faith in the Code alone will enable you to beat me, but look at you!"

He thrust his arms out, salmon eyes seething. "You thought you could seize the Sacred Heart from a Jackal through belief?!" Spit flew from his bleeding teeth. "Through the Code?! Your ideals are blackened, rotting, and dead!"

But as Lucian raged, the fire from the cruisers behind him expanding slowly, a swiftly moving silhouette stepped through them.

Flames parting before it, the shadow limped through, the ends of the long jacket it wore flying backward. Though it moved with a slight hunch to its posture, though a piece of debris almost sent it stumbling back into the flames, it didn't show any signs of stopping.

It refused to stop, even as it shattered Lucian's rant with a simple gravelly rasp.

"Bloody hogwash."

Lucian's expression of anger sloughed off. The Ignis in his eyes winked out, leaving them unimpressively ordinary, and replacing giddy fury with an astounded, horrified realization.

We jerked our head up. Prince leapt to his feet, bottom lip trembling. Jezna rose to a knee, legs and shoulders quaking with similar emotion.

And Lucian pivoted slowly, wanting to wake from whatever nightmare he acted like he was caught in, and turned to see the silhouette emerge from the flaming wreckage.

He was still just as pale, ragged, and tired, but his fear looked to have been obliterated.

Fear was something this man had conquered long ago.

"Blackened?" he continued, tightening the white bandana covered in gold serpents wrapped around his forehead. "Mayhaps. Rotting? Most definitely. All bones, books, and blades do . . . But *dead*?"

He threw back the sides of the white-and-gold swashbuckling jacket he wore to reveal a long silver sheath. And though his hand wrapped around the hilt rigidly, he drew the glittering blade with unbelievable grace.

White flames poured out of the Sword. The diamond inferno seething around him might as well have been the waves of the Grand Sea lapping against a galleon deck. They might as well have been the unified spirits of every Navigator that had ever lived rallying to his cause.

And when he lifted the Sword to point directly at Lucian's heart, there was a faint smile on his lips.

"I'd like to see you try."

CHAPTER 78

Enoch / Murta

Lucian opened twenty more portals with a roar. Tentacles burst from the dark triangles, all at scattered points in time, varying between seconds and milliseconds to throw Kaleo off. Enoch shouted his name as if it would ring through the dragon's mouth without Murta saying it, but rather than crumble under the pressure, the opposite occurred.

Kaleo had been left back at Carbonek. The Leviathan was here.

Not mirages of him, like we'd seen in the manor every so often, but the Brotherhood's Champion. The Navigator that had freed cities, sailed every speck of sea, stopped wars, and leveled fleets. The one that had wrestled with gods and demons.

When Kaleo moved, he moved with purpose. Nothing was short and choppy or long and overexaggerated. His attacks, adjustments, and evasions bled into the next. A dance, one where Kaleo practically swam across the sand. Like a leviathan through the sea.

We were watching a master craftsman at work. All fights that we'd seen and taken part of paled in comparison. We had been finger-painting; Kaleo erected castle murals.

Lucian's tentacles moved faster than we could comprehend, but here Kaleo was taking on all of them with nothing but an Ignis-infused sword. He severed several of the limbs in great arcing swipes and deflected the rest, creating brief explosions of white Ignis where the Sword collided with them.

Murta's voice emerged first. *He's . . . winning.*

Enoch wrapped his hands back around the strand that was Murta's spirit, slowly sinking back into the gold flame. We spiritually became one once more; the dragon's scales fled back to brilliant white as the spirit of the Other was dashed.

Yeah, Enoch echoed. *He is.*

Jezna stepped into our line of vision. Prince popped up from the other side.

"If we join," Jezna said, "our chances of winning will only increase, right?"

Murta remained quiet, but Enoch spiritually smiled. Murta was itching to enter the fight to be able to say that he fought alongside the Leviathan; he'd just never be caught admitting it.

Prince rapped a fist against our forehead. "Hellooooo? You all awake in there?"

Enoch felt Murta fold into him, offering his silent emotional agreement. Then together, we lifted ourselves back up onto one paw. Prince yelped as particles of sand were dumped off of our wings and we raised ourselves to full height, belching a green-gold fireball into the sky.

"I'll take that as a 'full speed ahead!'" Prince saluted.

We bombarded Lucian. Now, he no longer had to worry about his front, but all 360 degrees. And instead of managing just the Leviathan, he now had a knight, a feisty treasure hunter, and a "connectiondrake," as Enoch had taken to calling us.

That's such a stupid name, said Murta.

Lucian created portals on every side of him to be ready for any attack we threw, but the one attack he'd *never* be ready for was another blast of fire. We kept our distance to provide space for the other three Navigators but continued to throw claw attacks just to remind Lucian that we were still here. As the fight continued and Lucian began to visibly sweat, we pulled back slightly. We steadily pulled back more and more, so when Lucian became so focused on dueling Kaleo that he forsook his back completely, we breathed a column of flame down on top of him.

Lucian was enveloped by the fire. Every portal winked out at once, taking its tentacles with them. Prince and Jezna leapt back. Kaleo lowered his Sword and looked up at us in disbelief.

In the center of the green-gold mass, Lucian dropped to his knees. Somehow, he still wasn't dead, nor did he shout. Nothing but eerie silence curled up out of the flames. We pushed our fire out harder, until the sand beneath Lucian smoked, yet still he lived. It was more than his cloak, more than his spirit.

Just as we'd waited for an opening in Lucian's game, he had done the same. When our fire started to wither, we quickly inhaled to excavate the rest of the flames from our chest but didn't get the chance.

Ripping off his burning, tattered cloak to reveal a torso littered with black scars, Lucian thrust the Sacred Heart into the sky.

"ENOUGH!"

The same dark-green energy that had seemingly been protecting him from being incinerated sprang out of the Heart and shot across the desert in every direction.

Prince, Jezna, and Kaleo all went flying. Prince's guns were tossed from his shoulders, Jezna's Ignis disappeared, and the Sword spun out of Kaleo's hands.

But whereas the blast had merely nicked everyone else, we were hit square in the scaled chest. Murta was flung out of the Other's body and tossed back into his own, coughing and shivering, and Enoch was knocked out of him, forced to take shape while flying through the sand.

Murta landed forty feet back with a sharp groan . . .

Enoch was thrown toward Lucian and collapsed in a ruined heap at his boots.

* * *

Lucian looked from the smoking Heart to the circle of scattered Navigators . . . then down at me. As he stuffed the Talisman back into his pants, his eyes spun with triumph.

Before I could crawl away, he seized me by the throat.

I struggled to escape his grip, but my body fought against me. Being back in physical form took its toll on me as the pain from all the injuries that I'd received over the past twenty-four hours added up to where I could barely move. And on top of that, my Ignis was completely spent from possessing Murta. I was powerless.

When Lucian's hand tightened around my neck, I figured my spinal cord would collapse before I ran out of breath. The Jackals truly were inhuman. Nightmares come to life.

"You know," Lucian said, "the more I've watched your squadmates work, the more I've begun to realize that it's not the Code that completely drives them. It's you, isn't it?"

I clawed at his grip, gagging breathlessly. My legs gave out, dropping me to my knees. Lucian's now-scarred face was terrifying, menacing pink eyes burning. He looked monstrous.

"You're incredibly special to them," he said. "A human Talisman. Not just to the knight and hunter, but also to the Shadarian. Although the Jackals sought to use you, I suppose there will always be others. And I have a friend within that can't have the Shadarian growing into something beyond mending. He's too important to us."

"Not . . . yours to control . . ." I rasped out but was silenced with a squeeze.

"And what do you know, Light Eyes? What do you know of us and the War? What do you know of the shadows in the rafters?"

"Enough . . ."

His teeth crackled when he gnashed them together. "I can assure you, far worse awaits you than furnaces and fire beams."

Spirit flaring with fear, I went for my last gambit: looking Lucian dead in the eyes in an attempt to possess him.

But before I could so much as reach for the cord that bound me to his flame, an invisible wall of energy collided with my mind, blocking me off.

My eyes bulged in their sockets as all hope was dashed.

Lucian lifted me so my feet dangled in the air. "Can't connect with those that feel no connection. Heh. It's a shame. Your quest had just begun . . ." He snapped his fingers, conjuring a portal just past his right shoulder. "And now it's over."

I stared into the portal, beyond the pink lines of Ignis into the demented nothingness, and watched the tentacle shoot out. There was a blur of familiar darkness, a slash of pink light, and the pain of a thousand wounds.

Lucian let go of my throat with a sickening smile.

The tentacle pierced my heart before hooking itself into my chest and yanking me into the shadow. The portal snapped shut behind me.

CHAPTER 79

Kaleo

Prince screamed.

It was a horrific sound. The kind that siblings made when one was killed. I'd heard it one too many times . . . I'd made it when I fought my way across the battlefield and found Lucian crumpled against Vendren, his chest covered in brutal bulletsword gashes.

And as a similar sound roared forth from Prince's lungs, Lucian clapped his hands together, stepping through the open air Enoch had just been dragged through. "Well, that was easy."

Attack.

When I appeared at Lucian's side, his eyes widened.

Attack.

I swung straight for his skull, but his crystal hummed, and he cartwheeled out of the way.

Attack.

Twirling the blade behind my back as I spun in the opposite direction back toward him, I guided the Sword with my Ignis, cutting at every inch of space where Lucian stood.

Tentacles raced back toward me. I cut through them all, the Sword moving so fast that the air splintered. White shards disoriented his vision, intensifying Lucian's dodges. He managed to snap his fingers and send two tentacles at me, but I blocked them both in the same swipe, cutting eight-foot-deep scars into their tips.

Cahis had taught me that move. Or at least tried to. I hadn't listened then.

I'd spent the next twenty years perfecting it, for this very moment.

"I don't know why you take your rage out on me," Lucian said. I ducked and rolled around the rest of his tentacles, leaving rainbow afterimages. "You train these children, yes? Then blame yourself. Can you live with that, Kal? Another group of failures?"

"The only failures," I said, "were your little posse. You were too weak, so you succumbed to the storm. Amon never succumbed."

"And who failed to spot the storm all those years back, I wonder? You were the only one capable of calming it." He blocked the Sword with four tentacles coming from different directions and leered inward to the point that I could taste the blood on his breath. "You were the weak one."

I sliced through the limbs with a scream, but Lucian just danced away, then snapped his fingers at Prince. A tentacle sped toward the Ignis-less, weaponless boy thirty paces from me.

Champ's hollow unblinking eyes flashed across my own.

"*NO*!" I couldn't make it there in time, so I threw the Sword. Ignis fled my body instantly, but it followed the burning blade, severing straight through the tentacle before it reached Prince.

As I leapt after the hilt, I heard Prince shout, "Help us, Murta!"

My stomach dropped out of my body. I scooped up the Sword, reigniting the blade painfully, and spun just to block three tentacles from snapping at Prince again. And beyond the spasm of pink Ignis, I saw the Shadarian kneeling in the sand forty feet away. He was clutching something in his right, black-clawed hand. It looked like bits of fleshy pulp, maybe even blood. But even rarer than that: His head was bowed.

I did this.

"He's beyond helping you," Lucian said, horrific demon eyes flicking toward where I stared beyond our clashing Ignis abilities. "Your Code didn't help you defeat me, nor strip the Heart from my hands. If anything, the Code is what killed Enoch. He's currently being digested in my Negative Realm. I'd like to see Eleri bring him back from that."

My rage overwhelmed me. As I blocked tentacle after tentacle with strikes that Bartholomew Norcus had worked me through night after night in the training halls, I saw the bowed, bloodied boy kneeling in the sand again.

And this time, a different boy flashed across my eyes: Mathias staring down at the bodies of seventeen dead Navigators—the first to have ever been slain in the War.

I wasn't the Light in the Darkness.

The coat didn't fit me anymore. I'd had to dig through piles of boxes to find it. I'd had to run faster than I'd ever run before to catch up to Barco's cruiser, to order him to turn back.

Because if anyone was going to find the Sacred Heart, it was going to be the one that the Shrouded Men had egged on for years.

Because if the jagged black lettering etched into the back of my jacket meant anything—the words fortuna favet fortibus, flanked by four dancing dragons—it meant that I needed to get my arse out of that stuffy old office and back out into the world.

But now, as the next tentacle flew into me, the Sword spun from my hands, landing point down a foot away from Lucian.

And my Ignis evaporated.

CHAPTER 80

Enoch

Am I dead?

I was too afraid to ask. But I could somehow still think.

Does that mean I'm alive?

No, I'd been stabbed through the heart by a tentacle and dragged into whatever nightmare world Lucian conjured them out of. A world built from shadow.

I tried tapping into Ignis but failed.

Maybe because I no longer have it. Maybe Ignis leaves your spirit when you die and returns to the Dragon Lords . . . Maybe I'm on my way to kingdom come now.

A sudden chill ripped through me.

Or maybe I'm in the other place. That would definitely explain the lack of light. It'd explain *a lot* about the situation I was in. *But what did I do wrong?*

Of course, there was no answer. There was never an answer.

Even the Lords themselves refused to connect with those to whom they'd bestowed their powers.

Combining my spirit with Murta hadn't even been enough to stop Lucian. Even after Kaleo arrived . . .

The legend that had helped me through the miserable Serapharus nights, then pushed me to leave the city and become a swashbuckler—then become a Navigator—had fought right in front of me.

But not even the Leviathan had been able to stop a Jackal.

The darkness around me became shaded cement streets, giving way to black alleyways and cathedral-like factories. The smoke and shadow entered into my lungs, coiling around my shattered heart.

This is what happens when you try to connect.

I'd stolen food from the Olders to give to the Youngers, and a Younger had betrayed me. The scar on my back had been the cause of someone I was trying to help. I'd been betrayed by connection, just like I'd been betrayed by the Younger. My own stupidity had brought about—

A scream pierced the darkness, ripping me from my misery. It was wordless, mindless, and growing closer. Like someone was running toward me.

Prince?

"Trying to best me in a physical fight is impossible," a cold voice drawled. "You would have a better chance of obtaining Ignis in your next life."

I froze. Lucian's voice was unmistakable. But it sounded far away and murky, like he spoke through mud. And it didn't sound directed at me as much as it did at the scream. At Prince.

Prince?! I tried again.

It didn't make any sense. I was dead, yet I heard what was still going on in Ryjen?

Prince, I'm here! It's Enoch!

Lucian spoke again. "And I would highly suggest you stop running at me unless you seek to join your squadmate."

The sounds of Jezna's armor crunching and Prince's moans of pain made me wish I could cover my ears. So this *was* the other place. I'd be forced to listen and observe the torment of my squadmates for the rest of eternity. I'd be forced to watch others suffer for being too weak, just like in Serapharus.

Let me go, I pleaded with the darkness. *Please. Let me leave . . .*

"Help us, Murta!" Prince said.

The silence that echoed after might as well have beaten my soul with a battering ram.

"He's beyond helping you," Lucian said. "Your Code didn't help you defeat me, nor strip the Heart from my hands . . . If anything, the Code is what killed Enoch. He's currently being digested in my Negative Realm. I'd like to see Eleri bring him back from that."

No! That's not true! I'm still here! I'm . . .

Realization crashed into me, then came with the fragments of something Murta had told me under the keep during what had been the lowest point of my life.

Remember on Aren's Steeple when I said that I've never had anything to believe in?

Searching for fire in a sea of shadows, drying my tears with darkness, I recalled the next two sentences.

Even after I almost killed you, you never gave up on me.

No. I'm dead, I reminded myself. *There's no way I'm alive . . . I'm dead. I'm . . .*

I remembered the finger pointing down at me, down at my heart. I remembered the hope in those eyes, the hope looking down at me and searching for the same in return.

So what the hell makes you think you can give up on yourself? You're our Charger, dammit.

I'm dead, I concluded. *That much is bloody evident.*

But my squad needs me. And because they need me, for now . . .

I have to at least try *to think immortal.*

Beyond the darkness there was sand and rage. But beyond that, there were others. Darkness or not, flames or not, I still had a connection to all of them. A connection that had grown into something greater. I'd cared for them. I didn't need to see their flames in the darkness to know they were there. I didn't have to see the spiritual cords of green Ignis leading to them.

I'd built myself a star system, and I lay at its center. I was the suns. After death, the remnants of a star still scattered out to the universe and helped craft the next generation of stars, the next suns that would give birth to the next star systems.

And I'd already danced among their dust every night in the Light Isles.

My body might be mortal, but my spirit never dies. My spirit: That's what's truly immortal. I'm not immortal, but my spirit is. So going by that . . .

I'm immortal.

A spark of emerald light ignited in the darkness, rising into a flame. It took me several blinking seconds to realize that the flame came from my fist.

I began to move the fire up through my arm, into my left shoulder, then into the rest of my body. I felt my whole body return. I felt myself become whole again, and although the darkness kept its depth, I could still clearly see myself floating.

That was slightly unnerving. I thought about a flat surface beneath my feet, and the darkness solidified under me. Much better.

Lucian was shouting more nonsense. The darkness rippled menacingly with every word, but I focused beyond the shadow and into the spirits that I couldn't see. And I recited their names:

Loc. Cowlin. Maddox. Biassis. Larry. Hektor. Eleri. Barco. Kaleo.

Jezna. Prince. Murta.

With every name, I felt my strength return. With every memory came another cord connected to another flame. They wrapped around me, collecting into my fist until the green flame grew to be the size of Aren's Steeple. The darkness recoiled from the light.

I built up Green Fire Fist until my brain bounced around the inside of my skull and entered what Murta had called the Twilight Realm. I delved deeper, further inward—*beyond* it.

Past pain. Past numbness. Past darkness.

Past death.

CHAPTER 81

Kaleo

I couldn't stand. Couldn't move. After years of letting my body go to shit, it'd finally given out on me.

Ignis sputtered from my spirit, my breaths coming out staggered. I was vaguely aware of the trainees around me: the kneeling knight, weeping treasure hunter, and silent Shadarian. They'd put their faith in me one last time . . .

"This is Carbonek's best?" Lucian said, closing all the portals decorating the air behind him. "This is what's become of what I once took pride in? Where is the training? The skill?" He looked at Murta. "The power?"

"The strength of one's Ignis ability," I said, focusing on the still-flaming Sword stuck in the sand just beyond Lucian's shoulder, "doesn't make the Navigator."

"You said that then as you say it now. And the only reason you ever did spew those lies was because you never gained full understanding of your own ability." Lucian lifted a hand to his face, watching pink fire dance between his gloved fingers. "You've never known what it's like to be *teeming* with power. If you'd felt the way we did, you would've joined His cause—"

I thrust out my hand.

There was the sound of a soft explosion, and the Sword flew toward Lucian. He slid out of the way in alarm, spinning the Sword back into my hand. Ignis surged back through me, reanimating my body. I slashed the Sword upward, sending a twenty-foot disc of white energy flying across the desert where it would've severed Lucian in half if his crystal hadn't forced him to dodge.

But as he dodged, he turned his spin into a backfist. My Ignis snapped out of existence. I hit the sand, seeing spots. Seeing Bartholomew Norcus growling over me, scolding me about how my own emotion had been turned against me.

"That," Lucian said, shaking his hand like it hurt, "was quite possibly the most satisfying thing I've ever done. Almost as satisfying as what I've done to your Code." Archengard lurched around me as he lifted me by the sides of my jacket. "Shadarian! Do you want to do the honors or shall I?"

"He's dead," Murta whispered.

Lucian frowned. "Who's dead? Kal? He's about to be, but . . ." He drifted off in disbelief. "You're still hung up on the swashbuckler?"

"You killed him."

"That's it." Lucian snapped my fingers impatiently, wrapping Murta in a tentacle. After the limb dropped him on the sand next to Jezna and Prince, he used it to shove me back toward them. Sand shifted under me, blubber and suckers nipped at my skin, and after the tentacle disappeared, I saw that the Sword was once again too far for me to reach and had returned to only a lifeless hilt.

Lucian eyed me coldly. "The Brotherhood builds up this idea that squads are invincible. But no one is invincible, especially those that take refuge in numbers. The War taught us that the individual will always be the strongest. Alone, there's nothing to hold you down. Nothing to hold you back."

He directed his words at the trainees. "Just now, Kal showed you a mere fraction of his power because if he were to go all out, you'd all be caught in the crossfire. This is what I mean. Murta Kaster should be able to transform into his true form as he pleases, but instead he hides behind a mask. A ridiculous ideal meant to enslave power, not let it grow. Emotion and attachment makes men weak.

"For centuries, the Brotherhood has failed at protecting Archengard. It's let it go to a twisted mess. Peace has yet to be restored in the Perpetual War, and the only way to see that true peace is restored is by obliterating the remains. Burn it to the ground. Seize the power we've been granted and use it how it should be used: to lead by example and destroy all who stand in our way. Until true peace is finally instilled."

"If lives have to be taken," I said, "it isn't peace. It'll never be."

"You're right. It's order."

"Something the Brotherhood was never meant to dictate. We're not a government—"

"But we should be! We should be *kings*! Lords above the Dragon Lords!"

Lucian's rage stabbed holes in my heart. Hatred for the Brotherhood was something that lively recruit had never harbored . . . yet here he was now.

"Is the Code not made up of laws?" Lucian shouted. "Should those laws not be followed by all?"

"That's the point of the Code. It's a choice." I felt the tears escaping now, but I didn't care. I needed him to know. Know that even after everything he and the rest of the Jackals had done, I still forgave them. *That they're still my brothers.* "And I chose wrong, Lucian. I failed every last of you.

"I'm so sorry."

A flicker of shock rippled across Lucian's face, stilling the rage for a single moment. And for that moment, all the unnatural energy in the crystal died, and he didn't look demonic, just scared. Like the innocent lad I'd once protected with all my might.

Then his eyes returned to sickly pink-black holes. "You didn't fail us, Kal. You failed Archengard."

I closed my eyes.

"So what now, Navigators?" Lucian gestured broadly. "Four against one, yet you still fail to do more than scratch me. Where is your brotherhood? Your fellowship? Where is your connection now?!"

He scoured our broken, beaten bodies in silence.

I didn't have any more tricks up my sleeve. I didn't have any will left to give.

Because everything he'd said was right.

Lucian nodded as though he'd expected it, then lifted a hand, eyes locked with mine. "Then farewell, Leviathan. Let this be a reminder of what He told you two decades ago: If change is what man seeks to create, then he must forever act as an isle . . . It's lonely, but it's *power*."

With the snap of his fingers, he opened a portal that would shoot the largest of his tentacles out to stab each of us through the heart.

I deserve it.

Except instead of opening away from Lucian, the portal opened *toward* him.

And instead of tentacles impaling the four of us, a fist immersed in emerald flame slammed into Lucian's face. Not even his crystal managed to detect it.

"*NO MAN IS AN ISLAND*!" the fist roared as Lucian was thrown ten feet through the air.

In that moment I was fourteen again, watching a blond-haired, black-suited boy make his way up an iron clock tower while dueling thirteen demons. I had watched that boy born from darkness use *overwhelming*, unbelievable light to keep the darkness that had once destroyed him at bay, and now I saw the same dauntlessness surging out of the figure before me.

Lucian sprang to his feet but almost fell over. He stumbled in place, eyes sputtering with Ignis as Archengard probably spun around him.

I couldn't believe it: a Jackal looking disoriented.

Standing in front of him, the last bits of fire clung to the swashbuckler's fist, his vest and dress shirt billowing with white smoke. The most smoke came from a tattered hole in both garments, directly where his heart was. The skin around it was scarred and glowed with green crystalline fragments, but it was closed.

Healed.

Enoch lifted his fist to his mouth and blew out the remaining wisps of flame. "Let the record show that that was done without any alcohol whatsoever."

"H-how?" Lucian stammered. "I destroyed your heart. That's *impossible*!"

"Is it?" Murta moved to stand beside Enoch and opened his closed fist. Coating his palm and between his fingers was the muddled bloody mess from before. Enoch peered at it with just as much shock as Lucian and I.

Until realization slammed into me.

A star of gold and green . . . I'd heard the Shrouded Man all those years ago say. Saw a ragged white-and-gold coat I'd abandoned blowing in the breeze atop a jagged crag.

Brilliant.

"You may have destroyed his heart," Murta said, eyes fixed with triumph. "But he has a new one now."

Enoch slowly looked down at his chest, fingering the hole in his shirt. Lucian kept staring in confusion, his mind unable to fathom how what had happened, happened . . . until the green fragments embedded in Enoch's tan skin began to look familiar. Lucian's hands sprang to his cloak pockets in a panic and found them . . . empty.

His body convulsed as he lifted his head to gawk at Murta. "DO YOU HAVE ANY IDEA WHAT YOU'VE—"

Lucian's head snapped back from the speed of a cacophonous right hook. Nowhere near as powerful as the initial punch, but just as dangerous.

He stumbled back, Ignis already swarming around him again, but this time, I was waiting. I laid the Sword against his cheek and saw him pause, then slowly glance over his shoulder. He tried to escape to the left, but another sword slid into view, this one a churning waterblade. He moved to scamper to the right, but the snap-hiss of an Aestus cannon echoed outward, and before he could lunge straight ahead, Enoch and Murta were already there, one holding a black claw full of gold flames and the other a familiar fist of green fire.

Lucian would probably have more nightmares about that fist than my Sword.

Scowling around the circle, Lucian slowly crept to my feet. I followed, keeping the blade inches from where his head met his neck.

"Oh, the irony," he muttered, but things like that didn't irritate me anymore.

"You've failed, Lucian," I said. "Take your defeat like a Nav . . . If you haven't forgotten what it means to be one. I'm sure you'll remember when you're on trial standing before the rest of the Council."

Lucian spun to stare at me. He looked deranged, his tattered facial features only heightening the hatred burning in his eyes.

"On trial? There will be no trial, Leviathan. Only the judgment. Look around you: The Jackals have won today. Ryjen has fallen. And though the Heart has been lost to us . . ." He swung his maniacal gaze back to Enoch. "It isn't lost completely."

"And the Brotherhood's job has always been protecting that which is lost," I said.

"For now." He turned about the circle, staring deep into the eyes of each of us. "Until the Brotherhood looks at the lost, declares them found, then puts them on the front lines to be slaughtered. Mark my words. If it happened once, it will happen again. He has seen it. The one you must face before it all ends."

Lucian paused on Enoch, but where I'd seen concern and distress in the eyes of Prince's and Jezna's posture, there was nothing of the sort in the swashbuckler's unwavering orange glare. Only fury.

He wanted to gut Lucian like a fish.

I heard the Jackal swallow uneasily, saw a black triangle form behind him, and before I could lunge forward, Lucian stepped through with two final words: "He knows."

CHAPTER 82

Enoch

We waited a minute after Lucian snapped out of existence.

Part of me expected him to return, for a hundred portals to pop up. Part of me figured that even though I'd broken out of his realm, my next few breaths would still be my last.

But time ticked on and the silence only grew. I made astonished eye contact with my squadmates near the tail end of the minute, then collapsed with them in unison.

Pained sighs hurled from each of us—except Murta, who merely grunted—as we finally acknowledged the pain of all of the injuries we'd received, but the moment was so bloody comedic that our cries quickly turned into maddened chuckles of relief.

I tried to join in, I really did, but was ultimately unable to shake away everything that had happened. When Prince piled on top of me, squeezing the life from my lungs, followed by Jezna lovingly ruffling my hair, I truly attempted to ground myself in the moment, in our first success as a squad, but couldn't.

Slowly reaching past them and ignoring Jezna's pleas for me to stay level with the ground, I rose to my feet.

Murta, of course, had already beaten me, standing with his back to the setting sun.

"You . . ." I coughed green smoke from my lungs and tried not to concentrate too hard on the odd fiery feeling in my chest. "You swapped my heart with the Sacred Heart, right?"

Murta looked down in remorse. "I call it castling. All shadedrakes can do it, exchange places with one thing or another. It was the only thing I could think of."

"But the Talisman . . . What about—"

"It's just a stupid artifact."

I poked the scars in my skin and the green crystal protruding from them. "How'd you know it would work?"

"Biorn. He said that the Heart didn't just have the ability to create death and destruction, but also life. It was capable of rekindling it."

Murta watched me continue to tap at my skin. "Just like any other heart," he added quickly, panic emerging through his tone. "It's not going to make you a different person or turn you into something like me. It—"

I threw myself at him, holding him and squeezing as tightly as possible.

Murta's words froze on his tongue. As did his body.

"You're perfectly fine, bruv," I whispered.

At first he remained rigid, probably waging an internal war with himself, but eventually relented with a soft intake of air. His hands wrapped stiffly around my back.

That broke down the dam. I choked and sniffled into his shoulder.

Murta's strong arms held me tight, the rhythm of his heartbeat against my new one filling me with relief, joy, and anger all at once. There was peace and hope, but there was also deep fixated frustration.

I never wanted to fail him again.

From now on, I'd train until I was just as strong as he was. Until we *truly* were equals. I swore on the Code.

"Thank you."

I felt him shake his head. "No. *Thank you.*"

I looked up from the hug but kept my arms secured around Murta's own. I looked up into the beautiful bright brown eyes I admired so much and finally saw similar admiration reflected in them. Murta didn't cry, smile, nor give any of the normal human cues that he was happy, but it was the most emotion he'd ever shown me.

And that was more than enough.

"Ahem."

We tensed, realizing who was still with us, and sprang apart to attention, suddenly side by side with Prince and Jezna.

Prince sniffled noisily, and Jezna's dented armor creaked, but neither one moved. We all stared straight ahead as Kaleo tiredly sheathed the Sword. When Ignis settled back into his spirit, he turned toward us, hands clenched behind his back. His scowl was as deep as the jagged scar he'd created in the desert, a remnant of one of his devastating strikes. A brutal reminder of what was about to happen to us.

Then, when Kaleo rinsed sand and blood from his hands, his scowl disappeared.

"It's become quite, er, clear that although I was right regarding many things, I was also very, *very* wrong. Particularly in the way that I treated you. So before I continue, I just wanted to say . . ." He looked straight at me. "That you were right. I'm scared, old, and foolish, and although you weren't ready, you were ready enough. I should never have said that I'd split such an impressive group of trainees up."

Just when we all started to relax, the scowl returned tenfold. I swallowed and tried to tilt my head higher without being blinded.

"But on the contrary." Kaleo paced down the line. "There's a far more important matter that needs discussing.

"First, you left your quarters while under lockdown. Then, you broke Kaster out of the containment device, attacked countless Nightguards, and stole a crab cruiser. After that, you flew it all the way to a city we have no dealings with, seized the Sacred Heart without Carbonek's consent, most definitely lied to the sultan about your positions in the Brotherhood, caused absolute chaos, tapped into an immensely dangerous power that one of you was restricted from using while the other possessed him, *and* took on multiple Ignis hunters and a Jackal.

"I might also add that all of this was done in order to impress the Brotherhood. You assumed that returning with the Sacred Heart would mean returning to active duty. Or being confirmed. But I don't see the Sacred Heart in any of your hands. You've put every one of your miserable lives in an insurmountable amount of danger. You should be banished from the Brotherhood immediately."

My new heart sank, but that only hammered the last nail into the coffin. Kaleo was right. The Heart was now inside me. If my real heart had been destroyed by Lucian, then removing its replacement would kill me. And who knew what just having it in me would do . . .

Kaleo slammed to a stop back where he'd started. And although his rigid posture didn't change, the air around him certainly did. Something seemed to expand in his eyes.

"But . . ." Kaleo curled a bloodied hand around the hilt of the Sword, turning toward Murta with flickering eyelids. "Maybe next time, try returning the Talisman instead of getting it stuck inside one of your squadmates." He extended a hand outward. "Aye?"

Prince fainted.

Murta's eyebrows furrowed emotionally as he gazed down at the hand before accepting it with a determined nod. "We'll try our best . . . *Leviathan*."

A smirk tickled Kaleo's face as he took to watching Jezna soak Prince with her Ignis ability. Prince eventually woke with a roar.

But I still couldn't shake my discomfort away. Not after we'd failed to save Ryjen. Not after I'd died.

"But we lost," I said, drawing the attention of everyone. "Ryjen's been completely overrun, and the Heart's stuck inside me!"

Kaleo swiveled to look at me. "And?"

I gaped.

"Lucian is partially correct," he said. "The Code is an imperfect system. The Brotherhood's ideology is impossible to carry out to the fullest. But that's exactly why we do it."

The wind whipped at the remains of his coat, tossing torn gold and white threads about.

"Adam Evenstar, Talen Vento, and Rebecca Newblood had a vision for Archengard—what it could be—but they knew that it'd be impossible to accomplish. They knew the darkness that human beings were capable of. And even as the rest of the world mocked them, they tried to realize their ideal anyway."

I stammered. "But Evenstar, Vento, and Newblood were—"

"Regarded as heroes and philosophers. The most important people of their time. Arguably the three most influential Navs in history. But they didn't start out that way. Far from it. The respect they gained had to be earned, oftentimes through tumultuous trial and error."

Kaleo gestured at Ryjen behind us. "That's because failure is part of the Brotherhood, the unsaid Fourth Law. Archengard is too impure, too consumed by violence to ever come close to the perfect world that we aim for, but that's what makes our quest that much more important . . . If we strive for it, at least there's a ghost of a chance."

The words struck my spirit.

A ghost of a chance.

Kaleo pointed to his heart. "Navigating isn't about navigating Archengard; it's about navigating *here*. You trip. You stumble. You fall. You fail spectacularly." He converted his hands into a triangle before pressing it against his chest. "The difference between ordinary men and Navigators is whether or not you get back up. A Navigational squadron doesn't quit after failure . . . They run 'til the rainbow's end."

Kaleo closed his eyes. "I might've failed to recall the Brotherhood's purpose, but you four defined it."

I couldn't believe it. Our quest had ended in complete and utter failure, yet I looked up into the face of the Leviathan and realized that it wasn't about winning.

It was about *navigating*.

Who knew what quests, dangers, and more near-death experiences we might face. The future was uncertain, but that was part of it. What mattered was that we moved forward together. What mattered was that we kept questing for the rainbow's end. The future wouldn't write itself; we had to seize the pen.

So I turned toward my squadmates, heart literally on fire, and lifted my fist.

"Immortal, we think. Immortal, we become," Prince declared, thrusting his wet fist outward while gripping his stomach. "And a pox on individualism . . . but not until I get some freaking food and take a ten-year nap."

Jezna sighed and stepped inward. "I swear I've basically become the mother of this group." She added her fist to the mix before looking at Prince. "But it's an honorable cause."

"Drenching people ain't."

I eyed Murta, busy scowling at the sand. "You know you love it."

He stepped inward. "I most certainly don't."

Yet as he said it, his fist completed the circle. All four of our knuckles connected in a disheveled, incredibly dirty cross.

I wouldn't have had it any other way.

Kaleo clapped his hands abruptly. "Well, Navigational Squadron . . . *327*."

Prince's mouth fell open. The Sacred Heart did a jig inside me.

Ignoring all our reactions, Kaleo looked out at the sun. "I'm missing Rolarns already. Never realized having only Tanten could get so annoying. How about we head back to Carbonek and get you confirmed before both the Government and the Noda show up asking to dissect Amon, aye?"

Prince put back on his sunglasses, scanning the horizon. "You got a cruiser nearby? Ours is wrecked, and one of that freaking Jackalope's tentacles split my new turner in half."

"I ran here," Kaleo said.

"You *what*?"

I looked around. "Everyone in good enough shape to at least make it to the next town?"

"There are no towns," Jezna said bleakly. "Nothing but sand."

"Suddenly, my legs feel as though they're nonexistent," Prince said.

"Jezna?" I asked.

Though she looked like a rusty garbage can, the knight smiled with her glowing eye slit. "If we can seize the Sacred Heart, we can run to Carbonek."

"Prince?"

"Eh, why not?" He took off with a whoop. "Should dry off faster, right?"

Expecting a snort of annoyance, I turned toward Murta, but he was already running beside Kaleo.

"Way ahead of you."

Before following, I returned to the great blackness in my mind that now seemed a galaxy of multicolored flames all bidding me godspeed. All promising that they walked beside me.

After failing, then dying, it was more than reassuring. And maybe it meant that failing—and dying, for that matter—were mere nuances of a Navigator's life.

Squad 327, I recited, catching up to Murta. *We're Navigators you can trust . . . Sounds bloody brilliant.*

The five of us fled the desert, our spirits towering over the bright shadows we threw behind us. We chased the sun until there were two of them, all the way back to Carbonek.

THE ~~END~~ BEGINNING

ACKNOWLEDGMENTS

First, to my incredible agent, Joshua Bilmes. For some reason, he decided to take the awkward dude that was stalking him at Balticon under his wing. Somehow he looked at what was a horrendous first draft and saw beyond it. I would be nowhere without his guidance and belief in me.

I swore from day one that I'd thank my sixth grade English teacher, Beth Topping, who's the solitary reason I stuck with writing and reading. By kindling the flames of my passion, she made sure those flames will burn until my dying day.

For Liam Harding and Tess McLaughlin who, alongside me, might've made up the very first Navigational squad. I wrote this book between our frequent bar adventures and it's fueled with all the fun we had. We have indeed heard the chimes at midnight.

To Emily Watson and Jessica Ayala—my cheerleaders throughout college. Akira Ritos and Claire Vanderlaan need thanking as well for their continued support.

And lastly, to everyone at Podium who helped make this happen. Brian, Kate, and my editor, Diana Gill.